Maizie Albright Star Detective

★ ★ ★ ★

19

CRIMINALS

★ ★ ★ ★

Wall Street Journal bestselling author

Larissa Reinhart

PRAISE FOR LARISSA REINHART

THE FINLEY GOODHART CRIME CAPER SERIES

"This is as fun a novel as it is moving and at times heart-breaking, never the more so when the final page comes and readers are only left wanting more."

CYNTHIA CHOW, *KING'S RIVER LIFE MAGAZINE*

"Con artists, murder, a cast of sinister characters, and some laughs along the way. Loved it."

TERRI L. AUSTIN, AUTHOR OF THE *ROSE STRICKLAND MYSTERIES*

THE MAIZIE ALBRIGHT STAR DETECTIVE SERIES

"The perfect combination of mystery, romance, and laughs."

DEVILISHLY DELICIOUS BOOK REVIEWS

"This was a fun read--a fast-paced caper that kept me entertained until the end."

TERRY AMBROSE, AUTHOR OF THE SEASIDE COVE MYSTERIES

"The mystery and detective cases drive the story, but Larissa Reinhart's characters steal the show every time."

THE GIRL WITH BOOK LUNGS

"Fans of cozy mysteries, southern chick lit, hick lit, crime capers, and humorous mysteries will love it."

JANE READS

"I encourage readers to delve into this lively, funny, and genuinely satisfying series."

CYNTHIA CHOW, *KINGS RIVER LIFE MAGAZINE*

"Larissa writes a delightful book. [Maizie's] a teen star grown up to new possibilities."

SHARON SALITURO, FRESH FICTION

"Sassy, sexy, and fun, 15 Minutes is hours of enjoyment."

PHOEBE FOX, AUTHOR OF *THE BREAKUP DOCTOR* SERIES

"Move over, Janet Evanovich. Reinhart is my new 'star mystery writer!'

PENNY WARNER, AUTHOR OF *DEATH OF A CHOCOLATE CHEATER* (15 MINUTES)

"Maizie's my new favorite escape from reality."

— GRETCHEN ARCHER, *USA TODAY*
BESTSELLING AUTHOR OF THE *DAVIS WAY
CRIME CAPER* SERIES (15 MINUTES)

THE CHERRY TUCKER MYSTERY SERIES

"A Composition in Murder is a rollicking good time."

TERRIE FARLEY MORAN, AGATHA AWARD-
WINNING AUTHOR OF *READ TO DEATH*

"This is a winning series that continues to grow stronger and never fails to entertain with laughs, a little snark, and a ton of heart."

KINGS RIVER LIFE MAGAZINE

"Cherry Tucker is a strong, sassy, Southern sleuth who keeps you on the edge of your seat."

TONYA KAPPES, *USA TODAY* BESTSELLING
AUTHOR

"Giggle-inducing, down-home fun."

BETTY WEBB, *MYSTERY SCENE MAGAZINE*

"The perfect blend of funny, intriguing, and sexy!"

– ANN CHARLES, *USA TODAY* BESTSELLING
AUTHOR OF THE *DEADWOOD* AND
JACKRABBIT JUNCTION MYSTERY SERIES

"Reinhart's charming, sweet-tea flavored series keeps getting better!"

GRETCHEN ARCHER, *USA TODAY* BESTSELLING AUTHOR OF THE *DAVIS WAY CRIME CAPER SERIES*

"Like front-porch lemonade, Reinhart's cast of characters offer a perfect balance of tart and sweet."

SOPHIE LITTLEFIELD, BESTSELLING AUTHOR OF *A BAD DAY FOR SORRY*

"Reinhart manages to braid a complicated plot into a tight and funny tale. Cozy fans will love this latest Cherry Tucker mystery."

MARY MARKS, *NEW YORK JOURNAL OF BOOKS*

"Readers who like a little small-town charm with their mysteries will enjoy Reinhart's series."

DENISE SWANSON, *NEW YORK TIMES* BESTSELLING AUTHOR OF THE *SCUMBLE RIVER MYSTERIES*

"This mystery keeps you laughing and guessing from the first page to the last. A whole-hearted five stars."

DENISE GROVER SWANK, *NEW YORK TIMES* AND *USA TODAY* BESTSELLING AUTHOR

"Highly recommended for anyone who likes their mysteries strong and their mint juleps stronger!"

– JENNIE BENTLEY, *NEW YORK TIMES* BESTSELLING AUTHOR OF *FLIPPED OUT*

"Reinhart is a truly talented author and this book was one of the best cozy mysteries we reviewed this year."

– *MYSTERY TRIBUNE*

"Cherry is a lovable riot, whether drooling over the town's hunky males, defending her dysfunctional family's honor, or snooping around murder scenes."

— *MYSTERY SCENE MAGAZINE*

19 CRIMINALS, Maizie Albright Star Detective #8

ePub ISBN-13: 979-8-2233530-6-5

ASIN: B0CHR1TBZR

Print ISBN-13: 978-1-7377550-4-3

Hardback ISBN-13: 978-1-7377550-5-0

Library of Congress Control Number: 2023915355

Past Perfect Press

This is a work of fiction. Names, characters, places, and incidents are either the products of the author's imagination or are used fictitiously, and any resemblance to actual persons, living or dead, business establishments, events, or locales is purely coincidental.

Printed in the USA

Author photo by Scott Asano

Original cover design by James of GoOnWrite

https://www.goonwrite.com/

BOOKS BY LARISSA REINHART

A CHERRY TUCKER MYSTERY SERIES (IN ORDER)

A CHRISTMAS QUICK SKETCH (prequel)

PORTRAIT OF A DEAD GUY

STILL LIFE IN BRUNSWICK STEW

HIJACK IN ABSTRACT

THE VIGILANTE VIGNETTE

DEATH IN PERSPECTIVE

THE BODY IN THE LANDSCAPE

A VIEW TO A CHILL

A COMPOSITION IN MURDER

A MOTHERLODE OF TROUBLE

Audio

PORTRAIT OF A DEAD GUY

STILL LIFE IN BRUNSWICK STEW

HIJACK IN ABSTRACT

DEATH IN PERSPECTIVE

THE BODY IN THE LANDSCAPE

A VIEW TO A CHILL in CRIMES MOST MERRY AND ALBRIGHT

A COMPOSITION IN MURDER

MAIZIE ALBRIGHT STAR DETECTIVE SERIES (IN ORDER)

15 MINUTES

16 MILLIMETERS

NC-17

A VIEW TO A CHILL

17.5 CARTRIDGES IN A PEAR TREE

18 CALIBER

18 1/2 DISGUISES

19 CRIMINALS

20 CARATS

Audio

15 MINUTES

16 MILLIMETERS

NC-17

CRIMES MOST MERRY AND ALBRIGHT

18 CALIBER

18 1/2 DISGUISES

19 CRIMINALS

20 CARATS

21 GUNS

A FINLEY GOODHART CRIME CAPER SERIES

PIG'N A POKE (prequel, short story)

THE CUPID CAPER

19 CRIMINALS

A ROMANTIC COMEDY MYSTERY NOVEL

MAIZIE ALBRIGHT STAR DETECTIVE
BOOK 8

LARISSA REINHART

Past Perfect Press

ACKNOWLEDGMENTS

I owe a huge debt of gratitude to:

Tracy Sands for stepping in as my beta reader. Thank you for all your cheerleading over the years!

To Susan Y Tanner for stepping in as my editor. I hate the circumstances for bringing you in, but I'm so grateful that you were able and willing to help me out! Thanks for bringing your big scissors to the table.

My readers who hung in with me for 2+ long years, waiting for this book to come out! (I hope it was worth it!) Especially to Elaine Embree, who's been waiting very patiently to find out what character she became in this book. (Elaine is not really a 15-year-old dog whisperer.)

The libraries for their enthusiastic support. Particularly those near my childhood hometown of Andover, IL—Woodhull, Cambridge, Geneseo, East Moline, and Orion. And my adult hometown library, Peachtree City, and the surrounding libraries in Fayette and Coweta County.

My friendships with other dog lovers, particularly Cinda Watson, Katie Sparkman, Holly Bender, Christine Gutshall, Irma Schwingshakl, and Diana Concepcion. (We hold nothing against cats, we just have dogs. lol)

My sister and mom for always encouraging me. And as voracious readers, telling me exactly what you think about not only my books, but books in general.

For my family, as always, for your support and for tiptoeing around me in the kitchen while I try to get some words in!

To Biscuit and His Friends
We miss you, Charlie & June!

Also, for Terri and Ritter.
I miss trying to make you laugh.
Writing has been very lonely without the two of you.

ONE

I SLIPPED a finger along the nape of my neck, felt beaded sweat, and hoped the glue held for the blonde wig covering my noticeably ginger hair. This bar—actually a micro-brewery filled with soccer fans watching Atlanta United on a projection screen —needed better ventilation. Beneath my wig, my hair steamed. Beneath my jersey and cutoffs, my body steamed. The bar also smelled like beer (naturally) and dog. For every two people, there seemed to be three dogs. Dogs pacing restlessly under the tall pub tables. Sitting in the aisles. Nosing into unattended purses and bags.

The dogs were bored. So was I.

Unlike their people, the dogs did not care about soccer (except for the Sheltie mix who ran before the screen chasing the two-dimensional ball) or beer (except for the golden retriever licking puddles of spillage on the floor) or hooking up (except for the lab mix and basset hound who seemed to eye each other).

I also did not care about soccer, or beer, or hooking up. But I had to pretend like I was interested in all three. This was much easier to do in a wood-paneled bar with low-lighting, soft music, and glasses of water with a slice of lime. A vodka tonic disguise.

When the option of alcohol was solely beer, my pretend drinking strategies were limited.

But I gasped dramatically with the crowd, sipped tepid near-beer, and didn't squirm as some kind of monstrous dog—bull-mastiff, possibly—licked my bare legs. I never broke character. I grew up in front of the camera. After all, I was Maizie Albright, the teen TV star and B-list celebrity. I was still Maizie Albright, but now I played the private investigator who never broke character.

Not even when the soccer fan sitting on the stool next to me slipped his hand onto my thigh and squeezed.

I leaned toward the man—Brian Hearn, husband and financial planner—and pretended to brush dog hair off his white and peach jersey. Leaving my hand on Brian's shoulder, I angled so our heads almost touched. A good Kodak moment.

Inside my head, I tried to recall Wyatt Nash's last GPS bearing and calculated the odds of my catching him after I left this micro-brewery. I wanted to shower off the scent of beer, dog, and cheater before locating him, but I was out of town and the timing wasn't good.

As the hand on my thigh crept higher, I adjusted my sit so the fingers naturally slipped off. I turned my head, allowing my breath to tickle Brian's neck. In this position, I could see a corner table where two women drank a flight of beer. One, small and fierce with a blue-tipped bob. The other, tallish with a dark ponytail and an equally intense disposition.

Hopefully, they caught Brian's squeeze and my sit and squirm on their hidden camera. I squinted in their direction, then blinked when I felt a contact slide in my right eye. The contacts were chocolate brown to cover my distinct sea glass-green, but they didn't fit well.

I giggled when Brian's hand moved to rest on the back of my stool. On the pretense of crossing my legs, I scooted my butt away from his hand.

I excelled at pretending, having pretended from early childhood into my adult life. Professionally. As an actress. Surreptitiously wriggling away from wayward hands was also something I was used to on- and off-screen.

This part of my job—my new job as a private detective—was depressing. I liked surveillance, research, and analysis. Felt pretty good at them, too. But busting cheaters wasn't where I wanted to make my mark in the world of investigations.

Career-wise things were going well, though. I worked in my chosen profession (instead of the acting profession chosen by my ex-manager/still-mother Vicki Albright) with three wonderful women.

My boyfriend, Wyatt Nash—Not boyish. Built like a stunt double for Dwayne Johnson—worked in a similar field and understanding of late-night, honey trap gigs. He didn't care if I showed smelling like beer, dogs, and cheaters, as long as I showed.

But lately, it felt like I was living a double life. It wasn't all the pretending. Something else was off.

"This place is awesome," said Tiffany through my earpiece.

"Agreed," said Annie, also into my earpiece. "I'm coming back after we're done with cheater patrol."

"Maizie needs to perk up," said Rhonda, the third in our quartet. Not into my earpiece, but closer to my shoulder, where she stood, supposedly watching the game and perusing the extensive beer menu. She also wore an ATL UTD jersey, one borrowed from a brother that hung like a tent over her generous curves and fell below her round knees. Rhonda had Extra-Extra-Extra Large brothers.

I didn't say anything. I couldn't. Although a microphone was strapped to my sweaty body beneath the slick soccer jersey, I had a fish on the hook and we were about to reel him in. Brian's posture had changed. His attention shifted from the game to gaze into my eyes.

"D'ya want to get out of here?" murmured Brian.

I scooted closer so the mike could catch his voice over the

cheering, barking, and growling. His ferocious bullmastiff didn't seem to like other dogs. Or people. Luckily, the lotion on my legs distracted him.

"Do you do this often?" I said in my best home-wrecker voice —deep and sultry with a side of stupid.

"Watch soccer at the Bark and Brew?"

Dropping the stupid, I said, "Pick up women at the Bark and Brew."

Brian smiled. Not an innocent, "that's funny" smile. The smug smile of a guilty man who enjoyed getting away with cheating. Possibly enjoyed it more than the cheating itself.

The smile told me everything I needed to know.

Unfortunately, lawyers and judges needed more than a smile.

"You're funny," he said. "And gorgeous. How can I resist?"

"Resist what?" I leaned toward him, laying the coy on thick. I played with the collar of his jersey. "You're not married, are you, Brian? You're single? I've been stung before."

He moved his lips toward my ear. "I'm free as a bird. Let's get out of here."

The mike wouldn't pick up whispers, particularly in this environment. I pulled back, but left my fingers on his collar. "Brian, I'm serious."

"Me, too." He grinned, and his hand landed on my thigh. Near the enormous nose of the bullmastiff.

The dog snarled. Brian's hand flew off my thigh. I glanced behind me for help, but Rhonda was inching away from the dog.

"Cuddles, no," scolded Brian.

"I think he likes my lotion."

"I think he likes your legs," said Brian. "I do, too."

Still not enough evidence for court.

"Mayday," said Tiffany in my earpiece. "Rhonda, you're about to back into—"

Behind me, something crashed. A dog yelped, followed by a cacophony of barking. Cuddles barked and snapped.

"Oh, sh—" muttered Annie. "I told her not to come here."

My eyes darted to the door. A woman was looking wildly around the large space. Amanda Hearn. Brian's wife. I sighed, dropped my hand from his shirt, and slipped off my stool.

"You're ready to go?" Brian had his back to the door and didn't realize he'd been busted prior to the bust his wife had paid us to do. He reached for me but froze at the deep growl from his dog. "Cuddles, what's wrong with you?"

Annie strode toward Amanda. Tiffany began slugging the remainder of the beer flight. I glanced behind me at Rhonda. She was bent backward over the bar, pinned by a standard poodle. His paws rested on her shoulders and his tongue lapped her face.

"Down," shouted Rhonda. "No lickies."

Below me, Cuddles growled and snatched at the leash Brian held. Nearby dogs backed away, barking. In the din, people shouted at their dogs and tugged on leashes. Atlanta United scored and the non-dog owners cheered, setting off howls.

I slapped a hand over my ear. Annie was speaking to Amanda Hearn. Annie's voice transmitted too fast and low to catch what she said over Rhonda's shouts. However, I knew our sting had been cut short. I slung my purse over my shoulder and moved away from the bar. A hand reached for my elbow and a shriek cut through the barking and howls.

"You said you were going to the dog park," screamed Amanda.

The hand slid off my elbow. Behind me, Cuddles' growl turned into a ferocious snap. The crowd moved and shifted with the dogs, blocking my view of Amanda.

"Baby," called Brian. "I just stopped in for a beer."

It would be impossible for Amanda to hear Brian. I don't think she would have listened, anyway. In my earpiece, Annie's pleas grew faster and louder but were still unintelligible.

Until she said, "gun."

That word cut through the clutter of noise.

My heart stuttered, then galloped. I rose on my toes, trying to see over the crowd. Tiffany swore in my earpiece. I spotted her sliding under the table to rifle through a bag of equipment. I glanced over my shoulder to see if Rhonda had heard the same thing.

Judging by the roundness of her eyes and the panic on her face, she had. She shoved the poodle off her body, dropped to the ground, and pulled the dog to her side. Then began gathering nearby dogs into her huddle.

"Get down," I screamed and spun to face the bartender. "Call 9-1-1."

The room quieted, then the sound swelled, cresting into a tidal of panicked barking and screaming. People flopped to the floor until only Amanda, Annie, Brian, and I remained standing.

Now I could see the gun she brandished. A small revolver.

Annie still spoke to Amanda, the words a jumbled rush in my ear. Brian also spoke in a jumbled rush. But not words of comfort. Mostly swearing about Amanda's idiocy and her audacity.

"What in the hell do you think you're doing, Amanda? My great-grandpa's Luger? He took that from a German officer after the Battle of the Bulge. And you're turning it on me?" Brian threw his hands up in the air. "Whatever. It's all rusty and corroded. No one's used it since the sixties. That thing doesn't even work."

Amanda pointed the gun at the ceiling and fired.

It worked.

TWO

FOR A MOMENT, the room stilled. The gunshot rang in my ears, scrambling my brain. I unclenched my teeth. My brain restarted. Before I could review my emergency training—emergency training that didn't include a canine hostage situation—the dogs snapped out of their shock.

All hell broke loose.

A cacophony of barks and cries resounded from the room. Ripping free from the grips on their leashes, the dogs ran toward the front doors. Stools and tables tied to leashes dragged behind various canines. People scrambled to move out of the way, scuttling along the cement floor like crazed crabs. Freed dogs leaped over crouching figures, jumped over chairs, and bounded over their smaller compatriots.

Except for Cuddles. He shook his large head, spraying me with drool and spittle, and turned toward Brian.

"Cuddles, stay. Stay. Stay," barked Brian. "Dammit, Cuddles."

"Don't talk to my dog that way," shouted Amanda. The arm holding the gun swooped and centered on Brian.

Holding up a hand, I shouted, "Amanda, think about what you're doing."

"He's done this to me." Amanda's eyes narrowed on Brian. "I'd rather be in prison than married to this lowlife."

"There are other options," muttered Tiffany in my earpiece. "I told you this woman was high-strung."

"All the cheaters' wives are high-strung," said Rhonda.

"This one's wound tighter than a six-day clock."

"Not now, Tiffany," snapped Annie. "I can't get to Amanda with all these dogs fighting at her feet. Maizie, get Brian out of the way."

I eyed Cuddles. "That's going to be tricky."

"Figure it out."

Ignoring the room, Cuddles growled at Brian. With his chest thrown out and teeth bared, the massive dog looked like he'd tripled in size. Cuddles stood almost three feet tall and probably weighed 150 pounds on a good day. The foam dripping from his mouth didn't help either.

Angling sideways, I inched toward Brian and bent my head toward my miked chest. "Are the police on their way?"

"Roger, that," said Tiffany. "I reported a hostage situation at a dog show. I thought it summed it up better."

"Get Brian on the floor," said Annie.

"If he goes down, I think his dog will eat him. It's like the dog knows what Brian's done."

"Probably been a long time coming," said Tiffany.

"Tiffany…" Annie snarled.

"She can't help it," said Rhonda. "She always gets sassy in nervy situations."

"What does Amanda want?" I said quickly. "In *Julia Pinkerton* Season 7, Episode 20, we did a hostage crisis. We need to seem empathetic if we're going to convince her to stand down. Ask her what she wants, Annie."

"Amanda, what do you want from Brian?" shouted Annie.

"I want to shoot him." Amanda's eyes narrowed. She shifted to avoid a yapping Chihuahua at her feet.

"I could've told you that," said Tiffany.

"Annie, empathy," I said. "Amanda has to understand we're listening. Like, 'we know what you've gone through with Brian, but don't you deserve a better life?'"

"At this point, she's going to lose everything in the divorce and go to jail," said Tiffany. "How's that better?"

"Amanda," hollered Annie. "We know what Brian's done to you. You deserve better."

"I know I do," she screamed back. "Ten years of putting up with him cheating on me and treating me like a second-class citizen. I deserve a medal."

"This isn't working," muttered Annie. "Dropkick Brian. Let the dog have him. When he hits the ground, she'll be distracted. I'm going for her knees."

I inched toward Brian. Cuddles snarled. I inched back.

"There are too many people and dogs in here," I said. "Tell Amanda Cuddles is ready to attack Brian. She should let everyone go because Cuddles has Brian pinned. She trusts her dog. She told us that in our meetings."

Annie relayed the message.

"Cuddles is protecting me." Amanda squinted. "Tell Cuddles to stay."

"Stay," I shouted. "Cuddles, stay."

Cuddles glanced over his gigantic shoulder and narrowed his eyes at me.

"Craptastic," I whispered. "Now Cuddles wants to eat me, too."

"Oh, Maizie," wailed Rhonda. "Protect your face. I don't think you'll do well with scarring on that face."

"Am I that vain?" I slithered back a step. "I mean, won't I be happy to be alive even if I'm disfigured?"

"It would take a lot more therapy," said Tiffany.

"Would you three stay on topic?" said Annie, then shouted, "Amanda, tell your dog not to kill my employee. And drop the gun."

Amanda's focus shifted from Brian to Cuddles. Her elbows

drew toward her chest. However, the gun remained pointed at Brian. "Cuddles doesn't want to kill her. He's waiting for another command."

"That's a relief," said Rhonda. "I can't see anything with this poodle in my face."

Blue and red lights flashed outside the glass doors. Whispers stole through the room. Pacing dogs whined and pawed at the door.

"The police are here, Amanda," shouted Annie.

"Look at what you've done, Amanda," yelled Brian. "You better hope you get a good lawyer who can prove how crazy you really are."

"Quiet, Brian," I shouted.

Cuddles shifted his focus from me to Brian and resumed growling.

Amanda glanced over her shoulder. Looking back, her face betrayed the shock of seeing the SWAT team exit their truck. "I didn't mean to scare these people and their dogs."

"Annie, tell Amanda, 'Of course, you didn't,'" I said. "Make it seem like it's her idea to let everyone go."

"Amanda, you didn't mean for this to happen. Let these people go home," said Annie. "Don't worry about Brian. Just turn over the gun."

"I didn't plan to do this." Amanda's shoulders drooped. "I knew he was going to take your bait. It made me so angry."

"Of course," said Annie. "Just hand me the gun."

"I didn't mean to hurt anyone." She lowered her arms. "Especially the dogs. I love dogs."

"The dogs will be okay. As soon as you give me your gun."

She stared at the Luger, then handed the pistol to Annie.

The crowd cheered and moved across the floor toward the exit. SWAT team members edged into view on either side of the doors. Dogs bounded between their owners and the door, barking excitedly.

I rolled my neck, feeling the tension that had held my body rigid.

Brian leaned against the bar and crossed his arms. His smug smile reappeared.

"Amanda, lower yourself to the floor and put your hands on top of your head," said Annie. "Show the police you're not dangerous."

We watched as Amanda dropped to her knees and gripped her head. I felt a little sorry for her now. We all had our crazed, heat-of-the-moment acts of regret. Mine never involved firing a gun into the ceiling of a crowded microbrewery filled with dogs. Mine were more of the "stumbling out of a club after getting sprayed with Dom Pérignon and getting caught by the paparazzi"-type acts.

Humiliating. Career-damaging. But at least I hadn't put anyone's life in real danger.

Amanda was in serious trouble. Her dog was still bent on protecting her, too. He leaned forward, teeth bared, and eyes on Brian. A continuous, low growl rumbled from him.

The doors opened. The SWAT team waded past the outpouring of people and dogs toward Amanda.

"Is that your dog?" said an officer, cuffing her upturned wrists.

"Yes," mumbled Amanda. "I trained him myself."

"Guess he's mine now," said Brian, in a voice a bit too triumphant than the situation warranted.

Amanda's eyes narrowed. A sneer unfurled from her lips.

Shizzles. I stepped away from Cuddles, then pushed into a backward run until I tripped over Rhonda. My butt hit the cement floor. The poodle vaulted from Rhonda's lap and slammed into me, shoving me down.

"Don't do it, Aman—" My cry was lost to the poodle's tongue licking my face.

"Cuddles. Go," shouted Amanda.

Cuddles snarled, and Brian screamed.

THREE

THE BARK and Brew wasn't in my hometown of Black Pine, but in another mountain town, Gilmore. The Gilmore police were not familiar with Albright Security Solutions private detective agency, so the interview process took longer than it would have in Black Pine. Several hours later, Tiffany, Rhonda, Annie and I stumbled out of the deserted Bark and Brew.

"Why bring a gun when you have that dog?" said Tiffany. "I think Brian would've preferred a gunshot wound."

"It's late. See y'all tomorrow." Rhonda waved, and they crossed the parking lot to Tiffany's Firebird.

Annie looked at me. "You still want to hit the surveillance at the Tiger Lounge? Our other cheater?"

"I guess," I said reluctantly.

"I'm kidding," said Annie. "Lighten up. But I could use a drink. A real drink."

Annie and I had never done drinks after work. I didn't drink anymore, but I didn't want to miss out on a bonding experience with my boss.

She paused before hitting the unlock button on her fob. "You were great in there. You kept your cool. Even though you know I don't approve of using *Julia Pinkerton* plots to problem-solve, this one came in handy."

I bobbed my head. "The producer had us meet with an FBI hostage negotiator to give us an 'air of authenticity.' The agent said the FBI would never let a teen detective deal with a criminal, and the entire plot was far-fetched and ridiculous. But they paid him well, so he gave us the pointers."

"He's right. But whatev." Annie shrugged and started across the parking lot to her Jeep.

I followed, feeling encouraged. "You know, I have a lot of ideas for breaking into other kinds of investigations. Beyond infidelity cases." I paused for Annie to comment. When she didn't, my voice rose. "I know I'm still an apprentice, but like you said, I was great in there. I have a lot more to offer than these honey trap characters. I'm starting to feel typecast."

"Using words like 'typecast' makes me think you're not ready for the majors. Don't start getting cocky, Albright." Annie snapped her gum, then slugged my shoulder. "Come on. Gilmore's got an old-school bar."

I nodded, fighting off resentment, and opened the passenger door. Before I could climb in, a jingling and patter of feet caught my attention. I spun around and was side-swiped by a massive body leaping into the Jeep.

"What the—" yelled Annie.

"It's Cuddles." The bullmastiff arranged himself in the passenger seat and smiled at me. Then turned toward Annie, bared his teeth, and growled.

Annie backed out of the Jeep. "Didn't Brian take him? Hang on, I've got his cell number in our paperwork." Annie popped the rear door and reached for her backpack.

Cuddles rose to follow her movements. The growl grew more menacing.

"Maizie, get that dog out of my Jeep."

"Come on, Cuddles," I coaxed.

The big dog glanced at me over its shoulder. A long strand a drool hung from his fang. He turned back to watch Annie.

"This is my Jeep," she said in her boss voice.

Cuddles snapped.

Annie jumped back. "Maizie, get over here and get my backpack."

"I don't want him to bite me, either."

"I don't think it's going to be a problem." She pointed at the dog, who looked expectantly at me. His tail brushed the seat.

"He likes my lotion." I walked around and retrieved the backpack.

Annie rifled through, pulled out the Hearn file, and called Brian. After a lot of eyeball rolling and wrinkling her nose, Annie hung up. "He doesn't want the dog."

"How can he abandon his dog?" I cried. "What kind of person does that?"

Annie looked at me.

"Right, it's Brian." I looked at Cuddles. "You did try to kill him."

He smiled.

"I'll call a rescue place in the morning," said Annie. "You've got him tonight."

"I can't take him to the cabin." For legal reasons, I lived with my father and his family. The requirements of my probation. I liked to think of it as a long-term family reunion. "I've seen the Jack Russells take on badgers and wild pigs. They only listen to Remi. The dogs are probably safe. Remi, come to think of it, too. But I need to worry about Daddy and Carol Lynn."

As Paul Bunyan's older doppelgänger, likely Daddy was also safe. But his wife, Carol Lynn, was the sweetest woman in the world. I'd never want to put her in danger.

Also, she was an amazing cook, but that had nothing to do with it.

"I'll take him to Nash's old office," I said. "The drool will match the furniture."

———

ANNIE RODE in the back seat. I drove with one hand, patting Cuddles to keep him calm. Before leaving Gilmore, I pulled into a Sip-N-Stop for supplies.

"This place better have bourbon." Annie jumped out of the Jeep before I turned off the engine. "What are you doing? Come on."

"That looks like Nash's truck." When I'd turned into the Sip-N-Stop, I'd noticed the Silverado in the parking lot of the Waffle Haus next door. "Why would he be in Gilmore this time of night?"

"Eating pancakes."

"Waffle Haus doesn't have pancakes."

"Georgia is too obsessed with waffles," groused Annie.

"You're grumpy. Maybe you need some waffles. Or eggs. Food will make you feel better."

She glared at me. "It's been a rough night. I want a glass of bourbon. Waffle Haus doesn't serve bourbon. I don't want to eat breakfast with your boyfriend."

"One minute." I held up a finger. "One minute to see if that's Nash. And another minute to buy dog food."

"If the Sip-N-Stop doesn't have bourbon, I'm going to get grumpier." Annie shoved a piece of gum in her mouth. "And if that dog eats my Jeep while you're spying on your boyfriend, you're out of a job."

I sprinted across the parking lot and slowed before hitting the sidewalk. Instead of walking to the door, I edged toward a window and peered in. I was right. Nash sat in the last booth with his back to the wall. A typical Nash spot. I felt pleased to know him so well, but not pleased that I didn't know him well enough to understand why he was eating waffles in Gilmore with a woman I didn't recognize.

They both had coffee and waffles, and seemed to share a plate of bacon and sausage. I focused on the woman, studying her profile. Her back was to me and her chestnut hair fell beneath her shoulders in waves. She was youngish and looked like she used the gym regularly. They seemed to be talking. No hand-holding or intense gazing. But Nash didn't believe in PDA.

He also didn't believe in cheating. And he preferred curvy gingers like me and his ex-wife, Jolene. I preferred not to think about Jolene at the best of times, and this was the opposite.

A fit of intense jealousy gripped me, but I forced myself to stalk back to the Sip-N-Stop. I found Annie in the snack aisle.

"Was it him?"

"Yep." I sighed.

"Sorry."

"I've never looked for him outside Black Pine. I guess I should've widened my circle." My shoulders drooped. "I'm going to get the dog food."

Annie patted my shoulder. "He'll tell you, eventually."

"It's killing me." I stared up at the dingy ceiling tiles. "Why would he take a case without me?"

"It's not a case—"

"You don't know Nash," I said. "It's a case. But why won't he let me help him?"

"Because he works for your dad's company and he's investigating your dad's company? Makes sense to me."

"It doesn't to me. I can waltz in and out of DeerNose HQ, poke my nose into all kinds of places, and nobody would think anything about it. I grew up around the management."

"Let him figure out what's going on. He'll tell you when he knows. Leave the stalking and spying for your real job."

"It's like he's living a double life."

"Says the person in the blonde wig and brown contacts."

I'd had some investigative success lately. I'd show Annie and Nash I could unravel Nash's DeerNose secrets and find a way to help him solve his case.

And wouldn't need the disguise to do it.

FOUR

#GOODBOYS #DOGWHISPERING

BACK IN BLACK PINE, I parked Annie's Jeep before the Dixie Kreme Donut building. The Dixie Kreme was housed in an old-timey brick storefront, where the best donuts in the world were made by Lamar, the sweetest ex-cop in the world. Nash Security Solutions had been housed on the second floor. Now it only housed Nash. The office hadn't disappeared, just the name after Nash lost the business. It's a long story involving my ex-manager/still mother, Nash's ex-wife, and me (although I had the best of intentions) that ended in Nash working as head of security for DeerNose, my father's business.

I felt eager to pull the scent of fried dough and sugar into my lungs and rid my nostrils of Eau de Cuddles. While we had argued in the Sip-N-Stop, Cuddles had eaten a bag of Doritos and a box of tissues, then rid himself of both on the curving mountain roads.

I had to pull over so Annie could do the same.

Upon opening my door, I stumbled out and fell sideways as Cuddles shoved past me. Annie climbed over the center console and slid into the driver's seat, grimacing.

"I love dogs, but this is a bit much," she said. "I'll start calling rescue places first thing. If we're lucky, someone will take him until Amanda posts bail."

"If we're not lucky?"

She snapped her gum. "He seems to like you. A lot."

I looked down at the dog. He had lifted his chocolate muzzle to stare up at me with soulful brown eyes. Eyes centered on a massive head. Eyes that had appeared to glow red when irked. "I can't take a dog. Particularly a dog this gigantic. I live with my dad's family. Where am I going to keep him?"

"I'd take him, but he doesn't like me."

"He could learn to like you."

"Cuddles," said Annie. "D'ya want to go home with me?"

One hundred fifty pounds plopped onto my feet. I whimpered. "I think he broke my toes."

"Good luck." Annie pulled the door shut and drove off.

"Come on, Cuddles." Grabbing his leash, I tugged. Cuddles rolled over, taking his leash with him. "Fine. Stay on the street. I'm going inside."

I dropped the leash, hefted the bag of dog food on my hip, and limped to the stoop flanking the doors to the Dixie Kreme Donut shop. I propped open the stairwell door, mounted the creaky stairs—skipping the one that sounded like a gunshot—and unlocked the office door on the second-floor landing. Dropping the dog food inside the door, I listened. Then hustled down the stairs and onto the stoop.

No dog.

"I'm sorry," I called. "Come back."

After limping around the block, I returned to the office to make fliers. Shredded paper covered the floor. Cuddles lay in a battered La-Z-Boy. A piece of the dog food bag was stuck to his muzzle.

"That's Lamar's chair." I crossed the room and patted the frayed couch. "Sleep here. It's bigger anyway."

Cuddles extended a leg over the armchair and closed one eye.

In one of Nash's dented file cabinets, I found two plastic bowls. I filled one with water and set it on the wooden floor. I pointed at the second empty bowl. "You could've had food in here and eaten like a normal human being. I mean, dog."

He closed both eyes.

"Look, I don't have time to babysit you. I've got research to do. I should write my notes while they're fresh in my mind."

Sighing, I walked into the inner office and retrieved my new laptop from its hiding place. While I waited for the laptop to power on, I jotted down my notes in my casebook.

"You barely blinked when Amanda fired that gun." I looked up. "That's interesting."

Turning back to the computer, I logged into my network file monitoring software and scanned the results. "Today Nash did the usual work stuff, but he is obsessing over the shipping and receiving logs again. And spending a lot of time on the security camera footage at a store in Denver."

A snore emanated from the other room.

"I know, boring stuff. We want to know who he met at the Waffle Haus tonight. I couldn't get a look at her face, thanks to you." I tapped on the app for the mobile phone spy software. "Although if it wasn't for buying dog food, I wouldn't have stopped at the Sip-N-Stop and seen Nash's truck."

The dog rolled over in the chair, slid to the floor, and climbed back on.

"No new phone numbers. How did he meet her?" I switched to the GPS tracker. "He was at a store in Gilmore earlier tonight. The Boot Scoot. Do you think he picked her up at the store and they went to the Waffle Haus together?"

Cuddles opened one eye and stared at me.

"The Boot Scoot. Sounds like a country boutique." Tapping my chin, I thought for a moment, then reached for my case log. "Doesn't make any sense. I'm still not great at memorizing a string of license plates. But I did write down the models of the vehicles in the Waffle Haus parking lot. She must be the owner of one of the cars."

I entered the vehicles into my spreadsheet tracker, switched off the laptop, and leaned back in the chair.

"This is a break. I'm getting closer. I can feel it. And as soon as I can pinpoint what Nash is investigating at DeerNose, I'll be able to help him." I looked at Cuddles, who still stared at me. But now with two eyes. "That's healthy, right? Wanting to help your future partner solve an investigation into your father's company? If DeerNose is in trouble, Nash is going to need support when facing Daddy. I don't know why he doesn't get that, but to keep the peace, I have stopped trying to reason with him. It's easier to investigate his investigation. Nash is one stubborn individual."

Cuddles yawned and turned in the chair.

"I know, I know. But spying on Nash is good practice for me. I'm still an apprentice PI."

The La-Z-Boy smacked the wall. A cloud of plaster exploded, raining a fine mist onto the bouncing chair. I stared for a moment. Blinked. Cuddles stood before the door, growling.

"What is it?" My heart thudded in my chest.

A moment later, I heard Nash's boots clomping up the squeaking stairs.

"Shiztastic." I slammed the laptop shut and shoved it in a file drawer beneath boxes of feminine products, hair care items, and makeup. "Cuddles, it's okay. It's just Nash. Just a minute. Hang on. Don't be alarmed."

The dog barked once—low and fierce. The boots paused. My phone rang.

I raced into the front room, shoved my phone between my chin and shoulder, and grabbed Cuddles' collar. "It's me. It's me. I'm here."

"Are you okay?" Nash's deep voice whispered.

"Fine, fine. We had a honey trap that went south."

"Is that a dog?"

"Yes. The result of the honey trap. Cuddles is the wife's dog. The husband abandoned him on the scene. The wife was arrested. I've got him tonight. We're looking for a rescue group in the morning."

"Cuddles?" Nash dropped the whisper. His boots resumed their clomp. "Pick him up so he doesn't get out. Be there in a minute."

"Um." I held the phone between my chin and shoulder. My hands grasped Cuddles' collar as he strained toward the door. Low growls coursed through him. "I don't think I could lift him if I tried. To be honest, I don't know if I can hold him."

Cuddles snapped a single ferocious bark.

Nash's footsteps halted. The phone went silent.

"Nash?"

"Maizie," said Nash. "What kind of dog is in my office? Is it as big as it sounds?"

"Well, yes … Cuddles is a bullmastiff. About 100 or 130 pounds. Or maybe 150 or 200."

"I see." He paused again. "Are you sure you're okay?"

"Yes. Apparently, Cuddles likes me."

"Does he like most people after he meets them?"

I bit my lip. "I haven't had a lot of experience with that, but so far … no."

"And why's he in my office?"

"I was afraid to bring him to the cabin. You know how the Jack Russells are."

"Did you have a plan for when I came back?"

I had a plan before I met Cuddles. Now not so much. Instead, I said, "First, let me get Cuddles into the inner office. Don't worry, I'll protect you."

A sigh emanated from the phone.

I ignored the sigh and tugged on Cuddles' collar. "Come on, boy. Ease up. It's just Nash. You'll like Nash. He's nothing like Brian."

Cuddles lunged toward the door. My fingers slipped from his collar. I fell onto the floor.

"Do you think it would be alright with Cuddles if you came out here?" said Nash.

"Cuddles, I'm going out there. I love Nash. He looks scary, but he loves me, too." I stood up. "Nash, tell him you love me. Make Cuddles feel reassured. His former father treated his mother horribly."

Nash's large silhouette appeared behind the door's wavy opaque glass. "I love Maizie. I'm not going to hurt her."

Cuddles growled.

"Nicer," I said. "In a happy voice."

Nash's deep voice rose an octave. "I love Maizie. And…" His voice dropped, "This is stupid."

A ferocious bark ripped from Cuddles.

"I'll buy you a box of biscuits if you just let me see for myself that Maizie is okay. Because if she isn't—"

"Happy voice."

"If she isn't," he continued in a bouncier tone. "I'm going to bail your momma out myself. I'm just getting out of debt, so that's a big sacrifice, now isn't it? Come on, boy, let me see Maizie. I haven't tasted those lips all day."

Cuddles cocked his head.

"Not what you thought," I said to Cuddles. "He likes to kiss me."

"Come on, Killer," pleaded Nash. "Calm down."

Cuddles looked up at me. Two thick lines of drool hung from his muzzle, but his teeth were no longer bared.

"Good boy," I said, then looked at Cuddles. "You're a good boy, too." I patted him and placed my hand on the door handle. Cuddles tensed and leaned toward the door. "No. Sit."

Cuddles sat.

"Stay."

His body hummed with tension, but Cuddles stayed. I placed my hand on the door again. Watching Cuddles, I cracked the door, slipped through, and shut it behind me. I waited for the slam of Cuddles' body against the door.

"He stayed. I can't believe he stayed," I exclaimed, then turned around.

Nash also stood wide-legged, chest thrown out, with his brawny arms flexed and wide shoulders tensed. The Paul Newman-blue eyes scanned me, then he grabbed my hand and pulled me against his hard body.

A low growl crawled through the door.

"It's okay," I called. "Stay, Cuddles."

"What'd you know? You're a dog whisperer." Nash's lips grazed my neck and began a slow trail of kisses toward my mouth.

"Good boy," I sighed.

FIVE

THE NEXT MORNING, Cuddles and I walked from the old office, Nash Security Solutions, to my new office, Albright Security Solutions—or A.S.S, as Tiffany had gleefully pointed out one day.

The day was clear, sunny, and smelled like donuts. I had spent the night at the office to prevent Cuddles from eating Nash. Cuddles slept in the La-Z-Boy. Nash and I had lain side-by-side on the hide-a-bed couch, afraid to make any sudden movements. After supervising the donut-making shift, Lamar knocked on the door, ready to take his morning nap. Before he could enter, Cuddles had bounded from the chair and attacked the door.

Thankfully, Lamar had a strong heart. As a retired Black Pine police officer, Lamar also knew dogs. Cuddles had eaten donuts for breakfast.

They were my donuts, but who's counting?

Me, apparently.

"Cuddles," I said, yanking on his leash. "It's been a treat. I guess. When we get to the office, we'll say our goodbyes. Please don't barf donuts in the office. Annie is a bit of a clean freak."

A bird flew past. Cuddles dragged me the length of the block but lost the bird. He ate a gum wrapper instead.

In front of the big shop window, I ordered Cuddles to sit and stay so I could catch my breath and massage my shoulder. "Listen," I panted. "Tiffany, Rhonda, and Annie. We like them. Annie's my boss, you met her. She's like an M&M. Hard shell, sweet center. Rhonda's a marshmallow. Tiffany's more like a jawbreaker."

A whine curled from somewhere deep in Cuddles' chest.

"Maybe I shouldn't use food analogies for you," I said. "Tiffany's actually a nail esthetician, and Rhonda's been working on her license to do hair. But because of unfortunate circumstances, they are no longer working for LA HAIR. Annie convinced Vicki to hire them. We're expanding the shop."

Cuddles looked at the glass where "Albright Security Solutions" had been painted to look old-timey, like the rest of the building. My ex-manager/still-mother Vicki Albright owned the business and had hired Annie to run it. As a Hollywood insider and an amazing businesswoman, Vicki believed architecture should tell a visual story. The story said *Maltese Falcon*. However, we thought of ourselves as *Charlie's Angels*.

In reality, we were more like a younger, crime-solving version of the *Golden Girls*.

"You got it? Don't hurt them. And don't eat anything."

We entered, and the bell above the door rang. Cuddles snarled and snapped at the bell. From the other side of the brick wall, voices bellowed over the buzz of saws and the whine of a condenser. Cuddles whipped around, growling at the wall. Rhonda shrieked and backed into the corner behind the desk. The door to the office slammed. Cuddles bounded toward the back of the room, pulling me along with him.

"Good grief, Cuddles," I said. "Sit. Stay."

Cuddles sat. Looked at me with pain in his eyes. But stayed.

Rhonda peered around the corner. The office door cracked. Annie and Tiffany poked their heads out.

"I figured you for one to get a purse-sized dog," said Tiffany. "I was way off."

"This is Amanda Hearn's dog. Brian wouldn't take him."

"We remember," Rhonda's voice shook.

I looked at Annie. "Any luck?"

"Not yet. The rescue places are calling around." Annie shoved a piece of gum in her mouth. "He's obeying you. That's an improvement."

I glanced at Cuddles. Drool ran from the corners of his mouth like long, slimy icicles. He looked at me. "No, stay."

Cuddles sighed.

"What are we going to do?" said Rhonda. "We've got a client coming any minute."

"Maizie, you're going to have to handle the dog while he's here," said Annie. "Take Cuddles for a walk or something."

Cuddles cocked his head and pawed at my leg.

"No. Stay." I turned back to Annie. "But I meet clients. I do the fieldwork. I need to get a feel for them."

Annie shrugged.

I looked at Rhonda. "Come meet Cuddles. He's actually very nice once he learns he doesn't want to kill you."

"No, thank you. I'm not taking something that big for a walk." She disappeared around the corner. "I'm good with him learning not to kill me from a distance."

"Tiffany?"

Tiffany laughed and backed into the office.

Cuddles' body vibrated. The door chimed.

"Stay." I pivoted to face the door, pushing my worry into a welcoming smile to greet the thirty-ish, bearded man walking inside. "Come in. Don't worry about this dog. He listens to me."

"I'm Derek Johnson." Average-height, fit, and lightly tatted, Derek looked like a modern-day boy next door.

"Happy to meet you, Derek," squeaked Rhonda, still flattened against the wall.

Derek looked at Cuddles. "You sure?"

The bullmastiff sat with his back to the door. But his ears had rotated back, his hair bristled, and the low hum of a growl vibrated from his massive body.

"Oh, yes." I nodded, smiling like a maniac. "But if you're more comfortable, we can have our meeting in the reception. Cuddles and I won't move from this spot."

"Okay." Derek slid onto a chair near the door. "Is he some kind of guard dog?"

"Something like that."

Tiffany and Annie emerged from the office and edged along the brick and shiplap walls, making a wide circuit around Cuddles. They slithered into the reception area, taking seats across the room from Derek. Rhonda slunk toward the reception desk, grabbed a notebook, and wedged herself beneath the desk, pulling the chair in front of her.

"How can we help you?" I shifted, trying to find a non-awkward stance without actually moving.

"It's my wife," said Derek. "I love her. But…"

We nodded sympathetically. We were used to these introductory statements from clients.

"But there's something going on," continued Derek. "I'm a cable person for Black Pine Studio. A cable guy." He laughed weakly.

"You do sound," I said. "You're a sound technician."

"Exactly. We moved here about two years ago from California. I like Georgia. I can afford a house. It seems like a great place to raise a family. Plus, I've built a sound studio in my house. It's something I've always wanted to do. Kind of a passion project, I guess."

We continued nodding.

"I thought Kristi liked it here, too. Kristi's my wife. She wanted to be an actress but had trouble breaking into the industry."

I could sympathize. I had broken into the industry in a big way, but I had Vicki as a manager who liked to break things.

"I thought Kristi might have a better chance out here. But she still hasn't gotten any roles. I feel bad about that. Maybe that's what this is about..." Derek bowed his head and wrung his hands.

We murmured sympathetically. But in our heads, we were urging Derek to hurry up with the details. At least I was. I worried Cuddles would quit his "stay" position.

Derek looked up. "But Kristi got a new job and seems to like it. She travels a lot. Which may be part of the problem." His head dropped. "I work twelve-hour shifts sometimes. Also part of the problem."

"Derek," I said gently. "These things are never black or white. And you don't know for sure what's going on. That's why you're here, right?"

"I guess so." Derek gusted a long breath and looked up. "What do I do?"

"We have some paperwork for you," said Annie. "Basic stuff. Any information you can give us now helps us to work faster."

While Annie said her spiel about fees, expenses, and retainers, Rhonda crawled out from underneath the desk. She inched along the wall, dropped a clipboard in Derek's lap, gave Cuddles a sidelong glance, and scurried beneath the desk.

"Is Kristi traveling now?" Because of my probation, leaving the state could be a hassle. Traveling to California would be impossible after Judge Ellis basically kicked me out of the state and forced me to live with Daddy in Georgia.

"She's home for now. I think." Derek rapped his pen on the clipboard. "The travel is kind of spontaneous. She's a secret shopper."

Rhonda's head poked above the desk. "She's a secret shopper and they pay her to travel? To travel to shops? Does she get to keep the stuff she buys at the stores?"

"Sometimes."

Rhonda hauled herself out from beneath the desk and sat in

her chair. "But it's like shopping for hemorrhoid cream, right? Athlete foot powder? Windshield wipers?"

"Mostly clothes, I think." Derek shrugged.

"She doesn't make much money, so that's why they let her keep the clothes?" continued Rhonda. "I bet she drives to these little Podunk towns with bad weather?"

"No, she gets paid pretty well. The only bad weather she's experienced was a snowstorm in Denver."

Rhonda cut me a look. I gave her one back. We were all thinking the same thing. We wanted to know where Kristi worked. And how she got that job.

Derek gusted another sigh. "But Kristi really wants to act. Maybe she feels I've let her down."

"But she gets paid to travel and shop," said Rhonda. "Maybe the clothes don't really fit her. Or aren't stylish?"

"I don't know much about fashion, but they looked pretty good on her," said Derek.

"Moving on, Rhonda," barked Annie.

"There's got to be a catch," muttered Rhonda.

"Why do you suspect Kristi might be … acting strangely?" I said. The words we used for cheating were always deliberately vague. Our clients didn't want to hear the words they were paying us to prove. A terrible business, I know. "When did you begin to get suspicious?"

"It's just a feeling." Derek fiddled with his pen. "It started soon after her getting the new job. Not long before we moved here, I guess. She started working as a secret shopper in California. Kristi didn't want to move, then suddenly she did. But she preferred North Georgia to Atlanta. Which I thought was weird. Atlanta is more convenient for travel."

"Don't worry, Mr. Johnson," said Annie. "As Maizie said, these things are never black or white. You don't know what's going on. Yet. We'll get to the bottom of it."

"Thanks so much." Derek blinked and ran a hand over his

eyes. "This is so hard to do. I don't want to think badly about Kristi."

"Hopefully we'll find there's nothing negative going on," I said. "You're both busy. Working a lot. Moving is stressful, especially when you don't have a support system here. If it's just a feeling, you could be wrong about what you suspect."

"Maybe it's more than a feeling." Derek sighed. "I spied on her last night. I followed her to another town. And saw her meet a man."

"Oh, Derek," whispered Rhonda.

Annie double-clicked her pen. "What town?"

"Gilmore."

"And what did the guy look like?" said Annie.

"Really big guy. Shaved head. Scar on his jaw."

Three heads swiveled to look at me. I stared at Derek. "Did Kristi and the man meet at a Waffle Haus?"

Derek nodded. "Wow, you're good. You put that together quickly."

"There's probably a reasonable explanation," said Annie.

Rhonda's big brown eyes flicked between me and Derek.

"Yep." I licked my lips. "I'm sure of it."

SIX

AFTER DEREK LEFT, Annie and Tiffany sidled into the back office. Rhonda pulled the desk against the wall and wedged herself behind it. Cuddles looked at me.

I sighed. "Walk?"

Thirty seconds later, Cuddles had pulled me to the Dixie Kreme Donut Shop. I couldn't blame him. The scent of donuts often lured me. A forgivable sin.

"Sit. Stay." I rubbed my arm and looked up at the second-story windows. The Silverado truck was not in its customary spot. Nash had gone to work at DeerNose.

"This will just take a minute." I yanked Cuddles away from a puddle of coffee and toward the stoop leading to the stairwell for the office. Upstairs, I unlocked the door, took off his leash, and unburied my laptop. Cuddles woofed. Looked at his bowl, then at me.

"You ate all the dog food last night."

Cuddles pawed his bowl.

"Just a minute." I rummaged in a file cabinet. "All I can find is a bag of sunflower seeds and a can of deviled ham."

Cuddles woofed.

I studied the can. "This can't be good for you."

Cuddles smacked his bowl.

I gave up.

Turning back to my laptop, I logged into the network file monitoring app and studied Nash's searches. "No hits on Kristi Johnson. Not even her home address."

Switching to the mobile phone spy software, I checked his phone data. "Nothing here, too. He's never called or texted her. He's never been near her home. Hasn't even looked her up on social media. Weird."

Cuddles yawned from the La-Z-Boy.

"She has to be part of his DeerNose case, right?" I thrummed my fingers on the desk. "Maybe I just can't retrieve the data because I'm looking in the wrong place. I've only got access to his work computer and cell phone. Do you think he's using a secret laptop, too?"

A snore rose from the La-Z-Boy.

"Right. Let's try this the other way around." I looked up Kristi on social media. "At least she's not dumb enough to take pictures of herself cheating. You can't imagine how many people are caught that way, Cuddles."

He rolled over.

"But Kristi isn't cheating with Nash. She's part of his investigation. Maybe last night, she was with someone who looks like Nash at another Waffle Haus in Gilmore. I'll figure it out, don't you worry." I hid my laptop and stood. Cuddles opened an eye. "We need to go back to the office."

Back at A.S.S. Cuddles licked the glass door. I massaged my arm and rolled the crick in my neck. "I get the sense that this walking thing is more of an A-to-B line between food stops for you. Remember, when we go in, you have to be nice."

Inside, Rhonda shrieked and climbed on top of her desk chair. Annie and Tiffany stayed barred in the back office.

"This is ridiculous," I said. "Rhonda, I need the desk."

Annie poked her head out of the office. "I'll do the desk work. You start the surveillance prep and take Cuddles with you."

"What about the rescue people?"

"I'll call you as soon as I hear anything. Take the company car." She threw the keys. Cuddles jerked out of my grip and darted toward the flying objects.

His mouth opened. Jowls flapped. Drool flew like a jet stream.

"No," I screamed. "Cuddles. No. Sit. Stay. Drop."

The keys landed on the floor. Cuddles looked over his shoulder and glared at me.

Rhonda clamped a hand over her mouth.

Tiffany chuckled. "Atta girl."

Annie slid out of the office. "You got him?"

I nodded.

She slowly approached Cuddles. He moved closer to me and curled his lip. Annie edged back. "I don't get it. I love dogs. Dogs love me. Why Maizie?"

"I think it's my lotion."

"I think it's got something to do with Amanda and Brian Johnson." Tiffany slid out of the office. "Amanda had him trained to attack."

"You think Amanda planned for Cuddles to attack Brian?" I looked at Cuddles. "You poor thing. She made you into a doggie hitman."

He looked up at me, panting, then swung his gaze around the room.

"He's kind of cute once you get used to his monster size," said Rhonda. "You know who else is cute? Derek."

"No." Annie folded her arms and popped her gum. "Don't go there. He's a client."

"A cute client," said Rhonda.

"We don't think our clients are cute," said Annie.

"Sure we do," said Rhonda. "But usually it's a different kind of cute, because we rarely get someone as cute as Derek."

"Derek's a married client," I pleaded. "Who desperately wants to learn his wife is not cheating on him."

"She's cheating on him," said Tiffany. "Sounds like a spoiled rotten—"

"We don't have opinions about clients," said Annie. "Or their spouses."

"I don't have an opinion," said Rhonda. "I just have a lot of sympathy for such a sweet guy who works really hard at making his spoiled wife happy while she cheats on him. All he wants in life is a happy wife and a sound studio in his house. Is that too much to ask?"

"I guess it's too much to ask when it comes to Kristi," said Tiffany.

"We are professionals." Annie glared at Tiffany. "Maizie, do some drive-bys and get to know the subject."

"You got it." I spun toward the door.

"And take the dog."

———

THE PURCHASE of the company car, a gray Chevy Impala, was a small coup for Annie. The Impala symbolized her financial success in building a successful private investigations office. The office expansion and new hires were the bigger coup. Vicki owned Albright Security Solution, but Annie was the real hard-working genius behind it. Previous to the Impala, Annie had focused on digital paper trails: background checks, skip tracing, subpoenas, and due diligence research. When I had proven myself in the field, she pushed us into the infidelity market. Because I drove the dirt bike I received as my fifteenth birthday gift (a long story involving bad credit, lack of funds, and the destruction of a Bronco), Annie had purchased a company car.

When Nash ran Nash Security Solutions, he'd focused on surveillance and security installs with a smattering of paper chase cases. Like me, he'd rather be out in the field than behind a desk. An excellent investigator with great instincts, he closed cases efficiently and quietly. The courts loved his no-nonsense style and attention to detail. For his security work, he relied on word-of-mouth testimony. Never bothered with paid advertisements.

The main difference between Annie and Nash's business style came down to billing.

Annie focused on getting paid. She loved crunching numbers.

Nash? Not so much. He had no issue hounding debtors professionally. Personally, he'd let his accounts receivable slide. Especially if the client was female and down-on-her-luck. Facing a financial crisis after an expensive hospital stay, Nash had lost his business and now worked for DeerNose Apparel's security department.

The financial crisis began when he'd hired a down-on-her-luck celebrity who brought enough negative attention to his company—because her ex-manager/still-mother sought to destroy her daughter's new career in order to force the daughter to return to her old profession, acting—and gotten him black-balled in the business community. His ex-wife didn't help when she'd opened a competing PI shop to punish him. A shop subsequently bought out by the celebrity's ex-manager/still-mother and introduced to the burgeoning film industry in Black Pine.

And hired Annie, a.k.a. Scrooge McDuck, to run it.

In other words, I hadn't the heart to tell Nash about the Impala. Or the expansion. He also thought Tiffany and Rhonda were just hanging out on their days off from LA HAIR.

No idea where he got that idea.

"I know," I said to Cuddles. "I'm lying to Nash. I'll tell him when the timing is better. He's been heartbroken about losing his business and having to work at DeerNose. I'm sure that's why he's so focused on whatever case he's investigating after hours."

I pulled a twig out of Cuddles' mouth and bloop-bleeped the key fob for the Impala. Opened the back door, checked the back seat for food and other items Cuddles would consume or destroy, then held my hand out. "Ride?"

The dog leapt into the backseat, sideswiping me. I rose from the sidewalk, shut the car door, and leaned against the car. Took in deep mouthfuls of non-doggy air. And readied myself to play *Turner & Hooch*.

First stop, the Johnson's home. Second stop, Kristi's weekly salon appointment. Third stop, her gym.

"I'm familiarizing myself with her surroundings," I explained to Cuddles as I drove into the parking lot of Pets And Peeps. "Her daily routine is all over the map, so it's going to be hard to follow her."

I turned around in my seat. "Can I leave you alone for a minute? The errand benefits you. I can't take you inside. This store has live chickens. I don't have a good feeling about how you will handle that situation."

Cuddles moaned.

"I know, but you want food, right?"

He shook his jowls.

"No chickens. I'll be right back." I cracked the windows and ran into the store. Ten minutes later, I ran out with a buggy full of dog accessories and a twenty-pound bag of food. After storing the food in the Impala's trunk, I poured water into a bowl and opened the back door.

Cuddles leaped out and charged toward the store. I dropped the water bottle and took off after him. A family of four exited the store, carrying two chickens. They froze on the sidewalk. The daughters and mother screamed. Flapping and squawking, the chickens fought to escape the arms of the children holding them. The family pivoted and ran back toward the doors.

"Cuddles," I yelled between gasps. "No. Sit. Stay. Heel."

The doors to Pets And Peeps zipped open. The family scurried inside, losing a chicken in the process. The lone chicken flew into the landscaping next to the building. Cuddles woofed and bounded into the bushes.

Three minutes later, I emerged from the bushes covered in leaves, feathers, and dog slime. But with Cuddles in tow. He climbed into the Impala's back seat without protest. I set his water bowl on the car mat, shut the door, and leaned against it. Pulled out my phone and called Annie.

"Rescue people?" I said.

"Not yet," said Annie. "But I did find a dog sitter who specializes in big dogs."

"When can she start?"

"She's going to call me back." Annie paused to pop her gum. "But you're doing great, kid. Cuddles seemed to like riding in the Jeep last night. Driving him around on stakeouts is no big deal, right?"

"What's the bad news?"

"What'd you mean?"

"Your voice got weird. You don't do chipper, Annie. That's my schtick."

Annie coughed. "I don't know what you're talking about. Anyway, this shouldn't take too long."

"Out with it."

"I spoke to Amanda Johnson's lawyer. For pointing the gun at Brian, they could charge her with aggravated assault since Georgia doesn't have attempted murder. But aggravated assault is actually a harsher penalty. And with the discharge of a weapon in a public place, even pointed at the ceiling..."

"Not good."

"Bail is set extremely high. Brian froze their accounts. She can't make bail."

I glanced through the passenger window. Cuddles had tipped his bowl and was lapping water from the car mat.

"Her arraignment is Monday. Hopefully, some family

members will show to help her make bail." Annie's voice lightened again. "But you're doing such a great job with Cuddles. No biggie, right? Just need to get through the weekend."

"Uh-huh. Just so you know, you're going to find some unusual charges to the shop's account," I said. "We owe a family a chicken. And possibly psychological counseling."

SEVEN

#INDUCTIVEDEDUCTIVE
#CALLOFFTHEDOGS

AFTER CHECKING the rest of Kristi Johnson's various haunts, Cuddles and I returned to the office.

"Her place of business wasn't on the list," I said. "Did we forget to get the name and address from Derek?"

"CrossHair Marketing," said Rhonda. "The company is online. She doesn't go to a brick and mortar."

"Listen to you, 'brick and mortar.'"

She glared at me. "Maizie Albright, you think I only know salon terms? Or you think because I'm from Small Town, Georgia, I don't know current phraseology? I read more than *Us* and *New Beauty*. I got the waiting room a subscription to *PI Magazine*, even though it never mentions style. I'm bored out of my mind, but I'm reading it. Because I am a professional."

Cuddles growled.

Rhonda looked at Cuddles. "What I meant to say was, 'yes, ma'am.'"

He dipped his head, eyeing her.

"Cuddles, no." I pointed to the floor, and he flopped onto his stomach. "You're an intelligent woman, Rhonda. I was just teasing."

"Me, too." She pouted. "How am I supposed to trash talk if your dog's threatening to kill me? Girl, that's no fun."

"He's not my dog."

She rolled her eyes and jerked a thumb toward the back office. "Annie wants to talk to you. Take your killer dog with you."

Cuddles and I walked across the room. I knocked and opened the door. Tiffany scuttled out.

"This is ridiculous. I thought you of all people could handle a scary-looking dog," I said. "You're notorious for your fierceness. The first time I met you, you punched me."

"I know how to handle people." Tiffany eyed Cuddles. "You punch that dog in the nose and he won't think twice about ripping your throat out. I saw what he did to Brian."

"You're not Brian. None of us are Brian." I gestured to Cuddles. "She's not Brian."

"Maybe so," said Tiffany. "But you know who Cuddles might believe is Brian? You better think about that carefully."

"What are you talking about?"

"I'm talking about Kristi Johnson, the cheater, hooking up with tall, bald, and scary." Tiffany swung a look around the room. "You're all thinking the same thing, right?"

I folded my arms. "Nash isn't bald. He shaves his head. And he's not hooking up with Kristi Johnson."

"Who did you see at the Waffle Haus?"

"If it was Nash and Kristi, they were just having waffles, not hooking up. He's moonlighting a case." I paused, thinking. "Kristi's a secret shopper. Nash's case involves DeerNose. Maybe she secret-shopped a DeerNose store, and Nash was interviewing her." I smiled triumphantly, proud of my on-the-fly-deductive skills.

"He interviewed her at a Waffle Haus at eleven o'clock at night?" Tiffany's left eyebrow rose.

"I'm sure there's a reasonable explanation."

"Are you going to ask Nash?" said Rhonda.

"I could … Or I—"

"Don't even think about it." Annie shook her head. "You can't ask Kristi. She's our subject."

"I was going to say, I could continue to monitor the situation. Objectively. That's what I have been doing all along. There's been no Kristi Johnson up until last night."

"How do you know?" said Rhonda.

"I've been tracking him with my covert software. I checked today. He's never even googled Kristi Johnson, let alone gone near her house or any of the other places on our surveillance list."

Annie popped her gum.

"Yeah, if he was going to see someone on the sly, Nash would know how to cover his tracks. But I am positive he's not doing that." I straightened my shoulders, feeling confident in my on-the-fly inductive skills, which were almost as good as my deductive skills.

Tiffany tipped her chin, swinging her blue-tipped bob. "Speaking as a woman who's been cheated on, I didn't want to know until I had to know."

"I've been cheated on, too." I shrugged. "Nash is working a case, not cheating on me."

"Just like poor Derek," said Rhonda. "That poor, sweet, incredibly handsome man. He doesn't want to know, but he knows."

"Speaking of Derek—and without the descriptive, since he's a client—let's get back to work," said Annie. "Maizie, create a surveillance schedule. And Rhonda—" Annie clapped a hand over her mouth.

A noxious order assaulted my nostrils. Rhonda pinched her nose. Tiffany's face contorted. I held my breath, and our gazes dropped to the ground where the snoring dog lay.

"What are you feeding him?" muttered Annie through her fingers.

"He eats everything he finds," I said, thinking of the deviled ham.

"Get him out of here. Start the surveillance and figure out the schedule in the car." Annie waved a hand before her face. "I'm going to call that dog sitter again."

———

I PARKED the Impala down the street from the Johnson house, angling so I could easily observe movement through windows, vehicles in their drive, and other activities. Cuddles snored from the backseat. I yawned from the front. The garage door opened. I slid down in my seat, picked up my binoculars, and trained them on the black Ford F-150 exiting the driveway.

Derek Johnson.

Twenty minutes later, a Toyota Prius shot out of the drive.

Kristi Johnson.

"Gotcha." I glanced in my rearview mirror. "Hang on, Cuddles."

I waited a few beats, then followed the Prius. Kristi wound through town, making pit stops at a bank and a dry cleaner before parking at Rounds of Grounds. While Kristi went inside, I backed into a space to watch the door. A large group of women sat at a table beneath a patio umbrella. The coffee shop was Black Pine trendy.

Pulling out my surveillance log, I notated Kristi's stops. The scent of coffee drifted into the car, followed by a whiff of baked goods. My stomach growled.

"This is the hardest part of surveillance, Cuddles. I really want a coffee, but I can't blow my cover. Also, if I get a coffee, I'll have to pee. If I leave to pee, something will happen."

Cuddles pawed at the door.

I turned halfway in my seat. "Do you have to pee? I shouldn't have mentioned it."

He looked at me and swiped the door again.

We made a circle of the parking lot's green space, stopping at each bush, tree, and blade of grass. While I yanked coffee stirrers, lids, and sugar packets from his mouth, I kept an eye on the coffee shop's doorway.

A bird flew past. Cuddles charged after it, pulling me with him. The bird darted toward the shop and perched on a folded umbrella. Jowls flapping, Cuddles lunged for the patio. The women screamed and ran for the door.

"No. Sit. Stay," I shouted. "Sorry, ladies. He was provoked by a bird."

The women yanked the door open. Inside, Kristi and a man sat at a table, a laptop open in front of them. Kristi looked up and our eyes met. The door slammed shut, breaking our eye contact.

"Shizzles. I think she recognized me." Ignoring me, Cuddles lapped a pool of whipped cream. "Not like taking a burn. The investigation just started. She wouldn't know I'm shadowing her yet. Like she really knew me."

Cuddles looked up. Whipped cream ran down his chin.

"Right. Of course, she knew who I was. I'm Maizie Albright. Except now that I'm Maizie-Maizie Albright, fewer people recognize me. My glam polish has worn off. I'm wearing almost real people's clothes." I gestured at my Co high-rise jeans and Port De Bras tank top. "It was like she knew me-knew me."

Cuddles' tongue made a few rounds across his muzzle.

"Back to the car. I want to get video of the guy at her table when he leaves. Standing in front of the shop while you drink a matcha creme isn't doing us any good."

Forty minutes later, Kristi left. I let her go, waiting for the man. Five minutes later, he exited the building. He looked to be in his mid-thirties. Gym fit, but not overly so. Good looking but not excessively. Dressed casually but nice enough for an office. As unobtrusive as male middle management could get.

With the Canon camcorder, I followed his movements to his

car—a blue BMW Z4 that gave me car envy. "I have a thing for blue convertibles."

Cuddles raised his head from his lean against the passenger door.

"They were my vehicle of choice back in California. Now I drive a green dirt bike. And a gray Impala while working. That's life." I shrugged. "Anyway, it looked like Kristi and the dude had a business meeting, not a clandestine rendezvous. Back to the shop. We'll upload the video, turn in our logs, and figure out tomorrow's plan of action."

He turned three times on the seat, curled up, and shut his eyes.

"You take a lot of naps." I pulled from the parking space. "All the eating. Maybe you have a thyroid problem. Did Amanda ever mention—Holy shizzles."

I shrank back against the seat and zipped past the Silverado parked at the far edge of the parking lot.

"What the heck is Nash doing here? He's supposed to be at DeerNose." I turned onto the street and glanced behind me. The tall, imposing figure wasn't looking at my car. He was typing on a laptop. "I knew it. It's a case. It has to be a case."

I looked at the snoring dog. "Really? Can't you hear the excitement in my voice? Don't you want to congratulate me or something?"

The dog opened one eye, glanced at me, shut his eye, and resumed snoring.

"We're going to DeerNose, Cuddles. I've been looking in the wrong places." At the stop sign, I made a U-turn and accelerated toward the other side of town. As we drove past Rounds of Grounds, I eyed the Silverado. "He's cheating, but not on me. He's cheating on DeerNose."

Which meant Nash was also cheating on my father. But that sounded weird, so forget it.

EIGHT

#OFFICEDALLIANCEDANCE #HOUNDING

DEERNOSE HEADQUARTERS WAS CARVED from a forest in the valley created by Black Pine Mountain. The Spayberrys, my father's people, had lived in the area since the days of muskets and log cabins. My father still owned muskets, along with a large assortment of rifles and other weaponry. He also still lived in a cabin—5,000 square feet with nine-foot ceilings and a sun deck—modest for a man of his means. The Spayberrys had fished, trapped, and hunted as a means of survival. My father had done the same. In his early days, the money normal people would allot toward the supermarket, he used to build his empire. An empire built on fishing, hunting, and general outdoorsing.

Or at least outfitting those who did. DeerNose was a garment company named for the camouflage that hid the hunters from their prey. Somehow, he and his team of apparel engineers had figured out how to scent the cloth with deer pee. Actually, a chemical that remarkably smelled the same.

Either way, gross.

I drove into DeerNose's parking lot, skipping the front entrance that looked more lodge than business, and headed toward the employee door in the back. As head of security,

Nash's office was between the administrative and manufacturing areas.

"It's probably not a good idea to bring you inside," I told Cuddles. As soon as the car had slowed, he'd woken up and pressed his nose against the passenger seat window. "This is a place of business. There are many people inside—nice people—and your social skills are not so hot."

He whined and pawed the door.

"I'm sorry, but no. I'll just be a minute." I cracked the windows. "Don't give me those sad eyes. You're trying to manipulate me."

Cuddles cocked his head, doing his best beseeching pout.

"Fine, but listen. Even if it smells like a deer, no tinkling. Also, no growling, barking, snapping, or lunging. Don't show your teeth. You have to be good."

We entered an empty hallway painted to look like a forest. Cuddles took no notice of the animals and birds peeking through the trees, nor of the sounds of nature lightly playing through hidden speakers. He had his nose on the floor, intent on vacuuming.

"Best behavior." I pulled up on Cuddles' leash.

We entered a smaller hall flanked by doors. I marched us to Nash's and knocked. Then used the key I had gained through Mrs. Peters, my father's executive assistant. Petey had known me my entire life and knew I could be trusted.

Although, I hadn't told her that Nash didn't know I had the key. But I also didn't tell her not to tell him. I figured she wouldn't mention it.

"I'm not spying on my boyfriend," I muttered and quietly shut the door. "I'm just trying to help him."

Cuddles snuffled the office floor, walked to the desk, and lifted his leg.

"No," I said. "That's just rude. Your tank has to be empty. You peed on every rock in the parking lot."

Sighing, he plopped on the ground.

"Good dog." I slipped my key logger in the USB port on Nash's computer and pressed the power button. Moving behind the desk, I rifled through his filing cabinets and his desk drawers before turning my attention back to his computer. "Do you think he'd use a code name for Kristi?"

Cuddles growled and paced to the door. I shut off the monitor and poised myself in a relaxed stance in Nash's chair. Then remembered Cuddles. Scrambling around the desk, I grabbed his leash and collar. The door began to open. Cuddles lunged, snapping and barking. The door banged shut.

"Who's in there?" said the deep voice of an older man.

"Just me, Maizie," I called. "Is that you, Marshy? I'm dog-sitting. Hang on."

"Honey, are you okay?"

"Yes, sir. Cuddles isn't a people person. Or a dog person. At least until he gets to know you. Hopefully. Hang on." I looked at Cuddles. "Marshall Roth has known me my whole life. He's my godfather, for heaven's sake. You need to calm yourself."

The bullmastiff lowered his head, rolling his lip.

"Stay down." I stood and tugged on the leash. "Sit. Stay."

The door cracked, then widened. Keeping his hand on the lever, Marshall Roth, my father's long-time friend and business partner, stepped inside the doorway. My father was a large man —tall, broad, and barrel-chested with thick ginger hair gone white. Marshall was shorter and leaner, with thinning hair and glasses. Still, he hunted, golfed, sailed, and fished. Could lift heavy bolts of cloth and knew how to thread sewing machines, repair steam presses, and reset the giant rollers on the heat fuser.

You wouldn't know to look at them, but my father was the creative and Marshall Roth the fixer. Not just of machines. Marshy was DeerNose's in-house lawyer and vice president of operations.

"Little M, what have you gotten yourself into now?" Marshy drawled, staring at Cuddles. "Whose dog is this, and why is he in the building?"

"A client's dog. His owner is in jail. We're sort of waiting on her to make bail." I tightened my grasp on the leash as Cuddles' growl intensified. "If I leave Cuddles in the car too long, he'll destroy it. He already ate a headrest and a seatbelt."

"Good Lord, girl." Marshy stepped backward, keeping his hand on the door lever. "I'm looking for Nash."

"He's not here. Yet," I hedged.

"Out again?" Marshall checked his watch. "How long have you been waiting for him?"

"Not long." I didn't want to get Nash in trouble. At least not with his boss. "I'm sure he'll be back any minute."

"Honey, I know you want to see him, but it's business hours." Marshy eyed the dog. "Alright. You might as well get. I'll tell Nash you stopped in."

"No need to do that," I said, my thoughts on the key logger still stuck in Nash's USB port.

Marshy moved his gaze from Cuddles to meet my eyes. "You two doing okay?"

"We're fine." I used my *Girl's World* smile, one of Marshy's favorites. "I just thought I'd surprise him. Nash's been busy working on a project."

Cuddles lowered his head and lifted his chest.

"Are you sure you're safe with that dog?" Marshall took another step back, bringing the door with him.

"We get along famously. He's suspicious of everyone else. Very protective." I waved away his concern, focused on my fishing expedition. "Anyway, Nash's big project. Do you know anything about it?"

Cuddles lunged. I yanked back on the leash. "No, Cuddles. No. Down. Sit. Stay."

The door shut. "Honey, I'm always glad to see you, but you need to get that dog out of the building," Marshall's voice carried through the door. "Now."

"Cuddles, that was rude." I hurried to the desk, ejected the key logger, and slipped it into my pocket. "But it worked."

I tapped on the computer to scroll through Nash's Outlook calendar. Except for invitations to meetings, he didn't use the calendar.

"What kind of code name would you give a girl named Kristi?" I moved the cursor over the search box.

Cuddles' ears pricked. Growling, he climbed to his feet and swung around to face the door. Taking my cue, I powered off the computer, shut off the monitor, and grabbed the leash. The door swung open. Nash filled the frame. His eyes darted from me to Cuddles, then swept over me again.

"What's he doing here?" Nash narrowed his eyes. "Actually, what are you doing here?"

I gave him a flirty *Cosmo* smile. Realizing that would never work, I switched to the *Mona Lisa* look I did for *GQ*.

"Where've you been?" I countered in the sultriest voice I could muster.

An eyebrow rose, followed by a crease between his eyes. His expression smoothed. He stepped into the room and closed the door behind him.

"Sit. Stay. Stay. Stay." Cuddles sniffed, cocked his head, and lowered his butt to the floor.

"Good dog," said Nash, then looked at me. "But have you been a good girl?"

I shifted tactics—from vixen to beguiling, minus any simpering. "I don't know what you mean."

"I think you do." He prowled the circumference of the room, avoiding Cuddles.

I followed with my eyes, then pivoted as he drew near. He stopped behind the desk. Cuddles, also watching Nash, turned and plopped on my feet. Nash laid a hand on his computer.

His eyebrows rose. "Warm. Interesting since I turned it off more than an hour ago."

"Who's Kristi Johnson to you?" I said, ignoring his implication.

"Kristi Johnson?" Nash didn't hide his confusion. "I don't

know a Kristi Johnson. Or at least, I don't remember a Kristi Johnson. Who's Kristi Johnson?"

"A client's wife."

"What kind of case?"

"Infidelity."

"Why would you think I know her?"

"She met someone at Rounds of Grounds today."

"Rounds of Grounds…" Nash paused a beat. "You saw me there."

I crossed my arms and nodded. "Among other places."

Nash glanced at Cuddles' posture and lightened his voice. "Why would I be tailing your client's wife?"

"What were you doing at Rounds of Grounds?"

"Getting coffee."

"You only like Lamar's coffee." Cuddles tensed. I changed my tone. "You call Rounds of Grounds 'fancy coffee.' You said it tastes like 'dirty flowers.' But you have never lied to me. You must have gotten coffee there. Did it taste like dirty flowers?"

"More like dirty pumpkin pie." His expression darkened. "Are you following me or your client?"

"Why would I be tailing you?"

"Because you are dying to know about my DeerNose investigation." He smirked. "I know you've been shadowing me."

"Have you seen me watching you?"

"No." His smirk disappeared. "But I know you are. Stop smiling."

"If you think I'm watching you but haven't seen me, that must mean I'm pretty good." My smile broadened. "Why won't you let me help you?"

"You know why. It would be too personal for you." He leaned over the desk. "This is your father's company, Maizie."

I stepped around Cuddles and placed my hands on the desk. "Exactly. If something hinky is going on, then I deserve to know."

Nash dropped his hands next to mine, angling closer. "This is me protecting you."

"Remember how we talked about Neanderthal tactics?"

"You can't keep a secret, and I'm not ready to bring this to Boomer." His Paul Newman-blue eyes sparkled, and a dimple appeared next to the scar that ran from his cheek to his chiseled chin. "Besides, you like some of my Neanderthal tactics."

I sucked in a breath, and his eyes dropped.

Shizzles. I did like some of his Neanderthal tactics. But I was supposed to be a feminist. His Neanderthal tactics left me feeling like I'd gladly sign up for cave-woman duty.

Minus the cave and diet. I tried Paleo and couldn't stick to it.

"When do you get off work?" he murmured.

"I'm following Kristi Johnson."

"All night?"

"As long as it takes."

"Care for a ride-a-long passenger? We can take my truck."

"If we share the same subject, that would be convenient for you." I raised my right eyebrow. A skill I honed for the *Julia Pinkerton* role.

"I told you, I don't know Kristi Johnson." His eyebrows waggled. "But I do know what can happen in a truck on a quiet street in the middle of the night."

"Neanderthal tactics," I breathed.

"The kind you like." His dimple deepened.

I paused to think. He didn't know Kristi Johnson, but he knew something. I could use the opportunity to check his reactions and interest. Note his behavior if Kristi did anything.

Nash drew closer until his lips hovered above mine. "I promise to behave myself. Or not. Your choice. We can listen to the Braves and do a proper stakeout. I'm good with that, too."

"You know I get bored listening to baseball."

"I count on it." He winked. His lips brushed mine. Once. Twice. The third time was less of a brush. More of a soft melding of scorching heat.

"I have a job to do," I muttered without much conviction. My thoughts had drifted to what can happen in a truck on a quiet street in the middle of the night. I closed my eyes and rose on my toes to reach his lips. And met empty space.

I opened my eyes.

Nash glared down at me.

Not at me. At the dog wedged between me and the desk. Giant paws rested near Nash's hands. The massive head hovered beneath my chin. Cuddles curled his lip, revealing a fang.

"When is he going home?" Nash whisked his hands from the desk and straightened.

"No," I said to Cuddles. "Sit. You're upsetting your new daddy."

Nash gave me a look.

"He's just like you." I smiled and grabbed Cuddles' leash.

Nash gave me another look.

"Cuddles is big and scary and protective. But really just a marshmallow inside. Soft and gooey. When it comes to me."

"I am not gooey." Nash folded his arms. "Except when it comes to you. Sometimes."

"Will I see you on my surveillance tonight?"

He grinned. "Stakeout in my truck?"

"I don't mean doing surveillance together." I tipped my chin up. "I mean, will I spot you watching my subject, Kristi Johnson?"

"I told you I don't know a Kristi Johnson."

"We'll see about that." I turned toward the door.

"Maizie."

I looked over my shoulder.

"I might not tell you everything, but I don't lie." Nash rubbed his chin. "And if I'm not telling you everything now, it's only because I'm not sure of what I know. It's to protect you."

I believed him. But it didn't change the fact that he wasn't telling me the whole truth.

NINE

WE DROVE BACK to the office in silence.

Too much silence.

"Cuddles." I glanced into the rearview mirror. "Is that stuffing exploding out of a hole in the backseat?"

Cuddles' eyes met mine in the rearview.

"Craptastic. You could at least try and look remorseful." I whipped my gaze back to the street. "You know, that's twice I didn't bring up the Waffle Haus. My ex-therapist Renata would say I'm falling back into non-confrontational patterns to reduce risk in our relationship. But by avoiding risk, I'm actually undermining our foundation and causing instability."

Cuddles woofed.

"You don't have to agree with me."

At A.S.S., everyone had left the office for the evening. I checked for new Kristi information and gathered my surveillance supplies. Hit the drive-through for dinner. And drove by the Johnson house.

The lights were on. Derek's black truck was parked in the drive.

"I don't see Kristi's car." I turned to look at Cuddles. "Okay, don't say anything. We should have followed her from the coffee shop instead of interrogating Nash. But I mean, come on. Of course, I'm going to interrogate Nash."

Cuddles pawed the door.

"Right, water some trees." I grabbed his leash and opened the car door. We looped the neighborhood. A block from the Impala, a man jogged toward us. Cuddles threw his chest out and growled. I did a, "Heel. Stay. Stop. Quit. No."

Jerking to a stop, the man tossed back the hood from his sweatshirt.

Derek Johnson.

"Aren't you from the detective agency?" he said, his eyes on Cuddles.

"Yes, I'm Maizie Albright. I think you remember Cuddles. We were just checking on your house."

"I thought you'd be following Kristi, not me."

Shizzles. I scrambled for an explanation. "We did earlier today. Then I did some … cross-checking. Cuddles and I were headed home for the night, but I just wanted to make sure every-thing was okay here."

"Oh, thanks," he said. "That's really nice. Do you want to come inside?"

Seeing the inside of their house could give me some insight on Kristi. But if Kristi came home, she would see me. Which was why we generally didn't go inside the couple's home.

I explained my dilemma.

"Kristi's at book club." His shoulders drooped. "Supposedly. Anyway, on book club night, she usually doesn't come home until late."

Craptastic. Snooping on Nash made me miss Kristi at "book club." Annie would kill me.

"Good to know." I gave Cuddles a meaningful "I want to see their house, so you better be good" look.

Cuddles sighed.

"Do you want to put him in my backyard?" said Derek. "I have a fence."

"Um. Okay."

"Great," Derek called over his shoulder, crossing the street and fast-walking up his drive. "I know he's your service dog, but he makes me a little nervous. Just bring him around to the right side and you'll see the gate."

"He's not my— Yeah, okay." A picket fence circled their quarter-acre lot. "Look, Cuddles. Lots of trees and bushes to water. You'll be fine for ten or fifteen minutes, right? Just wait for me here."

I opened the gate, led him through, and shut the gate. He plopped on the ground and closed his eyes.

"Or just take a nap. That's good. I won't take long." I walked backward, watching Cuddles through the slats in the fence. When he didn't move, I dashed around the corner of the house and met Derek in his garage.

Derek opened the door to the house. We stepped into his kitchen. "Want a cup of coffee or something?"

"I'm good, thanks." I glanced around the kitchen. Avocado green appliances, oak cabinets, chicken wallpaper. I couldn't learn much about Kristi in this room, other than possibly she was into chickens. Or she didn't secret shop in appliance stores.

"We need to do some updates," Derek said apologetically. "I got the house for a great price. Let me show you my studio."

"Okay." I followed him into the living room. As I walked, I scanned the room, looking for Kristi's touches. A wedding photo in a ceramic frame rested on one table. A flat-screen hung above the fireplace. Built-in shelves flanked the fireplace. On one side, albums—both LPs and CDs—lined the floor-to-ceiling shelves. The other side held a smattering of novels, a shelf of scripts, and two shelves of DVDs. I stopped to check the titles.

"I still use a Blu-Ray player." He blushed. "I keep all the films and TV shows I work on."

"Me, too." I shrugged. "I don't watch them, though."

"I don't watch them, I just listen to them."

"You're a craftsman. You're reviewing your work for the sound quality."

"I knew you'd understand. Most people don't get it." Derek smiled. "I like being a python wrangler. You know, handling the cables. It's an interesting gig, but I'm ready to move up. Some guys want to become a Foley artist or do other sound effects. My goal is music editor."

"That's great."

"That's one of the reasons I decided to learn for sure if Kristi is cheating on me. This whole thing is messing with my head. I'm really distracted at work. The mixer needs to know he can trust me."

"Oh no, I'm so sorry to hear that."

"We've talked about me moving up to booms."

"Boom operator? That's a good step in the right direction."

"Yeah, pays better than what I'm doing now, although I'd rather go into mixing. There's more leeway in Georgia than in California between career tracts, which is nice. Here's my real passion, though."

He ushered me through a door. Control boards, recording equipment, and a mega-ton of cords and wires filled the long room. A large window looked into two smaller rooms. Album cover posters covered the doors and walls.

"This wing was for a study or family room, but I converted it to the studio." He pointed to a control board. "You see this one? I got it for a steal. One of the later versions of *Cats* was recorded with this board. Cool, right? And this one? It's from Mussel Shoals. I bid on it. Needed new wiring, but no big deal. Just think of who could have recorded on this board—Aretha, Wilson Pickett, Dylan, Lynyrd Skynyrd. Even the Stones. Right?"

I nodded and smiled. This told me nothing about Kristi other than she lost an office or family room to a recording studio. The studio was impressive, though.

He pointed to one of the two sound booths. "See that drum

set? I got it from Tokic's Bomb Shelter in Nashville. And that microphone? That's a Shure SM58. Got it used on eBay."

"This is super cool," I said. "But you know what would be really helpful? If you can show me some of Kristi's things."

"Oh, right." Derek's shoulders slumped. "Yeah, that makes sense."

"Unless she's into recording, too?"

"Not really."

We schlepped back through the living room and up the stairs.

"This is our bedroom," he said, opening a door to a room with a king-sized bed and matching furniture.

I walked through, noting the lack of photos. Daddy and Carol Lynn's bedroom had framed photos of me, Remi, the dogs, their extended family, and themselves over every available space, including the walls. Even antiquey-looking photographs of their ancestors that gave me the shivers. Vicki also had framed photos in her designer bedroom. Mainly red carpet and award-night pictures, but still. The absence of personal pictures felt strange to me.

I mentioned the lack of photos to Derek.

"Kristi doesn't have any family. And mine are in California, but we're not really close." He shrugged. "Her dad took off before she was born, and her mom died when she was a kid. Overdose, unfortunately. No siblings. She grew up in foster care."

"That's so sad. Poor Kristi."

"She said her foster parents were nice enough. But she doesn't really talk to them much. Christmas cards and that sort of thing. When I met her, she was focused on her acting career."

"How did you meet?"

"I was working on a TV series. Just as a runner. She was background."

"That's a meet cute. An assistant and an extra."

"Our relationship started a lot later." Derek shook his head.

"Kristi was hoping I knew people. Wanted me to put in a word for her, you know. I did get her on as a feature."

"A featured extra? That's great, especially for a series."

He nodded. "But she didn't stay past the season we were shooting. Kristi got a day player job at another set. Bit part. She had a few lines."

"Did she get her SAG card?"

"Yeah, but that was her only speaking part." He grimaced. "Kristi struggles with landing an agent. She got most of her jobs through word of mouth. In California, she took classes and would audition when she heard of something. Or use casting notices."

"That's rough. A really hard way to get parts."

"Yeah." He sighed. "We both have dreams and this industry can be harsh. That's why I thought we might have a better shot in Georgia."

"How does she like her new job?"

"She seems to like it." He paused. "She doesn't talk about it much."

"What can you tell me about CrossHair Marketing? The company, I mean."

"Not much. They seem to treat her well."

"Do you know where they're based? Who her boss or coworkers are?"

"No idea. We don't talk about it much." His gaze dropped to his feet. "We don't talk about anything much."

A clatter followed by a loud crack caused my stomach to tighten. I couldn't tell if it came from inside or outside the house.

"What was that?" Derek cocked his head.

"I should probably get going. I don't like to leave Cuddles too long."

"You're really attached to that dog. That's sweet."

I gave him a tight-lipped grin. Sweet had nothing to do with it. More like self-preservation.

———

IN THE DOORWAY to the kitchen, Derek halted. "That's odd. I don't remember opening the fridge."

Shizzles.

As discreetly as I could, I pushed past him and into the kitchen. The refrigerator door stood open. I couldn't spot anything on the ground—no splatters, spills, carcasses. I blew out a breath, closed the fridge, and felt a breeze.

Not an air-conditioning breeze. The breeze had the sweet tang of grass and pine. An outdoor breeze.

"You have a doggy door?" I said, repressing the anxiousness in my tone.

Derek smacked his head. "Oh, right. We don't have a pet, so I totally forgot about it. But I sealed it off with a piece of plywood. Until I get time to put in a new door."

As casually as I could muster, I fast-strolled past the fridge to the breakfast nook. Spotted the back door and suppressed a gasp. I wrenched open the door with the gaping hole, stepping over the splinters and bent nails. Outside, a piece of mangled and chewed wood had been left on the concrete patio. Also, what appeared to be the metal and plastic frame to what once must have been a doggy door.

"Cuddles?"

A moment later, the giant galloped toward me and stopped a few feet away. He pawed the ground, spotted the evidence of his destruction, and backed away. His tail hooked over his butt, and he plonked his back haunches onto the concrete.

"What did you do?" I spoke in a furious whisper. "You destroyed this man's door? And what else?"

Raising his chin, he cast his eyes toward the tree line.

"What did you eat? Stay right there, you bad dog." I stalked across the patio to the gate. In the light cast from Derek's patio, I found pieces of a pizza box, a milk jug, and an egg carton.

"And a can of ... What is this? Beans?" I shouted, picking up the mangled can missing a label. Then spotted the bottles of ketchup and ranch dressing. "OMG, Cuddles. I was gone for ten minutes. Ten. Minutes. Twenty tops."

I picked up the trash and stomped back to the patio. Cuddles moved his gaze to the sunset. Gave me the side-eye.

"This is a client," I hissed. "It's one thing to eat all of my food and destroy the company car. But a client? What was I thinking? I should have left you to further destroy the Impala. Twenty. Minutes. Twenty minutes and you destroyed a door and ate the contents of a refrigerator."

Cuddles stared at the power lines.

"What am I going to do? I can't charge it to the company or Annie will find out I was at the Johnsons' house. I'm going to have to pay for this myself. How much does a door cost, Cuddles? I don't even know."

I tried to gather the wood with the destroyed trash. Lost the bottles. Then the cans. Dropping the pieces of the pizza box, I squatted on the ground and covered my face with my hands.

"Hey, don't cry." Derek dropped his hand to my shoulder. "It's not that big of a deal. He's just a dog."

"Half of your door is missing," I wailed. "And he's not just a dog. He's like seven dogs in one. Maybe eight."

"That's true. But really, don't worry." He squeezed my shoulder.

"I'm so sorry." I rose, holding the empty bottle of ranch dressing. "We'll pay for all this. I'll find someone to come out and fix your door. Or install a new one. And if you give me a list of the groceries, I'll get those now."

"Really, it's okay." Derek took the bottle from my hands. "I mostly eat at Crafty. Kristi doesn't cook. I don't really either."

"No, it's not okay. Craft Services is wonderful, but you need food at home, too." I pinched the skin between my thumb and pointer finger to ward off tears. "I knew I couldn't trust Cuddles. I should have left him in the car. Or not come in at all. Today he ate a chicken and the backseat of the Impala."

"That sounds … bad." Derek wrung the punctured bottle between his hands. "But really, I can fix the door. For now, I'll just tack a tarp over the hole."

"That's really nice of you. But what will Kristi say?" My lip trembled, thinking about the implications. He'd have to tell Kristi. She'd know he had hired us. It would damage their already precarious marriage. I ruined the investigation and a marriage. Annie would kill me for destroying his house and losing the client.

"Kristi won't notice. Trust me. I've got all kinds of projects at the house going on all the time. She's constantly annoyed by them, so I gave up explaining a long time ago. If she notices, she'll roll her eyes. I'll shrug and tell her it'll get fixed soon. She's wanted to get rid of that doggy door for a long time, anyway."

I sniffed and swiped at a runaway tear. "I'll get your groceries at least."

Derek patted my hand. "No, no. I'm good. They weren't really groceries."

"Are you kidding me? Pizza's real." I gulped back a small sob. Noticed he hadn't let go of my hand. I slipped mine out. "I'll go to the store now."

"How will you go in the store if you can't take your dog? Why don't you come inside? I'll fix you something to drink."

"That's a very nice offer." I blinked away tears. "But I don't think it's a good idea, Derek. We're working for you. And my dog just destroyed your kitchen. I'll just go. I'll have someone bring you the groceries. Thank you."

"Right. Okay. Maybe another time."

I called over Cuddles. He pressed against my leg, but turned his head away. "I am sorry. I will pay for all this."

"Maizie," Derek said gently, "maybe you should talk to your trainer about Cuddles. I think service dogs are required to behave … differently."

I coughed back a snort. "I wish I could, Derek."

TEN
#DROOLANDDONUTS
#CHEEZEDANDPAUFED

WE RETURNED to A.S.S. Cuddles wouldn't look at me. I didn't want to look at him. After ordering a delivery of groceries to the Johnsons, I found a sleeping bag in Annie's office. I bedded in the sleeping bag. I didn't know where Cuddles slept, and to be honest, I didn't care.

The next morning I woke exhausted. During the night, a giant dog had tried to crawl into the sleeping bag with me. A battle of wills ensued. I lost. But gained a hot and hairy blanket draped half across my body. A blanket that drooled and snored. Loudly.

After a walk that included a stop for donuts and coffee, I filled out an expense report that looked more like a damage report. Cuddles and I were out the door before Annie returned and questioned my decision to enter the Johnson house.

I'd already questioned that decision and concluded it hadn't been a good one. But I was determined to do better. Each day is a new opportunity to succeed.

Anyway, that's what my therapist used to say.

From our position down the street from the Johnson's house, it looked like Derek had left but Kristi was home. Hopefully, the wine flowed at book club and she hadn't noticed the giant hole in her back door.

Soon after arriving, we shadowed the Prius. No coffee shop meeting this time. Gym. Lunch. Home. All by herself. After several hours, my butt was numb. The car smelled like dog. I smelled like dog. I called Annie and reported my "no news is good news."

I am always hopeful that the client's infidelity doubts are wrong.

"We don't have opinions on the client's marriage—good or bad," said Annie. "But I'll take over tonight. Go home. Get some rest. Saturday's date night, right?"

"And you'll take Cuddles?"

No such luck.

After a Hot Clucks stop and walk along the lake where Cuddles might have eaten a duck (I didn't look), we motored to the old office. We grabbed a bag of day olds and climbed the stairs. Cuddles remembered to skip the step that sounded like a gunshot. He hopped into Lamar's chair. I pulled out my secret laptop. Later, I convinced him not to kill Nash. We'd settled into a routine.

Cuddles slept in the chair. Nash slept in his office. I slept on the couch. In the morning, while I walked Cuddles, Nash made his escape and called me.

"I'm hanging out with Lamar," said Nash. "How long do you plan to keep this up?"

"Until we find a dog sitter, I guess. I'm thinking of getting t-shirts made that say, 'Free Amanda Hearn.' I'm on surveillance duty tonight. You'll get your couch back."

"I'm more concerned with getting you back."

Grinning, I said my goodbyes. "We need to prepare for tonight, Cuddles. If it's as boring as yesterday, we're going to need good snacks."

His tail wagged.

"By good, I mean healthy."

He sighed.

I knew how he felt.

———

AFTER RUNNING OUR ERRANDS, we parked down the street from Kristi's house. Cuddles snored in the backseat. I tried not to do the same in the front. Out of boredom, I turned to my backpack to look over my stock. Pulled out my binoculars, camcorder, and case log notebook. The newest issue of *InStyle*. And *Elle*. Plus the Saint Laurent Lookbook I had borrowed from Vicki. Cuddles' new collapsible bowls.

Cuddles woke from his nap with a snort. Sniffed the air.

"Getting ready for an all-nighter." I popped the collapsible bowls open, poured water into one, and reached over the seat to set it on the floor.

Cuddles ignored the water and stretched from the backseat to hang over the passenger armrest. He nosed at my backpack.

"Get out of there." I tossed the backpack on the floor. "Nothing but healthy for you from now on."

Cuddles looked at me.

"I know, but—" I bit off my words.

The Johnson's garage door had opened. Kristi's Prius backed out of the driveway.

"Get ready. Sit." I jerked a thumb toward the backseat and started the Impala. The Prius shot down the road. "Hang on."

I watched my distance, careful to not get burned. Black Pine didn't have a real rush hour, but it was dinnertime and the town was on the move. I maintained one car between us and watched for choke points. Kristi turned right onto the highway leading out of town. I sped up to the intersection, then slowed my turn to not draw attention to the Impala.

Cuddles climbed onto the middle console.

"What are you doing? Get down."

He clambered into the front seat. The magazines and bags of

food slid to the floor. I reached for the binoculars and camcorder and shoved them in the console. I glanced over. He sat on his haunches watching the black Toyota Tundra in front of us.

"That's not Kristi. She's in the Prius. If this guy doesn't speed up, I'm going to have to pass him. That's tricky. He's behind Kristi."

He flopped down and closed his eyes.

"We're headed toward Gilmore. Derek's out of town. He said his show is filming at a remote location so he won't be home for a few days. We might catch her tonight."

I grimaced. "Actually, I hope not. I always want the suspicious spouse to be wrong. I have this fantasy. We'll find the suspect in self-improvement seminars or secretly helping the poor. The spouses will reconcile and have a vow renewal. They'll invite us to the wedding and…"

The Tundra's back lights flared.

"Oh, she turned. Hang on." I sped, then slowed onto Gilmore's business highway and positioned myself behind a minivan. "Where are we going?"

The Prius turned into a neighborhood. I slowed to a crawl, irritating the truck behind me, and turned onto a pretty street of newer homes meant for growing families. "Maybe she's visiting a friend."

Kristi took a right, moving out of the neighborhood and onto a busier road, then shot onto a side street behind the stores. A quieter street leading to a newish apartment complex: Windmere.

The Prius wound between apartment buildings and parked before building C. I idled next to D. Kristi popped out of the Prius, carrying a grocery bag and a sunflower-printed duffle. Her long legs made quick work over the sidewalk and up the outside stairs to the second floor. I watched her place the duffle on the ground, take a key from her purse, and open the door. I backed into a spot across from C and looked at Cuddles.

"Are you kidding me? You ate all the—" I stopped, turning

my attention to the blue BMW Z4 that had driven up to building C. I squirmed down in my seat, readied my camera, and raised it to hover just below the window.

The driver's door opened, and a pair of legs drew out. A pair of oxblood brogues shod the feet. Paired with dark chinos, they sharpened the trendy, urban look. The body attached to the legs emerged from the car in a slow, graceful arc.

"It's the guy from the coffee shop," I muttered.

I left the video running, capturing the BMW's plates. With my lens, I followed the man as he climbed the stairs to the apartment Kristi had entered. He pulled keys from his pocket, unlocked the door, and went inside.

"Bingo," I said without enthusiasm. I had hoped Kristi was cat-sitting. Or dog-sitting. Fish-sitting would be good.

I swept the lens across the windows of the apartment, but the blinds had been pulled. I angled the camera down the building. A glint of light caught my eye. Leaving the camera on, I peered through the passenger window. Noted a Silverado backed into a space behind Building E.

The driver held a pair of binoculars before his eyes. Paul Newman-blue eyes. Not that I could tell from here. I just knew the color by heart.

ELEVEN

I WAS ON A SHIP. A squall rose in the distance. The rhythmic undulation beneath my head matched the heavy whistle of wind. The ship smelled musky and musty. Not terrible, but not pleasant. Or at least the fur-lined bunk I'd curled up on reeked of the odor. Like dehydrated cheese and … dog.

I blinked and focused on the ceiling of the bunk, which looked a lot like the gray headliner of the Impala. Pulling a Cheeze Pauf off my face, I untangled my legs from below the steering wheel and shimmied my elbow beneath me. My head was wedged between Cuddles' belly and the passenger seat. Using my elbow as a lever, I hoisted my stiff body.

The Silverado and BMW were gone. However, the Prius was still parked before Building C. Dawn hadn't quite broken, but a few people were on the move, leaving for work.

"Cuddles," I hissed. "We fell asleep on watch. We've got to get out of here before someone sees us."

Cuddles rolled over and resumed snoring.

I glanced back at the apartment. "This doesn't bode well for poor Derek. Kristi had an all-nighter with the BMW guy. Now I have to figure out who he is." I brightened. "Maybe a cousin? Or she's friends with the BMW guy's wife and the wife is sick? Wouldn't that be great?"

A low moan broke my reverie.

"I don't mean it's great that BMW's wife is sick … Okay. Right." I bent over, shuffled through the partially chewed trash below the passenger seat, then rifled through my backpack. I looked up. "You ate a whole bag of Denta-Bonz? It's not like I can tell by your breath."

Cuddles nosed through the trash and jerked his head to the side, tossing his bowl at me.

"I get it. Fine. We're going. But we're coming back."

———

AT THE GAS STATION, I bought dog food, a bag of breakfast sandwiches, and a large coffee. I couldn't risk walking Cuddles around the apartment complex and stopped at Gilmore's dog park. Ironically, the park was full of squirrels, not dogs. Maybe due to the time of day. Sunrise was not a time to encounter dog park dogs.

I relaxed against the fence, relieved Cuddles could run, sniff, and pee to his heart's content. If a squirrel was chomped, that was less of a social faux pas and more Darwinian.

Pulling out my phone, I texted Annie and gave her the basic outline of my surveillance. My phone rang two seconds after I hit send.

"You're up?" I said.

"I always hit the gym before work." Annie paused. "So BMW guy … too bad we can't run his plates. That'd make life easier. Next time you see that car, follow him instead of her. Get more pictures. Stake out the apartment. Watch to see if she takes out the trash. A little garbology might reveal a name or something."

I grimaced at the thought of garbology.

"You need me to take over for a bit?"

"I could use a shower," I said. "And a break from Cuddles would be nice."

Annie puffed out a long breath.

"Are you lifting weights or something?"

"No, I'm already at the office. I'm working on a dog sitter. The one I thought I had fell through. Hang tight. I'll be there in an hour. If Kristi moves, ping me your location."

I slipped my phone back in my pocket and gazed at the dog park field. Empty. My heart stuttered. My eyes swept the fence line, checking for breaks. I looked down. Cuddles lay pressed up against the gate, sleeping.

"Are you kidding me? You use the time to take a nap?" I shook my head and opened the gate.

Cuddles opened an eye.

"Come on. We've got to get back to our stakeout."

He closed his eye.

"Breakfast is waiting."

He shot out of the gate, heading toward the Impala. I ran after him. Opened the door to the back seat and gasped. The stitching between two of the seats had rent, exposing thick foam. Pocked foam. Pocked with teeth marks. Worse yet, the underside of the seat had also been chewed.

Cuddles hopped in the back seat and climbed between the seats to the front.

"Annie is going to kill me." I slammed the door shut. "This is a new pre-owned car. You are eating a car. Who eats cars? Besides Godzilla?"

I unlocked the trunk, filled his food bowl, and opened the driver's door. Reaching behind the seats, I set his collapsible bowl filled with food on the floor. He looked at me. Glanced at the back seat. I raised my brows. Moaning, he clambered onto the center console and poised to jump into the back.

Feeling wise with my newfound dog-savvy, I grabbed the bag with my breakfast sandwich from where I had left it on the roof of the car. Climbed into the car and reached to shut the door.

Felt the bag rip from my hands.

If Annie didn't find a dog sitter soon, I was going to quit.

———

WE RETURNED TO WINDMERE. In the parking lot, the Prius hadn't moved. Other spots had opened. I positioned us catty-corner from Building C. We resumed our watch. I sipped coffee. Cuddles slept.

And occasionally farted.

Okay, more than occasionally.

The sun rose higher and the parking lot grew busy with people leaving for work. No one took notice of me. Many did of Cuddles. Mainly because he went nuts anytime a person (Or a leaf. Bug. Candy wrapper.) got within fifty feet of the car. As a ruse, I pretended to get ready for work.

By the time I had applied my eighth coat of mascara, I thought I might lose my mind. Not just from Cuddles' *Cujo* act, but from wondering when Annie would call. Wondering what time the Silverado had left the previous night.

Also wondering why Nash had been watching Kristi Johnson when he supposedly didn't know her.

Nash wasn't lying when he said didn't lie. If he didn't want me to know something, he wouldn't tell me. A fuzzy gray line. But it was fair. Everyone had secrets. It wasn't like he was cheating on me.

But what was he doing? If he didn't know Kristi, did he know BMW guy?

There was an idea. Maybe BMW had been at the Waffle Haus, too. We were investigating opposite ends of an illicit romance. Except Nash was no longer a PI. He worked security for Deer-Nose. And was supposedly investigating something in DeerNose.

Did BMW work for DeerNose?

Movement at Building C caught my eye. I straightened in my seat. In the back seat, Cuddles woke with a snort, bounded over the center console, and nosedived into the passenger seat.

"Get ready."

I centered my camera on the apartment's stairwell. A moment later, Kristi popped into view, carrying the sunflower duffle. My Canon whirred. She wore jeans and a t-shirt with her hair in a ponytail. Surprising for a secret shopper with access to designer duds. She moved slowly, pausing between unlocking the car and opening the trunk. Took a few beats before getting in.

"She's thinking about something."

I pulled out of our spot and followed Kristi from the apartment complex. Twenty minutes later, we were on the outskirts of Black Pine. My phone rang.

"Where are you?" said Annie. "Do you want me to take over?"

"We're on the move toward Black Pine. We just passed the Piggly Wiggly and coming toward the place that serves chicken and pimento sandwiches."

"Maizie, I told you to learn street names. I can't map a route by your favorite lunch destinations."

"Hang on."

Kristi turned off the local highway and onto a street. One I knew well. "She's on Buckshot Drive. Why is she on Buckshot? I thought she'd go home."

"I'm in the Jeep," said Annie. "Heading toward Buckshot. I'm going to relieve you. Shouldn't be hard to find her on Buckshot. It dead ends…"

"At DeerNose," I interrupted. "I'm very familiar with this particular street. Why is she here?"

Because Nash worked at DeerNose? I didn't want to say it out loud, but I had a feeling Annie was thinking the same thing.

"You can go home. Shower and rest. I'll take over," said Annie.

"Nash was doing surveillance at that apartment complex, too," I said. "But he says he doesn't know Kristi."

"Nash was at Windmere? He *says* he doesn't know Kristi? You didn't include this information in your report earlier. When were you going to tell me this?"

"I thought it wasn't relevant."

"Do you understand relevancy? How is a man watching our subject not relevant?"

"Because he's a PI."

"Not anymore he's not and even if he is a PI, he's still relevant."

"Nash says he doesn't know Kristi. Something is weird."

"You're off the case."

"What?"

"You heard me," barked Annie. "And you know why."

"Nash doesn't lie. I couldn't find any evidence that he knows her."

"You know this because you're spying on him. Illegally tapping his computer and phone. A DeerNose computer and phone, by the way. I've pretended I don't know what you're doing because I didn't want to implicate myself, but you're going to get us in a helluva big lawsuit. This ends now. I'm taking over."

"But we're here. I can just go in and ask him."

"No. You don't ask him. All surveillance and questions related to the Johnsons stop now." Annie's gum chomping crescendoed with her agitation. "I'm here. Go home."

"Let me park anyway." I drove the Impala toward a line of cars pulling through the gates. Kristi's Prius was three cars ahead of me. Somewhere behind me was Annie's Jeep. I stayed in the line of people arriving at work, wondering where the Prius would park. In front, in the visitors' section?

Nope. Shizzles.

Kristi drove around to the side. Near the factory. Near the side door where I always entered. By Nash's office.

Chewing my lip, I drove closer and parked two rows behind her. Watched as Kristi shuffled toward the door, mixing in with another group of women. They looked like seamstresses. I recognized a few who had been with DeerNose for years. They took no notice of Kristi, too busy chatting and waving hellos. Kristi walked into the building. Like she belonged.

I looked at Cuddles. He stared back at me. "What is going on?"

Cuddles barked, catapulted off his seat, and lunged for the window.

"Down," I yelled. "Sit." I turned to the window, half-expecting to see Nash.

Not Nash.

Annie's jaw firmed, and her eyes flashed.

I grabbed Cuddles' collar with one hand and zipped down the window.

"I told you to go home," said Annie.

"But she … Kristi went inside with the seamstresses. Nobody noticed her. She could be—" I had no idea what she could be doing. Cheating on her secret shopper job? "Why would she dress like a seamstress?"

Annie's head jerked back. But her eyes softened. "You've been up all night. Time to get some rest. I'll take over from here. I promise to tell you what I find out."

"But—" I swallowed hard. Annie thought … what did she think? But that didn't make sense. If Kristi and Nash were having clandestine meetings at DeerNose, why would she pretend to work in the factory?

"BMW," I chirped. "I'll work on figuring out who the BMW driver is."

Annie shook her head. "You're nothing to do with this case. We've got this. Go home."

"But—"

"You're done. Go home."

TWELVE
#DOGGEDDEFEAT #FASHIONFAUXPAWED

I'D HEARD those words before—"You're done. Go home."—but never from Annie. From a producer when I left for rehab. I wanted to finish the movie shoot first, but they digitally subbed me in for the few retakes I had left.

The digitally enhanced version of myself did a better job than my real self. I'm surprised Hollywood hasn't gone completely AI. According to my writer friends, they use artificial intelligence to save on paying scriptwriters all the time now.

But this case was real and now and very confusing. I wasn't even completely sure Kristi was cheating on Derek. Or if Nash was cheating on DeerNose.

I needed to clear my head, but needed a shower even more. I smelled like dog.

And defeat.

Thirty minutes later, I pulled up to the gate, marking the drive to my father's cabin. He took an ATV to work every day, cutting down his commute by cutting through the forest that stood between his home and office. I drove on roads like a normal person. Which took twice as long. But still.

While I waited for the gate to open, I turned to my partner and gave him my most serious look. "Listen Cuddles. This is

Daddy's cabin. Children live here. Actually, one. Remi. My half-sister. If you try to chomp her, she'll take you on. I seriously don't know who would win, but she's only six, so let's not try anything, okay?"

Cuddles sighed.

"A lot of dogs live here, too. They're Jack Russell terriers and a lot like Remi. They will also take you on. Just stay in my room and ignore everyone. And please don't scare Daddy's wife, Carol Lynn. She's the sweetest woman in the world and possibly the best cook, too. If you were smart, you'd work Carol Lynn to your advantage."

I let him stew on that advice while I steered the half-eaten Impala up the long and winding drive and parked in front of the cabin. Knowing the kitchen was likely the most populated room, I led Cuddles through the front door to my bedroom. After locking the door and giving Cuddles a "Sit" and "Stay," I headed into the shower to think.

While I sudsed with Whamisa and conditioned with Weleda, I realized the key to my conundrum was likely Kristi's employer. DeerNose and CrossHair Marketing, the secret apparel shopping company, had to be the link. I needed to get back to the office and look at Rhonda's research on the company. Show Annie that Nash's connection was only peripheral.

I sped through my beauty routine, dressed, and exited the bathroom. Halted two steps into my bedroom. And picked my jaw off the floor.

Cuddles lay on my bed. Not surprising. However, instead of drool, he was engulfed in sparkles. And tulle. And what looked to be my Victoria Beckham Beauty midnight lid luster. Circling his eyes and covering most of his forehead.

"And my Bobbi Brown?" I exclaimed. "Dude. That's brand new."

Remi dropped the gold lipstick tube and kicked it under the bed. "Is his name Bobbi Brown?" She jerked her thumb at the made-over dog.

"His name is Cuddles." I pressed my hands against the sides of my face. "He let you do this to him?"

"He didn't complain." Remi cut Cuddles the side-eye. "Much. The Jacks won't sit still long enough for me to dress them."

"OMG, Remi. He could've bitten you. Badly."

She turned to examine Cuddles. "You bite?"

Cuddles buried his head beneath the green tutu, knocking off his tiara.

"I don't think he bites."

"How did you get in here, anyway? I locked the door."

"I forget." She squinted at me. "Where've you been?"

"On a stakeout. Leave the dog alone. I'm dog-sitting. He's not friendly." I cocked my head. "Hang on, has Daddy left for work yet?"

"I already ate breakfast." She folded her arms.

Remi was lying, but I didn't have the time or energy to fight that battle. Her campaign against eating was more of a reverse siege. One I couldn't comprehend. Gordon Ramsay wouldn't find fault with Carol Lynn's home cooking.

The strength and subterfuge of Remi's rebelliousness made me fear her teenage years.

"Is Daddy still here?" I gave her my best adulting, hard-eyed look. "Yes or no."

She shrugged, then nodded.

"On second thought, stay with Cuddles. I need to talk to Daddy before he leaves for work."

Daddy was no longer eating but in his study. A room *Field & Stream* might have designed. Framed prints of camouflage and gun cases lined the wood-paneled room. Daddy—who often appeared in *Field & Stream*—stood before one of the gun cases, stroking his beard and rocking on his heels.

"What's wrong?" I blurted, hoping he wasn't worried about Nash. Particularly while staring at his deer rifles.

"Mornin' sunshine." He pivoted, dropping his hand from his

beard to smile at me. But his eyes had lost their usual luster and his forehead remained pinched. "Just some things going on with work. Nothing to worry yourself about."

"Staff issues?" I hinted.

"Naw. I've got the best crew in the world." This time, his smile was real. "Never you mind, hon'."

"Nash is working on a big project. How's that coming? Causing you any stress?"

"Is he now?" Daddy blinked. "I'm not detailed in security, so I wouldn't know about that."

I needed different lures for this conversation. "Has there been any internal issues Nash would need to focus on? Maybe with the seamstresses?"

"Seamstresses? Those gals are reliable, as the day is long. I'd trust them with anything. You must be mistaken, baby girl. But that Wyatt Nash is a self-starter. Wouldn't surprise me if he's burning the midnight oil. Security's got a big reach and is involved in things across the globe as we expand. It's a big job. If he's not always available for a date night, you're going to have to give him a pass. Just take heart that we appreciate Wyatt Nash's 110% all-in attitude."

I sighed. My lures didn't work. I'd have to use traps. Or outright honesty. But I didn't know enough about the situation for either of those schemes.

"I tell you what does have me in a pickle," Daddy continued.

I brightened. "Tell me about your pickle."

"My latest samples I got back are nothing like the tech packs I sent. I don't know what happened. This could put us back in production. We'll lose our place in the market."

My brightness dimmed. Tech packs were the spec designs Daddy created for his clothing lines. Nothing to do with Nash. "Why did you outsource the samples? Don't you usually have them made in-house?"

"We've grown too big, hon'. It's been years since we've made everything at DeerNose HQ. All we do locally is small batch specialty stuff. And the designing, of course."

"You mean you outsource the *prêt-à-porter* and make the *haute couture* in-house?" I grinned.

He rolled his eyes. "Girl, don't throw those fashionista terms around this house. But, yes. I suppose so. We have some high-rollin' hunters who like the bespoke stuff." He frowned. "I shouldn't have let Marshall talk me out of keeping the samples at home, though."

Custom-made hunting clothes smelling of deer pee. High fashion knew no bounds. "What happened to your samples?"

"They sent these." Stepping away from the gun cabinet, he revealed a narrow rack of clothing hiding behind his giant body. He grabbed a hanger and held it before him. "Can you believe it? Our manufacturer thought my tech packs were some kind of joke or gimmick, but they made the samples without question and sent them, anyway."

I examined the booted overalls. "I don't know. Pink sequined fish are cute."

"On waders?" He shot me a look of disgust. "Those sequins will catch the light and alert the fish. Not to mention the color will tip them off."

"Fish are that smart?" I cocked my head.

He glared at me. "Yes."

"Can't you just have the manufacturer skip the sequins and change the color?"

"Look more carefully." He shook the waders. "What's the material?"

I rubbed the thick cotton. "Nice touch with the linen. This will keep your fishermen cool."

"Good grief, girl. Why would someone want to stand in a stream in linen?"

"Daddy, I don't understand why someone would want to stand in a stream at all."

"Waterproof. They are supposed to be waterproof. A water-proofed polyester microfiber high-density taffeta."

"Taffeta," I breathed. "Now you're speaking my language. I love taffeta."

"Not what you're thinking of. Look at this one." He held up a large t-shirt. More pink. Emblazoned with a hunter hugging a deer.

"'Make Love, Not War.'" I smiled. "Also cute."

Daddy lowered his brows. "Not to me. I almost fired the manu-facturer for their mistake when the sample maker showed my signature on the tech pack proofs. Someone goofed somewhere down the line. I've got to send in another round of designs."

"Why don't you resend the designs you already made?"

"Because I don't know where those are, honey." Daddy scowled. "And if someone else has them, they've got my spring lineup. I can't risk releasing a line that could be compromised."

"I'm sorry, Daddy. Anything I can do to help?"

"We'll figure this out. In the meantime, I'll be burning the midnight oil to create a whole new line." He sighed. "Sometimes I long for the days when DeerNose was still small, and I had more control of what we did. At least if a mistake was made, I could see the when, where, why, who, and how. And correct it. Now, most things are out of my hands. But I've still got to answer to the board for those mistakes."

"This is so odd, though." I rifled through the pink clothing trimmed in sequins, fringe, and shiny rickrack. "I hope you get Nash involved. He'll get to the bottom of it."

Daddy grunted. "Did you need something, Maizie?"

I glanced at him. "I almost forgot. Do you know a young woman named Kristi Johnson? She might be a seamstress."

He shook his head. "I know all those gals. Never heard of Kristi Johnson. I did know a Christy Anderson once. Nice girl. Great marksman."

"Never mind." I hugged him and grabbed the pink deer t-shirt. "I hope you find your tech packs quickly. Maybe it's not too late."

"Thanks, hon. You're taking that t-shirt?"

"Unless you need it for evidence." I winked. "I love fashion samples." I couldn't tell him he finally had a line I would willingly wear.

And not only did I love fashion samples, but I also loved evidence.

———

OUTFITTED IN MY DEERNOSE BLING, I returned to DeerNose. With Cuddles. Minus the tutu and tiara. But not all of my lip gloss, because Remi had used a semi-permanent lip stain.

The ruined tech packs were the perfect excuse. If Annie found me, I legitimately had a reason to return to DeerNose that had nothing to do with the Johnsons. Since Annie's Jeep was not in the parking lot, I didn't have to worry about an excuse.

Kristi's Prius was also gone, explaining Annie's disappearance. Giving me the freedom to question the seamstresses. Except for one minor detail.

Cuddles.

I supposed Annie kicking me off the case would count as a detail. But we all knew (or at least I did), I wouldn't drop the case.

"Can I trust you in the car for thirty minutes?" I said to the empty backseat. "The air is cool and overcast. I'll leave water. It would be so helpful, Cuddles. You could nap. You love naps."

His head popped up.

I pulled a piece of foam off his fang and sighed. "Okay, I can't risk dog hair in the production area. We'll try the break room. But if I spy a cake, we're not staying. I'm not ruining someone's birthday for a chance to learn why Kristi was hanging with the sewers."

We entered the building, turned left, and before reaching the big doors for the workspace, I hung a right into a short hall housing bathrooms and a break room. Cuddles lifted his head, pulled in a long breath. And charged toward the break room, towing me with him.

"My arm," I shrieked. "Wait. Stop. Halt. Sit. Stay."

Cuddles' haunches hit the floor, but his nose pressed against the door. His ears flicked back while his tongue mopped the door.

"Stay." I rubbed my arm, pushed on the door, and peeked inside. Two middle-aged women holding coffee mugs stood at the counter, staring at me.

"Hi," I said, wedging my body into the frame of the door. I held the leash in one hand and kept the door closed against my body with the other. "How are you?"

"Good, how are y'all?" said one.

"Is that a dog?" said the other.

"Yes," I said. "He's just visiting, but I'm not letting him in here. I'm looking for a seamstress. Kristi Johnson. Do you know her?"

The ladies looked at each other and shook their heads.

"I thought I saw her come in with everyone this morning. Dark hair in a ponytail. T-shirt. Jeans."

They glanced down at their t-shirts and jeans and shrugged.

"She might be new? Youngish?"

"Hon, we know everyone who works here," said the woman on the right. "Don't you remember me?"

Shiztastic. I'd offended a seamstress. Daddy was going to kill me.

"Sure," I hedged and dimpled a smile. "At the Christmas party, you always bring the … what was it?"

"That's right." She straightened and gave her friend a knowing look. "My deviled eggs are always a hit."

"Baby, you are thinking of my deviled eggs," implored the other woman. "Everyone loves them. I use Duke's. I won a prize at the family picnic. You probably remember that."

I didn't remember any specific deviled eggs. There were always deviled eggs at the parties. A plethora of deviled eggs. "You know, both kinds were so good. I just felt lucky to eat either."

The first woman nodded. "I heard you weren't allowed to eat mayo as a kid."

"Shame." The second woman shook her head.

"That's showbiz." I shrugged my shoulders and gave them a big smile. "Anyhoo, you didn't notice an extra seamstress today? Maybe there's one in training?"

"If someone's in training, we'd be training them and not standing here, hon."

"Okey dokey. Thank you!" I backed out of the doorway and looked down at Cuddles. He'd gone to sleep again. "Wakey-wakey. We're going to Nash's office."

Cuddles took his time stretching.

"Come on." I jiggled the leash. "You like Nash. Nash is a good boy."

He sighed and stood.

"Mainly a good boy," I muttered. "Let's go see what he was doing at Windmere last night."

THIRTEEN

I KNOCKED on Nash's office door, then entered at his call. He looked from me to Cuddles and back to me. "What's going on?"

I closed the door and dropped the leash. Cuddles nosed the ground, walked over to the desk, and lifted his leg. "No. Sit."

Cuddles sat. Nash stood. Cuddles curled his lip, and Nash stayed behind the desk.

Giving an impatient sigh, Nash placed his hands on his hips and gave me an exasperated look.

I strolled to the desk. "I spoke with Daddy this morning. He showed me the goofed samples."

"I noticed your t-shirt." He smiled. "Looks good on you, even if it doesn't fit the DeerNose image."

I caught my bottom lip with my teeth, enjoying his admiration. Shook it off and got down to business. "Do you know what happened to the tech packs?"

"No. Not yet." His warm look became guarded.

I sat on the edge of the desk, turning to face him. Cuddles leaned against my leg. I rubbed his ears. "It sounds like it wasn't the first time something like this happened."

"Industrial espionage is part of the business. Also part of my job." He sat on the desk opposite me. "You know this. You also know I shouldn't talk about it."

"Daddy already told me about the stolen tech packs. If he can tell me, you can, too."

Nash's gaze dropped to the desk. He played with a paperclip and dropped it. "He told you they were stolen?"

"They had to have been stolen, right? Daddy is very thorough. He wouldn't have signed off on tech packs without looking at them."

"You think someone forged his signature?" He drew a circle on the desk near my hip.

"Something like that." I watched his finger draw a second circle. "Or switched out his designs after he signed them."

"As far as I know, those samples were a one-off." The circles drew closer to my hip. "The digital files could have corrupted."

"Daddy won't use digital for that reason. The patterns are scanned digitally, but he always draws by hand. He's not very trusting."

His fingers stroked the desk, brushing my thigh. "I think Boomer's very trusting. Maybe too trusting."

I watched his finger skim the desk from my thigh to my hip. "Daddy did say he was too trusting with Vicki when he let her take me to California. He thought we'd be back in a few months, not move there permanently."

The fingers stopped. "Vicki hoodwinked Boomer?"

"He said she moved the goalposts once she got there." I looked up and found his gaze on me. "You weren't home last night."

"We talked about this. We were both working."

"Do you know where my surveillance was?"

"Where?" He smiled. The fingers played near my hip again. "At the Bark and Brew again? Did y'all come back with another dog?"

He was joking, but he also didn't seem to know. Maybe he

still didn't recognize the Impala. Did I want to tell him I was at Windmere? "Where was your surveillance?'

"Gilmore."

"Where in Gilmore?"

The fingers stilled. "Sugar, we decided to leave this be. I'm not going to play twenty questions because I'm not talking about my case."

"Your case is a DeerNose investigation?"

He frowned. "Yes."

"Did you look up Kristi Johnson?"

"No, because that's your case." He leaned forward to kiss me and drew back as Cuddles' head landed on my lap. "Fair's fair. If I ask you to stay out of my work, I'm staying out of yours."

He swooped in to kiss my forehead and hopped off the desk at Cuddles' growl. "Unless you ask, of course. Then I'd love to help."

Cuddles jerked his head off my lap and lunged toward the door, snarling and barking. I hopped from the desk and grabbed the leash. "Cuddles, come on. Sit. Stay."

"This is getting old."

I looked over my shoulder. "He's getting better, though. He didn't try to bite your fingers."

"I was being careful." Nash's gaze moved to the door. "Somebody there? Maizie's in here with me. She's dog-sitting."

"It's just me, Mr. Nash," said a familiar voice. "Hey, honey. Sounds like a big dog you're watching."

"Petey," I exclaimed and wedged myself into the frame. "How are you?"

The tall, older woman regarded me. Although her personality seemed to lend itself to sweater sets and pants suits, she was loyal to the brand. Her athletic, sixty-something body modeled DeerNose's activewear line. Aqua camo flared yoga pants with a matching long-sleeve tee. Her tortoise-shell readers hung from a beaded chain around her neck. Despite the athletic wear, she still hot-rolled her white hair, spritzed Elizabeth Arden, and regularly applied her Estee Lauder red lipstick.

"Honey, you shouldn't have a dog in the building. We can't have the hair floating around so close to the production room."

"I'm sorry." I leaned forward so we could hug. "I can't leave him alone. He ate the car."

"Let me see the fur baby."

I opened the door with a sharp "stay." Petey crouched in the hallway and held out a hand.

"Hello, sweetie," she said in her low, gentle tones. "You're a big fellow, aren't you?"

Cuddles looked at me, then looked back at her. I held tight to the leash. He stepped toward Petey's hand. Sniffed it, then returned to plop on my feet.

"I'll be damned," said Nash. "Maybe he just hates men."

"Cuddles isn't fond of Annie, Tiffany, or Rhonda, either."

Petey straightened from her crouch. "He's territorial for sure. But he's also fearful. Let's get him away from the facility and allow Mr. Nash to get back to work. Come down to my office, honey. You can catch me up with a cup of coffee. You look like you need one."

"I'm a little tired."

"Mr. Nash looks like he needs a coffee, too." Petey pursed her lips. "I can tell you're both exhausted."

"We're tired individually," I blurted. We were all grownups, but Petey had changed my diapers. There were some ideas you didn't want floating around people who had changed your diapers. "Not tired together. We were both on stakeouts. By ourselves."

"Stakeouts. How exciting." She glanced at Nash, then at me. "You can tell me all about it."

———

THE ADMINISTRATIVE SIDE of DeerNose was timber and glass and more chirping bird sounds. If a Bass Pro shop was an office building, it would look like DeerNose. Potted trees and shrubs abounded. In the lobby, mannequins wearing the latest lines posed on block pedestals. A large glass case held a forested scene with dummies poised as hunters wearing Daddy's OG's.

Cuddles ignored the faux woodlands and mannequins and kept his nose to the tile. From the lobby, we hooked a right into the executive hall. We passed a conference room, Marshy's office, and knocked on Petey's door. The last stop before my father's room at the end of the hall. Coffee was waiting on her desk, along with cookies on a china plate. Below the desk rested a bowl of water and another plate holding a dog biscuit.

Cuddles towed me to the desk, inhaled the biscuit, lapped the water, and knocked the plate across the room. I scrambled to retrieve it, but Petey picked it up and walked it to the desk.

"Sit, honey." She waved at a leather chair, then looked at Cuddles. "You sit, too. Tell me about your work and your new friend."

I caught her up on A.S.S. and the Bark and Brew fiasco while she sipped coffee.

"I'm so proud of you, honey. Your daddy was worried about you in California, you know."

Oh, I knew.

"He wanted you to come home before … all the nonsense. He'd always hoped you'd work at DeerNose. Originally, he thought you might have a flair for design, like him."

"I do love fashion." Not a super big fan of camouflage, though. But I didn't want to disappoint the woman who was like a grandmother to me. "I don't think I inherited that kind of creativity."

"I understand. And we've seen your aptitude for investigative work. When you get more experience and finish your apprenticeship, maybe you could take over security for us. We'd love to have you here, honey."

My head jerked up and the cookie I had just picked up fell on the plate. "What about Nash?"

"Mr. Nash will have moved on by then, I'm sure." Her smile was sweet, but her look was pointed. "We respect him tremendously. But we also understand him. He doesn't seem the sort to stay in one place for long. Unless he's working for himself, I suppose."

True, DeerNose Security was temporary in Nash's mind. He needed the paycheck until he could get Nash Security Solutions back on its feet. Uncomfortable to hear it put so bluntly, though. However, Petey had always been a straight shooter.

"Nash seems pretty fixed for now, anyway." I shifted in my chair. "In fact, there's some big project that has him super busy. Do you know anything about that?"

"Big project? Maybe the sabotaged tech packs? I see by your t-shirt, your Daddy told you about the samples." She shook her head. "Terrible shame. All that work Boomer did is just gone."

"Do you have any clue as to what happened?"

"I don't rightly know." Petey sipped her coffee. "I hope Mr. Nash can figure it out. There must be a spy amongst us. Was his stakeout anything to do with the compromised tech packs?"

"I honestly don't know. Nash is tight-lipped about anything to do with DeerNose. He has strong beliefs about separating…" I bit my lip, not wanting to explain his protecting me from his suspicions about something fishy at DeerNose. I also realized I hadn't told Nash about seeing Kristi enter DeerNose. I considered telling Petey, then thought that news better wait for the head of security.

"Separating work and pleasure?" continued Petey. She smiled. "I hope Nash can get to the bottom of it. Boomer is so upset. He's having difficulty concentrating on new designs. That bothers him more than anything. It's the pressure to be innovative but also to stay relevant. Marshall and I leave him alone so Boomer can focus on what he does best."

"Daddy did say he felt a little out of touch about what's going on in the company."

"Marshall and I don't like the business frustrations to upset Boomer. But of course, when the samples came back, it was obvious what was going on. Someone's trying to sabotage us."

"I don't know if industrial spying was obvious to Daddy. He thought there'd been some kind of switch up or mistake."

"Of course, Boomer's a technophobe, so he'd like to blame it on a software glitch or something like that. But sequins and linen, dear? It's so upsetting to Boomer. All that work he did. Not to mention all the money and time that will be lost in production and marketing."

"I think Daddy feels too much is out of his hands now."

"You know your father. With a company this size, he can't control everything."

"Too true. Daddy is a bit of a control freak."

"I wouldn't call him that. Boomer has a particular way of doing things. He has high expectations for himself and for others. I think everyone at DeerNose appreciates that. His principles are why the company has grown from his garage to what it is today."

I'd heard that story a million times over. I nodded and smiled.

"But to handle the operations and the creative is too much for one man. He learned that early on and that's why he leaves the operations to Marshall. Marshall, of course, gives him the overview in their meetings. Boomer has a say in the big decisions. Your father has to answer to the board, in the end."

"Are you worried about Daddy getting the new designs done on time?"

"Your father will finish the new designs. There is no question about that. He has always met deadlines. Despite such a cruel prank played on him, he'll succeed in the end."

"Do you think it could have been a practical joke? By

someone in the company? It looked as though the sequins and deer-hugging graphics were meant to be ironic."

"It's not a joke, sweetie. It's too expensive and hits our bottom line. Who would do such a thing to Boomer? Boomer's hard-working and a good man. Everyone at this company likes and respects him."

"If they don't?"

She blinked, looking dazed. "Not respect Boomer? That's not possible."

FOURTEEN

#DOGOLOGY #B&EMYHEART

A CUP OF COFFEE LATER, I returned to A.S.S. with Cuddles in tow. Actually, the other way around. I still didn't know why Nash was investigating Kristi. Or why Kristi had dressed like a seamstress and entered DeerNose. But I knew the two had to be related. Annie's words—"You're done. Go home."—still smarted. I wasn't ready to face her. I also wasn't ready to give up the investigation on Kristi.

If anything, I'd dug my heels deeper into this investigation.

At the office door, Cuddles stopped, snorted, and hunkered.

"Not in front of the—" Too late.

While waiting for Cuddles to finish his business, I studied the name on the front window—Albright Security Solutions. The mention of Maizie Albright used to open exclusive doors to boutiques, restaurants, and clubs. Even the doors to prestigious producers and directors at certain studios. I had a household name.

Now I couldn't even keep a case at the office with my name on it. Not only that, it seemed I'd been demoted to pooper-scooper.

After cleaning up the sidewalk, I tugged Cuddles through the door, setting off the tinkling bell. Cuddles barked and lunged.

Rhonda shrieked. The back door slammed. I calmed Cuddles and collapsed into a chair.

"I'm getting tired of this," I said to the empty room and Cuddles.

"Good news," said Rhonda from under the desk. "We might have a dog sitter in the area."

"When can they start?"

"I don't know."

"How is that good news?"

"It's better than the bad news," said Tiffany, peeking out from the back office door. "Amanda didn't make bail. And we can't find any friends or family to take Cuddles."

I looked at Cuddles, who stared back with bright eyes. One fang poked out of his mouth. He pawed at my leg. "He's not that bad."

"That's what we told Amanda's people," said Rhonda from under the desk. "Once you get to know him and he gets to know you, there's little likelihood he'll tear your face off. Unless he doesn't like you. Then we couldn't guarantee anything."

Cuddles turned around three times, flopped on the floor, and closed his eyes. Rhonda and Tiffany emerged from their dens.

"How was the surveillance?" said Rhonda. "Did you catch Kristi at anything?"

I rose from my chair and deposited the video camera on the desk. "I followed her to an apartment complex in Gilmore. Windmere. The man from the coffee shop met her there."

Rhonda clasped her hands together. "Poor Derek."

"Maybe he's her cousin. You never know. Hope for the best."

"Girl." Tiffany rolled her eyes.

"There's been an interesting development." I busied myself with removing the micro-card from the camera. "Nash was also doing surveillance at Windmere last night. This morning, Kristi drove to DeerNose and entered the building with the seamstresses."

"Girl," Tiffany and Rhonda chorused.

"That dog," growled Tiffany.

Cuddles looked up.

"Not you," she exclaimed.

"Then what happened?" said Rhonda.

"Annie showed up, told me to go home, and said I was off the case." I handed Tiffany the memory card. "I got some shots of the guy who was with Kristi. Can you upload them for me?"

"I want to see him." Rhonda tore the memory card from Tiffany's hand and shoved it into an external drive connected to her computer. "That cheating whore is not getting away with wrecking poor Derek's life."

Tiffany and I looked at each other.

"Anyway," I continued. "If Annie isn't going to let me watch Kristi, I have a couple of other options. I'll do surveillance on the BMW guy. I also want to know more about Kristi's employer. If she's a secret shopper, there must be some connection with DeerNose. Although I can't think of what a secret shopper would do at the factory instead of a retail shop."

"She could work for CrossHair Marketing, just not as a secret shopper. Maybe she's in management," said Tiffany. "It is possible Derek doesn't recognize that his wife has moved up the corporate ladder."

"I checked LinkedIn and Kristi's not on it," said Rhonda. "Don't you think if she's management, she'd be on LinkedIn?"

"There's another route you can take," said Tiffany. "It might answer more questions. The questions you really want answered."

"What route?"

"Do surveillance on Nash. You're already cyber-stalking him. Might as well go full-blown paranoid girlfriend on him."

I winced.

"I can do it if you won't." Tiffany's eyes gleamed. "I've had a lot of practice stalking boyfriends and my ex-husband. It's a hobby."

"This is about the case. Two cases. Mine and his. His has to do with my father's company. It's not about our relationship."

"We could go together. Tonight. After work."

Rhonda looked up from her computer monitor. "Y'all can't do a GNO without me."

"This is not a Girl's Night Out," I said. "I can't do a stakeout on Nash. Or Kristi. Only on BMW guy."

Ignoring me, Rhonda looked at Tiffany. "We should do take-out. And a bottle of tequila."

"No tequila," I said. "No night out. Normal research. Working hours' research.

"Suits me," said Tiffany. "Better than hanging around here."

"You should go through Kristi's garbage." Rhonda smirked. "That's fieldwork. Your department."

"But I'm off the case." I smiled, thinking of Annie. "Someone else is going to have to go through her garbage."

Cuddles looked up.

"Not you," I said. "You'd eat the evidence before anyone could examine it."

WE DECIDED against garbology and for checking Windmere again. Cuddles rode shotgun while Rhonda and Tiffany took the backseat. After covering it in towels. And trying to shove the ripped stuffing back inside the seats.

"It's so lumpy," complained Rhonda on the way to Wind-mere. "And smells."

"Not to mention all the dog hair and stuffing everywhere. I can't breathe." Tiffany sucked on her vape and blew smoke out the window. "Annie's going to kill you."

"How is it my fault?" I kept a firm grip on Cuddles' collar with my right hand while steering through Windmere's parking lot with my left. "Annie should've thought more about the consequences of Cuddles as a ride-along. She knows what he's like."

Cuddles looked at me.

I released the collar to rub his neck. "It's okay. You can't help yourself."

"We need better screening of our clients," said Rhonda. "Maybe add to the questionnaire, 'Do you have an attack dog?' And, 'If you do time, will your dog try to eat our staff?'"

"Staff and staff vehicles," added Tiffany.

"Poor Cuddles," I said. "Another childhood victim of abandonment and incarceration."

"I think in dog years, he's middle-aged," said Tiffany. "Old enough to know better."

"Like all grown children from dysfunctional families, he needs a good therapist."

"Now you're talking," said Tiffany. "I have a thing for Cesar Milan. Use your connections and get that man to work his magic on Cuddles the Killer while I work my magic on Cesar."

"No, pet psychic," crowed Rhonda. "Please, I've always wanted to get a pet psychic, but I heard it doesn't work on goldfish."

"Maybe the dog sitter can help him. You're going to be good for the sitter, aren't you, Cuddles?" I rubbed his ears. Cuddles flopped onto his back. His legs fell open and his foot smacked the stereo on the dash. I turned off *My Favorite Murder* podcast and parked the car.

"I still think he needs a pet psychic," grumbled Rhonda. "I'm sure there's something in Cuddles' past making him aggressive."

"Um ... maybe Amanda teaching Cuddles to attack her husband?" said Tiffany. "I'm not psychic, and I figured that one out."

Rhonda waved a hand in front of her face. "I'm not talking to a non-believer."

"I'm not talking to a crazy person," snapped Tiffany.

"And I'm glad we didn't bring tequila," I said brightly and turned off the engine. "The BMW isn't here. Let's snoop. First order of business is to see if we can get a name for BMW guy. The apartment's on the second floor facing this parking lot, right-side."

Cuddles jerked his head up, flipped over, and slammed against the passenger door. Rhonda and Tiffany scrambled out of the Impala. He looked at me. I shook my head. He pawed at the door and whined.

"Do not chew up this car," I warned, cracking the windows. "We'll be back in a second."

We hurried into the building's overhang, up the stairs, and stopped before apartment 204C. The girls looked at me. I looked at them.

"Now we know the apartment number."

"This is why Annie says you're good at fieldwork?" Tiffany rolled her eyes.

"We can do a reverse search with the address and see what hits we get for names. That's progress."

Rhonda bent over, flipped up the welcome mat, and picked up a key. She held it up. "Here's more progress."

I shook my head. "That's breaking and entering. We don't do that."

Rhonda eyed Tiffany.

"I'm also on probation," said Tiffany. "You're the only one with a clean record."

"Don't do it," I said. "Let's go to the mailboxes and see if we can learn the name that way. That's good snooping, too."

"Your snooping is boring, Maizie Albright," said Rhonda.

"My snooping is legal."

"*Charlie's Angels* broke into places all the time, didn't they?"

"I really don't—"

The sound of feet plodding up the stairs echoed in the narrow space.

"Quick," I whispered. "Hide."

I darted for the stairs, hustled to the third floor, and peered over the edge. A man in a blue-collared shirt and a ball cap shuffled up the stairs to the second floor. He carried a large, red metal toolbox.

"Maizie," hissed Tiffany.

I turned with my finger in front of my lips. And noticed Tiffany was alone. "Where's—" I hung over the railing. "Shizzles."

Tiffany joined me at the rail. "She's just standing there. Rhonda, get out of there."

Rhonda looked up, waved, and met the repairman at the stair. "Are you coming to 204C?"

The man halted, looked at Rhonda, and cocked his head. "Well, now, I thought 205, but just a minute." He set his toolbox on the stair and drew out a clipboard. "Were you the one with the refrigeration issue?"

Rhonda held out the key. "You want to check? It's probably the ice maker."

"Y'all are likely froze up. Happens all the time. Now, don't you worry, ma'am. I got my own master key." He shuffled to the door. "This won't take too long."

"Do you want me to wait out here?" Rhonda's voice had taken on a sultry lilt. "Will it bother you to have me inside while you work?"

Tiffany and I looked at each other.

"No ma'am. You can come in." The man shifted. His chest rose and his voice deepened. "I don't mind. Not a bit."

"My girlfriends will be here in a minute. You don't mind if they come in, too?" She played with her hair.

"No, ma'am." He stooped to pick up his toolbox, keeping his eyes on Rhonda. "No reason why your girlfriends can't come in."

"Well, okay then." She beamed and stepped back. "After you."

His hand went to his belt. With a flourish, he zipped out a key on a retractable cord. He opened the door and stood against it, ushering in Rhonda. She looked up, winked, and fluttered her fingers.

I looked at Tiffany. "I don't know if that is legal or not."

"She's inside. Doesn't matter now."

"If Annie finds out, she'll kill us."

Tiffany rolled her eyes. "Isn't Annie the one who told you to not work the case? She's going to kill you anyway."

FIFTEEN

#FERGALICIOUS #INTHEDOGHOUSE

WHILE SHE SWEET-TALKED THE REPAIRMAN—
JOE Ferguson. UGA fan. Once met Champ Bailey at a Popeye's
—Tiffany and I scanned the apartment.

"Everything looks sort-of new," Tiffany whispered, smacking
a cushion on the couch. "And uncomfortable. No give. If they're
doing the nasty, they're gonna get back problems."

I let that remark slide. "The furniture does look rented. And
no personal pictures or tchotchkes. No magazines. No books.
Hotel art on the walls. This place feels temporary."

"Maybe he doesn't care about art. He might not like clutter."
She pressed the remote. "TV works. Maybe they're not readers."

While Joe broke down UGA's offensive line stats for Rhonda,
Tiffany and I sauntered into the hallway off the living area.

"Something about this place is hinky." I entered the first of
two bedrooms. "Here's the master. The bed looks slept in."

"Point against Kristi."

I opened a dresser drawer. "Not much in here. Men's clothes,
though." I slid open the drawer beneath it. "This one's empty.
Check the closet."

Tiffany cocked her head. "You're right. Something is off."

I approached her. "Like a smell?"

"No, the clothes. Check it out."

The closet was mostly empty, except for a selection of men's outfits inside dry cleaner's bags. "Sorted by color. I like that." I skimmed a hand over a plastic bundle. "Each outfit bundled together in one bag."

"Now that's weird," said Tiffany.

"The only thing weird is that it's all activewear. Maybe he uses a personal styling service."

"What kind of adult man would rely on Garanimals?"

"Some need help putting together looks if they want to appear polished. That's normal."

"Not in Black Pine." Tiffany shook her head. "You were right. Something's off. Let's check out the other room. Probably severed heads in that closet."

We poked our heads into the hall, listened for the rumble of Joe and Rhonda's bubbly reply, then tiptoed toward the next bedroom. Besides a desk and a stack of cardboard next to a printer stand, the room was empty.

"Office?" said Tiffany.

"Remember, we're looking for a name."

"I'm checking the closet." Tiffany pushed open the folding doors. "More Garanimals. Ugh. Women's. Can these people do nothing for themselves? How hard is it to put together a t-shirt and leggings?"

"Wait. What?" I strode across the room. Outfits swathed in dry-cleaning plastic filled the closet. More leisurewear. "These ensembles are all different sizes."

"A room for people who can't pick out clothes and also can't do laundry?" Tiffany shook her head. "They dry clean everything. Who dry cleans leggings?"

"Were the men's clothes different sizes, too?" I pawed through the various bags.

"Now that you mention it, yes. The guy is a nut-job."

"Kristi wants to be an actress," I said slowly. "Maybe she's not having an affair."

"Didn't she spend the night here?" Tiffany held an outfit against her small frame. "You think they'd miss this one?"

"These aren't dry-cleaning bags. These are costumes. This is wardrobe."

"This isn't a theater."

"No, but it fits with the rented furniture. Maybe they're using this apartment for auditions or fittings."

"All-night auditions?"

I shrugged. I still had hope for Derek and Kristi. "I think these are costumes."

"Shouldn't they be fancier?" Tiffany shoved the outfit back into the closet. "Costumes are like ruffly dresses or whatever."

"That's ridiculous. It depends on the production. Maybe it's a TV production about athletes. Or a play, like *Red Speedo*. Or it could be a musical or dance production. The avant-garde troupes sometimes wear athletic wear."

"In Black Pine?"

I thought about Kristi walking into DeerNose with the other seamstresses. Dressed in flannel with a ponytail. "Maybe she's learning a role at DeerNose. She could be a Method actor. Maybe she got a part in a local production of *Real Women Have Curves* and didn't want to tell Derek for some reason. That would explain the late nights. She's rehearsing. Although it wouldn't explain how she got the role, because I don't think Kristi's Latina. Unless they changed all the cultural motifs in the story. Which wouldn't surprise me. It's been done before." I tsked and shook my head.

"A local production of anything wouldn't explain this apartment. I say they're into weird stuff. Maybe there's more people involved, which explains the different sizes."

"Why do you and Rhonda want Kristi to be a cheater so badly?" I stalked to the desk. "I think this apartment proves something else is going on. I'm going to figure it out."

"Because we believe in Derek," whispered Rhonda. "And something is going on."

Tiffany and I turned to the doorway. Rhonda quietly shut the door and held her finger before her lips.

"What's going on?" I said.

"Fergy stole a banana."

"The singer?"

"The repairman. He took a banana right off the counter and ate it in front of me. I'm not interested in someone who steals another person's banana."

"I didn't know you were interested in Fergy at all," said Tiffany. "I thought you were pretending to be interested, so Sherlock and I could sweep the apartment for clues. I thought you were hot for Derek."

"Right." Rhonda tapped her chin. "Just saying."

"Where's Fergy now?" I inched open the door. "Did he leave?"

"He's talking to someone on his radio."

"Who?"

"The guy whose freezer is really froze up. Fergy didn't find anything wrong with this freezer. What do we do now?"

"Fergy's leaving?"

Rhonda nodded.

"We'll wait for him to go, then slip out." I walked over to the desk. "Keep a lookout to see when he's out the door."

"I think Fergy's suspicious," hissed Rhonda. "He's talking to management about us."

"Shiztastic," I whisper-shouted. "This is why you don't break into people's apartments." I spun away from the desk. "We're breaking the law. I'm still on probation. OMG. Annie's going to fire us."

"Calm down, Maizie," said Tiffany. "Rhonda, ask Fergy about his banana. That will distract him."

"I can't ask him about a banana he stole." Rhonda clasped her hands together. "What are we going to do?"

"Why did I let you guys talk me into this?" I muttered,

pacing before the desk. "Cuddles has probably eaten the entire backseat by now."

"Don't throw us under the bus, Albright." Tiffany folded her arms. "You didn't have to follow us. You could have stayed in the car."

"Annie would have killed me either way." I threw my hands up in the air. "This never happened with Nash."

"Why are you bringing Nash into this?" Rhonda cocked her hip. "What happened to *Charlie's Angels*? Cheryl Ladd never turned on the Angels like this."

"And why am I always Cheryl? Why can't I be Jacquelyn Smith?"

"Obviously, I'm Jacquelyn—"

"Put a pin in the *Charlie's Angels'* argument." Tiffany jerked a thumb toward the door. "We need to get out of here first, remember?"

"Hells." I bit down on my thumbnail, yanked it from my mouth, and pulled on a lock of hair. Then glanced at the desk. "I didn't get to rifle the drawers. There's definitely something fishy going on. Maybe just local theater fishy, though. If we've already B-and-E'd, I should rifle. To confirm for Derek that Kristi's just had all-night rehearsals."

"Rehearsals." Tiffany finger-quoted the words and rolled her eyes.

Rhonda nodded. "Poor Derek"

"Do it." Tiffany slipped into the doorway. "I'll keep an eye out."

I ran to the desk and yanked on the handles. "Who locks all their desk drawers?"

"People who have secrets," whispered Rhonda. "Hurry."

Giving up on the drawers, I spotted a trash can. "Office garbology. Better than regular garbology. Hopefully, he eats in the kitchen."

"Fergy's leaving," whispered Rhonda. "Do you think I should say goodbye?"

"Probably not." I yanked an eight-by-ten photograph from the bin. "This looks like a headshot."

"Uh, Maizie."

"Yep?" I flipped the headshot over and scanned the bio.

"BWM guy. Basic-looking white dude? Mid-30s?"

I looked up. "Why?"

"I think he's here. Talking to Fergy in the doorway."

I abandoned the headshot and scurried to the hall door.

Tiffany hustled toward us. "You think this place has a back door?"

"It's an apartment." I jerked in a breath and pushed it out. "Frig. Hells. Shiz."

"You're running out of fake swear words," said Tiffany. "We should probably hide."

"Hide?" My jerky breath bounced on the word. "Fergy's going to tell him we're in here. Hiding will make it worse."

"The truth will make it worse," said Tiffany.

"I should tell BMW about the banana," said Rhonda.

"No." I deliberately slowed my breathing. "We're going to improvise. I can do this. I'm an actress."

"You best act your way out of hyperventilating," said Tiffany. "I say we try the balcony."

"I don't know, Tiff," said Rhonda. "I like it. This sounds like an idea that would come to the Angels. Not Cheryl, though. More like Farrah."

"I'm not taking this from a guy who steals bananas." Tiffany thrust her chin up and placed her hand on her hips. "Leave this to me." She shot out the door.

Rhonda grimaced. "I don't think this will end well. It's the kind of situation that lands Tiffany in probation."

"We should follow her." I pushed Rhonda toward the door.

"You're right," said Rhonda over her shoulder. "The Angels always had each other's backs. Even though the camera seemed more focused on their chests."

SIXTEEN

#BANANABUST #PAWPATROL

BEFORE TIFFANY COULD REACH the front door, I zipped around her and clasped Fergy's arm. "Thanks so much, Fergy. Your freezer tutelage has convinced us that refrigeration school is our best option."

"What?" Fergy turned to look at Rhonda. "You really were interested in learning how to blow out the condenser? I thought—"

"I know what you thought," said Rhonda tersely. "But I won't let that bother me."

"Fergy." Tiffany stepped in front of Rhonda and glowered at him. "Before you say another word, you should know how strongly Rhonda feels about respecting personal property. For example, she would never walk into someone's home and use their amenities without asking. Let alone eat their food."

Fergy blushed and turned back to the two men standing on the landing. "It was a mixup, y'all. I'm sorry."

"You should be happy a qualified technician has serviced your freezer," said Rhonda to BMW. "That will keep you from a freeze-up in the future. But if you have a card or give us your name and number, we'll check in to see how your freezer is doing."

"I'm not concerned about a freeze-up." BMW's tones were crisp, clipped, and surprisingly British. "I just want to get into my apartment. If you would excuse me."

He cut between Tiffany and Rhonda and shut the door behind him.

"You and your apprentices still need to fix my freezer," said the guy next door.

"He's British?" I said to no one in particular.

"I guess," said Next Door. "He's not very neighborly."

"What's his name?" I continued.

"Dunno," said Next Door. "I told you, he's not neighborly."

"Has he lived here long?"

"Six months, at least. And not once would he give me the time of day." Next Door looked at Fergy. "Your staff is nice enough, but I've got to get back to work. Can y'all get to my freezer?"

"I'm sorry, but one more question," I said. "Does a woman with dark hair visit him often? Her name's Kristi Johnson. She was here last night."

Next Door shrugged.

Fergy looked at Rhonda. "Are you coming?"

"I don't think so." Rhonda folded her arms. "I know what you did."

"What'd I do?" He glanced at Tiffany. "What'd I do?"

"We've got to go." I grabbed Tiffany's arm and yanked on Rhonda's shirt. "Thanks, Fergy. Good luck with the freezer."

We hurried down the stairs. "That's just great," I whispered. "We've been made. How am I supposed to follow this guy when he's seen us face-to-face? That's why we're supposed to keep a distance in surveillance."

"You must be glad to have us heere." Tiffany's snark-infused tones were not lost on me. "When you're doing surveillance alone, you have no one to gripe at."

"Do you know who you sound like?" said Rhonda. "Nash. Or Annie. Annie-Nash. We got stuff done. We learned things we wouldn't have learned just sitting in a car that smells like dog."

It was true we'd learned some things about BMW. Things we didn't understand. Also true about the car smelling like dog. And I did sound like Annie or Nash. Maybe because I had used them for character development in practicing my role as a professional private investigator. Maybe because there were rules for private investigating that Rhonda and Tiffany didn't like to follow.

Honestly, they didn't like rules in general. No surprise there.

"You know what else is true?" I huffed. "We left our dog in that smelly car longer than five minutes. He's probably destroyed it."

"He's not our dog," said Tiffany.

"Our temporary dog. I really need that dog sitter. I can't leave him alone for more than a few minutes." I halted just before hitting the sidewalk. "Where is the dog?"

"What d'ya mean?" said Tiffany. "We can barely see the car."

"Do you and Cuddles have a psychic connection?" Rhonda cheered. "The pet psychic is going to love you."

"Look. No, listen." I pointed. Across the parking lot, a teenage girl stood next to the Impala. "If Cuddles were in the car, he'd be going bonkers. A bird flies past, he loses his mind. The car rocks when a bug hits the window. I hear nothing, and the Impala is not shaking. He's gone."

The girl looked up and spotted us.

"Have you seen a big dog?" I shouted. "Really big? Kind of fierce? Probably looks like he's hunting for a cheeseburger? Did he make a hole in the car?"

Her head tilted and her long braids slid over her shoulders. She wrapped her arms around her slim frame and stepped away from the Impala.

"It's okay, honey," called Rhonda. "She's not crazy. She thinks she lost her dog. But it's not really her dog. He is big and vicious, though. If you see him, you best run."

"No," I yelled. "Don't run. Stand really still and don't look at him. Otherwise, he might mistake you for a cheeseburger. But have you seen a dog?"

The girl's shoulders hunched. She backed up a few more steps. A yip sounded from the car. Cuddles' face appeared in the window.

"There he is," I crowed and rushed over. "Such a good boy, Cuddles. You've really turned a corner."

He tipped his head back and smiled. As I beamed back, a June bug buzzed past my shoulder and hit the window. Cuddles lunged at the door, scrabbling and howling. Foam spattered the window. I could hear fabric ripping as he tried to claw his way out the door.

"I don't think he turned a corner," said Tiffany.

"Hey, girl." I spun toward the sidewalk. "Did he do that to you?"

The girl stopped mid-stride and looked back. "For a minute. Then he listened to me and calmed down."

"What'd you say?" said Rhonda. "Must've been good if he listened."

The girl shrugged. "Just dog stuff."

"What's dog stuff?" said Tiffany. "How he wanted to kill you but let you live?"

"No, ma'am. About how he doesn't like it when his mom's gone. He worries about her."

"Aww." I clasped my hands together. "That is so sweet."

"She's psychic," hissed Rhonda.

"I told him you'd be back soon, and you were fine. Then he calmed right down. He's just anxious is all." Placing a hand on her hip, she slanted a look at me. "But I can tell he's not trained well. And the training he's had hasn't been to his benefit. Y'all should be ashamed of yourselves, teaching this guy to attack like that. He doesn't know how to direct that aggression. It's all pent-up with no place to go."

Tiffany, Rhonda, and I looked at each other.

My face burned. "He's not really our—"

Rhonda held up a hand. "How old are you? Why aren't you in school?"

"I'm homeschooled, ma'am." The girl's chin jerked up. "Finished my classes for the day already. You can speak to my mother if y'all got a problem with that."

"No prob—" I began.

"We don't have a problem," continued Rhonda. "We have a solution."

I looked at Rhonda. "What?"

"This girl could be the solution to our dog problem," said Rhonda.

"I thought you got a sitter."

Rhonda pressed her lips together and blinked.

"Tell her," said Tiffany.

"Well…" Rhonda drawled. "We sort of did, but when I sent a picture of Cuddles, she backed out. However, there's still one more on our list that I haven't talked to."

"I wouldn't count on that sitter," said Tiffany. "His voicemail box is full. He might be dead."

I looked at the sky, then dropped my gaze to Cuddles. "You're just misunderstood. You have a giant body because it has to hold your big heart."

"I don't think the size of his body is the problem," muttered Tiffany. "It's the size of his teeth when he's not smiling."

"Also, when he's smiling," said Rhonda. "The smiling picture didn't help either."

"Your solution is to ask a little girl to dog sit?"

"She's not that little," argued Rhonda. "She's probably in high school."

"Or middle school," said Tiffany. "Old enough to use big words."

"Doesn't matter." I gazed in the direction the girl had fled. "She's gone. And we didn't get a name."

Tiffany slapped my back. "Good thing you're an investigator. Just add her to your list."

SEVENTEEN

#DOGSMACKED #COSTUMECONUNDRUM

BACK AT THE OFFICE, we used the Windmere apartment address to look up a name for BMW. *We* meaning *me*. Cuddles slept. Rhonda left to "buy office supplies." On the other side of the wall, the construction crew blasted Norteño music. Tiffany slipped into Annie's office to "think."

"Annie's the kind to check her computer history," I said to the closed door. "If you're playing video poker, she'll figure it out."

"Not if it's on my phone," shouted Tiffany.

Getting a name from an apartment address was difficult. Property records didn't work, apartments leases weren't public. However, they're also not confidential unless a confidentiality clause was signed. The problem wasn't finding a name. It was getting the right name. I suspected another person had signed the lease. Possibly the apartment was even sublet to BMW.

My bigger problem in name searching was finding a juvenile dog sitter. It also felt creepy, so I set that problem aside and focused on my theater and film connections to look for BMW. An hour later, I'd learned no one knew the leaser's name nor of an "unfriendly" British guy temporarily staying in the area.

"Y'all!" Rhonda banged through the door. She backed out. I

calmed Cuddles. She reentered, carrying bags from the boutique shop two blocks down and a liquor shop on the other side of town. "Did you find the girl yet?"

"I've been focused on finding BMW."

"What did you learn?" said Tiffany, emerging from the back office.

"Not much," I admitted. "I'm rethinking the producer-director thing. First off, I checked the Windmere records. The name on the apartment lease is Dee Dixon."

Rhonda tapped her chin. "He doesn't look like a Dee."

"Second, he's unfriendly."

"How's that relevant?" said Tiffany.

"If he's a theater director or producer, he's going to talk about the production to his neighbors. To anyone he meets. Not only to drum up business, but because he won't be able to help himself. I've never met an unfriendly theater director. At least in terms of off-off-off-Broadway directors. They have to be outgoing. Their livelihood depends on it. Until they make it big, then they can afford to be as unfriendly as they want. But if BMW's made it big, he wouldn't have a leased apartment in Gilmore."

"So he's not a director. Maybe he's an actor or a ..." Tiffany rolled her hand. "A whatever else there is."

"If he was a costume designer, there would be more sewing equipment. If he's an actor, there wouldn't be outfits of different sizes in his closet."

"Maybe he's an agent," said Rhonda.

I shook my head. "Still doesn't explain the clothes in the closets."

The bell rang. Annie waited while I hooked a thumb in Cuddles' collar. She entered carrying bags of office supplies.

"Rhonda," she barked. "Where are we on the dog sitter?"

Rhonda cast a look at me. "We sort of found one, but we're checking to see if she's available."

"Get on it, now." Annie eyed me. "What've you been doing?"

"Researching Windmere apartment leases," I said. "The name

on 204C is Dee Dixon. The guy Kristi visited must be subletting. Or house sitting."

Glaring at me, Annie crossed her arms.

"You don't need to say it. You told me I'm off the case. I agree I have a conflict of interest with the case, but—"

Annie snorted.

"But I can still be of value."

Annie nodded. "Your value is getting this dog out of here in case a client decides to visit the shop."

I looked at Cuddles.

He looked at me.

I looked at Annie. "I'm back on fieldwork?"

She shook her head.

"I'm the dog sitter."

She nodded.

"Come on, that's not fair. I've done a lot of legwork on this case."

She shrugged and walked to her office. "You find a dog sitter. I'll find you something else to do."

———

AS A DOG SITTER, I felt obliged to take Cuddles to a dog park. That it happened to be a dog park in Gilmore near Windmere Apartment Homes was something I couldn't help. What did I know of area dog parks other than the one near Windmere?

That Cuddles refused to go into the dog park and instead wanted to sleep in the car while I drove around and into Windmere also couldn't be helped. What other places did I know near the dog park to wait out Cuddles' nap?

Cuddles was becoming an asset instead of a hindrance in my case. The case I wasn't supposed to work.

"We're looking for the dog sitter," I told him. He opened one eye and sniffed the air. Noticing there was no scent of junk food in his vicinity, he shut his eye.

"However, if we do some surveillance on BMW in the meantime, I can't help that. Win-win all around, I'd say."

I prepared my camera and focused it on the parking lot in front of Building C. I used the viewfinder to scan the surrounding area and stopped on a pickup entering the parking lot. The Silverado backed into a space behind Building A.

"Cuddles, Nash is here. What am I going to do?" I slid toward the floor. "I could walk over there and confront him about Kristi Johnson and BMW. That doesn't seem to work, though. But with my conflict of interest, I'm not really supposed to be confronting him either."

Cuddles yawned.

"No, I'm not chickening out. It's just that I can learn more this way."

Cuddles guided his head under my hand. I scratched his ears and watched the Silverado from below the steering wheel. Occasionally, I'd glance at 204C, but nothing was going on there. After an hour of battling sleep and impulses to march across the parking lot to the Silverado, the Prius drove into the parking lot and parked in front of Building C.

"Kristi Johnson," I said to Cuddles. "Now we're getting somewhere."

Cuddles sat up.

"Stay down," I hissed. "Nash will see you."

Ignoring me, he put his paws on the dash and leaned toward the windshield.

"Shizzles. Do you see Annie?" I hopped up. Remembered Nash. Slunk to the floor, then wiggled to just below the steering wheel. "I almost forgot our alibi. If Annie sees us, we're watching for the dog sitter. Nothing wrong with that. But get down. Unless you see the dog sitter, then let me know. Except we can't very well get out and chase her down with Nash in the parking lot."

Cuddles glanced over his shoulder at me. Might have rolled his eyes.

"Anyway, what's Kristi doing?" I shifted the camera lens to the bottom of the window and watched her from the viewer. Grabbed shots of her exiting the car, carrying hangers of clothes in dry cleaner's bags. "Maybe she's his costumer? What if she went to DeerNose to learn tips from Daddy's seamstresses? What if they're doing a show about fishermen? She might need to know how to sew Gortex or something. If BMW is in the industry, Kristi could've been meeting with him to go over her wardrobe designs. All night. But they could be on a tight schedule…"

Cuddles looked at me.

"I know, I know. I really believe in giving people the benefit of the doubt, though. Derek is so nice. Why would anyone cheat on him?"

My camera angled toward the Silverado. The shutter whirred.

"I mean, isn't anybody honest anymore?"

EIGHTEEN

#QUIDPRONO #WELLHEELED

AFTER A FEW HOURS of semi-unbearable parking lot sitting, we followed Kristi home.

Okay, we followed Nash, following Kristi home. Super tricky. As a former PI, Nash had mastered the art of mobile surveillance. I kept an eye on his route with my mobile tracking app, stayed on parallel roads as best I could, and followed at a safe distance when I had no choice but to take the highway back to Black Pine. Passing Kristi's street, I parked on the next street and double-backed on foot. Cuddles plodded along, taking my pauses to check for lurking Silverados as a chance to lie down. Or eat.

At the corner of Kristi's street, I peered from behind a tree. Squinting, I spotted a Jeep at the far end of the street. The Silverado was three doors down from Derek and Kristi's house.

Cuddles and I hurried back to the Impala. A big black pickup had parked across the street. We corrected our hurry into a normal "girl takes dog for a stroll" in case anyone was watching, then hopped into the car.

"We're not running from Annie and Nash," I explained once we were seat-belted inside the car. "There's no need to cover a subject if two other PIs are doing surveillance. Also, I don't want to get fired. Or caught stalking."

Cuddles woofed his approval. We set out for A.S.S.

Then remembered, I wasn't allowed at the office. Hooked a U-ey and headed home.

———

CUDDLES and the Jack Russells had such a similar tee-tee schedule that separating them became nightmarish. I was also running out of makeup and tiaras. Remi had used a tube of Bobbi Brown's Tahiti Crushed Shine Jelly stick for a Cuddles makeover. I wouldn't take "he likes the taste" as an excuse.

Remi howled. Cuddles howled. The Jacks howled.

Cuddles and I headed back to the office. Nash's old office.

Before going inside the Dixie Kreme building, we pulled in deep mouthfuls of donut-scented air. Inside, I snagged a bag of day-olds, and we galloped up the stairs for dinner. We settled into our new routine. I cracked open my secret laptop. Cuddles flopped on his back and worked on pumping donuts through his system while snoring. When he leaped to his feet, I hid my laptop. A moment later, Cuddles committed a full-blown berserk. A man's silhouette appeared in the door's frosted glass.

"It's just Nash," I said, grabbing Cuddles' collar. "We like him."

"His owner hasn't been bailed out yet?" yelled Nash through the door.

"Happy voice," I reminded him.

"How much is bail?" said Nash. "Because I'm willing to go back in the red to return this—"

"Happier."

"Nice, little insane beast of a doggy," he said in the sweetest voice he could muster. "I need to talk to your friend, Cuddles. She and I are long overdue for a nice, little—"

"PG-13 only please."

"I was going to say chat."

He wasn't going to say chat.

"Miss Albright." His voice gentled to a croon. "Maizie. Darlin'."

I turned to Cuddles. "You need to calm down. It's Nash. You like him." This wasn't the truth, but I thought some psychology might work on him.

Cuddles gave me a look to let me know he didn't do psychology.

"Cuddles, I will give you a bag of Cheeze Paufs if you let Nash in. And promise not to hurt him."

Cuddles relented.

"Who's a good doggy?" I said, handing him a Cheeze Pauf from the bag I had stashed on top of the file cabinet. "Sit. Stay. No eating Nash."

Nash came in and stared at us. "He really hates me."

"He has bad luck with men. His father was a terrible person. He's just overprotective."

Nash folded his arms. "Maybe there's another reason."

"Possibly it's your aftershave or body wash. He does have a thing for more feminine scents."

"I meant more along the lines of you following me. You're suspicious of me, so he's suspicious of me."

"You saw us."

"When did you get the Impala?" The little scar on his chin had whitened with the clenching of his jaw.

"It's not mine. It's Annie's."

"Annie drives a Jeep. She's following me, too."

"We're not following you." I crossed my fingers behind my back and gave him my friendly *InStyle* smile. I was following him. But Annie wasn't. I only needed a half-finger cross. "We're doing surveillance on Kristi Johnson. Who you claim you're not tailing, but you are."

Nash's polar blue eyes narrowed. "I'm not following Kristi

Johnson. I'm following—" He stopped abruptly and ran a hand over his head. "Dammit."

"You are following someone. What does Kristi have to do with DeerNose? She was in the building today."

Behind us, Cuddles barked. I threw him a Cheeze Pauf and reminded him we liked Nash and to be a good dog.

"Let me get this straight. Kristi Johnson—your infidelity case suspect—was in DeerNose?"

"Who is she to you?"

Nash's eyebrow rose. "I told you, I have no idea who Kristi Johnson is. Did she have a meeting at DeerNose? With who?"

I ignored his questions. "You were at her house."

"Tell me what you know about Kristi Johnson." His brows lowered.

"Tell me what you know about whoever it is you think you're following."

A low growl reverberated from the massive body pressed against my legs.

Nash glanced down, then flicked his gaze to me. "Never mind."

"No wait," I lightened my voice, placed a hand on Cuddles' head, and scratched his ears. "I want to exchange information."

"But I don't want to exchange information," Nash smirked. "And now I don't need to exchange information."

"Hey, that's not fair. You got a name from me, give me one back."

"This was fun." He smiled. "Let's exchange something else."

I glared at him. "Think again, buddy."

Cuddles shook his head, splattering Nash's pants with foam.

Nash reached to wipe his pants, then jerked back his hand before Cuddles could lunge. "How long are you going to have this dog?"

"As long as it takes." I snagged the bag of Cheeze Paufs, my backpack, and Cuddles' leash. "See you later."

"You're not staying? Come on, darlin', don't be mad. You know this isn't personal."

"You're investigating my father's company. How is that not personal?"

"You're right. It is personal. That's why I can't talk about it."

"Your logic is all over the map, Nash. You make these rules and expect me to follow them."

"This isn't a rule. The rules were for when we were working. Rules to protect you."

"The no hugging rule? That was to protect me?"

"Believe me," he flashed a dark smile, "that was to protect you."

"Well, guess what, buddy? I'm making some rules of my own. Rule number one, no 'hugging,'" I finger-quoted, "while there are secrets between us."

"Really?" Nash raised a brow. "You don't think that's a little hypocritical?"

Possibly. Well, yes. Definitely hypocritical. But I wasn't going to tell him that. "Are you going to agree to this rule?"

"I don't want to agree to this rule." He leaned in. "I don't think you want to agree to this rule. I think we can do our own investigations and still 'hug.'" He ended with a mock finger-quote and used the fingers to brush a wisp of hair behind my ear.

I batted his hand away but dropped my backpack, the leash, and Cheese Paufs. Cuddles grabbed the bag of Paufs and carried it to the La-Z-Boy. I opened my mouth to call over Cuddles, glanced at Nash, and closed my mouth. His eyes had darkened, and a dimple had appeared next to his scar.

"You love investigating, don't you, Miss Albright?" His voice had dropped to a low murmur.

"You know I do. But I don't see what that has to do with—"

His thumb brushed my bottom lip, stopping my words. "The thing is, I enjoy seeing how much you enjoy investigating."

"Oh?"

"You really light up when you think you're on to something." He stroked the side of my face. "I can almost see the gears working in your head. It's exciting to witness."

"Oh," I sighed.

His hand trailed down my neck, curved over my shoulder, and drew me toward him until we were inches apart.

"It's mighty attractive." His deep voice stirred the tendrils near my ear.

"Really?"

"Really." The hand moved to stroke the small of my back. "I've got an inkling you felt the same watching me pace the floorboards."

I did. Nash was a magnificent pacer. Like a lion planning his attack. Male lions don't stalk in a pride. They corner their prey strategically in order to face them.

"But we're not working together." I splayed my hands against his chest. "I'm investigating—" I stopped myself before saying *you*. "A *subject*. If we worked together, it would be … mutually beneficial."

He pressed his lips to my temple. "I'd argue it's the *subject* you find particularly stimulating." His lips dusted my hairline. "If I worked with you, you'd no longer get to enjoy that particular *investigation*."

True. My Nash-snooping felt a lot more exciting than it should.

"The point is, all this stimulation…" he murmured. "Really makes us feel like hugging."

The lips followed the curve of my cheek and hovered below my jaw. The hand on my back trailed lower. He breathed in my scent. I closed my eyes.

"I say," Nash continued, "let's change your rule. We can have our secrets as long as the secrets only involve our investigations."

The little resolve I had wavered. This wasn't cheater patrol.

Tracking Nash was a turn-on. He'd caught on to the *Mr. & Mrs. Smith*-thing between us.

But I needed to know why he was following Kristi Johnson. And I needed to know if my father's company was in trouble.

I crossed my arms to show Nash I meant business. Difficult in the tight space. I hadn't enough gumption to back out of our non-hug hug.

Nash pressed me closer until my crossed arms fitted against his chest. His hand wiggled into the gap between my side and arm. He slipped his fingers through mine. "Remember how we broke my no-hugging rule? Remember how good it felt?"

It'd felt like fate. Kismet. Like the inevitable had finally happened. We were meant to be together. We'd grown into a relationship.

But a relationship meant he should know I'd want to know what was going on in my father's company.

Wait, he did know. He thought he could prevent me from finding out. Which meant his investigation must be pretty big. Making me more determined to learn what the big secret was. When it came to clandestine activities, Nash had more experience than me.

However, I had experience in breaking men.

I mean, getting my boyfriends to give up their secrets.

Although their secrets generally doomed the relationship.

But this was a different kind of secret.

I lifted my chin. It bumped against Nash's collarbone. Dropping my arms, I angled my head back to better eye him. "This is different. This isn't just a regular investigation. Like you said, it is personal. Therefore, we shouldn't involve ourselves personally until we can share personally."

"I'm not following," Nash murmured, sliding his hands to my hips. "But I can tell you really want to hug this out."

"No, I don't."

"Honey, I beg to differ. You're rubbing my back and staring at my lips. You can't make this rule because you can't possibly mean it."

I stopped stroking his back and brought my gaze to eye level. "Of course I can agree to the rule I just created."

"I don't think you can." He dropped his lips to my ear. "You're a hugger, Maizie. You can't fight your nature."

"Sure I can," I murmured, tilting my head back. Not just in case he wanted to slide his lips from my ear to my neck. "For the right reason, I can do anything."

"Darlin', I am not going to tell you about my work at Deer-Nose. I told you, I'd never deliberately lie to you, but I'm also not going to share." He dropped a kiss on my cheek. "I adore you, Maizie. And I care deeply for you. So deeply that I will stick to your ridiculous rule in order to save my investigation and, therefore, protect you."

He gently pushed me away. Walked over to the couch and sat down.

I shivered. I felt cold and hot and juiced up by hormones and slightly annoyed. But more than slightly aroused. "That wasn't fair."

"Your rule isn't fair."

"The rule stays."

"Fine." He shrugged.

"Fine?"

"Fine."

I pressed my lips together, feeling like I had lost a battle instead of proving a point. "I guess I'll be going."

"See you later." He winked. "Possibly."

"Possibly?"

"Possibly." He winked again. "Who knows where our *investigations* will take us?"

I narrowed my eyes. "You're on." I snapped my fingers. "Come on, Cuddles."

A snore emanated from the La-Z-Boy. Neon orange dust

covered the chair and the dog. Shreds of plastic bag littered the floor.

Nash smirked.

"Cuddles," I called. "Come. Now."

Cuddles leaped off the recliner, trotted over, and plopped at my feet.

At least one male in my life obeyed.

Sort of.

NINETEEN

#DOGDAYS #TRUELIES

I DIDN'T KNOW where else to go, so Cuddles and I snuck into A.S.S. At least it was quiet. I let out a long sigh, filled Cuddles' bowls, and looked around.

Okay, began snooping for any information about the Johnson case that might have come to light after I'd been kicked off the case.

There were new folders on Rhonda's desk. Some subpoena work (Tiffany's favorite) and a new infidelity case (Rhonda's favorite).

"I'm getting the sleeping bag from Annie's office," I said to Cuddles. "I'll be right back."

He looked at me like he knew I wasn't just looking for a sleeping bag.

"Ok, so maybe I'll look at the Johnson file. We're not supposed to be here anyway, so how's checking on the file going to hurt anything?"

I entered Annie's office and turned on her computer. We all knew the password (BoAndLuke4EVA*!) to use the laptop, but she'd protected the Johnson file with another passcode. After trying every password I could think of related to the *Dukes of Hazzard* and Jeeps, I gave up.

———

AROUND THREE, I jerked awake, unable to breathe under the weight of the problems that had kept me in a fitful sleep. I was temporarily homeless. Sort of jobless. Stuck with a behemoth monster dog I could barely control and could never allow out of my sight.

Even worse, my relationship with Nash had taken a weird turn. Playing *Mr. & Mrs. Smith* was fun, but the reality meant we were lying to each other. We were cultivating our separate investigations to the detriment of our relationship.

What were we doing? Was his investigation more important to him than my feelings? Was my wanting to crack that secret more important than our relationship?

I stifled a sob and gasped for breath. My arms were pinned against my sides. I struggled to move. Remembering the signs of previous panic attacks, I began to reassess the physical symptoms.

And realized a 150-pound weight stretched across my chest. A weight emanating a noxious smell.

I gagged and buried my nose in the sleeping bag. Then yanked an arm out and pushed at Cuddles. He rose, curled along my body, and pressed his nose into my armpit.

"I don't know what I'm going to do. Should I even continue this investigation? It's making a wreck of me, my relationship, and my career. But I need to know what's happening at Deer-Nose. Why it involves Kristi. I'm really worried about Daddy, too."

Cuddles snuffled my armpit.

I sighed. "Lack of sleep is making me a little nutty. But I want it all, Cuddles. I want the job, the man, and to save my Daddy's business." I wrapped an arm around his neck, he licked my hand, and we fell back asleep.

———

CUDDLES and I were out the door and in the Impala before Annie could kick us out of the office. We drove a block, parked in the alley between a printer and a jewelry store, and walked to Dixie Kreme Donuts. Chatted with Lamar until a customer wanted to enter. Exited out the back before Cuddles attacked the customer. Took our bags of donuts and coffee back to the Impala and watched for Nash's Silverado to leave his parking space in front of the Dixie Kreme building.

A few minutes later Nash strolled out of the side door, stopped on the stoop to glance around, spotted us, and waved. Cuddles barked. I started the car.

We followed him to the DeerNose factory. At the gate, we were stopped by one of DeerNose's security officers. Judging by the camp chair he'd hopped out of, he'd been waiting at the entrance for me. The guard, Joel Dewillis, played the elf to Daddy's Santa at the company Christmas party every year. I rolled down my window, grabbed Cuddles' collar, and stopped him from snapping at Joel's looming face.

"Hey Miss Maizie," said Joel, stepping back. "I heard you got a dog. He's bigger than I thought."

"He's not my dog, but yes." I smiled. "How are you, Joel? How's your family?"

"Good, good. Nice to see you, honey. Been a while." Joel played with his DeerNose camouflage tie and peered over my shoulder at the behemoth dog. "Nash said you can't come in."

"Really?" I said, as if I hadn't guessed that's why I'd been stopped. "I can't come in to see my father?"

"Nash said no dogs on the premises unless you have paperwork stating the dog is a trained support animal."

I pressed my lips together and winced at Cuddles' booming bark. I daintily wiped away dog spittle from my cheek and turned back to Joel. "If that's the case, do you think you could watch my dog for a teensy bit while I go in the building?"

"Nash said you'd probably ask me to do that and even

though I've known you since you were in diapers, I should refuse if I wanted to keep my job."

I gasped. "That's horrible."

"Direct quote." Joel winked. "Don't worry. I don't think he'd really fire me. He's just trying to make a point."

Shizzles.

"Besides that, honey, you couldn't pay me enough to watch that dog. He's ready to tear my face off."

"It's all for show. He's really a teddy bear." I glanced at Cuddles, who growled like he was ready to tear off a face. "Actually, he's not keen on men. What about asking Linda or Amy to watch him for a minute while I go inside?"

"No can do, Miss Maizie. Sorry. You're to turn yourself around and skedaddle. Your daddy's not here yet, anyway. I think he's meeting with some folks. That's what I heard, anyway."

I paused before shifting the Impala into drive. "Hey, Joel. Is there a new seamstress with a green Prius? Or have you seen a green Prius in the parking lot lately?"

"Green Prius?" Joel rocked back on his heels and glanced toward the parking lot. "Seems to me I've seen one recently, now that you mention it. Kind of stood out."

Considering pickups or SUVs were the standard vehicle for DeerNose, I thought a Prius might catch Joel's attention.

"Could you let me know if you spot that car at DeerNose again? Give me a call?"

"I guess I could do that. Nash didn't say nothin' about a green Prius or calling you."

"You're very dutiful, aren't you, Joel?"

"Nash is a good guy. Smart, too. I don't mind working for a younger guy if he don't act like it."

"That's good to hear."

"Hang on, girl." Joel held up his hand. I turned in my seat to watch him hustle toward a vehicle approaching the gate. "Just a minute there, honey," he called to the slowing Jeep.

I looked at Cuddles. "Annie's not going to like that one bit. Even though it's a custom down here, she's not gotten used to terms of endearment in everyday speech."

Cuddles woofed.

"I don't mind it. But I grew up around Daddy. There's nothing behind it. The babies and honeys just pop out of their mouths like the ma'am's and sirs." I paused. "Oh wait, you meant, why's Joel stopping Annie? Good question."

I grabbed Cuddles' collar and zipped down the passenger window so I could hear them.

"It ain't like this is public property, ma'am," said Joel to Annie. "Mr. Nash can keep out anyone he pleases."

"That's not the issue," said Annie. "I'm asking if my Jeep or name was specifically put on a refuse entry list."

"Yes, ma'am. Also Rhonda Robinson and Tiffany West were, too. I think one drives a Firebird and the other a … green dirt bike?"

"No, that's mine," I hollered through the window while tugging Cuddles to keep him on my lap. "Good morning, Annie."

"You better not be here because of the Johnson case," growled Annie.

"No, she wanted to see her daddy," said Joel. "But he's not here, so she can't come in."

"What if Daddy were here?" I said hopefully. "We didn't cover that."

"Then I escort you to his office and back to your vehicle," said Joel. "But you can't come through the gate with a dog."

"Jeesh," said Annie. "Did Cuddles bite Nash?"

"They don't get on," I said. "You promised me a dog sitter."

Cuddles swung his head around and gave me a look.

"It's not personal. But you're not making it easy for me to have a life."

"We're working on it," said Annie. "But you're also not working right now anyway, remember?"

"Just not on the Johnson case."

"Sorry, Maizie, but I can't see you doing anything right now. Not until we get the Cuddles situation sorted. And you stop stalking your boyfriend." Annie tossed her arm over the back of her seat, reversed into the road, and sped off.

"What'd she mean by stalking your boyfriend?" said Joel.

"Inside joke." I smiled without my teeth. Then glanced at Cuddles. "Don't look at me like that."

TWENTY

I THOUGHT about following Annie but didn't want to press my luck.

"I can't follow Kristi when Annie's also watching her. We'll focus on BMW. Drive-bys of his known spots—the coffee shop and the apartment. In between, I'm going to keep making calls to my old network. That apartment smells like theater."

Cuddles cocked his head.

"Not literally. More like balsam or cedar. I think there was a candle in the kitchen." I sighed. "If Kristi's just preparing for a role, why the clandestine activity? Why not tell her husband about the show?"

He shoved his head into my palm. I scratched. "I agree. Even if they don't talk—and it sounded very much like Kristi and Derek have communication issues—there's something more than theater going on, particularly now that I know about the stolen tech packs. CrossHair Marketing is the only relationship between Kristi and DeerNose that makes sense. But with no brick-and-mortar store, how do I learn more about CrossHair?"

Cuddles pawed my shirt.

"You're right. It'll come to me. In the meantime, we continue our surveillance."

He nudged my backpack.

"Oh, right. Good idea. We'll hit Nash's office first."

He looked at me pointedly.

"And yes, we'll go to Dixie Kreme Donuts while we're there. I could use one, too."

———

WITHOUT A NAME, I couldn't do my usual skip-tracing searches. I scoured the internet for local theater productions and nearby TV and film shoots, then expanded that search to Atlanta and beyond. No *Real Women Have Curves* reboots. Nor *Intimate Apparel*, *The Dressmaker* (now a musical), *The Seamstress*, or even an American version of *The Factory Girls*.

I took another look at CrossHair Marketing. Nothing stood out. I entered my information on an employment application and hoped an interview with the firm might give me some background and leads.

"Without a name, that's all I can do online," I told Cuddles. "Let's go for a ride."

He jumped off Lamar's chair, bounded to the door, and pulled me down the stairs to the Impala.

"First stop, Rounds of Grounds. That's where we first saw BMW. If he doesn't show there, it's back to Windmere. Maybe we'll run into your future dog sitter there. Pray we don't run into Annie."

Or Nash.

Or maybe I did want to run into Nash. I felt all discombobulated after last night's encounter. Was I mad at him or at myself? Or worried we might have screwed up something wonderful?

"I just keep circling back to Daddy," I told Cuddles. "Which sounds weird. But Nash knows something he'd want me to keep from my father. I can't let that go. Particularly when Kristi's connected."

Cuddles woofed.

"Of course, you'd say that. You're biased. You'll hold anything against Nash you can."

———

ONE "ALMOND MILK, HONEY, FLAT WHITE" and one "just milk with extra cream hold the sugar" later, we scored more than drinks at Rounds of Grounds. The blue BMW had pulled into the parking lot and parked near the entrance.

"Bingo." I put down my coffee cup and picked up the camera.

BMW exited his BMW. I examined him through the camera lens. Today he'd added dark-framed glasses to his trendy, dapper repertoire. He glanced around and headed into the coffee shop.

"Kristi's not with him, so we're safe. If she shows, we'll have to skedaddle. Annie will be on her tail." I looked over at Cuddles. "You're oozing cream. That's the last time I'm buying you a drink."

He flopped onto the seat and closed his eyes.

"I wonder if BMW locked his car. I didn't hear a bloop-bleep. Did you hear a bloop-bleep?"

Cuddles opened his eyes and sat up.

"No, you're staying here. This is an extremely risky move. I'm going to check out the car while he's in line for coffee. I can't chance you setting the car alarm off."

He whined and pawed my arm.

"You just tinkled."

He clawed the door and looked over his shoulder.

"Really?"

I sighed, clipped the leash on his harness, and opened the door. We walked toward the blue convertible.

"Go over there to do your business." I pointed toward a set of shrubs lining the parking lot's greenbelt.

I could sense his eye roll as he wandered toward the shrubs.

Honestly, in four days, it felt like I'd gone from puppyhood to dog-sitting a teenager. When Cuddles had gotten into his sniffing zone, I moved closer to the BMW's passenger door. I let out the extra lead on the leash. Edged toward the door. Peered through the window. Gym bag in the back seat. Folder on the front passenger seat.

I bumped against the door. When the alarm didn't go off, I slipped my fingers into the door handle, held my breath, and pulled. The latch opened. My heart pounded. Glanced around. Cuddles was circling a spot. The drive-thru was empty. Parking lot, quiet. I opened the door, grabbed the folder, and shut the door. Leafed through the printed applications. They looked a lot like the form I had filled out online for CrossHair.

Double bingo.

Triple because I felt this was the evidence I needed to prove Kristi wasn't cheating on Derek. BMW was a coworker or her boss. She'd been working.

Overnight at her employer's sublet. But still.

As an eternal cock-eyed optimist, I felt ninety-nine percent better. I had a viable connection between CrossHair Marketing and DeerNose. It justified me …

What? Spying on Nash?

Shizzles. Is this what I was really looking for?

After a quick glance at the coffeehouse, I popped the latch on the car door, ready to slip the folder back on the seat. Before I could get my arm inside, Cuddles shot between my body and the door.

"No. Oh, no. No. No. No."

He grinned at me from the seat of the blue BMW. Milky drool foamed from his mouth. He shook his head and splattered the dash, window, seat, and windshield with slobber.

"Cuddles," I hissed. "Get out. Out. Out. Now. Out."

He turned three times and collapsed on the seat. I yanked on the leash, accomplishing nothing.

"Please, please, please get out of this car. I'm committing a crime and you're an accomplice. Frig. Shiz. Frick." I tugged the leash. Set the folder on the ground to get a better grip. A breeze popped open the top of the folder. I stepped on it before the sheets blew, grabbed the leash with both hands, and pulled. "Cuddles. Out. Now."

Cuddles jumped out of the car. I grabbed the folder, threw it on the seat, and slammed the door.

I looked around the parking lot. No one had seen me. I checked the car. The folder had shoe prints on it. The papers had slid out, littering the leather seats and floor. White slime dripped from the dashboard onto the floor mats.

"How am I going to get this car cleaned up?" I spun around and glared at Cuddles. "This is your fault. Why are you doing this to me?"

He stared up at me. His chocolate-brown eyes full of regret and sorrow. A droolcicle hung from his jowls. The single fang popped out.

"I know, I know. My fault, too. You miss Amanda. I'm a substitute mom and not a good one. But Amanda gave you a complex. This negative attention cycle is damaging to us both—"

The Rounds of Grounds door opened.

"Shiz. Fraptastic. We've got to get out of here."

TWENTY-ONE
#DOGINTHENIGHTTIME #FELONYFLEA

WE RETURNED TO WINDMERE. It would take BMW some time to clean his BMW. I would use that time to interview his neighbors and poke around. There was nothing else I could do, other than grand theft auto to get the convertible to a detail shop.

At least that's what I told myself. In reality, my shame meter had tipped toward the first time I had tried red bull vodkas and did an impromptu burlesque show at Bootsy Bellows in West Hollywood. Then decorated their bathroom in a style similar to what Cuddles had done to the BMW, just less white.

Not only had I committed Entering Auto, but I'd also committed Destruction of Personal Property. Technically, Cuddles had done the act, but I was the responsible party.

At the moment, I felt just as sick as I did after the Bootsy Bellows performance. Who had I become? Defying my boss. Breaking rules. Committing felonies. While still on probation. And instead of apologizing to BMW and offering to pay for the cleaning, I'd fled the scene of the crime.

"You're staying in the car while I visit the neighbors," I said to Cuddles. "Take a nap. Don't eat the headrests. Take the time to reflect on the causality between destroying private property and lack of freedom."

Using flyers I had picked up in the Windmere office reception, I canvased Building C.

"Just dropping off Windmere Satisfaction Surveys," I said to the young lady in 101C and beamed my *People Magazine* smile. "How do you feel about your neighbors? Anything strange going on you'd like to report?"

"Everything's fine. I've got a leaky bathroom faucet, though."

"Good to know. I'll have someone over to fix it." I noted it on the back of a survey. "What about your neighbors? We've heard a complaint about the man in 204C. I believe he's subletting, so I don't know his name…"

"Not sure. He's cute, but not friendly."

"Yes." I bobbed my head. "No idea what his name is?"

"Sorry."

Skipping 204C and 205C, I tried eight apartments in the block of ten and moved to the next building. Only five people were home. No one knew BMW's name. He kept to himself. Quiet. Not home regularly. I toured the Dumpster but quickly gave up on garbology. Finding something useful among forty apartments' garbage bags would take time. More importantly, emptying hundreds of bags of garbage while wrestling with Cuddles would draw attention.

However, I'd sunk low enough that dumpster diving would have been a step up.

I dragged myself back to the Impala. Stopped a few feet away. The girl with the long braids stood next to the car. Her hand pressed against the window. Cuddles' muzzle was barely visible through the smeared glass. He'd been licking her hand.

A stab of jealousy rocketed through me. I shook it off.

"Girl," I called out. "Dog-whispering girl, please don't go. I need to talk to you."

She turned. "Y'all need to stop leaving your dog in the car."

"I know, I know," I jabbered. "But I can't take him with me when I visit apartments. He's too ferocious and destructive."

She turned to give me a teenage eyeball full of contempt. "And whose fault is that?"

"It's a long story. Listen, I have a job for you. But I need to meet your mother."

———

ELAINE EMBREE AND HER MOTHER, Victoria, lived in a neighborhood of ranch homes behind Windmere. Each day, after Elaine finished her online schooling, she walked through Windmere to a shopping area to visit her mother, who owned a dog grooming business.

"She won't let me work there unless I'm licensed," complained Elaine.

Victoria lifted her chin and peered down her nose at Elaine. "I follow rules."

I bit my lip. Recently, rules were not my forte.

"But I could watch Cuddles." Elaine patted his head. He beamed back at her. I felt another stab of jealousy. "Couldn't I, Momma?"

"I'll think about it," said Victoria.

"A few hours a day would help." I had already explained my meet-cute with Cuddles and the subsequent eating of everything. "It's my fault he destroyed a subject's car and a client's house. He can't be left unattended. Don't forget, it's temporary. Just until one of the Hearns takes him. Or when Amanda returns home." Although that didn't seem likely anytime soon.

"He needs me, Momma." Elaine and Cuddles looked at Victoria with the same pleading look.

"I've got to go back to work," said Victoria. "I have a Pekinese and a pair of Dalmatians at five, then back-to-back poodle mixes until eight. We'll do a trial run now. Elaine has school in the morning. Tomorrow is also piano and tennis. We'll talk about her schedule later."

"Yay!" Elaine threw her arms around Cuddles' neck. He nuzzled her face.

"Thank you." I edged to the door. "See you around eight." I waited a beat. "Cuddles, I'm leaving."

He had flopped onto his back with his legs sprawled so Elaine could rub his belly.

"Cuddles," I called in my smoochy-dog voice. "I'm going now. Are you going to be okay?"

"He'll be fine," said Victoria. "Don't you have suspects to watch or something?"

I nodded and exited the house. Then watched the girl and dog through the front window for a minute or two longer.

Relief was a strange feeling. It felt a lot like guilt.

TWENTY-TWO

#LITTLEGAPPERS #DOGMOM

I MOTORED TO WINDMERE, feeling strangely bereft. And angsty. Possibly more angst than in my late teens, although that angst had been somewhat deadened by pharmaceuticals, so hard to tell.

"Get a grip," I told myself, backing into a parking space. "He's happy. It's a much better situation for him. You broke a bunch of rules and several laws because of him. He ate a car and a refrigerator. If anything, his diet will improve at Elaine's."

I continued this sort of dialogue while I watched building C. I moved the car after an hour. Parked at D. I tried a new character for building D—woman who talks on the phone in her car because of her nosey roommate—when the blue convertible drove past me.

"Bingo," I said and realized I spoke to myself. Sighed and picked up my camera.

BMW was alone. He hurried toward building C, carrying the gym bag. I grimaced and wondered if he'd spent the past hour cleaning his car. Also, wondered if anyone in the coffee shop had seen me. If the coffee shop had security cameras in their parking lot. If I should check on his car.

And why I was such a dolt.

"Shizzles." Could I risk taking a burn to see if my subject's BMW was still covered in dog slobber? Anyway, Cuddles would somehow jump in …

Hold on.

I scanned the parking lot, got out of the Impala, and checked if 204C's windows remained shaded. Ran across the parking lot. Strolled to the BMW and casually glanced inside.

No visible dog slobber. The folder was in the front seat. The shoe imprint remained, but it was faint.

I scurried back to the Impala. Spied BMW hurrying out of building C. The back of my neck grew hot, my palms grew moist, and I talked myself out of hyperventilating. He didn't look my way. Got into his convertible. I blew out a long breath and started the Impala.

We were off.

He drove through Gilmore, turned onto the business highway, and followed it north out of town, into the mountains. A difficult area for tailing. We were near the North Carolina border. The winding one-lane road hugged the mountainside. Not a lot of traffic. I fell back, but glimpsed the blue convertible exiting a turn. Sped up. Decelerated to a crawl at the apex in case the BMW had slowed around the corner.

Gripping the wheel, I focused on the upcoming embankment and spotted a bit of blue disappearing up a mountain lane on the left. I shot past the lane, took two more turns, and pulled into the drive for a touristy overlook restaurant and store. Whipped the car around and pulled back onto the highway. Sped around the two turns, slowed, and took a right onto the mountain lane.

The drive was steep and wooded. Paved, yet bumpy. A dense forest shrouded the lane, and the Impala's automatic lights came on. I switched them off and crept along. Logging trails branched off the lane, but they appeared unused. The road ended at an impressive wrought-iron gate. A fence stretched in either direction. Beyond the gate, a long drive extended into the woods. I peered through my windshield but couldn't see anything.

There was no number on the gate. No mailbox. No call box. Not even a security camera.

I turned around and drove back to the mountain highway, searching the woods for signs. Just before I turned back toward Gilmore, my phone rang.

"Where are you?" said Nash.

"I have no idea."

"Are you serious?"

"Yes. I might be in North Carolina. I was concentrating too hard to pay attention to the signs."

"How do you concentrate on driving and miss signs? Never mind. Are you coming back soon?"

"Why?" My voice pitched. "Do you want to get dinner? A dinner date? It's been a while. I could go for a dinner date."

"What about Cuddles?"

"I found a dog sitter. Hopefully. We're doing a trial run. But I think she goes to bed at eight, so our date has a curfew."

"Do dates fit in with your rules?" His voice deepened. "Or have you decided to give up on the no-hugging clause?"

"What? No." Actually, I had forgotten about the clause. Which said a lot about my willpower. Or lack thereof. "A dinner date that doesn't include hugging fits in with the rule. It can even be a business dinner."

"Then it's not a date."

Shizzles.

"You're still spying on me, then?" he continued. "I've spotted Ms. Cox's Jeep around town."

"No." I hadn't spied on him since Joel Dewillis stopped me from entering DeerNose. That much was true. I'd been too busy spying on a nameless guy who had just disappeared. I was a terrible spy. Also, a terrible girlfriend.

If only Nash would tell me about Kristi and DeerNose, then we could get back to hugging and I wouldn't have to break laws, plant GPS devices in Nash's truck, or lie to people.

The lying bothered me more than the breaking of laws. I

was an honest person. Really. Even back when I performed, or even now when I did honey traps, authenticity was important to me. Although I guess authenticity and honesty were two different things. But I still felt like an honest person.

Deep down.

Feeling confused, I checked my GPS tracker to find Nash's location. It seemed he'd found my tracker and returned it. Either that or he'd been at A.S.S. all day.

"So dinner. Depending on where you are," I hinted. "I can probably get to Black Pine in an hour."

"That's a short business dinner."

Shizzles. "Even shorter because my dog sitter lives in Gilmore."

"Sounds like it won't work out. Maybe I'll catch you—"

I waited, but I could tell something had pulled his attention away from our conversation. "Nash, are you still there?"

"Gotta go. Call you later."

He hung up.

I opened my mobile phone spy software app. The app showed Nash's call to me, Lamar at the Dixie Kreme shop, and the local tire shop. His received calls included a few spam numbers and one from Jolene Sweeney. Nash's ex-wife. The call duration for Jolene was longer than the call he had just made to me.

This was why spying on your boyfriend was a bad idea.

———

I SET ASIDE those thoughts and accompanying feelings and turned left onto the highway. Instead of heading back to Gilmore, I used my non-Cuddles time to learn about the mysterious property where BMW had disappeared. Four cups of coffee later, I had visited with everyone who worked at the overlook restaurant, gift shop, and connected gas station. Also at the post office, hair salon, and convenience store in the nearby mountain village of Little Gap.

I finally had a name

The Mercers had owned the property. The name seemed familiar, but Mercer was a common family name in Georgia. When one heard the name, you couldn't help but hum *Moon River*.

I learned the Mercer land had been in the family for generations. "Didn't have the big gate and fence back then," said more than one resident of Little Gap. A little over twenty years ago, they sold the property. It changed hands a few times. The previous resident had put in the "big fence."

"That lane is a bugger in the winter. If you're not mountain folk, ya cain't handle it too well," said Tim Creary of Little Gap Automotive. "Thought he was somethin' else with that fence, didn't he?"

"It is an impressive gate," I said.

Tim snorted. I guessed that meant the gate didn't impress him.

"Now the latest up t'ar is a lady," said Tim. "Don't think she's got a family. Keeps to herself."

"A recluse?" *Grey Gardens* popped into my mind. Of course, the Hamptons were not Little Gap, North Carolina. Still, an intriguing concept. Did she rely on Amazon or Door Dash? Uber Eats? Did a local deliver the necessities and care for the grounds? Did she only allow women to enter the old Mercer property?

I had so many questions, but none pertaining to my search for BMW and his relationship to Kristi and therefore Nash and DeerNose. I forced myself to put the *Grey Gardens* of Little Gap out of my head.

"Do you know her name?" I said.

"Nawp," said Tim. "Some think she's from Asheville."

"Asheville. Maybe she's an artist or creative?" I was on another *Grey Gardens* goose chase. I shook it off. "Have you seen a blue BMW convertible around much?"

"Yes, ma'am." Tim brightened at the car talk. "He gets gas here sometimes."

"Sounds like he's a regular visitor to the old Mercer place?"

"Could be. Thought he was a tourist myself. British guy. Sometimes they come up to hike, ya know?"

"I believe he lives in Gilmore."

"What's he want with Gilmore?"

"I have no idea." Tim and I took a moment to ponder that one. I noted the garage's deepening gloom. The sunset had come and gone. "Oh no! I've got to get to the sitter's."

"You best be on your way." We exited the garage and walked to the Impala. "Careful on those roads, now. Your kids will want you back in one piece."

"Kids? Oh, I don't have kids. I'm not even engaged." I sighed. "I'm in a relationship, but usually engaged by this point. Things are a little foggy at the moment."

"More's the pity." Tim patted my shoulder. "Looks like you'd make a good mother."

"Really?" I fiddled with the car fob to hide my blush. "Why's that?"

"Dunno. You remind me of my Bailey. She's got a few rug rats now. Wonderful mom to my grandkids."

"Aw, thanks." I grinned. "I'm watching this dog named Cuddles. He's at the sitter for the first time. I've done a pretty good job with him, though. That's practice for kids, right? He's a little destructive, but he's coming along."

"I know folks say that. I suppose it helps to care for a dog before having children, but the love you have for your kids can't compare. They're a much bigger responsibility, too."

"You have a point. Taking care of Cuddles is a *little* easier than watching my six-year-old sister." I clasped my hands together. "I really hope things work out with Nash. He hasn't said anything about wanting children, but he's great with Remi. Much better than he is with Cuddles."

"That's a good sign." Tim nodded. "He'll come around to kids if y'all get hitched. We usually do."

"I think he might be gun shy about getting married, though. He's divorced. Do you think that's why he hasn't proposed yet?"

"Cain't really say, now can I? I guess you need to get going, don't you, hon?" Tim opened the car door for me. Glanced in and did a double-take. "What happened to your interior?"

"Um, that would be Cuddles."

He straightened and backed up a step. "The dog that's *'coming along?'*"

I nodded.

He stared at the car and shook his head. "I think you might want to take your time in finding the right guy before you jump in t'anything with kids. Just my advice."

TWENTY-THREE
#DOWHATISAYNOTASIDO #DOGDISSED

IT SEEMED stupid to cry just because Tim Creary of Little Gap Automotive didn't think I was ready for motherhood. He didn't know Cuddles, but that was no consolation. I knew Cuddles, and I knew myself. Just because Cuddles liked me didn't mean I could control him.

He was like everyone else in my life. Sure, he responded to a few commands. People told me what I wanted to hear. But they still did what *they* wanted. What they knew I *expressly* didn't want.

Like eating a car. Creating a reality show for me to star in. Or looking into my father's company's secrets and pretending he wasn't doing exactly that.

I pulled into Victoria Embree's drive at eight forty-nine. The door flew open before I reached the front porch.

"If you can't read a clock, this is not going to work," said Victoria.

"I'm so sorry. I was all the way in Little Gap. What did he do? Did he destroy your kitchen? Living room? Back yard? Just list the damages. I'll have a contractor come out. Unless you have someone you'd rather use, then just bill us."

"Cuddles didn't do anything." Victoria crossed her arms. "It's your inability to be on time where I have the issue."

Elaine popped up behind her mother. "I'm glad you're late. It gave me more time with Cuddles. He's such a good boy."

"Good boy?" My neck stopped sweating, but my stomach still twisted. "He didn't destroy anything?"

"Naw, he was fine," said Elaine. "We went for some walks. I took him to the dog park. We played. But mostly he laid around while I did homework and watched TV."

"But he ate everything in sight, right?"

"I redirected him to healthier options." Elaine popped a fist on her hip. "He's learned some bad food habits."

"I have this love of trans-fats and carbs. My ex-therapist calls it emotional eating. Plus, there's the forbidden fruit complex because of my previous acting career, when I couldn't eat any of the unhealthy stuff that puts on weight. My ex-manager put it in my contract. She was also my mother, so it became emotional eating…" I was rambling. But I was also trying to peer around Victoria and Elaine to see Cuddles. Where was he? Why wouldn't he come bounding out to see me?

Where was my happy reunion?

Had I made a mistake leaving him with Elaine? Had they shoved him in a crate? He might have been ornery and destructive with me, but at least he'd been free …

Cuddles' muzzle popped out of the doorway behind them. He moseyed into the room to sit next to Elaine. She laid a hand on his head. He craned his neck to lick her hand.

"Cuddles? It's me. Maizie. Are you ready to go?"

He disappeared behind Elaine.

"It's time to go. How about on the way home, we'll stop by…" Elaine's eyes narrowed. I caught myself before saying Hot Clucks. "The dog park. You can have a healthy runaround."

Victoria looked at Elaine. "Help Maizie get Cuddles in her vehicle."

"Can he come over again tomorrow, Momma?"

She sighed. "After your work is done. And piano." Victoria looked at me. "Tennis is at six. You have to be on time."

"I'll do better. I promise."

———

ON OUR WAY back to Black Pine, Cuddles ignored me.

Of course, he didn't want to go home with me. Home was this car. I was a terrible dog sitter. Maybe nobody minded me because I wasn't any better at minding them. I wasn't even minding the law lately. Or my boss. Was there anybody in my life that I was being honest with?

I bit my lip.

"Let's find Nash," I said in the perkiest voice I could muster. "We're going to find him without the aid of electronics. When we find him, we'll talk about anything but Kristi Johnson and DeerNose."

The Silverado pickup wasn't parked at Dixie Kreme Donuts. When I called him, the number went to voice mail.

"Okay," I told Cuddles, who had climbed in the passenger seat to press his nose against the window and stare at the donut shop. "Maybe just this time, we'll use the help of electronics. Only because I want to apologize to him in person about this whole Kristi Johnson business and for spying on him."

I checked the GPS tracking app, then remembered it no longer worked. My neck heated and my palms began to sweat. "We can't go on like this. How am I supposed to do my job and let him do his, when his job is intruding on mine? Am I right? I mean, I know I'm not supposed to be doing this particular job. But our work life is overlapping and he won't tell me why."

Cuddles turned to look at me.

"I'm not having a tantrum. Okay, maybe a little one."

Fifteen minutes later, we parked across the street from the Johnson house. I didn't see Nash's truck. Or Annie's Jeep. But I did see massive plumes of smoke rising from the roof. Flames encased one side of the house. The sound studio end of the house. Derek's truck was in the drive.

"Holy shizzoli." I looked at Cuddles. "Stay."

I dialed 9-1-1, jumped out of the car, and ran toward the house. I hung up on the dispatcher to call Derek. While the phone rang, I checked his truck. Sirens wailed in the distance. I ran to the side of the house, through the gate, and into the back-yard. Spotted Derek, attempting to spray the house with his garden hose.

"Derek," I screamed. "I called 9-1-1."

He spun around, drenching me with the hose. "My studio."

"I know. I'm sorry," was all I could think to say.

He aimed the hose back at the house. "I thought I could put it out myself."

"I'm so sorry. The fire trucks are here." I laid a hand on his arm. "You did your best. The fire's too big. But you need to put the hose down and come with me."

TWENTY-FOUR

#FIREITUP #DALMATIONNATION

I STAYED with Derek Johnson until Black Pine Fire and Rescue took over for me. After answering a few questions, I drove to A.S.S. and listened to the police scanner. When it sounded like they'd put the fire out, we headed back.

The Johnsons' street had been cordoned off. I parked on the next block behind the black truck again and walked closer. Half of the roof was gone. What was left was charred and smoking. Firemen milled about. The police were there, too, and one ambulance, although its lights were off.

A small crowd of neighbors and newspeople had clustered at the end of the street closer to the Johnson house. We circled behind them, crossing through lawns to maintain our distance. Cuddles sniffed the air, but seemed uninterested in the hubbub.

"All these people and you're not going berserk," I remarked. "Either Elaine Embree put a whammy on you or it's not the crowds you mind, it's individuals."

I spotted Nash down the street. Arms folded, leaning against his truck. Before I could charge toward him, Annie grabbed my arm.

Cuddles snarled.

"Cripes," said Annie, stepping back slowly. "You brought him here?"

"What else can I do? Hang on." I settled Cuddles and gave him a healthy snack Elaine had shared with me. Cuddles plopped his haunches on my feet and stared up at me, waiting for another treat. "What's going on?"

"Doesn't look good for Derek." Annie's jaw worked furiously. I felt bad for her gum. "I talked to a fireman who was first on the scene. The fire took out the studio."

"Oh no," I wailed. Considering Annie's mandate, I was careful to react to the fire as if I had not already witnessed Derek trying to put it out with a hose. "The studio is Derek's dream."

"Whatever. Listen, they found a body in there. The firemen couldn't resuscitate her. She was already dead."

"She? Dead?" I didn't need to perform to react with shock this time. A shudder ran through me. "Who, she?"

"Take a wild guess." The gum popped between Annie's lips. She sucked it back in. "Kristi."

"That's horrific." I gazed at the ambulance. "Poor Derek. How awful."

"Poor Derek's okay. Minor burns and smoke inhalation." Annie yanked my arm again. Cuddles growled. She dropped her hand. I gave Cuddles another treat and wondered if behavioral rewards would work on Annie. Maybe I should start carrying Juicy Fruit.

"I also talked to a cop," Annie continued. "After the hospital clears Derek, Black Pine PD is bringing him in for questioning."

"Derek? Why? Was the fire his fault?" My gaze swung from Annie to the ambulance and back to Annie. "Wait. Kristi was already dead. Like … she was already dead before the fire, already dead?"

"Yeah. Maybe. I didn't get details. The cop just said, 'already dead,' but the way he said it…"

"No."

Annie shrugged.

"Derek's such a nice guy."

"It happens."

"It happens?" I looked up at the sky, then at the ground. Remembered Nash and turned around. No Nash. His truck was gone. I whirled back to Annie. "How could this happen? His wife dead and a fire in his studio? Wait, what about your surveillance on Kristi? Did you see anything?"

Annie looked at me sheepishly. A look I'd never seen on her. I'd seen mulish. Doggedness. Cat-like. But never sheepish.

"You lost her?" I guessed.

She sucked on her gum and cut her eyes away from me.

"When?"

"Today. This morning." She sighed. "I thought she might show at DeerNose again. When Barney Fife wouldn't let us in, I parked down the road but never saw the Prius. I hit Windmere, her gym, house, all the haunts. Never found her again."

"What about the day before at DeerNose?" I said, pretending I didn't know Annie had followed Kristi to Windmere. "Did she stick around? Where'd she go after that?"

"Couldn't read my files?"

I arched a brow. "As if I'm going to hack into your computer to read case files." Since my hacking prowess ended in guessing passwords, it was a moot point.

"Kristi left DeerNose and went home. Later went to Gilmore. But nothing interesting happened. She didn't stay long. Returned home. Lights went off around ten. I left and came back early the next morning. I figured if she didn't stay at Windmere earlier, she wouldn't go anywhere in the middle of the night. I had to catch up on paperwork at the office." She curled her lip. "It's hard to keep up with the details at the office and do all the surveillance."

I almost said, "If you hadn't taken me off the job, this wouldn't have happened," but I didn't. We were both staring at Cuddles, and it made me feel guilty. I was also at fault for getting caught stalking Nash.

Instead, I replied, "What happened?"

"I arrived at the Johnson house before dawn. No evidence that anything had changed." Annie looked sheepish again. "But I fell asleep watching their house. I don't know how it happened. It couldn't have been more than twenty to thirty minutes. I woke up. Tried calling the house. No one answered. I figured she'd left, so I drove around for hours, trying to find her."

I felt my mouth form an "Oh," and snapped it shut. I couldn't believe it. My PI mentor had really slipped up. Lost a suspect who later died suspiciously? I don't think even I had done that. "Could've happened to anybody. You were tired—"

"I wonder…" Annie narrowed her eyes.

"What do you wonder?"

"Maybe Kristi never left the house. Maybe Derek came back, killed her while I was looking for her, and started the fire to cover it up."

"No way."

She leaned toward me. The gum crackled between her teeth. "Don't tell Nash about the surveillance. Or what I learned about Kristi's death."

The shock of her ask stopped my confession. "Why? He's going to hear the same thing, if not more, from Black Pine PD. He's got a lot of friends on the force."

Annie sunk back on her heels. She contemplated me with a steely glint. "If not more?"

I shrugged. "He grew up here. It's a small town."

"Not that small."

"Maybe not now, but Black Pine was when he was growing up. Besides, he's been in the business for a while. His best friend, Lamar, is a retired cop."

"If Nash is in the know, find out what he knows." She glowered for a long beat. "I don't like his involvement. What's Kristi to him?"

"That's what I was trying to find out before you yanked me from the case."

"Kristi's dead. We don't have a case."

I grimaced. "That's harsh."

"That's life." Annie folded her arms. "But I still want to know Nash's involvement."

"You don't want to know Derek's?"

"That's for the police."

"What if he didn't do it? What if our client is innocent?"

"He hired us to prove his wife was sleeping around, not to prove he didn't kill his wife." Annie paused. "But he might want to change the directive now. We'll visit him. Whenever they allow him visitors. Probably after his arraignment."

Her point sounded a bit mercenary for my taste. But I agreed. I really wanted to hear Derek's side of the story.

But more than that, I wanted Nash's.

TWENTY-FIVE
#GOODBADBOY #FAILARMY

WE DROVE BACK to the Dixie Kreme office. My heart felt heavy. My head about to explode for want of information. After trying to find Nash electronically, I stretched onto the couch. Stared at the stained ceiling and tried not to think about Kristi and Derek. Tried harder not to think about Nash. Or DeerNose. Or that Tim Creary of Little Gap had found me wanting as a mother to humans and dogs.

About the time I had reached the point of wondering where my life was going in a borrowed Impala with a boyfriend who kept a lot of secrets, I fell asleep. I woke up to a loud bang, followed by frenzied barking and growling. My phone rang.

I fished the phone out of the back of the couch. "Hello?"

"Honey, can you let me in?" said Lamar. "I finished making the donuts. The girls are opening the store. I need a nap."

I calmed Cuddles down, let Lamar in, and hauled Cuddles onto the couch next to me.

Lamar looked at us and shook his head. "You're a mess. Both of y'all."

"I know." I blew out a breath and flopped back on the couch. "Nash never came back."

"Don't worry about Nash. What's going on with you?"

I told him about Kristi Johnson. Everything. Except for the spying on Nash. And the illegal enterings. Even though Lamar was just Lamar, in the back of my mind, Lamar was also a retired cop. I did include Cuddles' destruction of the Johnson kitchen. That was now destroyed again.

"A fire with a suspicious death is nasty business." From the recliner, Lamar folded his hands on his belly. "No wonder you're so upset."

That wasn't why I was so upset, but I didn't want to seem even more pathetic than I already was, so I nodded. "The police are acting like Derek's a suspect."

"Of course he is," said Lamar. "He was at the scene. He's a husband who hired a private investigation company to see if his wife was having an affair. And he never mentioned to you that Mrs. Johnson was in the house."

"Maybe he didn't know Kristi was in the house. I got the feeling he'd just gotten home and found the house on fire."

"Why didn't he immediately call 9-1-1? Or check to make sure his wife wasn't in the home?" Lamar shook his head. "Attacking a house fire with a hose?"

"It sounds strange, yes..." I thought back to my encounter with Derek. "But at the time, it seemed reasonable that he'd grab a hose and try to put the fire out. It was his studio. I think he panicked."

Lamar shrugged. "Sounds suspicious to me. I'd take him in for questioning, for sure."

"Do you know where Nash is? I haven't been able to reach him since yesterday afternoon. We were talking, and he had to cut off the conversation. I saw him at the fire, but then he took off before I could talk to him. I'm worried about him."

"I worry about Nash, too, honey. He's not great at relationships. Especially if he's on the hunt. His blinders go up when he's narrowing in on a target. Which is frustrating for those around him."

"What is he hunting? I know it's something to do with Deer-Nose, but he won't tell me."

"If he doesn't tell you, he has a good reason. Nash is very protective of his people. He loves you. He's just not always great about showing it."

"I'm having a hard time with this, Lamar."

"I feel for you, honey. You know, I watched out for him when Nash was a kid. His momma was … not too attentive. Kind of wrapped up in her own dramas. But she loved that boy as well as she could, and he took care of her as best he could."

"You never told me how you got involved with Nash."

Lamar studied his hands. "We had a couple of domestics at the Nash residence before his dad took off. I kept my eye on Mrs. Nash and Wyatt, particularly when she started dating again. He was smart. Hard worker. Hated to see him get caught up in his momma's entanglements. He liked riding in the patrol car. Then he'd find me, wanting to learn about being a cop. I started bringing him home. Olivia would fuss over him. Cook for him. Then the boy grew up." Lamar chuckled. "But he kept coming back. We're family."

"That was really sweet of you both."

"That was nothing." Lamar waved away the compliment. "He was a good boy deep down. Olivia knew about the family. A lot of families go back quite a way, like yours. We just knew everybody."

"Things have certainly changed. That was when DeerNose was just starting out."

"Yep. And before this movie business." Lamar's eyes drifted shut. "More people and businesses now, but Black Pine's still a small town. Old dramas still flare up."

"And new dramas cause fires," I said, thinking about the Johnsons.

"My advice to you," Lamar murmured, "you might need to let him go for a while, honey. Nash's a good boy, but he's not quite domesticated. He's not going to take well to you sticking your nose into his business. He's a serious man when it comes to his work. Move on to the next case."

TWENTY-SIX

CUDDLES and I returned to A.S.S. to break the bad news to Tiffany and Rhonda. They had already heard about Kristi and Derek. I wasn't surprised. Years of working in the salon had plugged them into Black Pine's gossip network. Now that they didn't work in the salon, they listened to the police scanner on the office laptop. However, the really good stuff was lost to those who still shampooed, cut, and colored.

"They arrested him," said Tiffany.

"No way did Derek do this," said Rhonda. "Anyone that cute and nice and handsome would not murder his wife and try to cover it up by setting a fire to his studio."

"I dunno," said Tiffany. "I bet Ted Bundy would've done that. Women found him cute and nice and handsome. There's no accounting for taste."

"I don't think Ted Bundy was married," I said. "Although it's been a while since I've seen *The Deliberate Stranger*. But I'm pretty sure Ted Bundy didn't have a recording studio."

"Do you think Derek could've killed Kristi?" Rhonda clasped her hands together. "Maizie, how did he seem?"

"He was genuinely panicked when I found him trying to put out the fire. I didn't see him after they found Kristi. They took him in an ambulance to get checked." I scowled. "He doesn't strike me as the wife-killing type, but…"

"But what?" Tiffany leaned forward.

"I mean, what do we really know about people?" I shrugged. "You think you know a person, but it's not like you can read their mind or anything."

"Are we talking about Derek or someone else?"

"Um." I snapped out of it. "Derek."

Tiffany exchanged a look with Rhonda, then stared at Cuddles. "This is the second case in less than two weeks that's ended in murder."

"First one was only attempted murder," said Rhonda. "I don't think that counts."

"Either way, our client has once again ended in the hoosegow. If this keeps up, Annie is going to have apoplexy over the accounts receivable."

"Maybe this will make her change her mind about infidelity cases," I suggested. "There's other stuff to investigate. There's got to be a kidnapping or a burglary victim out there who needs our help."

"Girl, those are too hard. Cheating spouses are easy money and a lot of fun. I love it when we catch the suspect red-handed," said Tiffany. "It's like busting my ex all over again."

"Tiff." Rhonda cocked her head. "That's not healthy."

"Neither are donuts, but I don't see either one of you cutting those out of your life."

"Hey," said Rhonda. "Don't get ugly. It's Maizie who has the real problem."

True. But still.

"Anyway," Rhonda continued. "This isn't an infidelity case anymore. It's a murder investigation. I've always wanted to investigate a murder."

"Nobody in their right mind wants to investigate a murder. It's horrible. And dangerous. And sad. You know how anxious I get."

"I think you secretly like investigating murder."

"The cases I've had involving murder never started with murder. I haven't gone out seeking to investigate a murder."

"How is this different? We have to help Derek." Rhonda folded her arms. "I don't think he did it."

"What if he did?"

"What if he didn't? Think of poor Derek sitting in jail. He just found his wife dead. He's mourning her behind bars." Rhonda stood and whipped her finger to point at us, getting into the role of the aggrieved. Her arms flew as her hands described the scene. "Going to prison, framed for a crime he didn't commit. He'll never get out. He might never see the open sky outside a prison yard. Won't be able to make any recordings no more. He'll start cutting tracks on the prison sound system with the deadbeat musicians and wannabe artists who wind up behind bars for killing a stripper during a blackout. What kind of life is that?"

"The kind of life you deserve if you murder your wife?" said Tiffany.

"Think about me." Rhonda's thumb jabbed her chest. "I'll become one of those crazy women who hooks up with a prisoner. Stuck moving into a little tract house near the yard so I can see him twice a month on weekends. What kind of life will that be for our kids?"

"You went there fast," said Tiffany.

"I was in the moment." Rhonda smoothed her top and sat down.

"Anyhoo," I segued, "whether Derek is guilty or not, I'm still dealing with the same question I've been wondering since the beginning."

"If Nash was cheating with Kristi?" said Tiffany.

"Maybe Nash killed Kristi," said Rhonda.

"Just stop." This time I took on the role of the indignant and pointed. "Nash wasn't cheating with Kristi, and no way did he kill her. But Kristi was involved in Nash's top-secret DeerNose project. I want to know why."

"Where's Nash now?" said Rhonda. "Have you talked to him since the fire?"

"No. But I went about this all wrong," I admitted. "Spying on Nash became a thing between us. I shouldn't have let it go down that road."

Rhonda arched an eyebrow at Tiffany. Tiffany rolled her eyes.

"What I mean is, he knew I was spying on him. I don't think Nash took me seriously."

"I guess it's serious now," said Tiffany. "Considering Kristi's dead."

"Nash didn't want to involve me in his DeerNose investigation because of my personal ties to DeerNose. He said he's protecting me and my family. I believe he *thinks* that's true. I just don't understand why it's such a big deal. One thing's for sure, there is some kind of industrial espionage and sabotaging going on. Maybe someone on the inside of DeerNose is a double agent."

"I don't get why he won't let you help him," said Rhonda. "Unless it's something to do with your dad. But your dad wouldn't be corporate spying on his company."

"What if Kristi and your dad … you know…" Tiffany made finger gestures.

"No way," I shouted. "Daddy would never cheat on Carol Lynn."

Rhonda and Tiffany did the eyebrow and eye roll thing again.

"Stop. Daddy is not the type."

"It makes sense." Rhonda shrugged. "Why else would Nash be trying to protect you?"

"No." My skin crawled. I shook off the idea. "I saw what happened to the tech packs. They were sabotaged. Mrs. Peters confirmed it. Kristi worked for CrossHair. Kristi snuck into Deer-Nose. Maybe it wasn't the first time. CrossHair must have something to do with it."

"Kristi would have easy access to DeerNose to do dirty work if she was … you know, doing dirty work." Tiffany made the gestures again. "Real easy if it was Boomer."

"Stop that. It's disgusting."

"Maybe somebody else in the company was doing Kristi?" said Rhonda. "Derek thought Kristi was cheating. It seems obvious to me. She used her body to gain access to … the secret deer pee-smell formula or whatever."

"Maybe. But isn't Kristi as Mata Hari too extreme? It'd be a lot easier for CrossHair to hire a hacker than to convince an actress to sleep with a company man to get some apparel design secrets."

"If you put it that way, I guess it doesn't make sense," said Tiffany.

"Except that Kristi was cheating on Derek," said Rhonda. "We know that to be true."

"We don't actually," I said. "In the little time we spent tailing Kristi, we didn't get any actual evidence."

"She spent the night at BMW's apartment."

"That's not enough proof. Remember, that apartment seemed more like an office for CrossHair."

"It had a bed and a couch," said Tiffany. "Uncomfortable and utilitarian but still horizontal."

"I'm convinced there's more to it than that. Why would a marketing firm have all those headshots?" I folded my arms and leaned back in the chair. "Kristi was an actress. She was acting the part of what … corporate spy? Is that why she snuck into DeerNose? Not to sleep with anyone, but to steal secrets?"

"Or both," said Rhonda. "She's a terrible woman."

"How can you say that? She's dead. Murdered. Possibly by Derek."

Rhonda shook her head. "Not Derek. Someone else. What about BMW?"

"She worked for BMW," said Tiffany. "Maybe sleeping with him, too. Derek could have killed her in a fit of jealous rage."

"Or BMW did."

"In her house, where Derek could catch them? That's a really dumb way to kill someone."

Rhonda opened her mouth. I held up a hand. "Hiring us makes it look doubly bad for Derek."

"Then you absolutely have to prove Derek didn't do it," said Rhonda.

We were back to square one.

"Okay, we'll work in figuring out who murdered Kristi by learning what Kristi had to do with DeerNose. Annie won't like it if we're not getting paid, though. Unless Derek calls us, we won't be able to talk to him. I'll see what I can find out from Ian."

"And Nash. Find out what he knows. He's plugged into the Black Pine investigation network."

"I'll try." I still felt uncomfortable with Annie's directive. "I also have another possible in with CrossHair. I've been tailing BMW. He went to Little Gap yesterday and visited the Old Mercer Place."

They looked at me blankly.

"You've never heard of it? A big old house up in the mountains just over the North Carolina border?" Maybe the Old Mercer Place was just common knowledge in Little Gap. Black Pine had a lot of big old houses on its mountain. The Mercer name still niggled my memory, but I chalked it up to my love of Mercer-Mancini collaborations. They provided the soundtrack to some of my favorite movies. Derek Johnson would understand as a sound engineer, but Tiffany and Rhonda didn't ground themselves in that kind of sentimentalism.

"Anyway," I continued, "I applied for a job with CrossHair. Except I used Rhonda's name."

Rhonda's eyes rounded. "You want me to play Mata Hari?"

"No, I'll do it. If CrossHair has a client who's stealing secrets from DeerNose, I couldn't use my name, could I?"

"You'll have to do it in disguise," said Rhonda. "You're still recognizable. Although in a shabbier way than when you were the old Maizie Albright. You're a lot more pitiful. But more authentic at the same time."

"Gee, thanks."

"What if they don't want Rhonda?" said Tiffany. "Kristi was an actress."

Rhonda's eyes grew round. "We could make me a dupe IMDb bio with *Kung Fu Kate* and your other shows in the credits. I could just be an extra, like Kristi. I've always wanted to be in the Internet Movie Database."

"She's got a point, even if it's for the wrong reason," said Tiffany. "If we use Maizie's headshot, it'll get recognized. We'll make Rhonda a fake resume and put it on IMDb, LinkedIn, and the other sites. Then we'll take it down when she gets the job."

"Yaas! I'm gonna be on IMBd." Rhonda did a chair dance. "I'm going to be famous."

"For about five minutes. And only to CrossHair," I reminded her.

"You are no fun, Maizie Albright."

———

WHILE RHONDA and Tiffany created an online alias, I returned to Nash's old office. Not that I thought I'd find anything about Kristi or DeerNose. But it'd be nice to know where he'd been the night before.

I might have searched his computer's system's memory with a special adaptor, but we won't talk about that since I had sworn off electronic surveillance.

"If he was moonlighting last night, he's back at DeerNose today," I said to Cuddles. At least I assumed he was at Deer-Nose. After Nash disabled my apps, I couldn't be sure unless I called him. But why make it easy (and awkward) for myself? "I can't take you to DeerNose unless we sneak in. But it's hard to be sneaky with you."

Cuddles opened an eye and looked at me from his prone position in Lamar's La-Z-Boy.

"I'm sorry, it's true. But I could sneak into DeerNose after I drop you at Elaine's. Not sneak but visit Daddy and drop by Nash's office unannounced. Maybe when he's not there."

At Elaine's name, Cuddles jumped off the chair and charged to the door. I folded my arms and blew out my breath. "To be honest, it kind of feels like you're cheating on me, too."

The words had popped out of my mouth. I took a moment to digest their meaning. "I don't think Nash is cheating on me. He's cheating on DeerNose … Maybe."

My phone rang. "What are you doing in the office?" said Nash.

My eyes narrowed. "How do you know I'm in your office? Are you spying on me?"

There was a long, what you might call pregnant, pause.

"Yes, I get the irony. But how did you know I'm at the office?"

Another pause. While he waited for me, I peered in the corners of the office, looking for hidden cameras. Particularly for one pointing at the computer.

"Never mind," I said, realizing if I was on camera, he'd see me looking for the cameras. "I need to talk to you about Kristi Johnson. Are you at DeerNose?"

"Of course. Is Cuddles with you?"

"He is."

"You can't bring him here."

"I know. The sitter has to finish her homework and piano lessons before I can take him, but that's all the way in Gilmore."

Another pause.

"What's with all the silence?"

"I'm thinking. Also, Mrs. Peters just dropped in to say hello."

"That's so sweet. Tell Petey I said hi. But listen, I need to talk to you about my client, Derek Johnson. Did you know Kristi Johnson was killed?"

"I do."

This time, I paused. Nash was not a chatty person, but this was a little ridiculous. Maybe he was angry at me for spying on him. "Did you talk to the police? I saw you at the fire last night."

"I saw you, too."

"Did you hear anything about the fire and Kristi?"

"I did."

"Are you going to tell me what you heard?"

"No."

"No? Really? Your answer is no?" My neck burned. I pressed my lips together, counted to ten, then forced them to relax. "I guess I'll ask Ian instead."

"I am not playing games with you," his voice sounded strangled. "Don't play them with me."

"I need information, Nash. Derek was our client."

"Mowry will take your asking the wrong way. Have Annie talk to him."

"I think you're taking this the wrong way."

"It's a guy thing."

"Okay then," I said with less irritation than I felt, but enough to imply my irritation. "Great *not* talking with you."

"I'm a little busy."

"I know you've got your rules about work and personal life and all that," I snapped. "But you didn't come home last night."

"I'm sorry." Nash sighed. "We'll talk later."

"*If* I see you later. Emphasis on *if*. If you get my point."

"I get it," he murmured. "Be patient, Miss Albright, please. I've got to go. Mrs. Peters is still here."

"Fine." I hung up and looked at Cuddles, who still stared at the door. He didn't want me either. "What is it with you men?"

Cuddles glanced at me, then turned back to the door.

"Fine. Okay, we'll go to Elaine's," I shouted. "Fine. Everything's just fine."

Except it wasn't.

TWENTY-SEVEN

WE HAD to wait for Elaine to squeeze Cuddles in between piano and tennis, so I took him with me to Black Pine Police Department. Normally, Detective Ian Mowry would usher me to his cubicle to discuss a case. I enjoyed visiting his cubicle. Not only did he decorate it with sticky notes, but he also plastered it with drawings by his six-year-old daughter. The cubicle also kept our discussions focused on casework.

Although I'd friend-zoned Ian almost from the start of our original meet-cute (featuring a disappearing body), we'd had a short dating history. We shared a mutual love of food and true crime podcasts. Ian also helped me with cases. But my heart hadn't been into it, having already settled on Nash.

Ian Mowry was a nice guy. He understood boundaries. I didn't feel like I was taking advantage of him. This meeting was about a client who might have murdered his wife. Our discussion wouldn't cross any lines in the sand.

Or rather, lines in the parking lot, which is where I met Ian, because I couldn't bring Cuddles to his cubicle.

From the visitor's entrance, Ian waved, then strode toward us. Like Cuddles, Ian had eyes the color of milk chocolate, although his wavy hair was darker. He also had a tall, athletic build, and was leaner and less barrel-chested than Cuddles.

Truthfully, Ian Mowry looked nothing like the dog. But they were both super cute in their own way.

"Don't get too close. This is Cuddles." I used my chin to motion toward the behemoth dog straining at his leash to take a chunk out of Ian. "I'm watching him for a client who's been arrested. It's a long story, but he's not good with people."

"I can tell." Ian halted, left his hands at his sides, and angled slightly so he wasn't looking at us straight on. "Can you handle him?"

"Cuddles doesn't trust men. Most people, to be honest. But he's gotten much better." I gave Ian the nutshell version of my history with Cuddles.

"I heard about that weapon discharge at the Bark and Brew," said Ian. "Gilmore police said it was one holy mess. Particularly what that dog did to the victim. You're certain you can hold him?"

"I'm safe enough. He likes me. I seem to bring out the worst in Cuddles' protective instincts."

Ian chuckled. "He wouldn't be the first guy to get overprotective of you."

I'd calmed Cuddles, but bristled at that comment. Ian had been good friends with Nash, but recently they'd begun a kind of alpha dance around me I didn't appreciate.

Now I had another alpha in my life, albeit a canine. I seemed to collect them. Was I giving off some kind of pheromone that encouraged this behavior? Too much tail-wagging on my part? Was my bark not threatening enough? I ground my teeth, wondering if I should start biting to make my point. Instead, I took direction from Elaine Embree by ignoring Ian's bad behavior and directing him toward good.

"How is Derek Johnson? I know he was arrested."

"The ambulance took him to be treated for smoke inhalation, but he's fine." Ian darted a look at Cuddles and took a step closer. "I saw you at the fire. What were you doing there?"

"Checking on Derek, of course." I told Ian about our investigation for Derek Johnson, minus the details of my personal investigation. And minus my visit to Derek's, where Cuddles had destroyed his kitchen. And the semi-breaking and entering of the mysterious BMW guy's apartment. And BMW.

To save time. And to not bring up anything arrest-worthy.

"I had no idea that Kristi was in the house when I was there earlier."

"Earlier? How much earlier?"

"I drove by on the way back from Gilmore," I hedged, not wanting to tell Ian that I'd really been looking for Nash. "Annie's doing the surveillance on Kristi Johnson, so I thought I'd check on Derek."

"Walk me through your check on Derek Johnson," said Ian.

"I drove up and saw the fire. I called 9-1-1 and found him in the back, trying to put out the fire with a hose. The fire seemed to come from his studio."

"You saw Derek Johnson putting out the fire? When was this?" He pulled a notebook out of his pocket and began jotting notes. "Did he say anything to you?"

"Not, really. I was focused on getting him to a safer spot so the fire crew could take over."

"He hadn't called emergency services?"

"I don't know." I tried to read Ian's face and couldn't. "Do they know what caused the fire?"

"We're waiting on the fire marshal's report." Ian pulled out a notebook, jotted down a note, then shoved it back in his pocket. "I'd like to see your notes and anything else you have on the Johnsons. How about I follow you to your office?"

"I've got to take Cuddles to Elaine's house."

At the mention of Elaine, Cuddles stiffened, pawed my leg, and stared up at me.

"We'll go in just a minute," I told him.

"How about you go later?" said Ian. "I'd like to see the Johnson file first."

I arched an eyebrow at Ian. "I'd need to ask Annie about that. Those files are private."

"Hon', we've got a suspicious death."

"Why did you arrest Derek? You must have something to hold him."

Cuddles whined and jerked toward the car. I laid a hand on his head and stroked his ears. He shook me off and pawed my leg.

"We had enough evidence to hold him." Ian kept his eyes on Cuddles. "To me, Johnson's explanation was unsatisfactory. His wife was found dead in his studio, where the fire started. We're expecting GBI to give us the cause of death soon and it's most likely not going to be from smoke inhalation."

"I already know that. Do you have an idea of what killed her?"

Ian's gaze shifted to me. His normally warm look had become deadpan. "Johnson said he had just gotten home. He was scheduled to be at a remote location for a few days, but yesterday's shoot was canceled. Because of a fire. Ironic, huh?"

I shrugged, noticing that Ian hadn't answered my question. Also feeling I should be keeping my cards closer to my chest. But Ian was right. That felt a teensy coincidental. Two fires on the same day. "What happened?"

"One of the trailers had a kitchen fire. Must have been disruptive enough to cancel that day's agenda. Or maybe it was a legal thing, canceling if there's a fire. I don't know. The plan was to get back on schedule the next day. Most stayed in the area, but not Derek. He came home."

"I guess they didn't need him, and he took the chance to come home," I said noncommittally.

"Johnson's a sound guy," said Ian. "Does that mean he knows a lot about wiring?"

"Sound cables are not the same as electrical wiring."

"But he'd understand basic electrical engineering."

"I suppose. But there are actual electricians on set. The sound technician jobs are specialized and get more creative as you rise in the industry. They're audio engineers. Derek's working his way up the ladder." Cuddles tugged toward the car. I pulled a treat out of my pocket and fed it to him.

"His wife probably wasn't expecting him at home," said Ian. "Why did Derek Johnson hire your services?"

"I'd rather Annie answer that question than me," I said carefully. "Why do you suspect Derek?"

Ian pressed his lips together, then relaxed them. "Do I need to spell it out for you?"

"I think you do. What was the evidence?"

"We don't want to release that yet." Ian stepped closer. "What's going on? Why are you still working for Derek Johnson?"

"I don't know if we are. We'd just like to know what happened."

"Did he say anything about his wife when you saw him trying to put out the fire?"

"Like I said, I didn't really talk to him. Right after I arrived, the fire trucks did, too. Derek was focused on putting out the fire." Cuddles pressed against me. I dropped a hand down to massage his ears. "I didn't know Kristi was there. I only saw Derek's truck in the drive. I feel kind of terrible about that. Maybe I could have done something."

Noting the wobble in my voice, Ian's features relaxed. "There's nothing you could have done for her, hon'. She was already dead." He reached for my hand but yanked it back at Cuddles' growl. "Drop your dog off, then give me a call when you get back to the office. I'll get a warrant for the Johnson file if Annie wants one."

"That's between you and Annie. She took me off the Johnson case. I've got one of my own."

"But you said…" Ian paused. "Was there something between you and Derek Johnson?"

"No," I gasped. "How could you think that?"

"There's something you're not telling me."

That something was Nash and the link between Kristi, Cross-Hair, and DeerNose. And possibly my father.

But I wasn't giving that bit of information to *Detective* Ian Mowry.

And probably not to Ian Mowry, my friend, either

TWENTY-EIGHT
#MOUNTAINMAMA #WORKLIKEADOG

ON THE WAY TO GILMORE, I shoved an earpiece in one ear and called A.S.S. "Tell Annie that Detective Ian Mowry is getting a warrant to look at the Johnson case files."

"How did that happen?" said Tiffany. "Annie's not going to like that."

"Stop crowding, Tiffany," said Rhonda. "Me and Tiffany are trying to share a headset for the computer phone. Why don't we have one of those speaker box thingies like Bosley uses on *Charlie's Angels*?"

"Because we're using a free phone app on the computer. Annie's too cheap to buy a real phone," sniped Tiffany. "Annie never met a penny she didn't like to squeeze."

"Ooh," squealed Rhonda. "She heard you say that. You're in trouble."

Scuffling and squawking sounds burned my ear, reminding me of the chicken incident. I winced at the memory.

"We have speaker phone ability with this app," announced Annie. Her voice sounded like she was calling from a distant galaxy, possibly underwater. "You two are unbelievable. Remind me again why I hired you?"

"Remind us again why *we'd* want to—" Tiffany's retort ended in an "oof." An oof likely caused by Rhonda's elbow. Or maybe her foot. A fist was possible.

"What's going on, Maizie?" continued Annie. "Where are you?"

"Taking Cuddles to Elaine's house."

At Elaine's name, Cuddles barked and pressed against the door. His window zipped down. With an excited woof, Cuddles shoved his head outside. My hair swirled. His jowls flapped. Drool spewed, coating the back seat's passenger window. I jammed my thumb on the window button. He arched his neck, following the window's ascent. I leaned over the console and yanked on a shoulder to pull him down. He scooted closer to the door and angled his head to keep his thick neck in the opening.

"Are you there?" bellowed Annie. "Hello? Are you in a tunnel?"

I gave up, grabbed my hair in a hand-held ponytail, and focused on the mountain road.

"Hi Annie," I said brightly. "Ian will probably show up with a warrant to look at the Johnson file. I thought I should warn you."

"What did you tell him?"

"Nothing really. He wouldn't tell me what evidence they have to hold Derek. Except there was a fire on set that stopped production for the day, so he came home unexpectedly."

"If he did it, it was a crime of passion," said Tiffany. "He probably came home and caught Kristi in the act."

"Derek didn't do it," cried Rhonda.

"It doesn't matter," seethed Annie. "If Mowry gets a warrant, I'll have to give him our case files. That's another case where we're not getting paid."

"If Maizie figures out who really killed Kristi, I betcha Derek would pay," said Rhonda. "He's that kind of guy. We'd be getting him out of jail. He'll be real happy about that. So happy he'll probably want to pay us extra."

I had opened my mouth to stop Rhonda but snapped it shut.

Rhonda was smart to appeal to the side of Annie's accounts receivable ledger.

"And what if Derek did it?" snapped Annie. "You think he'll pay us extra to prove he killed his wife? Solving a murder case will take a lot of time and manpower. What about the other cases that need our attention while we're following up on Johnson leads? That's more non-payment. Do you want to lose your jobs for real? If the office isn't getting paid, you're not getting paid."

To break the uncomfortable silence, I mumbled something about Gilmore and Cuddles and talking to them later. I regretted using Rhonda's identity to get into CrossHair. I'd have to find another way to learn more about CrossHair.

AFTER DROPPING Cuddles off at Elaine's, I used my only lead and drove to Little Gap. Before reaching the Old Mercer Place gate, I stopped, pulled out my phone, and searched for Wi-Fi. There were two signals—both random numbers and letters—one stronger than the other. I exited the car with my phone in hand and opened an app that used my phone's magnetometer, the built-in compass function, to sense electromagnetic fields. Very handy for searching for bugs in clients' rooms. Also handy for detecting the camera on a tree positioned to focus on the gate.

"One mystery solved," I muttered. "Someone calls the house. Whoever's home checks the camera and opens the gate. That makes sense. Being a recluse is much easier when you can afford the security measures. Really, it's just an upgraded doorbell camera."

I looked down to see Cuddles' reaction and realized I'd been talking to myself. "That's just great."

I was still speaking to myself, so I clamped my lips shut. On a whim, I tried the gate.

Unlocked. Weird, considering the extreme privacy. I thought

about the hidden camera and rolled the dice on anyone watching. After all, the gate was open.

I slipped through the gate and darted off the drive, into the tree line. Halfway up the climb, the house appeared. I'd expected a Victorian monstrosity or even a decadent robber-baron manor house like Vicki had purchased. The house was impressive, but not ostentatious. More of a gigantic modern tree house, built on posts to rise above the ground, level with the surrounding nature. Two floors of floor-to-ceiling windows and a wraparound terrace provided the homeowner with spectacular views.

It also provided me with an interior view. I could see two figures outlined in an upper-story window. A man and a woman. Lots of hand gestures from the man. Maybe an argument. The woman crossed her arms and stepped back.

Definitely an argument.

Since I couldn't see much else, I skirted the front of the house and approached the side without windows. I navigated down the embankment to the area below the house. Crept along a wall that eventually gave way to the open, beamed area that made the house look suspended in the trees. The walls wrapping the three sides of the embankment created a garage. Cement steps inside the garage led to a back door into the house.

In the semi-enclosed area, BMW had parked his BMW next to a Lexus SUV. I glanced into the BMW, then approached the Lexus. Despite the slick styling of the house and car, the SUV interior was a mess. A mess I understood. Lookbooks and fashion magazines covered the front passenger seat. Sunglasses, assorted pencils, and a small sketch pad were left in the open console. In the back seat, more art supplies overflowed from a tote stuffed with fabric samples.

I clasped my hands together and bounced on my toes. I knew this woman.

Well, didn't *know her* know her. But knew what she was about.

My gaze drifted back to the BMW. I stopped bouncing. What did I think? That I was going to make a new friend?

Anyway, why was a fashion designer hanging out with the CrossHair Marketing dude? They must be in a relationship. Possibly a business relationship. But they were likely seeing each other if he was often in this remote location—and according to Little Gap, he was.

Were they a *Barefoot in the Park* couple? A stuffy businessman and creative freethinker love match? Maybe CrossHair's secret shopping was their meet-cute.

I released a happy sigh and clasped my hands together again. Then got serious. I needed his name, not their relationship status.

But hang on. The girls—and I, admittedly—thought BMW was having a thing with Kristi Johnson. Did he know she was dead? Was he upset and hiding it because he'd been two-timing? Maybe the argument stemmed from his guilt and grief. Had he been cheating on the cheater? Or cheating on his fashion designer with Kristi?

Why could I not find a faithful couple in this business?

Wait. Maybe BMW and the fashion designer were brother and sister. Brothers and sisters argue.

Feeling right with the world again, I heaved a sigh of relief. My ex-therapist Renata always reminded me that, without knowing all the facts, attributing positive motives to a possible negative situation kept stress hormones at bay. Happy thoughts made for a happier person.

And bonus, fewer stress hormones meant easier weight loss.

Somewhere above me, a door creaked and shut. Footsteps clomped on wood. I froze next to the cars, then jogged forward, wincing at the sound of my Common Projects sneakers crunching on gravel. Outside the garage, I listened, trying to determine from which side to sneak back into the woods. What if they finished their argument and were enjoying the view? With a glass of wine. Or as brother and sister, maybe a friendly post-argument beer?

My positive motive thoughts were not helping to keep my stress hormones at bay. All my hormones focused on my trespassing on private property and getting caught.

I suddenly craved a donut. Or six.

Stupid stress hormones.

"Be reasonable," said a man's voice from somewhere above me. "It's enough, innit?"

Had to be BMW. Definitely British. His long vowels and dropped T's sounded working class. My ear could never identify the regional differences outside the Queen's English. Probably why I never got a British-speaking role.

"I'm not the one who messed up here, Simon," said a woman, sounding cool and firm. Also, with a strong accent. Georgian mountain twang.

Probably not his sister. How disappointing. Maybe Simon was a distant cousin of this local. Or just a friend, I thought, trying to keep my cortisol happy.

But more importantly, I had a name. I bounced in place, then tiptoed across the gravel to stand beneath the front overhang to better hear their conversation.

"Luella went overboard. That's not my fault, Dee. I didn't ask her to do any of it."

Dee. Great. Making progress. But now some last names, please.

"Bring Luella here," said Dee. "I appreciate what she's doing for us."

"I don't think it's a good idea," said Simon. "Come on, Dee. Too risky."

"Don't you want me to show her my appreciation? Why would you begrudge that of me, Simon?"

"It could blow up in our faces and where'd we be, then?"

"You don't trust me?"

"Of course, I trust you, Dee. You know I do. But I don't like mixing—"

"It's all business, sugar. It's always business."

Her tone had lightened, but I still detected a calculating coolness. This was one steel magnolia. I should know. Vicki had a similar accent. I could pick up the nuances in her tones like a seasoned translator.

They moved above me. Sounding like they'd gone closer to the stairs, I snuck to the opposite side and judged the distance from the tree line. Not a lot of cover until I could get deeper into the woods. They might hear me crunching on the fallen leaves and forest debris.

I could wait and hope they'd go back in the house.

They'd gone silent except for some rustling that I wasn't sure came from them or nature. I snuck over to the staircase and peeked. They stood in a clincher at the top.

I poked my head out, trying to see Dee. Simon's back was to me. With their faces glued together, I could only tell she was tall and blonde. Athletic looking.

This was some heavy-duty kissing. Trying to glimpse her face, I sidled forward. Dee pulled back from Simon. This time, I got a good look. Too good. I shrank back.

Her eyes had been opened. And she'd spotted me.

TWENTY-NINE
#SMALLBORE #JUNKYARDDOG

I TOOK off toward the opposite side of the house and slipped around the outside wall. Inched my way toward the back of the house. Paused there with my heart beating in my throat.

Above me, the door slammed and feet pounded the stairs.

"Hey," called Simon. "Who's out there?"

A crack rent the air. A sound I was familiar with—a rifle. Holy Shizolis. Sweat broke on my temple. It seemed Dee had my mother's accent and my father's gun collection.

"Dee, what in the bloody hell are you doin'?" yelled Simon.

"I take grave offense to anyone trespassing on my property," hollered Dee. "That was a warning shot. I was the junior small-bore rifle winner in high school. I don't compete anymore, but I still practice."

Frigalicious. Bragging rights on how easily she can shoot me.

I eyed the tree line. An uphill climb from the rear side of the house. Lots of time for my back to be exposed to a rifle. If I went right, parallel to the drive, another easy shot.

"I know you're there. Come on out," shouted Dee.

My heart backed into my throat and my stomach dropped to my toes. I couldn't get made. Simon had seen me at his apartment. He'd know I was following him. It would be the undoing of all my surveillance on him. He was my only link to Kristi.

I heard the crunch of gravel. Simon. Trying to find me.

"Y'all better haul ass out here where I can see you," warned Dee.

Hells. I had little choice. I sped over scenes when Julia Pinkerton had been cornered. Julia always confronted the subjects. Used her mouth to outsmart them. A few times, she'd been kidnapped or beaten up, but it depended on the kind of villain. What kind of villains were these?

A trigger-happy reclusive fashion designer and a British marketing consultant who was some sort of Don Juan.

Of course, maybe he had an open relationship understanding with these women. It wouldn't work for me, but there are all types.

Get a grip. Stop thinking about BMW—I mean, Simon's relationship status? Bigger things at stake, Maizie.

More importantly, the Don Juan (and possibly the trigger-happy fashion designer) might have something to do with Kristi's murder.

Shizzles. I'd have to take my chances. I was going with Season 7, Episode 3, "To Breathe Or Not To Breathe," when Julia Pinkerton snuck into a hospital to spy on a nurse she suspected of selling stolen EpiPens. A nurse and a dastardly orderly caught Julia. Pretending to be lost, she talked her way out of it and they let her go. Unfortunately, in the season's cliffhanger, they'd kidnapped her and put her in an induced coma. The final shot of the episode was Julia's boyfriend kissing her. In "True Lie's Kiss," Episode 1 of Season 8, she'd woken up.

So romantic.

Of course, she'd had to kill the boyfriend in episode five when she discovered the nurse had been his babysitter. He'd used the black market EpiPen scam to pay for his gaming addiction, which had used up his college 529 plan. Nice twist, even though it had broken Julia's heart. She'd gone to homecoming without a date.

I grabbed a hat and a pair of sunglasses from my backpack purse, shoved them on, and ran around the garage toward the stairs. Slipped my sunglasses down my nose and peered through the open understructure. Simon was standing in the drive, looking out toward the woods. I tiptoed halfway up the stairs, then knocked on the wood siding.

"Knock knock," I called in a ditzy sing-song voice. "So sorry for the interruption. I wandered up here, then realized you had company. I didn't want to interrupt and was so embarrassed, I snuck off. I was just leaving when you found me and fired that … uh, warning shot."

Dee appeared at the top of the stairs. With her rifle. "How'd you get in here? Where's your vehicle?"

"The gate was unlocked. I didn't see a call box, so I walked up." Of course, if Dee checked her security footage, she'd see me cutting into the woods when walking up. Before she could ask me why I'd come, I plunged in. "I drove up from Atlanta to hike and got lost. Cell service is terrible up here, isn't it? I saw your gate and thought you might help. So sorry for the interruption."

Dee lowered her rifle and eyed me. I took a better look at the blonde. The hard set to her features made her look older, but she was probably in her mid-thirties. And wearing snazzy camo activewear—appropriate for her modern mountain dwelling.

Which was a dumb thing to appreciate, but I couldn't help myself when it came to fashion.

"Hey, is that DeerNose you're wearing?" I said, searching for something to lighten the mood. "I like that blue and purple color combo."

"No." Her eyes narrowed. "Simon, get up here."

"Sorry to disturb you." I backed down the stairs. "I'll just go. I'll give up on finding the trail and just follow the road back. That's what I should have done in the first place."

"You found her, love?" called Simon. "Hang on."

I turned to hurry down the stairs. At the bottom, Simon blocked me.

"Hello there," he said. "Got caught trespassing, did you? Naughty girl."

"Sure did." I forced a chuckle. "Didn't mean any harm. I'll just be going."

He looked up at Dee. "Are we letting her go?"

The shizzles. What did that mean? I quickly tried to smooth my surprise over with another chuckle.

"She's coming up for a drink," said Dee. "I'm sure you're thirsty after that walk, right?"

"Oh, no worries." I patted my backpack. "I have a water bottle with me."

"You're our guest. We insist." Simon gestured. "You don't want to be rude, now, do ya?"

He stepped up, forcing me to back up the stairs. I climbed.

"Lovely view, yeah?"

I nodded. The view was lovely.

Dee gestured to a set of Adirondack chairs. "Have a seat. We'll grab some drinks. Will just be a moment."

I thought about an escape plan. They could easily see me through the windows. Besides, it would look even more suspicious. Hopefully, the hat and sunglasses would be enough of a disguise for Simon. I moved to the railing and leaned out. Julia Pinkerton was all well and good, but after all, she had writers and a long story arc. It'd probably be better to get in the WWND mindset—What Would Nash Do? Annie would never get herself in this situation. Nash didn't mind bending the rules if he thought the results worth it.

I'd play along. See what information I could get. Hoped they didn't plan to shoot me.

Had one of them killed Kristi?

The door creaked. I turned, greeting them with a smile.

Simon carried a tray of ice tea. Dee had left her rifle inside. I felt the tension run from my body and took a chair before my rubbery legs collapsed.

"Hope you like sweet tea," said Dee.

"Thank you. I hate being such an imposition." I gave them my friendly *Us* cover smile and reached for a tea. "I'm embarrassed to say I was about to come up your stairs when I spotted you kissing at the top. That's when I bolted and thought I should sneak away."

"There you go, Dee," Simon laughed. "I told you she's harmless."

"Yep, harmless is a good way to describe me." I kept my smile pasted on.

"What do you do?" said Dee. "You said you live in Atlanta?"

I took a sip of tea. "So, Atlanta. I moved here recently from California. Just trying to get my foot in the door."

"What door?"

Dee no longer had her rifle, but she was quick to fire off questions. Still suspicious. Instead of using improv to create a quick backstory, I returned to WWND. When Nash didn't want to reveal he was a PI, he kept some truth to the lie to make things more believable. "Acting. I was an actress in California."

"Thought you looked familiar," said Simon. "Was just trying to place you."

I choked on the tea. "I get that a lot."

"Anything I'd know?" said Dee.

"Mostly kid shows when I was younger. Reality shows as an adult. I thought I'd come out here and try for a refresh."

"Did you do *Dancing With The Stars*?"

"Unfortunately, no. My trainer had hoped for me to use *DWTS* as a boot camp, but I'd secretly told my agent to reject any offers." I saw their quizzical looks. "You had to know Jerry, my trainer. He takes intensity to a whole new level."

"Too bad," said Dee. "I love that show."

"More of a *Love Island* guy myself," said Simon. "Actress, though. Interesting that."

Dee looked at Simon.

"Why?" I said. "What do you do?"

"We've got this marketing firm," said Simon. "If you're looking for work, an acting background would be helpful. In fact, we employ a lot of actors."

"Really?" I leaned forward in my chair. This was going a lot easier than I thought. "How do you use actors?"

"Market research. Mystery shopping. It includes chatting up the store clerks and managers to learn more about a brand and how it's doing in the store without the clerks realizing it. You need a good memory and an eye for detail. It's a natural fit for actors."

"Who are some of the actresses you've used? Anybody I'd know?"

"No one famous," said Simon. "That would blow their cover, right?"

"That makes sense. But what about anybody local? Since moving here, I've been networking. Maybe I know them."

"I guess it's possible." Simon smiled and relaxed in his chair. "We have tiers in mystery shopping. Some work is more advanced. The basic secret shoppers are a much larger group. We do hire locally. But we've got employees nationwide."

I snapped my fingers. "I know an actor who was a secret shopper. Kristi and her husband live around here. She moved here recently from California, too. Kristi and I did some extra work before she moved to Black Pine."

I studied Simon, who was watching me carefully without appearing to do so. I recognized that look because Nash used it a lot. I glanced at Dee. She seemed bored with the conversation. Maybe she didn't know Kristi.

"Kristi Johnson?" I continued. "Her husband is in the industry, too. Sound guy."

"The name's not familiar. Sorry. I do employ a lot of people, though." Simon looked at Dee. "D'ya know her?"

Dee shrugged. "Johnson's a pretty common name in these parts."

"Dee, do you also work for Cro—" I caught myself. Had they told me the name of the company? "The marketing firm?"

"I'm the founder. Simon runs it. I don't really know the employees. I trust him, so I can do my own thing."

"Oh." I felt disappointed that we couldn't gush over fashion, but maybe that was better. I needed to stay focused. "Is your business nearby?"

She shook her head. "We're online. I work from home."

I noted she didn't explain Simon's Gilmore apartment. "Beautiful house, by the way. I love how the architecture is incorporated into the landscape. By your accent, you sound like you grew up around here."

"Thank you. It's family land." She had that look in her eye I recognized from Daddy. He got it whenever he was about to spill forth about family history, property rights, and freedom. "We lost it a long time ago. A horrible fire took out the house I grew up in. Terrible tragedy for my people. But after a lot of work, I'm proud to say I got the land back recently."

"I'm so sorry to hear that. Did you build the house?"

"No, ma'am. A former owner built it, so it's not quite the same. It'll never be the same. You can't make some wrongs right, no matter how hard you try. But it's a pretty house."

She sipped her tea while I pondered her meaning. Dee felt passionate about the fire. Maybe they couldn't afford to rebuild, causing her family to lose their land. Was she a Mercer? "What's your family's name? That had the land?"

She gave me a sharp look. "My name is Dee Dixon."

"Right then," said Simon. "It's been lovely meeting you. D'you need a ride somewhere? Where exactly did you get lost?"

I blinked. I'd almost forgotten why we'd started this cozy

chat. "Uh, no. I'll walk back to my car. I'll drive into Little Gap and ask about trails."

"Are you sure? I don't mind taking you. I was leaving soon anyway." Simon leaned forward. "Wouldn't mind telling you more about the company. As an actress, I wondered if you need a gig? The hours are flexible if you're auditioning and that sort of thing."

"When can I start?" I gave him my best *People* smile.

Rhonda was going to kill me.

THIRTY

#UNBECOMING #THEUNDERDOG

SQUINTING THROUGH MY BUG-SPLATTERED WINDSHIELD, I continued the argument via my phone's Bluetooth, "It's not like I'm actually going to be a secret shopper, Rhonda. I'm just trying to learn more about CrossHair. BMW Simon acted like he didn't know Kristi, but obviously, he did."

"But Maizie, I already picked out my outfit for the interview," pleaded Rhonda. "We created my fake resume online with all the social medias and whatnots. I even rehearsed the interview with Tiffany."

"I'm sorry, but I couldn't let the opportunity pass. I don't know yet if he really thinks I'm an actress who'd make a good secret shopper, or if he remembers me from Windmere and they're trying to work out who I really am. I had to take a burn on this."

"For my strengths and weaknesses, I was gonna say style as a strength, obviously," continued Rhonda. "But my weakness would be working harder than everyone else and them getting jealous. You see what I did there?"

"I told her to flip that one," said Tiffany.

"Oh, here comes Simon," I said. "He was telling the truth about leaving soon."

I had parked at a scenic overlook a mile from the Old Mercer Place a.k.a Dee's Mountain Hideaway. The BMW flashed by. I waited a moment before pulling onto the highway. "Heading back to Gilmore. Can you see if you find anything about a house fire at the Old Mercer Place in Little Gap? Dee said she grew up there. Twenty to thirty years ago?"

"Is she a Mercer?" said Tiffany.

"No, a Dixon. And he's Simon Craig."

"Dee Dixon holds the lease to his apartment, remember?" said Rhonda. "That boy has himself a sugar mama."

"She's the founder of CrossHair, but doesn't seem too interested in the company."

"Maybe she fronted the money to give her gold digger a job," said Tiffany. "Maybe Simon got tired of her apron strings and had a thing with Kristi."

"Do you think Dee Dixon could have killed Kristi?" said Rhonda.

"It's possible. But I can't get over how neither showed any surprise over my bringing up her name. I even described Derek and said they lived in Black Pine."

"They're good," said Tiffany.

"The BMW just took the turnoff for Gilmore. I'll call back later. Don't tell Annie about any of this. She's being a stickler about extracurricular investigating."

"What should we tell Annie you're doing?" said Tiffany, who had no issues with lying to bosses.

"Taking care of Cuddles. Which I did by dropping him off at Elaine's." I pouted. "He likes Elaine more than me."

"Thank your lucky stars," said Tiffany. "When are you heading back?"

"I wanted to check in at DeerNose while I didn't have Cuddles with me," I said. "It depends on how long it takes to tail Simon. I have to pick up Cuddles by six. Elaine has debate practice tonight."

"DeerNose, huh?" said Rhonda. "Will you be spying or snuggling?"

"Spying. I want to see if there have been any more sabotage attempts."

"No secret shopping?" said Rhonda.

"Don't worry. I have enough secrets right now and no time to shop." Both thoughts made me sad. But if I could figure out what was going on with Nash at DeerNose, that could all change.

———

SIMON CRAIG A.K.A BMW (as I still thought of him) ran a bunch of boring errands in Gilmore before turning back on the highway toward Little Gap.

I supposed even murder suspects had to buy toilet paper.

Leaving him to restock his sugar mama with Charmin, I made a beeline for DeerNose. I hadn't much time before I had to return to Gilmore to pick up Cuddles. At the DeerNose gate, Joel Dewillis checked the car for giant dogs and let me in. I parked in the visitor's section, went in through the front door, and made a beeline toward my father's office. His door was cracked, so I entered.

He wasn't inside. It'd been a while since I'd visited his studio. An artist's table tilted to a 45-degree angle faced a large window overlooking the woods. Natural light spilled onto design sketches and camo cloth swatches. Built-in shelves held lookbooks, catalogs, and magazines that spanned the almost thirty years DeerNose had been in business. The shelves also held awards and framed photos.

While I waited, I glanced at the new designs scattered on his drafting table, then moved around his desk to scan the photos on the shelves. I skipped over the award and family photos and focused on DeerNose-related pictures. Several shots of the DeerNose execs and business associates with hunting trophies. Smiles all around, but ugh, also a dead animal.

I turned at a swift rap. The door opened and Petey strode in. Today's abstract camo design was swirly and muted and the cut complementary to Petey's athletic yet older frame. I liked it.

"Who are you here to see, dear?" said Petey. "Your father? He and Marshall have a meeting with a distributor."

"I can wait."

"I am sorry, sweetie, but after the meeting and factory tour, they're taking the distributor to dinner. You're better off catching Boomer at the cabin later tonight. Is it urgent? I can get a message to him."

I sighed. "Not that urgent. I'll talk to him at home."

"Does Mr. Nash know you're here, dear?"

"No," I blurted. "I'm not here to see Nash."

"I see," she murmured, then pointed at a grouped leather settee and chairs. "Do you want to talk about it?"

I didn't, but nodded and plopped onto the soft couch.

"Something happened?" She lowered herself next to me.

I nodded again. "Someone died."

"I wasn't expecting that. I'm so sorry. Were you close to them, honey?"

"Not at all. I never even talked to her. I sort of knew her husband. He was a client."

"That's terrible. It sounds sudden."

"Sudden and unexpected. The police think her husband did it."

"'*Did it*?'" Petey blanched. "This wife of your client was … murdered?"

I laid my head back on the couch and stared at the ceiling. "Yep."

"Oh, my word." She paused. "How?"

"There was a fire. The husband claimed he didn't know she was in the house. He was trying to put out the fire, though."

"She died in the fire? Oh, my stars."

"The police said it wasn't the fire that killed her. She was murdered before the fire started."

"Oh." She winced. "How upsetting. It's terrible. Just horrible."

"Yes." I pushed out a long breath. "Derek didn't do it, though. I'm pretty sure. Like eighty-nine percent sure. Or at least seventy-five percent."

"Who did it then?"

"I don't know." I pressed my lips together. "I'm going to figure it out."

"If you don't mind my nosiness, I thought you were upset with Mr. Nash. I wasn't expecting a murder."

"Truth be told, Nash and I are going through a rough patch. But it's not worth talking about."

"Is this what you wanted to talk to your father about? The murder?"

"Sort of," I admitted.

"Does Boomer know the deceased?"

"I don't think so."

"Honey, please don't bother your daddy with this sort of thing. He's got so much on his plate right now. He's absolutely worried to distraction about the disruptions. Boomer doesn't need one more thing to disturb him. A murdered client? Heavens."

"What about Marshy?"

"Does Marshall know the deceased?"

"I'm not sure. I didn't think Kristi had anything to do with..."

"With what?"

I couldn't say DeerNose. DeerNose was Petey's life. I was already upsetting her. I couldn't make her more upset.

"Did you know a Kristi Johnson?"

Her forehead wrinkled. "I don't think so. She doesn't work here. Is she from town?"

"She's from California."

"Definitely not." Petey gave me a smile, but concern still

marked her brow. "I just wanted to check on you. You looked upset, and I worry. But it's time for me to get back to work. Should I walk you out?"

"That's okay," I said. "Thanks for listening."

"Anytime, sweetie."

Petey stood and looked down at me. "Maizie, I know you feel you've found your niche in private investigations. It's just..." She paused, thinking. "It's wonderful what your father has built here. He's created jobs for so many families, put money into the economy, and put Black Pine's name on the map—at least in the outdoor sporting apparel world. That's really something, isn't it?"

"It is." I looked up at her, feeling small and guilty.

"Your mother has put Black Pine on the map, too, in her way. Maybe not exactly with a positive contribution considering that reality show. But still, it's really lovely of all the places Vicki could live, she chose to come home."

I nodded.

"And you became so famous. We were so proud of you, honey. You came home, too." She tilted her head, not saying what we all knew—my return had everything to do with my probationary requirements. "But now you deal with what? Cheating spouses, child support dodgers, criminal subpoenas? And clients who murder their spouses. It's all so..." She searched for words. "Unbecoming, isn't it? A little too sordid."

"It's not pretty, that's true." I rose. "Not glamorous or edifying. It's pretty dirty work."

"Please don't say, 'But somebody's got to do it.' I don't believe that."

I tried to find a smile. "But sometimes that's true. Like Derek. Whom I'm sixty-eight percent sure didn't murder his spouse. It's important to help him, right?"

"But does it have to be you?"

Considering Annie didn't want to take his case unless he paid here, then yep. It had to be me. "Unfortunately, it looks that way. The police don't have any other leads. Derek had the motive, opportunity, and means. Maybe the autopsy or forensics will reveal something else, but as everyone keeps telling me, it's not looking too good for Derek."

Her eyebrows drew together. "Honey, it sounds like you should let the police handle this."

"Don't worry about me, Petey." I gave her a hug. "Just take care of Daddy."

"Oh, I will. His work won't get interrupted if I have anything to say about it. Don't you worry." Her head lifted and shoulders squared. "We've come too far to see DeerNose falter on account of some sneaky good-for-nothing who's too lazy and under-handed to really compete in the marketplace against us."

"I wanted to talk to Daddy about this corporate sabotage situation. Anything I can do there?"

"Hopefully, Mr. Nash will soon discover how this happened and who's behind it." She shook her head. "Your father doesn't deserve this."

"Nash will figure it out." And if he couldn't, I would.

THIRTY-ONE

#BREAKROOMBREAKDOWN
#HAIROFTHEDOG

I STRODE down the executive hall and through the atrium. If I couldn't talk to Daddy and Marshy, there was one employee I'd try to see before I left. The more I thought about seeing Nash at Kristi Johnson's house, the more upset I felt. He knew her. He'd talked to her. And just like BMW—I mean, Simon—he acted like he didn't know her.

Okay, that's weird, right? Both guys knew her. But her name hadn't meant anything to them. But Nash was at her house. So he must have known her name. Or did he find her house after I said her name?

I couldn't remember. My thoughts kept circling. I was confusing myself. Instead of hooking a left through the doors leading to Nash's office, I turned right toward the break room. I needed chocolate. Or salt. Or caffeine. Maybe all three.

A group of seamstresses sat around a table, sharing a box of donuts with their coffee. I recognized several of the older ladies, who waved me over with the offer of a donut.

They didn't need to ask me twice.

"Nice to see you, honey. We've got a machine down, so we're working in smaller groups today. Almost quitting time, though," said Miss Cheryl, who had bandaged my ankle after a three-legged race at a long-ago company picnic. "Who are you visiting? Your daddy or your beau?"

"Daddy mainly, but he isn't available." I helped myself to an old-fashioned. "He and Marshy are in a meeting."

Cheryl looked at the seamstresses. "Poor Boomer. That man hates to play corporate, but Marshall always makes him, don't he, Bonnie?"

"Heavy the head that wears the crown," said Bonnie. "Can't feel too sorry for him, now can you?"

"I remember the early days when Marshall would beat the bushes, looking for investors and retailers. Back then, he'd left Boomer to create his designs and work with us seamstresses. I bet Boomer misses that." Cheryl sighed. "I miss it, too. We really felt a part of something special, didn't we? Although, I never thought DeerNose would grow into what it is today."

"Mr. Spayberry worked back here with us?" said one of the younger women.

"We didn't have this building, then," said Bonnie. "They rented from an old textile company for a few years. Shared space. Maizie, do you remember, before Boomer had his office and the cabin, he would sketch out on his land? He had this portable easel that he'd strap to his back. Of course, you were just a baby back then. Your daddy would sit out in the woods for hours, drawing."

"Then he'd bring those sketches to us," interrupted Cheryl. "I was a pattern maker. He'd say, 'Miss Cheryl, what do you think? Can you work with this design? I'm fixing to have Mercer make this print.' I was right proud, wasn't I? He trusted me to take his sketch and create the pattern for it."

"Did you say, *Mercer*?" Having heard these stories before, I hadn't been paying full attention, but I'd latched onto that name. "Who's Mercer?"

"Oh, Randy Mercer," said Bonnie. "He owned Mercer Textile,

where we shared space. We got the material from him for a while. Until he went out of business. Sad story."

"Is he a Little Gap Mercer?"

"Little Gap? Over yonder?" Cheryl waved, as if we could see through the wall, forest, and mountain blocking our view of Little Gap. "Possibly. Mercers have been in the area forever. Didn't Randy's great-granddaddy start Mercer Textile, Jeanette?"

"Mercer Textile was in Shake Rag," said Jeanette. "I worked there before coming over to DeerNose. Shake Rag is between Gilmore and Black Pine. Nothing there except for Mercer's and a shanty corner store. Used to be a grist mill on the river, back in the old days. I think the Mercers did have a place in Little Gap. On the mountain. Family land, you know, for hunting and that sort of thing. But they were really town folk."

"I met someone living at the Old Mercer Place in Little Gap," I said. "Dee Dixon. Except it's not the original Mercer place. It's rebuilt. Dee said it used to be family land, but there was a fire."

"Maybe she's a cousin or something," said Jeannette. "Her being a Dixon and all."

"Maybe she's married," said Cheryl. "She could have been a Mercer."

"I don't think she's married," I said, thinking of Simon. "But you never know these days."

"No, you don't," said Jeannette. "I don't know nothin' about a fire. Randy Mercer died. Killed himself. I think his family left these parts after that."

"Killed himself?" I gasped. "That's terrible."

"About twenty years ago," said Jeannette. "But that was after DeerNose left Mercer's Textile. By that time, Boomer had the money to build the shop on his family land. Things had started rolling for DeerNose, so I followed over with some other textile ladies. Soon after that, Boomer built the office space and the fancy part up front."

"That must have been when they figured out the secret Deer-Nose ingredient," I smirked.

"Naw, that was when all Marshall's cold calls paid off," said Cheryl. "That and your Daddy's designs winning all those awards. They started the scent at Mercer Textile. Paid this scientist to come up with the process to bind the scent in the dyeing process."

I smiled. "It's pretty wonderful that there are so many Deer-Nose employees who've been with Daddy since the beginning and can tell these stories."

"We have a lot of loyalty to Boomer and Marshall," said Jeanette. "But we're as proud as peaches for our success, too. The execs here don't forget their roots. Those of us who stick around are rewarded for it."

"I marvel how Daddy and Mrs. Peters know everyone here by name. For example, when I asked if Kristi Johnson worked here, Petey knew right away she didn't," I said, feeling pleased to find a natural way to tie the conversation back to Kristi. Even if the ladies didn't know her name, they might remember a stranger in their midst.

"Peters is right," said Cheryl. "There's no one working here by that name. Friend of yours?"

"Not a friend, no. But a few days ago, I saw Kristi come in through the factory door at the start of the first shift. You didn't notice her?"

"We would have noticed a new girl," said Bonnie. "What was she doing coming into the factory like that?"

"I don't know. You're sure you didn't see her? She walked right in with a group of seamstresses."

"Didn't follow us on the floor, honey. We would have seen her." Jeannette shot a worried look at Cheryl. "If she walked in with some of us, she easily could have snuck into the offices."

"Cameras would have caught that," said Cheryl. "Mr. Nash would be on top of it."

Cameras. Duh. Why didn't I think of that?

I KNOCKED on Nash's door, peeked in, and entered. He looked up from his computer, smiled, then frowned.

"What are you doing here?" He rose and walked around his desk. "Where's your big friend?"

"At the dog sitter." I kept my hands clamped behind my back. They were itching to touch him, but I was following the no-hug rule. "I need to pick Cuddles up soon, but wanted to stop in and say hi."

"Hi," he said warily. "And…?"

"I'd like to look at your security feed from a few days ago."

"Why?"

"I want to see who entered the factory for the first shift."

A lone eyebrow rose. "Why?"

I had a dilemma. If I explained seeing Kristi enter the building, there was a chance he would run with that ball by himself. He had assumed she'd had a meeting at DeerNose, and I'd not corrected him. He might have checked on the security footage already. Nash was thorough.

"You're playing chess with me in your head. I don't have to show you DeerNose security footage. It's private and you have no legal claim to it." He held out his hands. "But I will for a hug. I miss you, Maizie."

He played dirty. How badly did I want to see this security footage?

Very.

How badly did I want a hug?

Embarrassingly more than I did the security footage. I missed him, too. But I couldn't let him get away with keeping secrets. I needed my own secrets.

Or did I? I was so confused.

"I miss you," he repeated. While I did mental gymnastics, he'd slid forward and taken my hand. He pressed his lips against my knuckles, then against my palm. "A lot."

For a man like Nash, that was the equivalent of the *Say*

Anything boombox serenade scene. A major declaration of love. A lengthy one at that.

He continued to kiss each finger. I continued trying to figure out my next move.

"It's been a long time since we've been alone." He paused on my pinky.

"My dad isn't having an affair, is he?"

Nash's eyes widened with my pinky still pressed against his lips. He pulled the finger off. "Lord, no. Why would you think such a thing?"

"I didn't think it. I don't believe it. Tiffany and Rhonda brought it up." I eyed him. "But it happens. Even to men who love their wives and children. They fall to temptation."

"He's not having an affair." Nash held my hand against his chest. "If Boomer Spayberry were caught in a trap, he'd gnaw his own leg off."

"True." I sighed, relieved even though I hadn't believed it myself. "What about Marshy?"

"Marshall Roth is the most intelligent man I've ever met. He'd see a trap a mile away and steer clear." He tilted his head. "You think your Kristi Johnson was having an affair with someone at DeerNose?"

This was what happened when Nash applied his lips to my body parts. He stayed sharp, whereas I couldn't think straight. But I'd enjoyed his trap. My fingers still tingled.

"The girls and I were trying to understand why you want to protect me from what you've learned about DeerNose." He dropped my hand. I crossed my arms. "I can help you."

"This is my job." He scowled. "I had hesitations about working for your father's company while starting a relationship with you. But I felt like I didn't have much of a choice."

It sounded a little like he didn't have a choice either way, but I let that go. "I know how seriously you take your responsibilities. You're a compartmentalizer. You like to keep work and personal life separate. I get that. Between me and DeerNose, personal and work life bleed into one another."

"Lately it's bled so much, it looks like a crime scene."

"Okay, ew."

"You're the one talking about bleeding."

"Aren't you being a little *extra* about all this?" I snapped. "I'm trying to help you unpack your feelings."

"What does that mean?" The tiny scar on his chin paled. His glacier blue eyes narrowed. "*Extra* what exactly?"

"An extra big pain in my—"

A knock sounded on the door. We turned as the door opened. Another DeerNose employee I'd known most of my life poked his head in. "Hey y'all, just coming in to pick up your recycling."

"Hey, Curtis," said Nash. "Come on in."

"Hi, Mr. Curtis." I gave him my *Tiger Beat* smile. "Nice to see you."

"Good to see you, too, honey. Still training to be a cop?"

"Not exactly a cop, no…" I began my explanation to Mr. Curtis, and Nash gave me an "I'll be back in a minute" signal. Feeling relieved by the interruption, I relaxed and kept up the chatter. I hated fighting. And tension. Hated negative feelings in general. My ex-therapist Renata attributed it to the result of my parents' divorce. I attributed it to most people don't like tension and negativity.

I guess that's why I wanted to unpack Nash's feelings.

Curtis grabbed the blue recycle box under Nash's desk, then looked at his trash can. "This fellow can't remember that all paper goes in the recycle. He only puts the newspaper in this."

"Let me help you." I took the small trash can and pulled the paper out to dump in the recycle box. I studied a torn piece with Nash's familiar scribbling on it. Hesitated. Then crumpled and shoved it in my pocket. I glanced at Curtis, but he was checking his phone. "Here you go."

"Thanks, honey. I'll get out of your hair now." He grabbed the blue box, dumped it in his wheelie, and opened the door.

"No worries, Mr. Curtis. I've got to get going myself." I followed him out the door and hurried down the hall toward the front atrium.

Thus avoiding Nash, so he wouldn't guess I'd just garbologized his trash.

THIRTY-TWO

RHONDA AND TIFFANY stared at the torn piece of paper on Rhonda's desk, while I chewed my lip.

"Nash is not going to like this." Rhonda folded her arms. "Not one bit."

"This makes no sense to me," said Tiffany. "Who are these fifteen people?"

"Not totally sure." I blew out my breath. "But Luella Haney's listed with an address matching Simon's apartment. 204-C Windmere."

"I can't get over you looking through Nash's trash," said Rhonda. "That's pretty cold."

"I didn't do it on purpose. It just kind of happened."

Rhonda held up a hand. "Girl, save your excuses. How are these names going to free poor Derek Johnson?"

"Simon and Dee mentioned the name Luella Haney. Simon said something about her going overboard, but Dee wanted to meet her. My guess is these fifteen names are CrossHair employees. Maybe Luella is an employee of the month or something."

"Why would Nash have these names?" said Tiffany. "And why is Luella living with BMW when Dee Dixon owns the lease? How many women is this man seeing? Anyway, it didn't look like there was a woman living there, other than the random outfits of different sizes. No way this Luella could yo-yo between my size and Rhonda's."

"Hey!" Rhonda skimmed a hand down her turquoise Lululemon-knockoff ensemble. "My body style is trending."

"You have a point, Tiffany," I interjected before a squabble got us off track. "I think the apartment's full of secret shopper wardrobes. The causal style makes sense for shoppers. Possibly designed by Dee Dixon. She wouldn't bite when I hinted at her being a designer, but her car told another story."

"What does this have to do with poor Derek Johnson?" Rhonda folded her arms and her eyebrow rose.

"What if Luella Haney was Kristi Johnson?"

"What?" Rhonda shook her head. "Where did you get that?"

"I just keep thinking how neither Nash nor Simon didn't even blink when I mention the name Kristi Johnson. But we know they knew her. Simon knows Luella Haney. Nash has her name on this list. Why else would he stakeout Windmere?"

"Why would Kristi have another name?" said Tiffany.

"Because she is an evil woman. A liar and a cheater," said Rhonda. "Poor Derek is rotting in jail because someone did in Luella Haney."

We stared at Rhonda.

"I think you're right," I said. "I don't know about the evil part. But maybe someone murdered Luella Haney, not Kristi Johnson."

Rhonda's brow furrowed. "Wait. What?"

"Kristi's an actress without a script. She was pretending to be Luella Haney, whoever that character is. And she did something that got her murdered." I sat on the edge of the desk. "I thought I had it. Now it's gone. Still doesn't make sense why anybody would kill her other than Derek."

"Hey," shouted Rhonda.

"Let's look up the other people on this list. Their addresses are all over the U.S. There's one in Canada, too."

"To see if they're also murdered?" said Tiffany. "Maybe it's a serial killer who hates secret shoppers."

"Another good point." I hopped off the desk. "Duh. Luella Haney is Kristi's stage name."

Rhonda tapped the mouse on her computer. "Yeah, I bet she uses BMW's address for all the bonus programs she signs up for while secret shopping. Kristi's greedy like that."

"Kristi is still a murder victim," I reminded her.

"Don't make her a saint," muttered Rhonda. "Bingo. Here's Luella Haney on Instagram."

I stared at the images. "Why didn't Derek tell us that Luella Haney is her stage name?"

"Maybe he doesn't know," said Tiffany. "It doesn't say anything about her being an actress in her bio. Are we sure that's Kristi? In all the pictures, she's got on sunglasses."

"That's because she's shady." Rhonda smirked.

"See if you can find Luella Haney on IMBD," I said.

Rhonda shook her head. "Kristi Johnson's on IMBD. Not Luella Haney."

"This is very confusing," I said. "Why would she make up a name for secret shopping? What's the big deal?"

"Doesn't she seem overly dramatic in these pictures?" said Rhonda. "Look at this one. She's got on a trench coat, sunglasses, and a finger to her pouty lips. It's like she's letting everyone know she's a secret shopper. She's standing in front of a Bass Pro shop. That's going to irritate the customers. Bass Pro customers aren't into overly dramatic."

"What does the caption say?"

Rhonda scrolled. "Some shopping rewards come with special bonuses. I love my work! I'm finally living my best life! The secret to my success? Always giving 110% to my career. The more I give, the more I get. #Bestlife #SuperFlySuperSpy."

"If you're going to be a super spy, you probably shouldn't announce it on social media," said Tiffany.

"This was her last post. Look at this. She's doing a *Charlie's*

Angels gun pointy thing with her fingers in her car." Rhonda rolled her eyes. "'Super pumped to take action. Super committed to our goals.' #SuperPumped #SuperFlySuperSpy."

"Can she say super one more time?" Tiffany snorted.

"And can she stop with the heart emojis?" said Rhonda.

"You're right. Kristi's coming off like a kook," I said. "But whose goals is she talking about?"

"CrossHair's?" said Tiffany.

"Obviously not hers and Derek's," said Rhonda. "Maybe Kristi's and Simon's. I'm starting to feel real bad for Dee Dixon, too."

"Take it down a notch," said Tiffany.

"You take it—"

"Hey, how about the Old Mercer Place fire?" I interrupted. "Did you find out anything about the fire?"

"First of all, we went over this," said Tiffany. "It's not the Old Mercer Place."

"There was a fire," said Rhonda. "After a guy died. Randy Mercer."

"The DeerNose ladies said Randy Mercer committed suicide."

"Yeah, there was a local news story about it. The guy went bankrupt. He had to sell the land, the factory, and their other house. Wife and kid left him."

"Pretty horrific," said Tiffany. "He set fire to the cabin so nobody could have it, then shot himself. If you read between the lines, he was struggling with drugs or alcohol, too."

"I'm kind of surprised Daddy would go into business with someone like that."

"These old rich families can't handle losing everything," said Tiffany. "When you're born with nothing, starting over again's not a big deal. The rich families are soft. They find it too humiliating to lose everything in front of their country club friends."

"Yeah, look at Maizie. She had everything and now she's got nothing. If the Spayberrys and your momma's folks had been ladi-da to begin with, you'd be a lot hotter mess than you are now. You're lucky you got some grit in your background."

Tiffany nodded.

Before I could get too offended, the bell above the office door tinkled. Annie strode in. "Good, you're all here. I've got a load of new skips to trace."

"I'm headed out," said Tiffany. "It's past closing time. I was just saying goodbye to everyone."

Rhonda switched off her computer and stood. "Yep, just clocking out."

Annie looked at me. "Where's the dog?"

"Waiting on me." I hurried toward the door, hoping she wouldn't think to ask exactly where he was waiting.

SOMEONE ELSE WAS WAITING on me.

Nash leaned against the Impala. He still wore his work clothes, but his tie had disappeared and his sleeves were rolled, exposing his thick forearms. The thick forearms were crossed, and he wore his resting Nash face. Which meant nothing and everything.

"You disappeared on me," said Nash. "I thought maybe Curtis had carted you off to the recycle dump."

"I have to pick up Cuddles by six." I hesitated before approaching him. I wouldn't put it past Nash to bug his Deer-Nose office with his own cameras. He might have seen me rooting through his trash.

"It's almost six now."

"I know, I know. Mrs. Embree is going to kill me. I needed to stop at the office for … to check in."

"I returned with donuts and coffee about ten minutes later. You and Curtis were gone. I thought you wanted to see our security feed."

"I'm sorry I didn't say goodbye. I had to rush." That was so sweet. How could I ever be annoyed with him? Oh, right. He was still withholding information from me. Information pertinent to my case. And my life. "I still want to check that security feed. Can I come back tomorrow?"

"Is that the only reason for seeing me tomorrow?"

I blushed. "Not the only reason."

A small smile cracked his stern countenance. Nash unfolded his arms and crooked a finger. "You're already going to be late. A few minutes more won't matter."

"Well, Mr. Nash." I fluttered my eyelashes. "Just what are you insinuating? That I break our little no-hug rule?"

He gave me a smoldering look that didn't require an answer. Before I could protest (or buckle), a truck pulled into the space next to us. Ian's Black Pine Police Tahoe.

"Great timing, as always," muttered Nash and refolded his arms.

"Evenin' folks," said Ian, exiting the truck. "Glad I caught you, Maizie. Nash, what are you doing here?"

"Why wouldn't I be here?" He scowled. "What do you want?"

"I got the warrant to look at the Derek Johnson case files. It would have been a lot easier if Miss Cox would just hand them over."

"I'm on my way to pick up Cuddles, but Annie's inside." I waved toward the door.

"That's too bad," said Ian. "I was hoping to talk to you."

Nash snorted.

"Do you have any new information on the case?" I said, ignoring Nash. I gave Ian my best *Cosmo* smile.

"Because of your involvement, I'm not sharing details."

"Involvement? Come on, Ian. Derek Johnson only hired us for an infidelity case." I switched to the smile I used for the *Men's Fitness* cover. "How about the cause of death?"

Ian grinned. "Blunt force trauma. But that's all you're going to get."

Nash snorted again.

"You got something to say, Nash?" said Ian.

"Looks like Cox's getting ready to leave." Nash jerked his chin toward A.S.S.'s storefront window. "Thought you might've forgotten why you'd come."

"I didn't forget." Ian glanced at the window. "Maizie, I'll talk to you tomorrow after I've read the case files. Nash, I need to talk to you, too."

I nodded, then waited for Ian to amble into the building before turning back to Nash. "Are we in trouble?"

He didn't speak for a long beat. "I'm not good at relationships, Maizie. I tried to warn you. Maybe you're right about the compartmentalizing stuff. I don't want it to be like this. I wish you'd let me work things out at DeerNose first. I promise you, I'll tell you everything as soon as I can."

"It's not my fault that my case collided with yours. I didn't ask Derek Johnson to investigate his wife. I didn't know you were involved with his wife. And I certainly didn't know his wife would be murdered."

"I wasn't involved with his wife. Her death makes it more complicated." He sighed. "You better go. It's six now."

THIRTY-THREE

MRS. EMBREE WAS NOT AMUSED by my tardiness. Her words, not mine. Cuddles was not amused either. The only one amused was Elaine, who would rather play with Cuddles than go to debate practice.

Driving through the streets of Gilmore, I mourned my relationship and Cuddles mourned the loss of his playmate. My phone rang. I pulled to the side of the road and checked the caller ID. Simon Craig.

"How about a trial run?" said Simon. "See what it's like working for CrossHair Marketing?"

"What do you mean?"

"There's a shop in Gilmore, The Boot Scoot. Meet me there now, yeah? I'll show you how it's done. Now's a good time, just before closing when the staff's distracted."

"I just picked up my dog from the sitter's." I didn't want to secret shop. But Kristi had gone to the Boot Scoot, maybe as Luella.

So had Nash.

"The thing is, he's a really big dog and not friendly. I can't leave him in my car because he'll destroy it. Could we do it tomorrow?"

"How bad d'you want this job, Maizie?"

"Can I call you back?"

I shoved in an earbud, dialed Rhonda, and started the car. "Simon wants me to meet him at the Boot Scoot in Gilmore, but I have Cuddles."

"Sounds like you've got yourself a real dilemma."

"I need help. Can you and Tiffany please watch Cuddles for me while I meet with Simon?"

"You're asking me to miss my dinner to watch a dog that would rather eat me for dinner while you steal my dream job?"

"I'm not stealing your dream job. What if BMW Simon murdered Derek's wife?"

"Okay, you've got a point there. I don't want to work for a murderer."

"Can you meet me at the Boot Scoot in Gilmore?"

———

THE BOOT SCOOT was a boutique Western wear shop in downtown Gilmore. Floor-to-ceiling shelves of cowboy boots filled the back rooms. Clothing and hats in the front. According to Daddy, this was a "fancy duds" shop. It surprised me to find the DeerNose brand amongst the plaid, fringe, and saddle stitching. But then again, his camo prints had gone haute couture in the outdoor world.

Luckily, the deer pee scent stayed in the non-haute couture world. The shop smelled like leather, not deer.

Simon and I huddled in the front corner of the shop among the displays of new items. One cashier was busy with paperwork at the counter. Another one was replacing boots in boxes and straightening shelves in the back. Simon and I pretended to shop, while he explained his method in a murmur.

I wanted to question Simon about Luella, but my eyes kept straying to the storefront window. Rhonda and Tiffany had struggled to keep Cuddles from charging in after me when I entered. They still struggled now.

"Take a few items from these racks." He motioned to the clothing hanging near us. "You're comparison shopping, so get different brands of a similar item. Ask the cashier for her opinion. Get her talking. We want to know her brand knowledge. Choose one to buy, doesn't matter which one."

"Okay, sounds easy enough." I glanced behind me. Cuddles had his paws on the window ledge and his face pressed against the glass. Behind him, Tiffany grasped the taut leash in two fists. Rhonda hid behind her.

"Go to it." Simon handed me a credit card. "I'll meet you in my car for a debrief."

I watched Simon leave the shop and glanced at the window. My eyes met Cuddles'. Foam splattered the window. He barked, and the glass shook.

The cashier looked up.

I grabbed three camo tunics from the rack and raced to the cashier's stand. "I have some questions."

"Can you wait one moment?" said the woman. "I need to ask those ladies to move their dog. He's going to scare people."

"I'm in a hurry," I said, imitating Vicki when she deigned to enter an actual store. Normally, her private shopper did any "retailing" and brought her finds to the house. "I'm trying to decide between these three tops."

The sales assistant glanced at the tops, looked at the window, and back at me. I'd hiked my shoulders back, my chin up, and my eyebrows down. She barely suppressed a sigh and gave me a faux-friendly smile. "Of course."

While she chatted about the tunics, I made mental notes and used my fashion knowledge to test her style IQ. "I'll take this one." I picked the DeerNose out of loyalty and handed her Simon's credit card.

"Great." She rang up the sale. "I think it'll look adorable on you."

Vicki never replied to trite remarks, so I didn't either. However, I bounced on my toes, anxious for Rhonda and Tiffany —a very non-Vicki trait. "Do you have another exit?"

"Oh no, are you worried about the dog?"

Yes, I was. But not for the reasons she thought. She escorted me past the boots and through the back room. "You must sell a lot of DeerNose," I said, waving at the DeerNose labeled boxes sitting near the back door.

"Oh, those are being returned. We had some issues."

"Oh, really? What kind of issues?"

"I don't really know." She shrugged. "My manager asked me to ready them to ship back. But don't worry, everything we put out has been checked for quality. That's why we're returning those."

She opened the back door. I walked down the alley and around the corner. Cuddles and the girls still patrolled the front of the shop. I crossed the street and got into Simon's BMW.

"Good deal," he said, taking the package and checking the top. "Give me a rundown of your conversation with the sales clerk."

While I spoke, I kept my line of sight on Cuddles.

"Right," said Simon. "You did a great job. Now return the top."

"Return it?" I looked at him. "I just bought it."

He nodded. "Take notes on the customer service and the process for the return."

"I have to go back inside the shop?" My patrol guard pulled the girls to the next shop. Cuddles placed his face against the window and peered inside. "I can't come back tomorrow?"

"This is the job," said Simon. "We're gauging the level of customer service. You can't worry about irritating the clerk."

"It's not that." But it was that, too. I always felt terrible doing a return. The sales assistants seemed to take it personally. "I don't want my d—"

He tossed the package onto my lap. "The shop is closing in

ten minutes. You have to go now. Unless you're not serious about the job."

His eyes narrowed. "Should I question your intentions, Maizie?"

THIRTY-FOUR
#MARGED #DAWGSABOTAGE

I WAITED until Cuddles had focused his attention on a neighboring shop's door, then pelted across the street. Cuddles barked. Tiffany and Rhonda shrieked. I ignored them and dashed for the door.

A web of slobber hit the back of my legs. I jerked the door open, slipped through, and shut it behind me. A violent thud slammed into the door. I closed my eyes for a moment, silently apologizing to Cuddles, and opened them. Daring not to look behind me, I kept my gaze directed at the saleswoman.

She'd been staring at the door, but snapped her attention to me. "That dog almost attacked you. Are you okay? You barely made it inside."

"I'm fine." I strode forward and held up the bag. "This isn't going to work for me."

"Wha—?" She shook off her discomposure. "Do you want to exchange it?"

"Not today," I lied. "I'll come back when I have more time to browse."

I dropped the bag on the counter. Cuddles slammed into the door, shaking the window. A little bell chimed with each bang. He was one giant thud away from opening it.

"I've got to speak to those ladies," said the shop girl. "Their dog's going to break our door."

"I'm in a hurry," I said in my Vicki voice. "That dog sounds worse than he really is. I think your door is weak."

"Fine," she blustered. She pulled out her scanner and fumbled for the tunic's tag.

The door banged open. Cuddles galloped inside and charged through a circular rack.

"Lord, help me," screamed Rhonda. "He's going to pull my arm off."

"Just let go of the leash," screeched Tiffany.

"You can't bring a dog in here," shouted the clerk. "Get him out of here."

"Let's get this done," I said, grabbing the tunic and hunting for the sales tag. "Why are there so many tags?"

Rhonda dropped the leash. Cuddles rushed out the other side of the rack wearing a green sundress. He shook off the hanger and the sleeveless dress slid over his face. Spotting me, he barked and shot forward. The dress bunched around his neck.

"Scan it," I shouted, holding out a tag.

"That's not the bar code," she cried. "Please ladies, grab the leash and hold him back from my customer."

"It's too late for that," said Tiffany. "Rhonda, block that stand."

I glanced at the tag. It pictured a graphic of a deer centered on a target. Bullet holes riddled the deer. The target had painted blood splashes.

A crash resounded behind me. I glanced over my shoulder. A revolving stand had toppled. Necklaces and sunglasses flew around the shop. A red beaded necklace hung over one of Cuddles' ears. Tiffany and Rhonda shouted, trying to herd him toward the door. He backed into another dress rack to avoid them.

"Get him out of here," shrieked the cashier. She looked over her shoulder. "Laurie, stop hiding and call the police."

"Just focus on the return," I growled, shoving the dress at the lady.

"Really?" she snapped. "That dog is destroying the store and you want me to do your return?"

"Yes." I waved the credit card at her. "Hurry, before he does more damage."

"Honestly." She grabbed the card. "I know who you are, you know. We get celebrities in here all the time. We pretend like we don't know who you are to be respectful and make you feel welcome. But nobody has ever treated me like this."

As much as I wanted to grovel, I had to remain in character. I needed Cuddles to heel without blowing my cover.

Wait a minute. I didn't have to blow my cover. She knew me as Maizie Albright.

I blew out an exaggerated sigh. "In *Julia Pinkerton, Teen Detective*, season two, I worked with a German Shepherd acting as a police K9 dog. Benji's trainer taught me some things. Let me see what I can do."

I turned around, faced the destruction. "Stop! Heel."

Cuddles popped out from under a rack with a blue ruffled dress covering the top of his head. The green strapless dress had worked its way under his doggy armpits. Red beads looped around his neck.

He looked like Marge Simpson.

"About time," yelled Tiffany.

"Put it all on this card," I said, handing her my A.S.S. card. "And I changed my mind. I'll keep the tunic."

———

CARRYING my recent purchases—two sundresses, a string of red beads, and six pairs of broken sunglasses, plus the DeerNose top—I exited the shop. Simon had taken off. Cuddles and I trudged three blocks back to the Impala, where we had parked.

Tiffany and Rhonda followed at a safe distance and waited for me to get in the car.

Cuddles' head fell into my lap and began snoring. I rolled down the window and rubbed his ears, feeling horrible for ignoring him while I did business. I also felt responsible for the damage he'd done to the Boot Scoot.

"It's not your fault," said Rhonda.

"Sure it is," said Tiffany. "You knew we couldn't handle this dog. When he got out of control, you waited until the last possible minute to give him a command."

"You know how this works," I said. "I can't blow my cover. Especially with Simon."

"You've already blown your cover with Simon." Rhonda raised her brows. "Twice."

"I planned to do this secret shopping thing to get him to trust me. Then start subtly questioning him about Kristi and Luella."

"I don't like the subtle stuff," said Tiffany. "Why not get to the point?"

"I don't want to scare him off if he does have something to do with Kristi's death. If he's involved, even accidentally, he's sticking around for a reason."

"What kind of reason?"

"Establishing an alibi? He'd look suspicious if he ran. Maybe Simon was having an affair with Kristi—"

"We're pretty sure he was having one with Luella. She listed his apartment as her work address."

"Maybe Dee Dixon killed her," said Tiffany. "Simon's covering up for Dee because she owns the company."

"I think Simon's in love with Dee Dixon," I said. "He was really vibing her at the mountain retreat. They make an odd pairing, but you can't control who you love."

"Yes, you can."

"Maybe Kristi got jealous, went crazy, and attacked Dee. Simon killed Kristi in self-defense, then covered it up with the fire," said Rhonda. "That sounds like something Kristi would do."

"Or the other way around," said Tiffany. "Dee found out about Kristi and killed her."

"None of this explains Kristi going into DeerNose and Nash meeting with her," I said. "However, there is something going on in the Boot Scoot related to DeerNose. And that's where Nash originally met up with Kristi."

I explained the stacked boxes and the weird tag on the clothing.

"Is that why Simon wanted you to test the sales assistant's customer service on a DeerNose brand?" said Rhonda. "Maybe DeerNose hired CrossHair Marketing because of their quality control issues. They'd want to know what shop assistants think of DeerNose."

"Simon didn't care which brand I chose. The quality control issues must relate to the sample sabotage." I took out the tunic and pulled the tag out. "Look at this. There's no way someone at DeerNose decided this was a good idea. Unless there's an internal saboteur."

We looked at the tag showing the bloody deer on the target.

"Is that supposed to be funny?" said Rhonda. "I'm not into irony."

"More people than Nash work there," said Tiffany. "Ask someone else."

Rhonda gave me a pointed look. "I think you're trying too hard with Nash. He's got his back up. You keep pushing. Something's gotta give."

She was right. And that something could be our relationship.

THIRTY-FIVE
#ACTING #HOUSEBROKE

RHONDA AND TIFFANY LEFT. Cuddles still used me for a pillow, so I made a few calls.

First Nash. Naturally, no answer.

I called Simon. "Can we get together and talk about today?"

"You didn't return the shirt. You failed your test."

"There was a disruption. My dog got in the shop—"

"Listen, this isn't going to work."

"Can I just meet with you?" I hated losing a job. Even one I didn't want. I also hated losing a fish on the line for learning more about Kristi. "It's about the advanced work. I think I'd be better at the advanced work."

"Yeah, I don't think so."

"Understood," I said, trying a new tactic. "I'll return the top tomorrow, anyway. I noticed something weird about the tag. I was going to mention it to the sales assistant. She said they were having quality issues with DeerNose gear…"

Simon quieted for a few beats. "She said that, did she? Anything else?"

"Are you nearby? I'm still in Gilmore."

He gave me the Windmere address.

I looked at Cuddles. "You're going to need to be a very good boy."

———

WHEN I PARKED AT WINDMERE, Cuddles moaned.

"I'm taking you with me this time."

He cocked his head.

"Only if you promise not to eat anything. Or anyone." I thought about the potential danger of meeting Simon in his lair. "Unless I ask you to."

As I gathered his leash in my hand, my phone rang. Nash.

"His timing is not great," I said to Cuddles. "But he's also hard to catch."

I answered the phone. "I just tried calling—"

"Maizie, this is important." Nash's usual drawl had quickened to a tempo closer to my own. "Did you get into my Deer-Nose computer files today?"

"Today? No." I thought about the note I stole. The trashcan was not a computer file. I was not lying. Thank goodness. "Why?"

"It's really important. Please be honest."

"No, I swear. I mean, okay, I did once before. Maybe twice. But not today. Honestly. Wait. Did someone hack into your computer? Is this part of the sabotage attacks that have been happening at DeerNose?"

He was silent for a long beat.

"Come on, I know about it from Daddy and Petey. I even saw some things at the Boot Scoot that made me think—"

"When were you at the Boot Scoot?"

"Just now."

"I really want you to drop this. Now. No more games. I'm serious."

"Why? Are you in trouble? You sound like you're in trouble…"

The call dropped. I called him back. Voicemail. Tried two more times, then looked at my call history. He hadn't called from his cell phone. I pressed the new number. Nothing.

No answer. No voicemail.

"He's using a burner phone. It's too hard to find pay phones, and the area code isn't in Georgia. But why?"

Cuddles had one ear back and one ear forward. He faced the window but was giving me the side-eye. "I know what you're thinking, but we're going to Simon's anyway."

———

AT THE DOOR to apartment 204C, Simon looked at me, then Cuddles. Cuddles stared back and began foaming. I gripped the leash, gave Simon my dazzling *GQ* smile, and handed him the Boot Scoot bag.

"Is this part of your advanced work?" I winked.

"Is he housebroken?"

"Yes, but I'm not," I purred.

That kind of thing would never work on Nash, but bad double entendres seemed to work on most men. I figured this guy had Romeo'd Kristi while seeing Dee. I needed him compliant. My 150-pound chaperone was ready if Simon tried anything funny. I flashed my *Maxim* smile and brushed my hip against him as I walked past.

Lately, I'd had a lot of practice playing the flirt.

Cuddles paced next to me. He was also acting. Acting like a well-behaved dog. But he'd flicked his ears forward. His tail pointed high and wagged slowly. His eyes darted, scanning the room. I didn't have much time.

I faked looking around the room in case Simon had forgotten I'd already been inside to pretend-fix his freezer. "Nice place."

Simon closed the door and tossed the bag onto the kitchen bar. "It's my temporary office. Not a home." Taking the sentinel cue from Cuddles, he leaned against the counter, folded his arms, and kept his eyes on me. "Tell me more about the Deer-Nose quality issues."

"I left through the Boot Scoot's back door. I saw boxes of DeerNose products they're sending back."

His expression didn't change. Despite the wariness, his eyes gleamed. I had to be careful. Not only because of Simon's relationship with Kristi, but also for Nash. Knowing Nash, he'd been building a case against CrossHair. I couldn't ruin that for him.

"Is DeerNose one of CrossHair's clients?"

"They are a target," he said.

"You're trying to get them as a client? Are you hoping to win them over by showing them where they went wrong?"

"Something like that."

"I didn't tell you this before, but I have a friend who works for you."

"You did mention someone, but sorry, the name didn't ring a bell."

"Someone else. Luella Haney."

Simon straightened from his lean. "Yeah? How do you know Luella, then?"

Cuddles tensed and bristled.

"You know." I lifted a shoulder in a mock shrug and stroked Cuddles' head. "From around town. We're both actresses."

"Right." Simon took a step toward me. A low rumble reverberated from Cuddles' chest. Simon glanced at the dog and backed up a step. "Both actresses. Except you're not just any actress. Luella hasn't broken into any great roles yet, has she?"

"I do have a SAG card, that's true."

"Bollocks. I know who you are, Maizie Albright. You work for your dad's company, yeah?"

"No, I don't work for my dad's company. I'm a private investigator."

"Okay, then." He folded his arms. "Did DeerNose hire you to investigate CrossHair Marketing?"

"Uh, no." This wasn't going exactly as planned. Not that I

had a solid plan. I figured I'd already been made, but not in the sense Simon thought. He didn't seem interested in Kristi. Or Luella. Only DeerNose. "Did a competitor for DeerNose hire you?"

A lone eyebrow rose. "Something like that."

"Why did you have me secret shop if you knew who I was?"

"To see what would happen, obviously. I suspect it's for the same reason you went through with the farce."

"Something like that." I tipped my head to the side. "What did Luella Haney do when she secret shopped?"

"Same as you did," he said briskly. "Right. I think we're done here."

"Who's your client?"

He walked to the door and opened it. "That is privileged information. I thought you didn't work for DeerNose."

"My client is Luella Haney's husband."

He rolled his eyes. "Luella Haney's not married."

I stopped in front of the door and faced him. "I think Luella Haney was a better actress than anyone gave her credit for."

THIRTY-SIX
#HEARTBURN #DOGGONE

I FELT WEARY. And confused. I needed headspace to sort out everything I learned about Kristi Johnson, that had somehow gotten wrapped in DeerNose camouflage and tied to my relationship with Nash. I needed real sleep. In a bed, not in a car or on a couch. After trying to call Nash again, I drove to the cabin.

"I'll talk to Daddy in the morning," I explained to Cuddles. "If I catch him at breakfast, he might be in a better mood. Dee Dixon and CrossHair are involved in the corporate shenanigans. I'm sure Nash already knows that much. Daddy might not know any details about CrossHair, but he'll shed some light on Dee's relationship with the Mercers. That can't be a coincidence. Maybe because of the Mercers, CrossHair's helping this other company assist in commercial espionage."

Cuddles gave me a look.

"Yes, I could try talking to Nash again, but he's not answering his phone. I also don't want to fight. Or give up my investigation when I'm so close. When we talk, I get confused. I want my focus on my job, not my love life."

He gave me another look.

"And yes, technically, this isn't my job."

———

"MAIZIE, WAKE UP," Daddy's voice broke through a dream where I held a pickle aloft while fighting off a pack of hyenas that were also a herd of elephants. Breaking through the mistiness of pickle protection, I realized the pounding of feet was actually a fist hammering on my bedroom door. The hyenas were actually one very large dog snarling and barking before the door.

I jerked upright, called Cuddles to heel, and shot to the door.

"What happened? Are you okay? Is it Carol Lynn?" I held Cuddles back, slipped out the door, and gripped Daddy's arm. "Is Remi okay?"

"Remi's always okay. Don't you worry about us." Daddy cleared his throat. "But honey, I've got some bad news."

"Just say it." I gulped. "What did Vicki do?"

"Not your mother." He gusted a sigh. "The Dixie Kreme shop, baby girl … There was a fire in the middle of the night."

"Nash. Lamar." I turned back to the door, but he placed a hand over mine before I could yank it open.

"I don't think anyone was in the shop, thank the Lord." He hugged me. "I knew you'd want to know immediately. I couldn't sleep and was sitting out on the deck. The noise from town drifts across the lake when the weather's good. I heard the sirens, checked the scanner, and made a few calls."

"Thank you for waking me." I hugged him back.

"It was an old building, honey. A lot of accumulated grease, I suspect. Or old wiring. Don't fret over much. They'll rebuild."

"Go get some sleep, Daddy. I'm not worried."

Except, I had a horrible feeling the fire had nothing to do with grease or wiring and everything to do with a homicidal pyromaniac.

———

THE DONUT SCENT WAS GONE. Nothing but the smell of acrid smoke and wet ash remained in the air. The charred brick front still stood, but the roof was mostly destroyed. If I had to guess, the insides were beyond saving. My heart felt heavy for Lamar's loss. His business had been an icon in our community, passed down through his family. And poor Nash. Besides his records and investigative supplies, all of Nash's worldly goods had gone up in flames. I'd lost my secret laptop and some other things, but my tears were for Lamar, Nash, and the people who worked at Dixie Kreme.

Lamar, Cuddles, and I leaned against Lamar's truck, watching the firemen and police finish their work. It felt déjà vu-ey. A rewind of the Johnson house. My hunch that this was the work of the Johnson firestarter could be wrong. Coincidences happen. The Dixie Kreme building was at least a century old.

But I didn't think so.

Besides, I wanted a person to blame for the loss, not a faulty wire. I'd watched Lamar supervise the daily cleaning. The culprit couldn't be grease.

"Stop crying, Maizie." Lamar hugged me to his side. "We'll rebuild. That's what insurance is for."

"Are they absolutely sure there was no one inside?" Neither of us had heard from Nash. He hadn't responded to our frantic texts and calls. I couldn't track him. He'd gone off the grid.

"He's fine. Remember what I said? If he's on a case, he won't be distracted. He would have heard on the scanner we're both safe. That's all he cares about."

I looked at my phone. Nash might have been ignoring my texts and calls, but he'd probably been tracking me. "When was the last time you heard from him?"

"Not sure. Maybe a few days ago?"

"Where would he go if he was hiding out?"

"He's not ducking you, girl." Lamar cut me a look. His expression changed as he considered my question. "You think someone's after him? They burned down the shop, knowing he sleeps here?"

I shrugged, then nodded.

"Lord Almighty." Lamar looked toward the breaking dawn and back at me. "I'll find him. You figure out who's responsible."

"I still don't have much to go on. Kristi Johnson a.k.a. Luella Haney was my link between CrossHair and DeerNose." I explained to Lamar what I'd seen at the Boot Scoot. "That confirmed my suspicions about CrossHair. Although Simon doesn't seem like a killer. He didn't even seem interested in Kristi-Luella, much less care about covering his connection to her."

"Good acting?"

"Maybe he's a sociopath."

"That kind of sociopath is not as common as people think," said Lamar. "Normal sociopathic criminals aren't Hannibal Lecter. Their IQs are usually lower than average."

"Come to think of it," I said. "Dee wanted Simon to invite Luella to her home. Obviously, Dee didn't know Kristi's dead. Or she was pretending because she killed Kristi. Or Simon's hiding Kristi's murder from Dee…"

Cuddles cocked his head. He was right. Something was off.

"You need more to go on," said Lamar. "You don't have evidence that this fire is related to the Johnson fire. Your best suspect for Kristi Johnson's death is still her husband. Somebody could have hired CrossHair to sabotage DeerNose, but Kristi Johnson's death might be a coincidence."

I sighed. "You're right. It just felt like too big of a coincidence."

"We'll know more after the Fire Marshal's report." Lamar shook his head at the charred remains of his business. "If this was arson, though…"

"Then Nash is in serious trouble," I finished. "If Simon or Dee killed Kristi, maybe they suspect Nash knows. He was following Kristi, so good chance Nash also suspects someone at CrossHair."

"Who else works for their company?"

"Good question. I found a list of names." I didn't say where I found the list. We didn't need to go there. "I'll start with that."

THIRTY-SEVEN

#BULLSEYE #DOGSBODY

AFTER HUGGING Lamar a few more times, I walked Cuddles to A.S.S. where we'd parked. I waved at the construction crew heading to the adjoining building and unlocked the door. Still early for Rhonda and Tiffany.

But not for Annie.

She sauntered from her office, chewing gum at a furious rate. "Heard about the fire. You okay?"

"Not really." I sighed.

"Everyone else okay?"

"Yes, but we can't find Nash. He wasn't sleeping in the office, though." I didn't know where he'd slept lately. Was he always on stakeouts? Or …

Anything else felt too overwhelming to contemplate. I forced my thoughts into a change of subject. "The Dixie Kreme fire feels a little too coincidental after the Johnson fire."

Annie arched a brow. "Aren't you jumping to conclusions? The Dixie Kreme fire wasn't covering up a death."

That we knew of. But I didn't say that. There was a lot I didn't say lately. I was either maturing or becoming disingenuous. I wasn't sure which.

"I still think Kristi Johnson's work for CrossHair relates to

Nash's DeerNose investigation. There's evidence of corporate espionage. It's possible another company hired CrossHair to sabotage DeerNose."

"And you can't find Nash. So you think, what exactly? That a marketing company is a fixer? CrossHair is trying to off the head of DeerNose security?"

"Well, not exactly…" I felt my face fire up.

"Is Nash ghosting you? Did he get tired of you stalking him?"

The bell chimed. Cuddles leaped up, barking. I turned, expecting Rhonda and Tiffany, but Ian strode through the door, saving me from coming up with a lame response for Annie.

"Morning, y'all." He beamed at us, then sobered his look. "Hoping to find you here. You okay, hon?"

"I'm fine." I avoided his eyes while settling Cuddles. "It's not me that everyone needs to worry about."

"I get that, but I was concerned anyway. I'm sure you'd grown attached to the building. And the people in it." He cleared his throat. "Glad no one was in the building last night."

"Me, too. Any word about a cause yet?"

"I haven't heard anything, but it'll take some time to trace it. Lamar kept that place spotless, so I'd guess the old wiring or something."

"That's what most people think."

"Not you?"

I shrugged.

"Do you know where Nash is?"

I shook my head.

"You sure you're okay, Maizie?"

"I've got an office to run," said Annie briskly. "Anything else, Detective Mowry?"

"I wanted to talk about the Johnson file. I went over it last night."

Annie glowered, crossed her arms, and worked her gum.

Ian looked at me and smiled. "Can I take you to breakfast?"

"Does your warrant cover breakfast?" said Annie.

"No, ma'am." He chuckled. "I know a great little place I think Maizie would love. You are welcome to come with us."

"I already ate breakfast," said Annie. "And we already gave you the information covered in the warrant. We don't need to do anything more."

"That's true," said Ian. "But I don't see why you wouldn't. It's not like you're working for Derek Johnson anymore, now is it?"

Annie stopped chewing and firmed her lips.

"Do you have any leads? Besides Derek, I mean?" I said, redirecting Ian. Annie's stiff jaw told me a lot. Was she working for Derek? I didn't think she could have talked to him before his arraignment. But Annie wasn't the pro bono type.

"Nothing really apparent. How about you?" Ian smiled. "We can play nice, see Ms. Cox?"

Annie gave him a steely-eyed scowl.

I couldn't see this conversation going anywhere productive. I also couldn't research the list of names with them around. Ian's friendliness only made me more worried about Nash. Hopefully, I'd find him at DeerNose. I needed to see those security videos. Learn more about the other fourteen people on the list.

"I've got to go. Thanks for the invite, Ian. I'll take a rain check on breakfast when I don't have this one with me." I used the leash to point toward Cuddles. Cuddles got the hint and trotted to the door.

"Wait," called Annie. "I have some skips for you."

I ducked through the door, pretending I hadn't heard her, and hurried to the Impala. My wingman took shotgun, and we pulled away.

———

"THAT WAS CLOSE," I told Cuddles. "I need to go to DeerNose, but I can't take you with me. It's too early to go to ..."

Cuddles stared at me expectantly. "E.L.A.I.N.E.'s house. I'm not going to say her name or you'll have trouble waiting. How about the dog park?"

He flopped down in the seat.

"I know. I feel like I'm spinning my wheels, too. Do you think Annie's showing sympathy for Derek?"

Cuddles shut his eyes.

"Yeah, it's hard to get a read on Annie. Losing money on cases puts her in a bad mood. She's not happy with me either."

He yawned.

"I wish I could find Nash," I continued. "I need a genuine conversation about DeerNose. It's so frustrating. Besides that, I'm worried about him."

My thoughts continued pinging around my brain while we drove. I slowed the car as we approached an exit before reaching Gilmore. "I've got an idea that's better than the dog park. Let's check out the old Mercer Textile factory. I don't know how Dee Dixon is related to the Mercers, but it's a lead I should check out."

Shake Rag was an unincorporated area outside Gilmore. The seamstresses were right about the town's abandoned appearance. There was a small mix of turn-of-the-century cottages and ranch-style homes. Several lots had crumbling architecture covered in vines and moss, with some cleared for trailers. Centrally, there was a tiny post office, a dollar store, and a small municipal building.

On the outskirts, I slowed, approaching a chain-link fence surrounding Mercer Textile. The sign had faded but was still legible on the brick building. I parked in front of the gate. Cuddles and I exited the Impala to sniff around.

Literally and figuratively.

I pushed on the gate. The latch gave, and we entered on foot. A truck drove by, catching Cuddles's attention. I ignored it to study the old building. It appeared in better condition than most structures in Shake Rag, despite its age. Cuddles seemed calm, crossing the weedy parking lot. I wasn't as calm.

The brick front had a small, covered stoop. A faded, illegible notice had been taped to the locked door. I squinted through the front windows. An empty hall with closed doors on either side led to bigger, open double doors. The hall looked fairly clean, relieving my worry about vagrants.

"Seems safe for you to roam." I unclipped Cuddles's leash. "I'm going to try more windows."

He followed me down the stairs. The front windows were set high off the ground. Dense overgrown bushes protected the area beneath them. I wrinkled my nose. Cuddles sniffed the bushes, lifted his leg, and looked at me.

"Let's try the back."

The back had more windows—bigger but still too high to see into—and two loading docks built about four feet off the ground. An accumulation of leaves and debris covered the bottom of one garage-type door. The other door wasn't completely closed. I stooped to peer inside the opening. Cuddles put his paws on the edge of the concrete and studied the gap.

I pushed up on the bottom of the metal door. It rose a few inches. I bit my lip. "It could be full of vermin."

Cuddles woofed.

"I'm not crazy about mice. Raccoons either. Have you seen a raccoon up close?" I shook my head. "Plus snakes. There could be snakes. Definitely spiders."

Cuddles scrabbled his paws on the concrete, trying to get a grip.

"What about meth-heads? It's an ideal location. What if they've taken over the factory, *Breaking Bad*-style? We could be entering a drug war zone."

He heaved himself onto the ledge and wiggled beneath the door.

"Okay, you're right. I didn't see any needles or bullet casings in the parking lot. Not a lot of trash at all." I clambered onto the sill, pushed the door higher, and crawled inside. "Still, spiders. Ugh."

Cuddles set to work, sniffing through the forest debris that had accumulated along the walls. I wiped away a web and looked around the open space. The machinery and usual detritus that one would find in a factory had been cleared. Overhead, a system of ductwork, pipes, and bracket-work used for pulleys, tracks, and chains remained. Except for a few damp spots from leaks, the dirty floor revealed only non-human prints.

"They must have sold everything."

A set of stairs led to a second-story open walkway. I climbed and looked over the railing at the massive space. "I'm surprised they haven't turned this place into loft apartments or something."

Cuddles trotted up the stairs. We peered into the grimy windows behind us that must have been offices. All empty.

"It's so weird," I said. "Kind of eerie. Why wasn't the building sold?"

At the end of the walkway, wide double doors stood open to the front area. "I don't know what I'm hoping to find in an empty building. Let's check out the front area, then we'll go. Hopefully Elai—"

Cuddles looked at me.

"The person whose name I will not yet mention will be done studying and can watch you."

In the front hall, I peeked into an empty conference room. The doors opposite opened into a reception area. Behind reception were more offices. At the end of the hall, a wooden door gave way when I put my shoulder against it. A single desk and chair faced the door. A big bin held mannequin arms and legs, stuck out at odd angles.

"Weird. I guess the leftovers were stored in here."

I moved behind the desk to check the drawers. Cuddles growled, then woofed. He shot into the hall, bumping the door on his way out. The door swung shut, revealing a dartboard with a picture stuck to it.

I hesitated before drawing closer. Pulling a dart from the picture, I gasped. My father's face looked back at me. Someone had ripped the faded, tattered picture from a magazine.

Barely recognizable, I still remembered it from my childhood. A hunting magazine had done a spread on Daddy's camo designs and the revolutionary DeerNose scent. I remember his excitement and the celebration in the new DeerNose building. They'd gotten a gigantic cake with the magazine picture painted on it to share with all the DeerNose employees.

The cake had been chocolate. The icing—thick, sweet, and delicious. At the time, Vicki didn't allow me to have sugar. Particularly, cake loaded with carbs and fat. We didn't tell her. It had been worth getting sick. A happy memory for DeerNose and for me.

I smoothed a curling edge and replaced the dart to hold the paper in place. Focused my gaze not on the image but on the small round holes dotting the paper. My stomach clenched. But the ill feeling I battled wasn't from remembered cake trauma.

Someone in this office had been throwing darts at my dad.

And judging by the number of holes, they'd been doing it for a long time.

THIRTY-EIGHT
#NOTSHINING #HELLHOUND

SOMEWHERE IN THE FACTORY, Cuddles yelped.

"Cuddles? Are you okay?" I yanked open the door and rushed into the hall.

The yelp switched to a ferocious warning bark. I took the corner out of reception too fast, slammed my hip against the frame, and stumble-ran through the big open doors. Reaching the factory area, I leaned over the railing and spotted him snarling at the opening in the dock door.

"It wasn't a raccoon, was it?" I shivered. "Good job. You scared it off."

Ignoring me, he continued growling and barking.

"It's okay, Cuddles. Nobody—" The words died in my mouth.

The tracks we'd made on the dirty floor had a strange pattern. From my aerial view, I could see my path from the factory floor to the stairs. Cuddles had two sets of doggy prints. One, the circuitous route to the stairs. The other was a direct route to the loading dock door.

But there was also a third set of prints, clearly different from my Bottega Veneta lug sole boots I had pulled on before rushing to the fire. One set of footprints hugged the walls. All the prints mixed closer to the stairs, but another path ran adja-cent to my lug sole amble from the stairs to the loading dock. Barely visible dusty toe prints were on the stairs and concrete landing. The prints led to the open double doors and disap-peared on the tile.

My nerves popped and snapped. The hair on the back of my neck stood. Someone had snuck in behind us.

This was worse than a raccoon. Maybe junkies and vagrants didn't always leave trash behind. In *Julia Pinkerton, Teen Detective*, the scenes portraying the homeless were always in sketchy areas of cities with garbage-strewn streets, graffiti-sprayed underpasses, and boarded-up buildings. The trashed rooms always had a few mattresses flopped on the floor.

No mattresses here. Not a hint of graffiti. Weird for an aban-doned factory. Possibly the *Julia Pinkerton* writers had relied on that trope too much. Or maybe the meth-heads in Shake Rag cleaned up after themselves.

Good for them.

I ran down the stairs to join Cuddles at the loading dock. Before I could reach him, he squeezed through the opening and disappeared.

"Cuddles," I called. "Come back."

I grabbed his leash and raced to the loading dock. Crawled out and dropped to the ground. Calling for Cuddles, I sped around to the front of the building and spied him across the parking lot with his nose to the ground. "Cuddles, come."

Giving up his hunt, he glanced at me and galloped in the opposite direction.

"Hey," I yelled. "Stop. Stay."

He looked over his shoulder. His tongue hung out and his ears stood up.

"Just stay there." I strode toward him while my pounding heart slowed to a mere thudding.

He dashed away. I broke into a jog. Then a run. I slowed. He stopped. When I neared, he ran.

"This. Is. Not. A game," I panted and grabbed the chain-link fence to lean over and wheeze.

A thick pink tongue swiped my face.

"Yehrg." I drew up and wiped my face. Looked down at the happy dog and rubbed his ears. He plopped on my feet and dropped his head for a quick snooze. "I guess you're no longer concerned. You scared them away. Good boy."

The parking lot was still empty. "We should go. After I get that picture. I can't leave it there. It'll haunt me."

I clipped his leash for our walk to the loading dock. Knowing someone had been inside with us made the empty factory spookier.

"It's strange. The building is accessible. Yet not one empty Thunderbird bottle to be found. Not even a Snickers' wrapper."

Nose down, Cuddles sniffed his way to the stairs. Up on the catwalk, he refocused—ears forward and nose in the air. His body hummed and his hackles rose.

"What is it?" I whispered. "Are they still inside?"

I listened. Caught a rustling that might have been mice or something else. Tiny shivers raced up and down my body. My mouth felt dry. I urged Cuddles to a faster trot through the open double doors. We snuck into reception. At the end of the hall, the office door still stood open.

Like it was waiting for us.

I had thoughts of *The Shining* but was more worried about getting trapped and ganked by a psychotic meth-head than hunted by ghosts. Unless the meth-head had been possessed by factory ghosts?

I shook off *The Shining* and marched forward. A low growl reverberated from Cuddles. I stopped halfway down the hall and shortened his lead.

"Hello? Anybody there?"

Cuddles' growl intensified. Closed doors stood on either side of us.

How badly did I want that picture?

I irrationally feared what might be behind the open door at the end of the hall rather than the closed doors on either side. Someone had attacked my father's picture with malevolence. It took some effort to make a target. Finding a picture. Attaching it to the dartboard. Not a difficult task, but a meaningful one.

Maybe the ghost threw darts. Maybe the ghost was Randy Mercer.

"If those creepy twins show up, I am so out of here," I whispered to Cuddles.

Frothy icicles hung from his mouth. He shook them off and pulled against the lead.

"Hello?" I called again. "I have a very large dog who is not friendly. It's better if you show yourself."

Cuddles tugged me toward the office.

"Seriously," I hollered. "In a minute, I won't be able to control him. If you're hiding, he will find you. It's instinct. A hunter-prey thing."

Cuddles strained at the leash. I stumbled behind him. At the entrance to the office, his nose dropped to the floor. I kicked the office door. It slammed into the wall. I let out a long breath that jerked back into my lungs, hearing the dartboard crash to the ground. I rounded the door and picked it up from the litter of darts beneath it.

The picture of my father was gone.

THIRTY-NINE

BACK INSIDE THE safety of the Impala, I let my brain click pieces together while we got the heck out of Shake Rag and away from the spooky Mercer Textile factory. "I didn't imagine it. That picture was on the dartboard, right?"

Cuddles woofed.

"Where could it have gone? If it had fallen apart when the dartboard fell, we'd see little pieces of paper, right? Do you think a raccoon took it?" I forced a chuckle. "I'm just kidding. But not really."

Cuddles looked at me.

I maneuvered the Impala back onto the county highway and maneuvered my thoughts back to the case. Except I wasn't sure which case I worked on anymore—DeerNose or Kristi Johnson's murder.

"New plan. I didn't get a chance to talk to Daddy this morning. The corporate sabotage thing could be a personal attack on him. Considering the darts thrown at his picture…" I shuddered. "When you go to Elaine's, I'll clue Nash in on what I've learned. I still want to see those security videos. Now that I know Cross-Hair's behind all this, he'll have to talk to me. Tell me about that list. Obviously, Nash has been concerned about Daddy, and he didn't want to worry me. That has to be what all the secrecy was about."

I sighed. "His protective instinct is romantic. Frustrating and irritating, but romantic. Wyatt Nash is a Neanderthal. I guess I like Neanderthals. As a modern woman, I probably should be into someone more enlightened, but as they say, you can't stop love."

My heart pounded, and my stomach fluttered, thinking about making up with my Neanderthal.

"I'll pick you up later. Okay?" I glanced at Cuddles.

He'd placed both paws on the dashboard to stare out the windshield. I'd said the magic Elaine word. He hadn't listened to anything else.

"Sit down." I leaned forward to bat down his paws. "That's dangerous. You should be in your seatbelt."

He shook his head and sprayed me with drool.

———

ELAINE WAS OVERJOYED to take Cuddles off my hands. Victoria was annoyed. "I have to go to work," she said. "Elaine needs to finish her studies before she does anything else."

"He'll just lie at my feet," pleaded Elaine.

"He loves taking naps," I added. "He already had a big morning. He chased—" I caught myself. "A big rabbit. Or maybe a large raccoon. In any case, he's had a lot of exercise already."

Victoria pressed her lips together.

"I promise to get everything done." Elaine had thrown her arms around Cuddles' neck. Her big brown eyes blinked up at her mother. Cuddles licked Elaine, then blinked his big brown eyes up at Victoria.

Hashtag Adorbs.

"Fine. Okay. Just this once." Victoria bent to rub Cuddles' head.

He was one smart dog.

I mumbled something about picking him up and shot back to Black Pine. At the DeerNose gate, I proved I wasn't hiding anything canine, parked in front, and raced inside. I hoped after talking to Daddy, I'd catch Nash, then convince him to go …

I had gotten so caught up in solving the DeerNose case, I'd almost forgotten about the Dixie Kreme fire. Poor Nash. Where could we go?

Wait. Where was he last night? Why hadn't he contacted me? Neanderthal or not, he owed me some communication. At least to let me know he was okay. No way was Annie right about him ghosting me, but—

"Oof." Lost in my thoughts, I literally ran into Marshy.

He turned our bump into a hug. "Hey Little M. What are you doing here? Where's your big fellow?"

"Cuddles?"

"Him, too. That dog wanted to take a hunk out of me." Marshy smiled, then sobered his reaction. "No, Wyatt Nash. Haven't heard from him either. Understandable with the fire, but I thought he'd at least call this morning. Let us know he's okay."

"Nash isn't at work?"

"Nope. Where is he?"

"I don't know." My heart tripped. Not in a good way. "I thought he'd be here."

"Listen, rumor says you're on the outs with Nash and he threatened to quit. I can't see Wyatt Nash doing something ridiculous like that, but you've both been a little odd lately. Is he okay? Besides the fire, I mean."

I didn't have an answer. My gut hurt like I'd been punched. I blinked away a few hot tears and pinched the skin by my thumb to make them stop. Marshy studied me, took me by the shoulder, and walked me to his office. He closed the door. I fell into a chair and sobbed.

"I don't know what's happening," I blubbered. "He won't talk to me. He's been working on the corporate espionage thing. He refuses to tell me anything, but Marshy, it's Daddy's company. I know my case overlaps with his case, but does Nash think I'll give away secrets? It shouldn't matter, especially now that I know about the trouble at DeerNose. We could work together."

I paused to blow my nose. Marshy patted my shoulder and mumbled, "It'll be okay, hon'."

"But with the fires and Kristi's murder and … and everyone thinks it's Derek, but I think maybe it was Simon or Dee or … or I don't know. I should know." I gulped back another sob. "I've done a terrible job with this case because I am totally distracted by Cuddles. Or maybe not. Maybe it's just me. I wanted to prove so badly that I'm good at this, and maybe all I'm good at is trapping cheaters, and …" I hiccuped, then wailed, "… and trapping cheaters is a terrible thing to be good at. Maybe Nash doesn't want my help because I'm no help at all."

Marshy stared at me for a long minute, then shoved a box of tissues at me. He cleared his throat. "Let me see if Boomer is free."

Poor Marshy. He didn't have daughters. Only a son who worked on a fishing boat in Alaska.

A moment later, Daddy hustled in. "What's the matter, baby girl? Is it the fire? I thought nobody was hurt. Don't you worry none. Marshall's got a plan to help rebuild the Dixie Kreme building. We're gonna meet with Lamar as soon as he's got a spare minute. We'll get the town involved, and Lamar will get his donut shop back lickety-split."

"That's lovely." Two fat tears splashed onto my thighs. "Thank you."

Daddy squatted in front of my chair—not an easy feat for a man that large—and took my hands. "Marshall also said something about you breaking up with Nash. I am here for you, sweetie. Did Wyatt Nash … did he … is he not the honest man we thought he was?"

"Oh no, Daddy, nothing like that." I cringed. How humiliating. For both of us.

"Well, honey, I am relieved." He lumbered to his feet and placed a large hand on my shoulder. "But something's happened, I can tell. What is it?"

I blew out a long breath. I wouldn't dwell on the rumors and gossip of my potential singledom. The best medicine for relationship failures was to busy my mind with something else. Besides that, Daddy and Marshy were also touched by Neaderthalitis. They wouldn't understand even if I could explain my tangle of emotions.

"Has Nash spoken to you about his findings with the sabotage attempts?" I moved my gaze from Daddy to Marshy. "Either of you?"

"Nash reports to me. We brought him on to deal with this problem," said Marshy. "Peters and I keep Boomer updated with the overall view, but not always the specifics."

"What has Nash reported?"

"Honey, I know you're worried about me, but why are you making this your business?" Daddy's expression had gone from concern to haggard. "I'm sure Nash and Marshall have a handle on it. Don't step on toes, girl."

"I can't help it. This security issue has gotten mixed up with one of my cases. There's been a murder. And a fire. Now two fires."

"Murder? How's that?" Daddy looked at Marshy. "Did you know about a murder?"

"No." Marshy folded his arms. "Nash hasn't said anything about a murder. Was there a break-in at a store or something? Robbery? He's been working with our service delivery team to investigate tampered shipments to stores. We have a compromised warehouse."

"No. Not like that." I stood to face them. "Here in town. A woman was found murdered in her home after a fire. I saw the woman, Kristi Johnson, enter the factory. She came in with the seamstresses. Nash was going to look at the security footage with me."

"When was this?" said Daddy.

"Monday morning," I sighed. "On Tuesday, her body was found in a house fire."

"What in tarnation?" Daddy planted his hands on his hips. "And Wyatt Nash?"

"I believe he's also investigating her, but from another angle. Kristi worked for a marketing company that's likely behind your quality issues. She was using an alias. Nash and I didn't realize we were following the same subject until it was too late." I grimaced. "I got a little cute with him, and it got out of hand."

"Merciful heavens." Daddy rubbed his face. "Nash can't go off half-cocked. He's in charge of security, not doing private investigations anymore. He needs to follow procedure."

My heart thudded. I didn't want to get Nash in trouble, I just wanted answers. "I think he was being careful. Making sure he had all the facts. Has he said anything about the Mercers?"

"Mercers?" Daddy looked at Marshy. "What's she talking about?"

Marshy glared at me. "I don't know."

"CrossHair, the marketing company that might be behind the sabotage attempts, is owned by Dee Dixon."

"Who's Dee Dixon?" said Marshy.

"I'm not sure, but she's living on Mercer land in Little Gap. She called it 'family property.'"

"Maizie, are you okay, sweetie?" called Petey. "I heard you were upset. So sorry to hear about the fire."

I turned toward the door, where she hovered. "I'm fine."

"Boomer and Marshall, y'all have a meeting," she said, striding in to join us. "Maizie honey, if you're okay, it's best you leave them to it."

"Daddy, wait," I pleaded. "I don't believe Nash has done anything wrong. I'm sure he's following procedure and keeping you apprised of facts. He won't share hunches or draw conclusions if he doesn't have hard evidence or proof. That's his way. He wouldn't want to lead you down the wrong path. But he will quietly investigate those hunches to see if they go anywhere. I'm sure that's what's going on."

"I get it," said Daddy. "But it's not how we do things here."

"Nash reports to Marshall. He should be telling Marshall everything," said Petey gently. "Especially if someone entered our building without our knowing."

Marshy nodded.

Desperate to show the other side of the story, I blurted, "On the other hand, I jump to conclusions. It's not good for the clients. Nash and Annie tell me that all the time. Like this murder and my belief that her husband didn't kill Kristi. I'm investigating it based on a hunch, even though we're no longer working for the husband."

"You're just starting out, Little M. You're learning." Marshy patted my arm. "Nash has been doing this longer and knows better."

"I hope you're still doing the job you're getting paid for." Daddy arched a brow.

Considering the job was dog sitting, I nodded.

"Where is Nash?" said Petey. "I've been trying to contact him."

"He must be dealing with insurance," I hedged. "He lost his home and all his possessions in that fire."

"Nash needs to tell us about CrossHair's connection to the Mercers." Marshy folded his arms. "Peters is right. Anything related to DeerNose, even a hunch, should be drawn to our attention. We don't have room for lone rangers in this company."

"He might not know the connection to the Mercers. I came across it in my investigation. I haven't … we haven't…" Frustrated, I drew my thoughts together. "Even though our cases have overlapped, Nash and I haven't shared much. He's been strictly professional. I may be Boomer Spayberry's daughter, but Nash will not divulge DeerNose security matters with me."

Daddy nodded, looking pleased.

"In other words, you don't know what Nash knows and can't help us." Petey hugged my shoulder. "It's okay, sweetie."

"Not really. Although if you can show me your security video feed, I could point out Kristi Johnson entering the factory."

"I'd like to see that," said Marshy. "Let's go."

"Boomer and Marshall, your meeting?" Petey checked her watch. "I let myself get sidetracked."

Marshy moved toward the door. "Boomer, is your presentation ready?"

Daddy studied me. "You okay, honey?"

"I'll take care of Maizie," said Petey. "I know how to pull up the security camera footage."

Marshy narrowed his eyes. "Peters, catch me up later. If the video caught that woman coming into our house, I want to see it."

FORTY

"WE CAN all access the security videos," Petey explained as we walked to her office. "If we find anything in the video feed, I'll show it to Marshall and Boomer."

At her desk, she logged in to the security app and moved the window to the biggest screen in her bank of screens. I pulled a chair to sit beside her.

"What day did this woman enter DeerNose?"

"Monday. When the first shift of seamstresses arrived. Kristi walked in with them."

While she tapped on her keys, I let my gaze travel the room. It stopped on a large framed picture hanging near the door. I hopped up from my seat and studied the magazine spread. The same photo of my father I had seen at the Mercer Textile factory. Except this one was preserved. His face wasn't pocked with dart holes.

"Petey, was this the shoot where we had that wonderful chocolate cake?"

She slid her glasses down her nose to study the photo. "Oh, goodness. I barely remember the cake. Quite a coup for us. We'd just moved into the new building. Your daddy's designs had caught the eye of *Hunting Life*. That's the magazine that took those pictures."

"I remember the cake. I got sick from eating too much."

"We loved to spoil you when you came home to us." She beamed at me. "We felt so sorry for you and Boomer. He missed you when you were in California with your mother. It's too bad you couldn't stay with him instead."

"I didn't have much say in that. I was pretty busy with the TV shows."

"Always working." She slid her cheaters back up her nose. "Boomer was so proud of you. But he still missed you. We all did."

"Well, I'm here now," I said in the perkiest voice I could muster, and pretended to study the picture so Petey wouldn't see my expression. I knew Petey meant well, but I felt guilty. I didn't have control over the terms of my custody until I was fifteen. By then, I starred in *Kung Fu Kate* followed by *Julia Pinkerton, Teen Detective*. I tried to spend as much time with Daddy as I could during my hiatuses. But during my breaks, there was also the push for other work, like TV movies and guest roles. The more on-screen time I had, the better positioning I'd have for bigger roles in the future.

And sometimes—just when I was at my lowest—I felt Daddy could have visited me more. Even if Vicki made it difficult. And though I loved Carol Lynn and Remi and would never wish a day without them in my life, it still hurt that Daddy had created a new family. Especially when I was stuck with Vicki and her maniacal focus on making me a star.

Renata, my ex-therapist, always wanted to explore those thoughts. I'd refused to discuss negative feelings toward my father. He hadn't wanted Vicki to leave him, after all. He'd tried his best to be a father across a continent. As Petey unintentionally pointed out, maybe Daddy didn't feel welcome to see me because I'd chosen work over him.

Although it seemed—only at my darkest times—he'd chosen work over me, too. DeerNose was his main excuse for not visiting.

I guess this was why children of divorce had such complicated feelings for their parents.

"And we're so glad to have you here now, dear," continued Petey. "It's too bad the career you chose has butted up with DeerNose in this way. I have to say I'm disappointed in Nash. And hearing you broke up with him, I guess I'm not the only one."

"Wait. What?" Childhood issues forgotten, I hurried back to my chair. "Where did you hear that?"

"Boomer and Marshy were talking earlier." She squeezed my hand. "It's not true? You know how small towns are. People talk. Don't worry about it though, sweetie."

Black Pine was as bad as Hollywood. The more you try to keep your relationship on the down-low, the more people talked. This was why Nash had so many rules. He valued his privacy. I'd trampled on that as a public figure. His working at DeerNose hadn't helped. I was like a daughter to everyone here. People would notice. And talk.

Particularly when I showed up at DeerNose to visit him. And to spy on him.

Annie and the girls were probably not the only ones who thought I'd been girlfriend-stalking him.

Was this all my fault? Maybe he *was* ghosting me …

"Oh, my heavens."

I shook off those cringey thoughts and turned my attention to Petey, who'd stopped clicking her mouse to rub her forehead. "What's wrong?"

"I can't find it."

"The factory door surveillance footage?"

"Not just that." She slid off her glasses and cast me an anxious look. "I can't find anything for Monday."

"Are you sure?" I leaned forward to study the screen and grabbed the mouse. "Could it be saved somewhere else? No, I see Tuesday. And Wednesday." I clicked through the app, searching. "How could this be?"

"I don't know. Wait. I've thought of something." Petey slid her glasses on. "The deleted files."

"Great idea." I tapped the cursor on File and found the trash. Empty. "What now?"

"We have an auditing program. Nash actually set this up for security tracking." She took the mouse from me. "Let's find out what happened to the video. Then we might figure out how to restore it."

She opened a program on a different screen. "Heavens. How could this—" After several minutes of tapping through folders and muttering, she stopped. Took a deep breath and rubbed her temple.

I leaned forward. "What am I seeing?"

"The program shows who's been accessing folders, the date, and what they did with them. Early on Tuesday, it was deleted. But someone else had accessed it on Monday."

"Who?"

"Unknown user."

"What does that mean?"

"Someone who doesn't work here. An encrypted account. If it were a DeerNose employee, it would show their name." She pointed at the screen. "Look at this. See?"

I did see. Just like I saw the name of the person who had deleted the file early on Tuesday. Wyatt Nash.

No wonder Petey had looked upset.

———

"WHY WOULD HE DO THAT? Without telling anyone?" said Petey. "What was he thinking?"

"Nash deleted the file after the unknown user accessed it. There had to be a good reason for it."

"Do you think these CrossHair people got into our system? Could that woman gotten access to one of our computers?"

"Without the security feed showing what rooms Kristi Johnson entered, there's no way of knowing. Unless a forensic analyst examines it."

"What do you mean? Hire an expert?"

I had meant the police. Ian already knew Kristi had entered DeerNose if he read our case notes.

Shiztastic. I should have taken that breakfast and learned what he knew.

Oh, hells. CrossHair hadn't been the only one to access Deer-Nose files recently. I'd been hacking into Nash's computer for the last few weeks, trying to figure out what he'd been working on.

Frigalicious. Humiliating and totally illegal. I'd violated my probation.

My heart hammered, and my vision spotted. I'd convinced myself I knew what I was doing. Why was I so stupid?

"Maizie, are you okay?" Petey patted my hand. "You don't look well."

"I … uh … well …" I cleared my throat and forced my tone to chipper. I sounded like a sliding whistle. "I need to make a few calls. Back in a bit."

"It's Nash, isn't it?" She gave me a pitying look. "I can't believe it myself."

I knew what she meant. The deleted file combined with his disappearance cast serious shade on Nash. "As soon as we hear from him, Nash will explain the missing security footage. I just need to find him."

"Do that. Bring him here. I sure hope he has a good explanation. Marshall will blow his top. I'll try to keep him calm, but…"

She didn't need to finish her sentence. I hurried from her office, wanting to talk to Nash before Ian. Not that I thought

Nash had anything to hide. He wouldn't delete that video without a good reason. I also wanted to warn him the police would likely confiscate his computer. In case he wanted to let Ian know about our little *Mr. & Mrs. Smith* game.

That was still a breach of security.

Making Nash look as bad as me.

FORTY-ONE
#BLACKCHAT #LYINGDOWNWITHDOGS

IN THE IMPALA, I called Nash from my visitor's spot at DeerNose. Naturally, he didn't pick up. I left a message explaining what I learned about the missing security feed. What the police would potentially see. And my next steps.

Plus, I might have lost it. Just a little.

"I'm so sorry. I just wanted to know what you found at Deer-Nose." I gulped. "I was worried about Daddy … and okay, I admit I was miffed you kept that information from me. I hacked your accounts to get even. To show you I could do it."

I pinched my thumb to quell any tears. "Okay, then. Well, if you're ghosting me, I understand. I can't expect you to cover for me because that would totally screw your future in security services." Welling panic bubbled and burst. "I guess I just screwed my chances of becoming a private investigator, too. Oh, God…"

I hung up. Pinched both thumbs. And called Ian.

"Ian, I need to talk to you about the Johnson case."

"That's great, hon'. Except I don't have time for lunch. I'm heading over to DeerNose. Need to talk to the big wigs there, including Boomer."

I thunked my head on the steering wheel.

"Real curious how y'all followed Kristi Johnson to DeerNose the day before she died. Great work on your part, by the way. Good surveillance."

"Thanks." I thunked my head again, then rubbed my forehead.

"I want a few words with Nash, too."

"He's not here."

"Here?" said Ian. "As in DeerNose? You're there and he's not? Where is he?"

"I don't know," I said glumly.

"I'm pulling into the parking lot now. Come outside and talk to me before my team goes inside."

"I'm sitting in the Impala near the front door."

A few minutes later, Ian rapped on my window. I exited the car and leaned against it.

"You look like you need a hug." Ian cocked his head. "What happened? Where's Nash?"

"I haven't seen him since yesterday when you stopped by the office to get the Johnson case file. Haven't really talked to him since then either."

"Yesterday afternoon? He hasn't talked to you? Even with the fire?"

I shook my head. "Lamar says he's too busy with his Deer-Nose casework. When he's on a hunt, he doesn't get distracted."

"I get it. But with the fire." Ian's forehead creased. "You must be worried."

"I am. But it's not just that." I blew out a breath. "I've got to confess something."

"Oh, boy." Ian rocked back on his heels. "Lay it on me."

I explained my cyber-stalking of Nash in the simplest terms I could. While avoiding eye contact. "Nash knew I was doing it, and—this is embarrassing—there was a cat-and-mouse element we both liked. I admit, I went too far and ticked him off."

"I've got to think about this. You crossed some boundaries. And laws." Ian winced. "Not good, Maizie."

"If my ex-therapist Renata were here, she'd call this a repeat performance of how I blew my acting career. Except I care about my investigations career a lot more."

But how much did I care about Nash if I'd violate his privacy and his career? That elephant sat between us, silently trumpeting my shame.

I hung my head. "If Annie finds out, she'll probably fire me. Vicki will use that excuse to pull me into a new reality show."

"I thought your probation restricted you from doing TV work."

"She'd find a loophole." I sighed.

"Are you done with the pity party?" Ian held out his arms. "I was kidding about the hug earlier, but I guess not."

I felt guilty after restricting Nash from hugging, but I really needed a hug. My head dropped to Ian's shoulder for a second too long, considering my history with him. Backing out, I looked up at him.

"You're going to be okay," said Ian.

"I won't get in trouble for pulling data from Nash's work computer in order to spy on him?"

"I meant you're going to be okay in general. Hopefully, that won't come out in the wash." Ian grimaced. "You should stop telling me things like that."

I nodded.

"I admire your honesty, though."

"That's nice to hear. I haven't felt very honest lately."

"Can I give you some advice when it comes to Nash?" At my nod, Ian gripped my shoulder. "You don't need to try so hard. You've got a lot to offer, and if he's reluctant to take it … well, that's his loss."

"Oh, okay. Um, thanks?" I felt heat spank my cheeks. "I wasn't stalking Nash for personal reasons. Just to learn what kept him from telling me about DeerNose's trouble. Although, I guess that's a personal reason, since Daddy's business is personal to me."

Ian squeezed my shoulder and let his hand drop. "Alright, enough said. I've got to do my thing now."

All I'd accomplished was making me look like a crazy ex-girlfriend and possible corporate spy. And making Nash look guilty in the process. When there were real corporate spies that might harbor a serious grudge against my father.

Serious enough to murder Kristi Johnson, though?

"Wait, Ian. In your investigation into Kristi Johnson's murder, has the name Mercer come up?"

"Mercer?" Ian's brow furrowed. "Who's Mercer?"

"As in Mercer Textile factory. They were in business with DeerNose twenty years ago. I think Randy Mercer was a supplier. They shared factory space in the early days. Mercer Textile is in Shake Rag. *Was* in Shake Rag. It's abandoned now."

"What does that have to do with Kristi Johnson?"

"I'm not sure, but CrossHair is owned by someone who might be related to Randy Mercer." I waved him on. "Never mind. Go on in. That's probably nothing to do with her murder."

Ian's hands went to his hips. He cocked his head. I knew that look. He was trying to get a read on me. "Is everything you know about Kristi Johnson in your case notes? I'm getting the feeling there's more."

"It's confusing. We were looking for evidence of Kristi Johnson having an affair. She stayed at the apartment overnight in Windmere, leased to Simon Craig. He claims it's his office for CrossHair. I don't think there's enough solid evidence Kristi and Simon were having an affair, because he seems to really vibe with Dee Dixon. Rhonda disagrees. But Rhonda has a thing for Derek Johnson."

I stopped. "Oh, I shouldn't have said that. Rhonda thinks Derek's cute. She's barely talked to him. It's not like she's acted on it."

"I get it. She's no Sam Spade." Ian pulled a notebook out of his pocket and began writing. "Keep going."

"Here's where our cases overlap. I followed Kristi to Deer-

Nose. Before that, I also saw her with Nash at a Waffle Haus in Gilmore."

"Stop. Nash interacted with Kristi Johnson?"

"I think he pretended to meet her at the Boot Scoot. I'm not sure how they ended up at the Waffle Haus..." I trailed off. Did he pretend to pick her up at the Boot Scoot and invited her out for a waffle? Was it planned? "The Boot Scoot is where I figured out CrossHair was behind the attacks on the DeerNose branch. And merchandise. They added inappropriate tags to the clothes."

"CrossHair did?"

"Honestly, I don't know if it was CrossHair, or if they were hired by a competitor and someone else is behind it. I was supposed to be secret shopping. Later, Simon Craig said Deer-Nose was the marketing target. He knew who I was."

"Why did he hire you to secret shop if he knew who you were?"

"To see what I would do. He thought DeerNose hired me to investigate them."

Ian tapped his pen against his pad. "Let's get back to Kristi. In your case notes, you followed her to DeerNose, then it dead-ended for you."

"Annie kicked me off the case because she thought I was stalking Nash." I bit my lip. "So instead of following Kristi, I investigated Simon Craig. And he led me to Dee Dixon. Who is somehow related to the Mercers."

"Why is that a big deal? Everybody is related to everybody around here."

"It's hinky. She owns CrossHair. DeerNose used to work with Mercer Textile. I think there was animosity between Mercer Textile and DeerNose." I was ready to launch into Daddy's magazine photo stuck with darts, but Ian held up a hand.

"Refocus on Kristi. The night of the fire, you went to the Johnson house after Annie told you to leave the case. Why?"

"Just to check on things..."

"To see if Nash was still following Kristi?"

"How did you know—" I blew out a breath. "Yes, he'd been following Kristi. I saw Nash at the Windmere apartment and a coffee shop, too. Because of the overlap in our cases. That's what I was trying to figure out. That's why I refocused on Simon Craig, because he was also at Windmere and the coffee shop."

"But Nash wasn't at the Johnson house that night."

"No, neither was Annie, who was also following Kristi."

"Annie couldn't find her that day, though. Did Nash?"

"I don't know." Why was Ian so focused on Nash?

"Where was Nash the day of the Johnson fire?"

"I don't know. I'd stopped monitoring him by then."

"You stopped, or he stopped you?"

"I—" Wait. What was going on here? "I saw him later at the Johnson's. When I returned. I left when the fire department arrived, so I wouldn't be in the way. When I came back, Annie and Nash were watching the scene. I didn't get a chance to talk to him because Annie caught me first…" And Nash disappeared before I could get to him.

"Neither you nor Annie had seen Kristi since the day before. Do you think Nash saw her on Tuesday, before the Johnson fire?"

"I don't know…" Before the fire, I'd followed Simon to Little Gap. "Wait, I talked to him on Tuesday. I was on the road."

"That's easy enough to check." Ian wrote something in his notebook.

"Check? Like Nash needs an alibi? What's going on, Ian?"

"Just trying to understand who were the last people to see Kristi alive. Standard stuff, hon'."

Worry didn't come close to how I was feeling. "What about the book club friends? Have you talked to them?"

Ian looked up from his notebook. "What do you mean, book club?"

"A couple days before, I missed Kristi going to book club because I'd…" Interrogated Nash instead. "Did Derek give you the name of the friend who held book club?" I could tell by Ian's face that Derek hadn't given him names. "She might have lied about going to book club."

"Or he lied about book club. I didn't see his mention of book club in your report." Ian cocked his head. "Something you forgot to write down?"

Frigalicous. Kristi was at book club during my visit when Cuddles destroyed the kitchen. Nobody knew about that except the expense reports that wouldn't show until the end of the month. "Okay, I saw Derek Friday night…" I explained my visit.

"He gave you a tour of the house?" Ian scribbled in his notebook.

"Derek was right to suspect Kristi. She was using an alias with CrossHair. Luella Haney. I don't know if she was having an affair like Derek thought, but she was into some shady stuff for CrossHair."

"I'm checking into that. It's why I'm here." Ian smiled. "You've been very helpful. Except for the holes in your story. You're covering for someone. Maybe not intentionally, but it's best to get this sorted. Come down to the station and do a report."

I realized my mouth hung open and snapped it shut. "I'm a person of interest?"

"You're an interesting person." Ian winked, then sobered his look to cop cool. "An interesting person with relevant facts about this case. I need a timeline. You have more information than what's in your case file. Pop down to my office. We'll do your statement. We can grab a bite after."

"Wait. What?"

"My associate is here. I'm going inside now." He waved at someone behind me and stepped onto the sidewalk. "Don't worry. We'll figure this out."

I whirled around. A patrol car had parked in the fire lane. A uniformed policeman waited at the front door. Ian hurried toward him.

Ian was on the wrong track. Suspecting Derek, I understood.

But why was he suspicious of Nash? Or me? I felt it in my bones that Kristi's involvement with CrossHair was behind her murder. Ian had swept that aside. Although he was going into DeerNose now to see the evidence of her entering with the seamstresses …

Oh hells.

I had forgotten to tell Ian that the footage had been erased. He was going to see who might have erased it. And build more of a case against Nash.

"Wait, Ian," I called. "I need to tell you something else."

"At the station." He waved and disappeared inside.

I hurried to the front door. No one was in the foyer. Voices carried from the executive hall, but the uniform blocked me from joining them. At the end of the hall, Marshy argued with Ian. Petey stood behind him, next to Daddy. He leaned in his office doorway, his face pale and drawn.

My heart tightened. Had Petey told them about the missing footage? Were they protecting Nash?

"Absolutely not." Marshy had drawn himself up to face off with Ian. "Not without a warrant."

"This isn't an unreasonable request," said Ian. "I'm surprised you're not willing to work with us on this, Mr. Roth. It's a murder investigation."

"We're a privately held company, Detective Mowry. I have to answer to our investors. They'll want more justification than your suspicion that the victim had been at DeerNose. A lot of people visit our factory. We don't know what else you're going to want to see. I have to draw the line somewhere."

"I'm just asking to see your security footage. What's the big deal?" Ian smiled and rocked back on his heels. "I promise not to look for your secret DeerNose formula."

"I'm sure Ian Mowry isn't up to anything, Marshall," said Daddy.

Petey patted Daddy's arm. "Let us handle this."

"It's not a joking matter." Marshy widened his stance and jutted out his chin. "I'm asking you to leave."

"I won't have any problem getting a warrant." Ian pushed past Marshy. "Mr. Spayberry are you okay?"

"I'm okay," he grunted, then clutched the arm he'd wedged against the doorframe.

"Daddy," I cried.

Petey grabbed Daddy around his middle, preventing him from sliding to the floor. "I've got you, Boomer," she said. "I'm going to walk you backward. You need to sit down."

Ian barked at the uniform to call emergency services. I dashed around the cop but was grabbed from behind before reaching the door.

"Give them a minute, Maizie," said Marshy, wrapping his arms around me. "He needs to breathe. It's the stress."

"Please, let me do something."

"Call Carol Lynn." He released me. "They'll take him to the ER like last time. He'll be okay."

"Last time?" My voice cracked. "This has happened before?"

"Once." He hesitated. "It's not my place to talk about it. Maybe Carol Lynn can clue you in if Boomer won't."

My cheeks heated. How could I have been blind to the state of my father's health?

Marshy's eyes blazed. "We need to stop this disruption to our business. That's what's getting to him."

"Did Nash know about Daddy's health?"

"I don't know, but he could probably guess," he said gruffly. "Find Nash. If he wants to keep his job, he'd better be looking for the responsible party. And doing something about it."

FORTY-TWO

#NOMOREMISTERNICEGIRL #OFFLEASH

ONCE THE AMBULANCE had rushed Daddy to the emergency room, we dispersed. Marshy followed Carol Lynn to the hospital. Ian left to get his warrant. Petey stayed to cancel meetings. I wanted to be with my father at the hospital, but I had a more important mission.

Babysit Remi.

"This car is so nasty," she said, watching me fit her booster seat into the backseat. "I betcha I can drink juice in here and you won't be able to tell."

I hoped Annie would find a similar silver lining when she next saw the Impala.

"Where's your dog?" Remi hopped into her seat.

"At the dog sitter." I handed her a bag of toys and snacks. "We're picking him up."

And after getting Cuddles, we were Nash hunting. I had a new policy. No more Mister Nice Girlfriend. He'd not only ignored too many of my calls, he'd also ignored important DeerNose calls. DeerNose needed him. This was killing my father.

I hoped not literally.

On my way from DeerNose to the cabin, I'd left Nash a series of messages about Daddy's collapse. An annoying beep had cut off each jumbled message.

As I drove, I tried again. "Marshy wants you to stop whoever's attacking DeerNose. But as soon as they see what happened to the deleted video, the police are going to look for you. With the fire and now this with Daddy..." I stifled a moan. "Where are you? How can you leave at a time like this? I need you."

I paused. "No, I'm not doing that. I'm trying to stay positive, Nash. That's who I am. But it's getting harder and harder to see the cup as half-full when it's looking empty."

No time for tears, anger, or dark thoughts. I had a six-and-a-half-year-old and a 150-pound dog to take care of. I needed to maintain my composure. And with those two, I needed to stay sharp.

I made it on time to the Embry house. For once. Victoria even smiled. Elaine and Cuddles did not. But upon spotting Remi in the Impala's backseat, Cuddles brightened from his normal "leaving Elaine" gloom.

I pulled out of the Embry drive, ready to head back to Black Pine, and heard Remi rummaging through her bag.

"You didn't bring no makeup."

"Cuddles doesn't like makeup."

"He never told me that." She paused. "He sure likes juice boxes, though. And Goldfish."

I gave myself a mental head slap.

I checked in at Nash's usual haunts. Gilroy's Got It. The corner gas station. The True-Buy supermarket.

I ran out of places. Nash wasn't a haunter. He worked, then kicked back with Lamar and listened to the Braves. Or went on surveillance with me.

He didn't even have a regular lunch place. I had twelve.

I tried Rounds of Grounds, the Johnson house, and Deer-Nose. Evening's deepening gloom had overtaken twilight when we parked in front of the Dixie Kreme Donut Shop. We stared out at the burned remnants of the brick building lit by the streetlight. The roof and windows were gone. Brick charred. Sidewalk cordoned off with orange cones and yellow police tape.

Cuddles whimpered. I wanted to do the same.

"Wow," said Remi, climbing into the front seat. Cuddles followed her. They had a brief altercation over who would sit in my lap. Remi won.

I called Lamar. He also hadn't heard from Nash.

"I'm sorry to hear about Boomer," said Lamar. "Let me know how he's doing. Can Olivia send a casserole to the house?"

"You've got enough to worry about with the fire, but thank you. I'll let Carol Lynn know that you and Olivia are thinking of them."

I hung up and smoothed Remi's hair. "I need to find Nash. I think he's following someone, but I don't know who."

"That happens with Teeny and the other dogs all the time," said Remi. "Usually I whistle and they'll come running, but sometimes they can't hear me. Daddy says they're so focused on a scent, they can't get distracted. It's tunnel vision with their nose."

"That's pretty much how Lamar described it. Except a lot of important things have happened, and Nash still doesn't hear my call." I pinched my thumb. "It's okay for dogs, but not for partners. Or boyfriends."

"It ain't okay for dogs, neither. If they're too focused, they might miss something dangerous like a snake. I've seen them with their nose to the ground, sniffing right up to a deer and they don't even see it."

"Good for the deer."

"Don't you know nothing? A deer can kill a little dog. A buck will go for a dog with its antlers. Doe's kick something fierce. That's what happened to Matilda. A deer broke her ribs. She was a nice dog, too. Daddy said Tilly got too close to the baby. But Tilly didn't even see the baby. That's what I'm saying."

I bit my lip. I'd never compared Nash to a Jack Russell terrier —he'd always seemed more German Shepherd-ish—but maybe

I'd been thinking about his lack of communication in the wrong way. Maybe he was in danger.

Or worse.

"Okay, last place to check is his ex—" I caught myself. I didn't want to explain Nash's divorce to Remi. Who knew what she would do with the information? "I mean, Miss Jolene's."

"Who's Miss Jolene?"

"Someone he used to know."

"He don't know her anymore? Then why would he be at her house?"

"I don't know. Get buckled up," I said irritably. "You, too, Cuddles."

FORTY-THREE

#TOPDOG #UPTONOGOOD

JOLENE LIVED on Black Pine Mountain in Platinum Ridge, a neighborhood that had a security gate with an actual security guard. Not because Black Pine had a high crime rate. Nor because the upper-middle-class to lower-wealthy-types who lived in this neighborhood were paranoid about crime. As Tiffany and Rhonda attested, having a security guard was "bougie."

The guard house impressed Remi, anyway. Cuddles not so much. But Remi kept him from lunging at the guard, which was a point in favor of bringing her on my mini-investigation.

"I'm surprised he let us go in," said Remi, turning in her seat so she could watch the little guard box through the rear window. "We could be up to no good. It's nighttime."

"If we're up to no good, they have our license plate on file. They can find us."

"By the time they find us, we've already done the no good."

I eyed her in my rearview mirror. I didn't hang out with six-year-olds much, but I had a feeling Remi didn't run true to type.

After navigating the maze of streets in Platinum Ridge, I did a drive-by of Jolene's house. Platinum Ridge homes stood on two-acre wooded lots. Jolene's house perched in the middle of her plot. Ornamental lighting in her garden beds shone on the two-story mini-mansion. However, the interior appeared dark.

"How many people live in that house?" said Remi.

"Just Jolene, I think."

"That's too bad. That's a mighty fine yard to play in."

I peered down her long drive. The side of her house wasn't lit, but she'd parked something near her garage. My neck prickled and some small, mean organism clawed at my stomach walls.

At the end of the street, I took a right on Dogwood Circle and the next right on Magnolia Curve. I parked before reaching the cul-de-sac. "We're going to take a walk."

"At night?" said Remi.

Cuddles pawed his door. I grabbed his leash and opened Remi's door. Cuddles and Remi jockeyed for position and shoved their way out. We walked to the end of the cul-de-sac.

"There's a golf cart path that runs through this neighborhood." I pointed to the blacktopped path and sign. "It eventually connects to Black Pine Resort's golf course."

"Cool." Remi darted down the path.

Cuddles and I jogged to keep up with her. "Go straight," I called, hoping the path would cut through to Jolene's street. The confusing paths meandered. Thankfully, it dumped us out on Jolene's street. That wasn't the tricky part, though.

I stopped just past her drive. Cuddles flopped to the ground. Remi danced around him, urging Cuddles to get up. I took advantage of their inattention to study the garage. The landscape lighting left the parking area before the garage in deep shadow. I assumed Jolene had movement-activated security lighting on the garage. Even for his ex-wife, Nash would have made sure her home had good security features.

Something was parked near her garage. Possibly a truck. But maybe not.

Chewing my lip, I told myself I made my situation worse by suspecting the worse.

The worse being, of course, Nash ghosting me while he stayed with his ex-wife.

Okay, not the worst, worst. But that would be the nail in the relationship coffin.

"But come on," I muttered. "That's not Nash. He doesn't lie, and he loves you. He'd never abandon Lamar, anyway. Not after the Dixie Kreme fire. That's not his truck at the end of Jolene's driveway."

Remi stopped dancing. "What did you say?"

I squinted at Jolene's drive. "Do you want to play a game?"

"Yes, yes, yes." She started dancing again. "What's the game?"

"It's a race."

"Woo-hoo!" She vibrated with joy. "Where? What kind? What do I win?"

Cuddles yawned and rose to his feet.

"Not you," I said to him. "Just Remi."

"I've got to race against somebody," she whined.

"You are racing against..." I thought for a moment. "Time and space."

She stopped dancing to consider the possibilities.

"Do you remember what Mr. Nash's truck looks like?"

She nodded.

"I want you to race to the end of Miss Jolene's driveway and back. See if that's Mr. Nash's truck at the end of her drive. But you have to be really fast and careful. There are lights that will go on if they catch your movement."

"I'll be super fast." She bent over into something like a runner's stance, then straightened. "You didn't tell me what I win."

"Ice cream."

"Okay." She bent over again.

I counted to three and said, "Go."

She took off down the drive. The lights came on. She returned.

"I lost." Her lip trembled. "I was going so fast I didn't look at the truck."

"It's okay. Nobody can beat time and space." I high-fived her. "You got second place and still get ice cream."

"Yes," she cried, fist-pumping.

Cuddles woofed.

We moseyed back to the car and drove to the Dairy Swirl, while Remi rambled on about new plans to beat time and space. Everyone got a cone except me.

I was the loser.

Nash's truck was parked at the end of Jolene's driveway.

———

THE NEXT MORNING, Carol Lynn hustled Remi to school and took off for the hospital. I hustled Cuddles through his morning routine and into the Impala. But while we hustled, I forced my thoughts into a slow deliberation.

There was a lot of damning evidence against Nash. His disappearance. The deleting of the video surveillance. His time spent with Kristi, and—perhaps less important to the murder investigation, but a small (large) blow to my pride—his truck parked at Jolene's.

I still believed in innocent until proven guilty. If I could remain hopeful through all our adultery investigations that there was always a good explanation for our subject's vehicle to be parked at a hotel at noon on a Tuesday, I could believe Nash had a very good explanation as well.

However, I couldn't count on Nash's explanation anytime soon. Therefore, I'd have to put a stop to the corporate sabotage myself. Daddy needed my help. Derek needed it, too. We no longer had the video surveillance footage that put Kristi at Deer-Nose. Our testimony in the Johnson case wasn't enough. Ian needed more evidence to show that Kristi was doing something more than cheating, and to show CrossHair was involved.

I could get the evidence for Ian.

I wanted to speak to Dee Dixon. Woman to woman. Mercer to Spayberry. Hopefully without her holding a gun on me. But if all my suspicions about her and Simon were correct, they'd known all along who I was and had been playing me like the proverbial fiddle.

"But maybe," I said to Cuddles, "I could play them if they don't know that I know what they pretend like they don't know."

He cocked his head.

"You're right. No more Mister Nice Girl for Nash and for CrossHair. I'm going to do whatever it takes to get that evidence. Including some blurring of lines and fudging of details in visiting the Old Mercer Place."

Cuddles whined.

"Yeah, I'm not so great at the whole girl power thing." Blowing out a breath, I backpedaled. "Rhonda's clever thinking had gotten us into Simon's apartment. I need help from my girls."

Cuddles and I drove to the office, hoping to catch Rhonda and Tiffany and not Annie. I was in luck. No Jeep. I parked and noted a piece of paper taped over the Albright Security Solutions logo in the window. "Albright Security and Investigation Solutions" had been Sharpied on the paper. Legible. But the printing tilted sideways and "Solutions" had to be crowded onto the right edge in smaller letters.

Inside, I found Tiffany doing Rhonda's nails at the reception desk. Cuddles forgot to growl at them and plopped on the floor for a snooze.

"We changed our name?" I pointed to the window.

"I changed it." Rhonda leaned back in her chair and blew on her nails. "I don't like working at a place whose acronym refers to my backside."

"I do," said Tiffany.

"That's the main reason I changed it. I'm tired of Tiff cutting up every time I answer the phone. What's going on? Have you saved Derek yet?"

I didn't have the heart to tell her that my conversation with Ian probably made things worse for Derek. I told her about my dad instead. They hugged me and said they'd deliver casseroles.

"Carol Lynn cooks a lot. I don't think she needs casseroles."

"It's what you do when someone's sick. You still have a lot to learn about Black Pine," said Rhonda. "What's your next step?"

"Talk to Dee Dixon. I want to get to the bottom of this Mercer thing. Look at what CrossHair is doing to my dad. I've got to stop them. Whatever I can do to speed up the murder investigation is helpful, too."

"Don't you have suspicions Dee Dixon might have killed Kristi?" asked Tiffany. "Is this the smart thing to do?"

"When has Maizie done the smart thing?" said Rhonda. "All this sneaking around is not so smart."

"Hey," I said. "My job is sneaking around. Sneakier the better."

"You know what I mean."

"Talking to Dee Dixon may not be smart, but I'm trying to understand her motives. My theory is Kristi started as a secret shopper who wanted to prove herself to Simon. Maybe it wasn't Derek's idea, but Kristi's, to move to Georgia from California. I bet Kristi wanted to be closer to Simon. He let her stay in the apartment, not knowing she was married. Dee Dixon's got a double motive for killing Kristi. As Luella, not only was Kristi cheating with Simon, she was also a loose cannon. Kristi went off-script."

"What she had loose were screws. The more I learn about Kristi, the nuttier she sounds," said Tiffany. "Creating a fake identity and pretending she was some super spy."

"She was acting in her own drama," I agreed. "I think Kristi picked up the secret shopping job. Found it fun, wanted more, and created a role for herself when she struggled to get the parts she wanted. Posing as the subversive was probably exciting, too."

"Whatever. She was a cheater *and* a criminal," said Rhonda. "But now there's a motive to get poor Derek released."

"Unfortunately, not until we have evidence that Dee Dixon or Simon did this."

We quieted on that thought. My normally glass-half-full attitude had nosedived back into mostly-empty.

"Hang on a minute," I intoned. "If Simon and Dee didn't know who Kristi was, how did they know where her house was in Black Pine? Her body was found in Kristi Johnson's house, not Luella Haney's apartment."

"Is it possible that Dee Dixon figured out Luella was lying about her identity?" said Tiffany. "That could have triggered Dee toward murder."

"I like it," said Rhonda. "Do what you need to do, Maizie."

"You're willing for Maizie to risk her life?" said Tiffany. "You just said her sneaking around was stupid."

To be honest, I wasn't willing to risk my life for Derek. I wasn't brave or courageous. I just wanted to find the missing link. Then let the police take over. Nash would be free to get back to his normal security job. And we could get back to smoothing out our relationship. "I thought maybe you two would go with me. Like as backup."

Rhonda inspected her nails. Tiffany started clearing her manicure supplies.

"Hello?"

"Uh, yeah, so Annie has given us a lot of diligence paperwork," said Tiffany. "And skips. Tons of skips. We should get back to work."

"Do your thing and let us know what happens," said Rhonda. "Besides, you have backup."

"Nash can't help me. I can't find him. And Annie will never go for this."

"I was talking about Cuddles."

FORTY-FOUR

BEFORE REACHING THE SCENIC OVERLOOK, I turned off the highway onto the Mercer Place lane. At the gate, I got out and waved at the camera in the tree. Nothing happened, so I tried the gate and found it unlocked.

"If we're going to snoop, I don't want to leave the Impala here." I turned the car around and parked on one of several logging trails branching off the lane.

Cuddles' ears flicked back and forward as he trotted. He was in surveillance mode. I was, too, despite my ears being fixed in place. I didn't trust Dee Dixon, especially on her own turf. At the gate, I waved at the cameras again, then entered, closing the gate behind us. As we drew closer to the house, I scanned the windows. No movement that I could see. Wood smoke scented the air, but no plumes rose from the chimney.

Reaching the house, I called out again. Nobody ran onto the deck and threatened to shoot me. "If she's not at home, why didn't she lock the gate?"

Cuddles looked at me. He didn't know either.

In the garage area, I found Dee's car. "Maybe Simon took Dee for a spin."

Cuddles sniffed the air, snorted, and turned from the garage.

I agreed with him. The garage smelled like spilled gas. "We'll go up the deck stairs. Just in case someone's home."

I still wasn't sure if Dee Dixon had committed murder, but I felt she was guilty of something. Like sabotaging my father's life work. Trying to ruin a business that employed a lot of wonderful people. And causing my dad to have something that bordered on a heart attack. Maybe someone else had paid CrossHair to do these subversive acts. But after seeing Daddy's picture on the dartboard, I thought Dee Dixon's personal reasons more likely overrode financial.

My personal feelings about the holes in that picture overrode my fear of getting caught.

On the deck, Cuddles flopped to the floor. I peeked through the windows. The house was still. I knocked. Called out. And tried the deck door. The lever moved and the door opened.

"If an alarm goes off, we'll have to wait for the police and improv an explanation. The video would have caught us walking up the drive."

Cuddles nestled his head on his paws. I unclipped his lead and secured the gate to the stairs. "I'll only take a minute."

Inside, I glanced around the open living and dining area. Whereas the Black Pine elite would choose contemporary furnishings in this very modern-looking mountain dwelling, Dee Dixon had chosen antiques.

An open fireplace stood between the two rooms. No wood in the fire and the fire-irons were missing from their holder, but the house smelled smoky. Dee needed to clean her flue. I skipped past the kitchen. A door opened to the descending cement stairs. I got a whiff of oil and chemicals mixed with sooty outdoors. Moved down the hall. Bathroom and a bedroom that looked unused.

Framed photos of family and friends hung on the walls. No one looked particularly familiar, but everyone looked vaguely familiar. That was mountain life. I peeked through the dresser and closet but found nothing unusual.

I moved to the floating staircase. The wood smoke scent was stronger on the second floor. The landing had a balcony over the living room and a short hall with two closed doors. I opened the front-facing room.

The light from the wall of windows dazzled my eyes. Blinking, I realized this was Dee's office. Sewing tables. Dummies with pinned material. Rolls of fabric on metal shelves. I skimmed my hand over the spandex, knits, polyester, and bamboo. Many were camouflage. Some prints I recognized from the athletic wear at the Windmere apartment. An old wooden desk in a back corner held a laptop with password protection. Since I'd taken so well to hacking, I tried a few passwords. CrossHair123, IHate-DeerNose, CamoFashion.

Thought for a minute. Typed, "MercerTextile."

I was in.

Nothing mentioning CrossHair. I found fashion design software—Adobe Illustrated and Blue Cherry. Files of her Double-D-Design apparel. I was right. CrossHair had been partly created to market her brand.

Also, a folder labeled "Dad."

The Dad folder held files containing links to news articles about Mercer Textile. And DeerNose. And the fire that burned the cabin with Randy Mercer inside. I opened a PDF file labeled "Post-Mortem Autopsy Results" and read the first paragraph. Results indicated Randy Mercer suffered from blunt force trauma. Just like Kristi Johnson.

I shivered, feeling sick. Blew out a long breath and sat back, unable to read more of the autopsy.

Wait. Everyone at DeerNose had said Randy Mercer had committed suicide. Wasn't that in Rhonda and Tiffany's research, too?

I hopped on DuckDuckGo and did a quick search. The Gilmore Gazette had a news article about the fire. The coroner had called it a suicide. Self-inflicted gunshot after setting the fire. There'd been a letter left at Mercer Textile. The business was in foreclosure. He'd had to sell the land. The Gilmore house, too. His wife had left him and taken their fifteen-year-old daughter. Deanna Mercer.

I tried her name on in my head. *Deanna Dixon Mercer? Dee Mercer Dixon?* Was Dixon her married name? Mother's name? Middle name? A lot of Black Pine people used family names for middle and first names.

Why hadn't I thought of that sooner?

I went back to the autopsy report. Dated ten years ago. Not the original post-mortem.

Holy shiz. She'd had Randy Mercer dug up.

I'd bet anything Dee had suspected all along that her father hadn't committed suicide. The report said the autopsy found a "traumatic brain injury," indicated by a "skull fracture with possible related diffuse axonal injury" and "cerebral contusion of the frontal lobe." Analysis showed the TBI preceded a gunshot wound that *may have* disguised the initial cause of morbidity. The gunshot had gone out the back of the head, whereas the skull fracture was in the front.

The cost of the autopsy was outrageous. She'd paid by credit card.

I don't know how long I sat there with my hand covering my mouth when the sound of Cuddles' deep woofs snapped me out of it. I shut down the laptop and dashed to the picture window. No vehicles driving down the lane. Had a squirrel woken him? Or something else?

I ran out of the workspace. Cuddles' snarling and barking grew louder. I squatted before the balcony rails, trying to see onto the deck. Only the backs of the Adirondack chairs were in view. I darted down a few steps and peered out. Cuddles was around the corner, near the deck stairs. In between barks, I heard a voice.

Shizalicious. Were they back? Had I missed their car in the drive?

I hovered on the stairs and ran through old *Julia Pinkerton* scenarios. She'd been caught in an arcade after hours once. Looking for a clue left in a reprogrammed game by a genius gamer who'd gone missing. She'd had to play Dance Dance Revolution 89 times in a row to win the clue. While babysitting the gamer's brother. The little boy had wandered up to the arcade window and been spotted. For some unbelievable reason —even after playing Dance Dance Revolution 89 times—Julia and the kid ran away from the security guard.

Besides that ridiculousness, I'd found Julia completely irresponsible to take a ten-year-old to an arcade illegally and past bedtime. But the audience bought it.

However, the big difference between me and *Julia Pinkerton, Teen Detective*, Season 1 Episode 2: "Dance Monkey," was Cuddles. Simon would recognize him as my dog. There was no point in running.

Moreover, Julia Pinkerton was in better shape. Then and now. Editing was my saving grace in that episode.

I listened. No more voices. But hard to tell with Cuddles' berserk barking.

Wait. Upper-floor windows on the other side of the house.

The other room—a bedroom with more heavy furniture and rumpled bedclothes—smelled like nail polish remover. I darted to the window.

Still barking, Cuddles paced before the gate to the stairs. No Simon or Dee. Okay, must have been a squirrel. A little early in the day for raccoons. I blew out a breath. My nerves were jumping between the trespassing and the autopsy results.

OMG. Someone covered up Randy Mercer's death.

Holy frickalations. Dee Dixon was after my father's company because...

Because what? She thought my father had killed her father? That was ridiculous.

OMG. Maybe that's why Nash was trying to protect me. Except Daddy would never kill someone. Even in an accidental death, he'd never make it look like a suicide.

Or would he? Cover up a death that would destroy not just his reputation, but an entire company that a town depended on?

No way. Daddy believed in Liberty and Justice For All, Amen. If he'd unintentionally killed someone, he'd throw himself on the mercy of the court.

Except he had a daughter who was in the literal limelight. And an ex-wife, who would never let him see his daughter again at any hint of scandal.

OMG.

FORTY-FIVE

#SHIZTASTIC #DOGSICK

I COULDN'T IMAGINE SUCH a thing could be true. But the thought kept roaring in my head. Had Daddy accidentally killed Randy Mercer and covered it up?

Hold on. Catch your breath.

Daddy wouldn't have forged a suicide note. Made it look like Randy Mercer had shot himself. Or set a fire as a coverup. That's super evil. Daddy went to church regularly with Carol Lynn. He prayed. He believed in forgiveness and repentance.

But the thing he harped on the most (at least to me) was accountability.

Was an autopsy report conclusive? It had to be wrong.

The thought of my father doing something so vile made me sick.

Holy Shiz. Nash was trying to protect me from something awful. This was so much worse than Daddy having an affair with Kristi Johnson.

I clamped a hand to my mouth, leaned my forehead against the cool glass of the window, and closed my eyes. I needed to talk to Nash. He must know something about this. Where was he?

Cuddles' constant barking had changed from low-pitched

growling and snapping to a higher-pitched yelp. I opened my eyes, looked out the window, but couldn't see him. A wispy cloud drifted past the window. Then another.

Smoke? I sniffed. Was there a forest fire? Was the smoldering wood we'd smelled on our walk to the house coming from the timber?

Time to get out. All I needed was for fire trucks to trap me on the mountain lane. I moved away from the window. Halted. Something was weird. I glanced back. The camo-print bedspread looked like someone had tossed it on the bed in a heap. Although the furniture didn't match, Dee kept the house tidy. Weird, she hadn't made her bed. And a comforter balled up in the middle?

The smoky scent grew stronger. The billowing before the window grew thicker. Cuddles' barking grew louder.

Wouldn't I have noticed a forest fire on the walk up the drive?

Holy shiz.

"No," I whimpered. "No fire. No dead bodies. I'm still processing what Daddy might have done. I can't take any more."

My hand slapped over my mouth.

No getting sick either. Get it together, Albright.

I tiptoed toward the bed. Poked the cover. Didn't feel like a body. My hand fell from my mouth, and I blew out a long breath.

Thank God.

I pivoted. Cried out. And pressed the hand back over my mouth. The en-suite bathroom door stood partially open. A foot blocked it from shutting. A man's bare foot. Simon's foot.

"Simon," I called. "Are you okay?"

No response from Simon. Not even a moan.

I touched his foot with a finger. Grasped it with my hand and shook it. Tried to take a pulse from his ankle. Didn't work.

"No. No. No," I whined. "I have to get out of here. I can't go in there."

I sounded like Willie Scott's bug chamber sequence in *Indiana*

Jones and the Temple of Doom. Except I would rather take giant bugs crawling all over me than a dead Simon. Instead of Indy and Short Round yelling at me in the spiked chamber, I had Cuddles barking at me from the deck.

"Okay." I blew out three Ujjayi breaths. Pushed and pulled on the bathroom door.

Nothing happened. His body blocked the doorway.

"No, no, no." I danced before the door. I couldn't leave a body in the fire. What if Simon was still alive?

Fire. Duh.

I yanked my phone out of my pocket and dialed 9-1-1. Reported the fire. And the body. And my possibly trapped situation. Ignored the dispatcher's ask to stay on the line.

Dialed Nash. Reported the fire. Simon. My possibly trapped situation. That I now knew my father might have killed Randy Mercer. Told him that his silence had done nothing but made things worse. Then apologized for my tone and told him I loved him.

I didn't want anger to be the last thing he heard from me.

Just in case.

Dialed Ian. Repeated everything except the part about Daddy, Randy Mercer, and Nash's silence. But in case I died in the fire, I apologized for trespassing.

Tried to open the bathroom door one more time. Gave up. Ran toward the stairs. Then back into the workroom. Grabbed Dee's laptop. Tried running down the floating stairs. Slowed—because the last thing I needed was a broken leg—then dashed to the deck door.

Cuddles' smeared saliva covered the glass, blurring the dog, who scrabbled on two feet to get inside.

"I'm sorry. I'm sorry. I'm sorry." I yanked open the door and bent to grab his leash.

He dashed inside and zipped to the back of the house.

"No. Outside. Stop. Stay," I screamed and waved the leash. "No Cuddles."

Shiz. Frick. Craptastic.

I darted inside to find Cuddles. Changed my mind. Ran out to check on the fire. The deck stairs were ablaze. Flames climbed the wooden sides of the house.

Shiz. Frick. Craptastic. No wonder he hoofed it into the house.

No way could I carry the laptop and deal with Cuddles in his manic state. I was too manic to carry it. I ran to the far side of the deck. Spied the fire catching that side of the house. Bit my lip to keep from crying. Tossed the laptop toward the slope. Even if it busted, the police might get the evidence off it.

Zipped back inside, calling for Cuddles. Gave up momentarily to hunt for a fire extinguisher in the kitchen. Didn't people keep them under the sink? After twenty seconds of frenzied searching, I left the hope of the fire extinguisher—What was I going to do anyway? Put out a whole house fire with it? I was as bad as Derek Johnson—to find Cuddles.

My thoughts slid sideways and backward, tumbling over each other. I needed to focus. I'd wasted time on tossing out evidence instead of looking for an escape route. The smoke seeped through the cracks and ventilation.

Escape plan. Yeah, that's the ticket.

Now my thoughts sounded like John Lovitz. Why couldn't I focus?

The windows had to be over fifteen feet off the ground. The fire on the outside stairs had trapped us. My mind spun in circles. There had to be another way out. The back of the house was on fire. Soon the deck would catch. Where was the safest place to wait for the fire department? The fireplace? It was open on both sides. Didn't the writers have Julia Pinkerton hide in a bathtub to wait out a fire? Or was that for a tornado? Did we need to wet sheets and wrap ourselves in them? If we did, how would we move?

Why was I thinking about sheets?

Cuddles burst out of the back bedroom and ran into the

kitchen. I ran toward the kitchen. He bounded past me. Found him pawing a closed door in the hall.

"Stay," I said as calmly as I could. "Sit. Stay. Leash?"

He bared his teeth and pawed the door. Fingers of smoke crept through the sides of the door.

Duh. Back stairs to the garage.

Except in every TV show and movie I'd been in involving a fire, the cars blew up and took the building out with them. Earlier, we'd smelled gas down there. I didn't know if that was real, but I positively did not want to get blown up. What if the garage was on fire?

"Not there. See the smoke? Come on, let me put the leash on you. We'll figure this out."

I bent toward Cuddles to clip the leash. He snapped at me. I jerked my hand back.

"Please, Cuddles," I pleaded. "Let me put the leash on you."

Maybe the bathtub scene was during a hurricane? Earthquake? No, maybe that was *Kung Fu Kate* ... why couldn't I remember?

Wait. It's stop, drop, and roll.

No, that was from kindergarten.

Barking and whining, Cuddles reared on his back legs and scrabbled at the door with his front.

"No, Cuddles. There's smoke. See?" I pushed wet hair away from my face and realized I was crying. "We could blow up. You might not know it because you're a dog, but you don't want to get blown up."

He dropped to four paws and body-slammed the door.

"Would you please quit?" I begged.

He rammed the door again.

"Fine, I give up. But I'm praying for no 'told you so' moments."

I yanked open the door. Smoke enveloped us. Cuddles had disappeared. "Cuddles?" I choked on my scream and hacked on the exhale.

Heat rose from the stairway. Fire crackled below. Unable to see, I crouched, leaned, and touched the first step with my finger. Cement. Hot but not scorching. Yet. A wet nose touched my arm. A tongue bathed my face.

"You're a good dog," I croaked. "A really good dog. You found a way out. But we can't go down there. Her car is parked down there and the fire will—"

He'd disappeared.

"Noooo," I wailed. I sat to crab-walk down the stairs after him. Smoke enveloped me. I drew my T-shirt past my nose and clasped my hand over the shirt. My skin felt like it would blister without touching a flame. I bumped down on my butt, one slow step at a time. My toes touched the cement and inched forward. No more stairs. Dropped to my hands and knees, and crawled in the direction I hoped was the exit from the open garage. My hip bumped into a car. Crying out, I skittered away.

We had to get out. Keep moving. Where was Cuddles? I couldn't hear anything except for a dull roar inside my head and my choked breath. Smoke rolled past me. I followed the smoke. Continued to crawl. Wasn't that what you were supposed to do? Heat rises.

Did I hear sirens? Or was that my imagination?

My hands touched gravel and dirt. I was out of the garage but still under the house. The blaze crescendoed above me. I made a sharp left. The loose rock scraped my knees and hands. I couldn't stay balanced. The rocks hurt my knees too much. I rose to a squat. Didn't have the stamina to squat-walk. Dropped my hands into a familiar yoga move, Down Dog. Coughing and hacking, I walked the Down Dog with my knees bent and my head down. When the gravel turned to grass, I pushed myself to get as far from the house as I could. Stumbled a few more steps and collapsed.

My lungs felt scorched. My eyes stung and watered. My muscles ached. I might have had a nosebleed. The gravel had ruined my manicure, not to mention my palms burned and my knees hurt like a house on fire.

Why had that phrase popped into my head at a time like this?

A tongue bathed my roasted face. "Cuddles," I croaked, leaving my eyes closed. "What a good dog. You made it. I'm so happy."

I felt him rise. A low, deep growl shook him. His collar jingled.

"'S'okay," I mumbled. "It's probably the fire department. S'all good."

His growling turned to raspy woofs. I tried to calm him. Coughing wracked me, twisting my lungs and burning my throat. I couldn't muster the energy. The firemen would have to handle Cuddles.

A crack like a gunshot rent the air. The fire thundered. Cuddles took off. Where were the firemen? Soot glued my eyes shut. My head weighed sixteen tons. Surely the fire crew would find me.

Someone was here. I could feel them nearby. With my eyes closed, I focused on sipping the air, trying not to cough. Lifted my head a few inches.

"Hello?" I wheezed.

Something slammed into the back of my head. My ears rang and colors exploded behind my eyelids.

FORTY-SIX

MY FIRST THOUGHT WAS CUDDLES. The second was Nash.

And oh, holy cannolis, Daddy.

It all came roaring back—Dee Dixon making Daddy pay for Randy Mercer's death. Simon in the bathroom. The fire.

My lungs burned. Throat hurt. Stomach ached. And my head was killing me.

I opened my eyes, expecting to see the blazing Old Mercer Place. But no, I was in a dimly lit hospital room. A machine blinked and hummed next to me. I had an IV in my arm and something on my finger. I yanked the oxygen mask off my face and jerked up to sitting.

My head throbbed. The room reeled. Nausea rose. Hearing movement next to me, I gingerly shifted toward the shadows.

"Nash?" I said, my voice rusty but hopeful.

"No, hon,' just me." Ian moved from a chair in the corner to the side of my bed. His warm brown eyes were full of concern. "How are you feeling? You're going to be just fine. Got a big knot on your head. Minor cuts and abrasions. They treated you for smoke inhalation."

I held up my bandaged hands. "Burns?"

"Thank the Lord, no. Other than you look like you've been to Panama City and forgot to put on sunscreen. Your hands were pretty scraped up, though." Ian's voice turned upbeat. "Annie and the girls have been by. They all wanted to stay in the ER waiting room, but I convinced them to go on home. The doctor's just keeping you for observation tonight because of the smoke and concussion. The night nurse told me you were pretty lucky. Your lungs are strong."

I nodded, fighting nausea. "Of all my teenage vices, I didn't pick up smoking. Too afraid of the damage to my skin and teeth. That's how vain I was." Ironically, I sounded like the chain-smoking ghost counselor from *Beetlejuice*. I felt like I, too, could exhale smoke from my neck.

"Ah, shoot." Ian shifted in place, looking uncomfortable. "That's nothing."

"How long have I been in here?" I rasped, stumbling over my words to get out the most pertinent questions. "What happened? Did you find Dee Dixon? How's Daddy? Where's Cuddles? Is he okay? Did he need to go to the vet? Has anyone found N—"

The last question died on my lips. If they had found Nash, he'd be here. I stared at my hands and talked myself out of crying. "Did they find any…" I blew out a breath. "Any bodies, other than Simon, in the house?"

"One question at a time." Ian handed me a glass of water. "To answer the last first, the answer is no. I went straight to the hospital but sent a couple of officers to the fire. They reported the Little Gap fire crew found you and rushed you here. We're in Gilmore. Closest hospital. That was early this afternoon. It's around ten at night now. You had a pretty fierce concussion. Weren't making sense. But you seem to be okay now. That'll please the nurses."

I touched the back of my head and felt gauze and tape. "My hair?"

He grimaced. "They had to shave some of it to stitch you up."

"Told you I was vain." I drank and handed him the empty cup. "What happened?"

"You don't remember?"

"The last thing I remember was crawling away from the house. Cuddles was with me. I thought the fire crew had arrived. And then…" I closed my eyes, wincing at the void that appeared between then and now. "I don't know. Did the firemen find Simon? I think he was … could they save him?"

Ian shook his head. "Got him out. Didn't find anyone else. Do you remember seeing anyone else there?" He let out a long breath and scooted his chair closer to the bed. "The firemen found a fire iron in the bedroom. Simon's body is with the medical examiner, but the officers on the scene are confident that's what did him in. Blow to the back of the head with the poker."

I touched the bandage on my head again. "You think this was —" I squeezed my eyes shut and opened them. "Someone tried to kill me?"

"Not with the iron. My officer said there was a chunk of wood nearby. Probably that. Except…" His eyes had hardened, but he blinked his anger away. He clasped his warm hands around mine. "My guys assisted the county deputies in combing the area. They found shell casings not far from you. One bullet was embedded in a tree directly beyond where you lay. Low to the ground."

"Dee Dixon," I murmured. "She must have shot at me. But how did she miss? I was lying on the ground. Even I'm not that bad of a shot."

"Yeah, I thought so, too. Bullet was low," his speech slowed, "but didn't hit the ground."

"Cuddles." I whimpered. "No. She didn't … Did she? Oh my God. Just tell me."

"I don't think she shot him, but they couldn't find him. My guess is she shot at him, and he took off."

"He's not scared of guns. Unless maybe if someone was shooting at him." My lip trembled. "I hope he got away."

"Oh, hon." Ian squeezed my hand. "He'll turn up. We would have found him otherwise. The deputies searched the woods and they're keeping someone on the scene. We'll put an APB out for him. They also discovered a torn scrap of fabric nearby with blood on it. Said it wasn't yours," continued Ian. "You remember anyone wearing dark gray camouflage? Kind of stretchy?"

"I don't think so."

"Cuddles might have attacked the culprit. There were punctures in the cloth that look like teeth marks."

"I hope he took a chunk of her, Ian. Dee Dixon's unhinged. Did you find the laptop?"

"In the house?"

"In the yard. I threw it off the deck so the police could find it."

He shook his head.

"Dee must have been there the whole time. She killed Simon and was preparing to torch the house while I was there. I smelled smoke but didn't see anything. I thought it came from a campfire or a nearby cabin. Cuddles and I also smelled gas in the garage. We must have interrupted her. As soon as I went inside, she really lit it up. Torched the deck stairs so we couldn't escape."

"But you did escape."

"Cuddles led me down the garage stairs. I thought the car might blow…" I rubbed my neck beneath the bandage. "I don't know why she killed Simon. Because of Kristi? Maybe Dee was jealous. Or to cover her tracks for something else? I don't understand her motives. I remember them talking about Luella. About her going overboard…"

I squinted, trying to remember that initial conversation between Simon and Dee, but it made my head ache. "I wish I could understand the relationship between the three of them."

"We'll find Dee Dixon. We'll find her and if she did this, we'll put her away. Don't fret. Just focus on healing."

"You need to protect Daddy, Ian." I explained Randy Mercer's autopsy results I'd found on the computer. "I think Dee believes Daddy had something to do with Randy Mercer's death. All this sabotage is a revenge plot. That's got to be what's going on. Why Nash has been protecting me from what he's found."

"Nash." Ian drew back, leaving my hand cold. "We got the warrant for DeerNose. I returned this morning. Nash deleted the security videos the day you said Kristi was at DeerNose."

"There must be an explanation for that. At least now we know why he was tracking Kristi."

Ian gave me a pained look. "We don't know yet. You have a suspicion."

"A reasonable suspicion. Is anyone looking for Nash besides me and Lamar?"

"We've got feelers out, of course. We want him for questioning. He may have been the last person to see Kristi alive. We want to know about his relationship with her."

"Aside from that, Ian," I tempered my rising voice but lost it to coughing. "If Dee Dixon knew Nash was investigating Kristi, he's in danger. He must have figured this out from another angle, but—"

"When was the last time you talked to Nash?"

I squeezed my eyes shut. Not that I didn't know the answer. "A couple of days ago."

"Before the fire at the Dixie Kreme shop?"

I nodded and opened my eyes. "Lamar thinks he's hyper-focused on the investigation. I get it—at least, I sort of get it—now that I've learned what happened to Randy Mercer. Maybe he's hunting for Dee Dixon himself, or—"

"Maizie, if Nash cared that much about your dad, he would have been at the hospital yesterday. Hell, he'd be here now, not me."

"It's just … I'm trying not to dwell on this, but I'm afraid for him. I found his truck at Jolene's, but—"

"You what?" Ian straightened.

"I'm sure there's a good explanation," I said primly. "I was going to say, even though I found his truck at Jolene's, I think he went off the grid because he knew someone was tampering with his computer. Maybe it was Kristi who deleted that video after she snuck into DeerNose. He went into stealth mode so Dee couldn't track him. That's why he left the truck at Jolene's. Probably borrowed a car—"

Ian's look stopped my words.

"Or Dee caught him and is holding him hostage. Or one of her minions. There was a list I found. There are more CrossHairs than Kristi Johnson."

He gave me another look. I didn't blame him. My first theory sounded like a *Julia Pinkerton* plot, but this one was more like *Kung Fu Kate*.

Kung Fu Kate's target audience was eight to twelve-year-olds.

"Or he's hurt or worse," I said pitifully.

"Hon', just…" Ian sighed. "Just worry about yourself for now. Heal up."

"We need to pursue this, Ian," I persisted. "Dee must have taken the laptop. Listen, I can't remember who did the autopsy, but they buried Randy Mercer around here. He's from this area. There can't be that many businesses that dig up bodies for autopsies. You could get a warrant for the autopsy results and—"

"I'll look into it." He rose from the bed and walked back to the chair. "You should sleep now. I'm going to stay here tonight. If it makes you more comfortable, I can sit outside your room. In the morning, a Gilmore officer will take over until you leave."

"Why?"

"Isn't it obvious? Someone just tried to kill you. They probably would have succeeded if the first responders hadn't arrived when they did." Ian blew out a long breath. "More than likely, they'll try again."

FORTY-SEVEN

AFTER A FITFUL, weird night—bad enough trying to sleep in a hospital, but try sleeping with a police detective in the same room—I had a plan. As soon as Ian left, I called Tiffany and Rhonda to explain the situation. Then buzzed the nurse. I crossed my fingers and let out a sigh of relief when a young woman in scrubs entered the room.

"I wonder if you could help me," I said. "I don't know if you know me. I'm Maizie Albright. I was an actress."

She brightened. "I thought you looked familiar. It's hard to tell with your hair looking the way it does."

I patted my hair and fought off a grimace. "Unfortunately, I was in a house fire yesterday. You'll probably hear about it on the news. A chunk of wood hit my head and gave me a concussion. But I'm feeling much better now."

"Let me check you out."

While she took my vitals, I carried on with a patter about the shows I'd been on and which she'd seen. Name-dropped a few actors. Watched for her eyes to light up before tossing a few juicy (only positive) details about their personal lives to warm her more. By the time she'd removed the IV from my arm, the conversation flowed.

"It's so embarrassing." I leaned forward so she could listen to my lungs again. "To have police here when I don't even use a personal bodyguard? But with the news crew following the fire, they were worried paparazzi would show up at the hospital and cause a fuss. Isn't that ridiculous?"

"Oh, that's why they're here? I wondered. Nobody said anything."

"I know," I exclaimed. "It's so annoying. The detective here last night is a friend. But because he's a cop, he's overprotective, you know? He has a real thing about personal privacy. I mean, the press used to be a problem. Especially when I first moved back; they wouldn't leave me alone. But now, not so much. Like, I'm not worried, so why should he be?"

"Right?" she said. "I haven't seen one photographer since I started my shift. What are they worried about?"

"Exactly. I just want to leave so I can go home. I'm dying to take a shower and suds off this funk. I keep smelling the smoke from the fire."

"You poor thing," she said. "You can shower here while you wait for the doctor to discharge you."

"What a great idea. It's too bad the fire completely ruined my clothes. If there are any paparazzi lurking about, I bet they'll love seeing me walk out in half-burned, soot-stained clothes. Ugh. Or a hospital gown? With my luck, they'll get a tushie shot."

"Would you like something else to put on? We have extra scrubs. Not very glamorous, but…"

"Oh my gosh, that would be perfect," I exclaimed. "Genius. Maybe I can put on a mask and they'll think I'm a nurse. That would be so awesome. I can go home without having to speak to anyone. I'll have the scrubs dry-cleaned and bring them back in a few days. Thank you so much."

I felt a little bad about manipulating Nurse Nightingale. But as they say, no harm, no foul.

A shower and change into scrubs later, I was told to wait for the discharge papers to come with the doctor's last check. Finally, the door opened. The doctor entered with his small entourage. Just as the door closed, a loud noise erupted from the hallway.

A noise sounding a lot like an overturned cart and a dropped vase of flowers. I slipped on a mask and followed the doctor out the door. A nurse was reprimanding a masked woman in scrubs. A visitor, also wearing a mask, squatted near the spilled vase.

The police officer watching the scene didn't seem to notice me walk toward the nurse's station, hook a left down a hallway, and hustle toward the stairs.

I hunkered in the back seat of Tiffany's Firebird until Rhonda and Tiffany climbed in.

"That was fun," said Tiffany. "I love that kind of stuff."

"I didn't like getting yelled at," said Rhonda. "I felt bad about the vase of flowers."

"It worked. We busted Maizie out without the cop even noticing."

"Girl," said Rhonda. "We're going to need to do something with your hair. That chick really messed you up. You look terrible."

I rubbed my neck below where they'd stitched the wound. I'd hoped showering might have helped. Guess not.

"You look sunburned and pale at the same time," said Tiffany. "Those dark circles aren't doing anything for you either. Maybe it's the scrubs."

"That shade of pink is not her color," agreed Rhonda.

"I'll worry about that later," I said. "I need the Impala. I have a very bad feeling. I don't think Ian quite understood the implications of finding that autopsy result. He said he's going to look into it, but they're focused on capturing Dee Dixon to question her about Simon's death."

"Is Derek off the hook?" said Rhonda.

"Not until they have evidence that someone else killed Kristi."

Nash wasn't off the hook yet, either. I didn't think he was a suspect, but Ian certainly thought he was acting suspiciously.

———

BEFORE TURNING on to the logging trail to retrieve the Impala, Tiffany drove up to the gates of the Old Mercer Place. Smoke billowed in the distance. The gate had been closed and festooned with police tape. Around the gate, the ground was churned up.

"Wow," said Rhonda. "You really know how to make an exit. I didn't think Dee Dixon would have tried to burn you up in her own house. I thought she'd just shoot you."

"I thought Cuddles would have eaten her," said Tiffany. "Guess we were wrong."

"It's okay. Just a little attempted murder." I slumped back in my seat.

I'd been hoping to see a gigantic dog with a chocolate muzzle napping behind the gate, waiting for me. Instead, a fire service truck with big knobby tires had parked on the other side of the gate. The volunteer fire fighter ambled forward to greet us. Tiffany leaned out the window and handed him an A.S.S. business card. I leaned out the window to show him my best picture of Cuddles and told him about the missing dog.

"I'm keeping an eye on the place," he drawled. "Working in shifts. Fire's pretty much out, but better safe'n sorry, ya know. The police think the owner may return, too."

"She's very dangerous," I said. "Please be careful."

He gave me a look that said he'd dealt with his fair share of dangerous women. For his sake, I hoped that was true.

"As for this here dog, I haven't seen nothing." The fireman studied the photo on my phone. "He's biggun?"

"Massive," said Rhonda. "You might mistake him for a bear."

"That right?" He straightened from his lean on the Firebird

and squinted into the distance. "Haven't heard no barking either. Might take a walk 'round the perimeter."

"He'll seem vicious. But he's really a scared teddy bear." I wiped away a tear. "Although I wouldn't get too close. You could lure him into your truck with food. But he might destroy your truck. Not on purpose. He's not very careful with his slobber, and he chews when he's bored."

Tiffany turned the car around and found the logging road before the highway turnoff. Emergency vehicle traffic had also churned the rutted dirt trail. We found the Impala splattered with dirt, covered in leaves, and stickered by Little Gap Sheriff's Department.

"Now the outside matches the inside," said Tiffany.

I dug in my backpack for the keys and pulled out another key chain. "Why do I have this? These are Nash's keys."

"Is that Roger Rabbit?" said Tiffany. "I wouldn't take Nash for a keychain guy. Especially a plastic toy keychain guy."

"I gave it to him as a joke. To match the Jessica Rabbit tattoo on his back."

"Who are Roger and Jessica Rabbit?" asked Rhonda. "Is that one of those Disney shows you have to pay to watch?"

"They're from a movie from the eighties," I murmured. My mind had wandered from the Jessica Rabbit tattoo and beyond for a few seconds. I brought myself back to earth. "You're right. He's not a keychain guy. They're an extra set."

"You okay?" said Rhonda. "Bad reminder on a lot of counts there."

"Nash must have slipped them in." I looked at the girls. "But I don't know when."

They nodded, studying me with sympathetic expressions.

"When I gave him the keychain, he told me Roger was his extra set. The set he'd give to me when I needed to use his truck."

Rhonda reached to pat my shoulder. "You're going to be okay, Maizie."

"I don't think you're getting it," my voice rose. "Nash planted this in my backpack on purpose. I just don't know when. It's a sign. Nash wants me to get his truck." I studied them. "I can tell you're not following my logic."

"Is it logic? Ow—" Tiffany shot Rhonda a dark look. "What was that for? You're thinking the same thing. That keychain could have been in her bag for—Ow. Stop jabbing me with your finger. Those acrylics are sharp."

"Tiff don't mean to be unsympathetic," said Rhonda. "She's just..."

"Yeah, I know. Keeping it real." I climbed out of the Firebird, trying not to feel dejected, and bloop-beeped the Impala's key fob.

"We'll follow you out, then head to the office," said Rhonda. "If the cops won't do their job, I'll look for Randy Mercer's autopsy myself."

"We'll monitor the police radio for you, too. Let you know if we hear of any Dee Dixon sightings," said Tiffany over Rhonda's shoulder. "Cuddles sightings, too."

I turned and smiled. "That's really sweet. It's the weekend."

"We know losing Cuddles is a low blow for you," said Tiffany. "Nash, too. Listen, don't read too much into a keychain —Ow." She glowered at Rhonda.

Rhonda shot Tiffany a hard look. "We believe in you, Maizie. We don't think you'll end up in rehab again over this. Don't worry."

———

BEFORE LEAVING THE MOUNTAIN, I'd called Victoria, who said she'd organize the lost dog effort. And made it clear where the fault lay in his missing status. But I was more upset about Cuddles than how the Embrees felt about me. On the way back to Black Pine, my brain ping-ponged between not-so-helpful scenarios. Tiffany had been right about the Roger

Rabbit keychain, too. I wanted to read more into it than I should.

Ian texted, asking to talk. I parked at a gas station and gazed at my splotchy face in the visor mirror.

A few rebellious tears squeezed out. I wiped them off and pinched the skin between my thumb and pointer finger until I gasped. Narrowed my eyes, lowered my head, and looked up at the mirror again.

"Stop being such a wuss," I said in Julia Pinkerton's snarky voice. "Derek Johnson is sitting in jail. Nash is missing. Your dad's one step away from a heart attack. And Dee Dixon is literally getting away with murder. 'You might be wearing a cheer skirt, but slip on some big girl panties underneath that spandex and get on with it.'"

That was a line that always took a few takes. Hard not to giggle with that writing. Today I recited it deadpan. It worked.

I should've done it sooner. Like a week ago.

I picked up the phone and called Ian.

"We got a lead on Simon Craig's BMW," said Ian. "A patrol car found it at Windmere Apartments in Gilmore. Gilmore police are following up, but I'm headed there, too."

I shuddered. "Thanks for letting me know. I hope you're able to bring her in safely."

"Me, too." He paused. "You didn't need to sneak out of the hospital like that. Just talk to me, hon."

"Would you have let me leave to find Cuddles?"

"I would have taken you to find Cuddles." He sighed. "To be honest, I probably would have argued that you should take it easy, and I should go looking for Cuddles."

"What about Nash? Would you have let me leave to find him?"

"Maizie, he's a person of interest in my homicide."

"He's also your friend."

"He's not been very friendly lately."

I let that one pass.

"I've got to do my job," he continued. "Part of that job is protecting you."

An uncomfortable silence grew between us. At least, uncomfortable for me. I felt more than a little flummoxed.

Ian cleared his throat. "Okay, that didn't come out the way I intended. You're an assault victim in a crime related to my homicide investigation. I have a reasonable suspicion that the perpetrator might attack you again. If you continue your investigation, that is."

"My investigation..." My investigation had changed to taking over Nash's investigation. But I shouldn't tell Ian that. "My main focus right now is finding Nash."

"I get it. I really do. If you find him, call me."

"And you do the same," I said in a tone meant to hurry the conversation along.

"Here's the thing," Ian's voice remained firm, although it rang with apology. I imagined his face stern, but cafe latte-brown eyes gentle. "I'm really struggling here, Maizie. As a cop, I don't like this. Not one bit. There's a suspect at large. We're looking at two homicides, possibly related. Several arsons. Assault, likely aggravated assault in your case. It's possible Derek Johnson killed his wife and set fire to his house, and we've got a copycat. Or he didn't, and we've got one perp who's done all the above. Either way, this person is extremely dangerous."

"Understood."

"I'm not finished. Until we get the suspect in custody and have evidence showing they are the perpetrator of these crimes, you're not safe. These are heinous felonies. We just don't see this kind of crime in Black Pine. It's not even gang activity or some kind of trafficking. Or at least it doesn't appear that way. Dee Dixon is the strongest suspect. You've gotten in the perp's way. Maybe they think you know too much. Or they resent your interference."

Or they hate my family, I thought, but didn't say.

"Could be the wrong time and place," continued Ian. "Whatever the case, I don't like your nosing around. Looking for Nash is nosing around."

"I'll be careful. But Ian, you know I've got to look for him."

"Do you, Maizie? Wyatt Nash is a grown man. He's not lost. It's not like he was hiking and fell into a ravine. If he's also hunting for this perp like you think he is, you would have caught wind of him. You know this."

"I know where his truck is. He swapped vehicles. Nash is really good at not getting burned in surveillance."

"I hope that's true. I'm warning you, though, if he's cut you off like this for an investigation, I'll deck him. Really clock him. I'm not kidding."

"Oh, Ian—"

"Forget it. Just listen Maizie," Ian interrupted, then blew out a long breath. "I'm going to say something to you that might hurt our friendship. I'm going to do it as your friend, not as a cop."

"I know what you're going to say."

"What am I going to say?" he said bitterly.

"The Dixie Kreme fire. We haven't heard from Nash since before the Dixie Kreme fire. The fire started upstairs, in his office, not in the kitchen, didn't it? I can tell by the damage."

Ian's silence confirmed my theory.

"You don't want me looking for Nash because you think Nash isn't missing. Or at least not missing in the sense that you think I believe. You were going to say, Nash might..." I gulped. "What if Nash is..." My voice broke, but I forced myself to continue.

"You don't want me looking for him because of what I might find. Wyatt Nash might be dead. That's what you want to say and you can't."

FORTY-EIGHT

#BIGGIRLPANTIES #DOGINTHEMANGER

IF DEE DIXON was hiding out at the Windmere apartment—kind of dumb but criminals have done dumber—I was safe enough heading back to Black Pine. I had two missions. Find Nash. And find evidence CrossHair was behind the DeerNose espionage. And find evidence that Dee Dixon was a *Kill Bill*-styled homicidal maniac who thought she was *The Equalizer*.

Okay, three missions. No, four. The fourth was Cuddles, but Victoria explicitly told me to leave her and Elaine to it.

I couldn't even be trusted to find a dog.

I also needed to check on Daddy. After changing out of Nurse Nightingale's scrubs, I found him fishing on his dock, a short walk from the cabin. Before the economic boon to Black Pine, he'd slowly bought up the area around his family land. Now he held prime real estate along Black Pine Lake with a view of Black Pine mountain.

I hoped it wasn't at the cost of Randy Mercer and his family.

"Weren't you supposed to be resting?" I said to him.

"Can't think of anything more restful than fishing." His normally twinkling blue eyes appeared dull. "I don't want you worrying about me. I'm fine. Or at least, I'll be fine. Those are the doctor's words, not mine."

"I'm sure the doctor had some advice on how you'll get to 'fine.'"

"That's why I'm fishing instead of working on new designs," he said grumpily. "Carol Lynn's packing us up to force me on a vacation. Why go away when I've got all this?"

I looked out at the lake instead of at him. "Paradise comes at a cost, I suppose."

"And what about you? Are you fine? You're the one who spent the night in the hospital."

"I have a headache, a skinned knee, and some abrasions on my palms." I patted my hair near the spot where they'd shaved and stitched my skull. My ponytail hid it. Mostly. "They kept me for observation because of the smoke and concussion. But I got out before the fire really got bad."

"You look a sight, but I'm glad you're okay, baby girl." He tugged my hand, forcing my eyes on his. "You had me worried. Detective Mowry said you were in Little Gap. A client's house. Was everyone okay?"

"More like a suspect and not really," I said carefully. "Have you been to Little Gap?"

He leaned back in his chair. "Oh, sure. I like that route up to Carolina. We took Remi to the Overlook once. Won't do that again. She thought she could try life as a goat."

Hints wouldn't be enough to get him to talk, but I didn't know if I had it in me to sling accusations at my father. More than anything, I wanted him safe and healthy. When Carol Lynn had pointed out where Daddy was "resting," the anxious look replacing her normally peaceful expression told me to slow my roll.

I sank onto the dock. Rested my back against his knees and dangled my feet over the dock. He placed a hand on the crown of my head and smoothed my hair.

"I wish you had told me about your problems at DeerNose."

"Didn't know too much about the problems until lately," he said. "I showed you my samples. In the operations meetings, they discussed some logistical issues and quality control problems. Marshall reckoned interference by a competitor. I figured he was overzealous in his suspicions. He gets that way, you know. He told me not to worry, that he'd handle it."

"When did these health problems start?"

"Hypertension runs in our genetics, baby girl." He squeezed my shoulder. "Don't start going on about diet and exercise. I don't just eat deer and other game meat because I enjoy hunting. It's lean meat. Heart healthy."

"So what happened?"

"I don't handle stress well." He sighed. "According to my doctor, my body doesn't. When I was younger, I'd go hunting or fishing to occupy my mind on something other than my worries. Chopping wood, tending fences, and the like, was good, too. Carol Lynn got me to church more. Serving the community's helped. But as the company grew, I have less time for the stress-relievers. And more stress."

I wondered about past stressors that contributed to his decline. Old regrets. Past sins. Was guilt haunting him and wreaking havoc on his body?

I bowed my head, hating myself. While we sat there, my thoughts roiled and bubbled, making my neck burn and my stomach clench. This terrible secret had to be what Nash wanted to keep from me.

Might have lost his life to keep me from learning this horrible truth.

A tear trickled down my face. I couldn't believe the worst. But to find him, I'd had to know more about what really happened twenty years ago.

Was it worth it? I'd played with fire, trying to learn Nash's secret. It might have cost me my relationship or worse. Did I want to do this to my father in his precarious state?

"Daddy, tell me about Randy Mercer," I heard myself saying.

"Randy?" he said and gasped.

I spun around. His line had gone taut. The pole arced and shook in his hand. Keeping a firm grip on the pole, he pushed out of his chair and jerked the line.

"Feels like a big'un. Kind of surprised me, this time of day." He cranked the reel. "Come on. Stay with me."

"Daddy, Randy Mercer?"

"Hang on, honey. Got to reel this baby in."

I watched him for a few minutes, then trudged back to the house. I wasn't up to fishing with Daddy. Not yet anyway. If I had to hook him, it would hurt both of us and my heart felt too heavy as it was.

———

I MOVED on with my missions. I could root around DeerNose for more clues to Nash's disappearance, but I had one lead on Nash that I'd been avoiding.

Even on a Saturday, I knew Jolene wouldn't be home. As a real estate agent, she'd be hustling for clients with similar tastes in mini-mansions. Her office was not in the old downtown, like Dixie Kreme Donuts and A.S.S. She worked in a trendier area of shops built with stacked stone, glass, and timber.

The moment Jolene met me—approximately six seconds after my move back to Black Pine—I knew she hated me. It happens. Sometimes women clash. We're both curvy gingers. Didn't help that when I met her, I was auditioning for the role of apprentice PI at Nash Security Solutions. She'd divorced Nash—mainly (from what I could tell) because his income and attention didn't meet her expectations—but she also didn't want to let him go.

I'd pegged Jolene's type, having known a handful like her in California. By this time, the fear and loathing were mutual.

Knowing Jolene could be showing houses, I called ahead to make an appointment. Knowing she wouldn't see me, I gave the receptionist a fake name—Nora Charles. *The Thin Man* reference would be lost on Jolene. I didn't bother with a disguise, but summoned up Nora's witty repartee for the job instead.

Getting into character would help me avoid all the feels. It wouldn't do to cry over Nash in front of Jolene. Jolene would love to see me cry. She'd take it as a triumph. She already held the ball in this game—Nash's truck in her drive.

But I had his keys. Which was another ball.

Or was it? I wasn't great at sports analogies.

Before stopping in reception, I slipped into a bathroom. At the cabin, I'd changed into an older pair of Free People jeans with an even older AC/DC concert t-shirt I'd once borrowed (taken) from Nash. Hopefully, Jolene wouldn't recognize it. I tucked the front of the t-shirt into my jeans. Ran a wet paper towel over my Doc Martens for a quick polish. Shook my hair out, moved a lock over my bald spot, and smoothed it back into a high ponytail. Good enough. Nora Charles would have worn a jaunty little hat and suit, but I also didn't have time to pluck my eyebrows pencil-thin, either.

After giving my name at the desk to the unsuspecting receptionist, Jolene appeared in the hall. Spotted me. Screwed up her face in a snarl and stalked back to her office. I smiled at the receptionist and hurried after Jolene.

Before opening Jolene's office door, I pictured Nash as Nick Charles, holding a martini in one hand and a gun in the other. "Keep the gun, darling," I whispered. "But I'm going to want that drink when I'm finished."

Nash drank beer, not martinis, so he'd oblige. Also, he was imaginary, so no problem.

I opened the door and swept inside, stopping before Jolene's desk. Doing the Myrna Loy sweep wasn't easy in lug soles.

She scowled up at me. "What do you want? I came back to the office for this fake appointment. I'm busy. And ticked off."

"I'm not here on a social call," I said, using Myrna Loy's lilt, and raised my chin. "Nash is missing. All I need is information."

Jolene rolled her eyes. "He's on a case. Get used to it. With a man like Wyatt Nash, you can't be so smothering."

"Jolene, dear," I said, getting into Nora Charles's brisk rhythm. A tinny jazz melody played in my head. "With a man like Nash, I'm the one at risk of being smothered."

That didn't sound right, so I hurried on. "We're working the same case from different ends, see? Nash disappeared after the fire. I know he swapped vehicles. He was at risk of being tracked down by a dangerous criminal."

"Really?" Jolene leaned forward to rest her arms on the desk. Her lips twitched. "A dangerous criminal?"

"A dame, too. A woman who's killed two already and gunning for a third. She'll stop at nothing. Nash is in danger if he hasn't already been captured."

Jolene rose and walked over to a wall unit that held a Keurig and cups on a tray. "Coffee?"

"With Nash missing, better make it a whisky."

"I thought you were on the wagon."

"Figure of speech. Anyway, are you going to give me any information or not?"

"Not." She thwacked a pod into the coffeemaker.

"Whaddaya mean 'not'?" Jolene seemed blasé about the danger. I guess a murderous rampage didn't do it for her. "I'm telling you, Nash is in danger. It's imperative I find him."

"Imperative, huh? I tell you what's imperative. You stop harassing me and Wyatt."

My mind fumbled, but I stuck with Nora. "What's the matter? Do I need to spell it out for you? I know you have his truck. Two people were murdered. Three buildings burned, including the Dixie Kreme. He's missing. Maybe it's a calculator you need, not a dictionary."

She spun around. "Why do you think I have his truck? Because he trusts me."

"He left me something, too."

Jolene's snarl froze. Her eyes panned down to his extra-large t-shirt tucked into my waist.

"Not that kind of something." I scoffed, then hunted through my bag and felt for Roger Rabbit. Yanking the key chain out, I dangled it before me. "His keys. He only wanted to hide his wheels at your house. I don't have a house. He planned for me to find the keys."

"By finding, you mean stealing."

"In my backpack? Then why did he park the truck in your drive and not hide it in your garage? He knew I would..." I could tell by the look on Jolene's face that Nash hadn't meant to park the truck in her drive. "What'd you do? Move the truck out when he asked you to hide it?"

She turned back to her coffee and reached for a bottle of Torani syrup.

"Hitting the hard stuff," I hid my discomfort in Nora's snark. "You screwed up, Jolene. Let's hope Dee Dixon doesn't know the make and model you gave Nash. Which was what?"

Her hand shook, grabbing the creamer.

"Process of elimination is not hard for me, Jolene. Save me the minute and tell me what Nash is driving. Unless you've already told the cops, that is."

"Cops?" Coffee sloshed out of the cup she stirred. "You mean Ian Mowry?"

"Detective Ian Mowry is exactly who I mean. There's an APB on Nash that covers the—" I almost said Tri-state area. A little too Nora. We were in North Georgia, not New York. "This is serious, Jolene. He's really missing."

She turned again, but her hands gripped the credenza. "Wyatt said I especially shouldn't talk to Ian Mowry."

"You lied to the police during a murder investigation?" I tsked. "Shame on you, Jolene."

Her face contorted. "I can't even tell if you're serious. Why are you so weird? Can't you just act normally?"

I dropped Nora's character. "Please tell me, Jolene. Anything you can. Nash is really missing. The murders are real. I'm completely serious."

"No." She straightened. "Wyatt's secrets are safe with me."

This was why I went to Jolene in character. Humiliation and frustration are easier to deal with when you pretended to be someone else.

FORTY-NINE

I CHECKED back at A.S.S. to see if Rhonda and Tiffany had made any headway with Randy Mercer's new autopsy. They moved out from behind Rhonda's desk to sit next to me on the client chairs.

"You're looking a little less shiny red and more dull red." Rhonda patted my leg. "Making progress."

"The red is not just from the fire. I tried to hustle Jolene for information and totally screwed it up."

"Which character did you use?" said Rhonda.

"Nora Charles."

"Never heard of her. That's probably why. You should stick with Julia Pinkerton. Everybody's watched that show. We're used to you talking like a sassy teenager."

I sighed. "Pretending I was in a *Thin Man* story helped me cope with Jolene."

"Her size is pretty intimidating," said Rhonda. "But I wouldn't call her thin. More like athletic. Except for her boobs and butt. Actually, she's more curvy than anything. If she's thin, I've got a shot at it, too."

"It's her personality that's intimidating," said Tiffany. "Not to me. But I can see how she'd intimidate Maizie. Maizie's too nice. That's why she can't get information from her."

"You want us to talk to Jolene?" said Rhonda. "Tiffany can be real intimidating, despite her size. Although Tiff's pretty thin."

"My meemaw calls it wiry. Our people aren't thin. You need money for thin."

Why did I bring up *The Thin Man*? It was like I sought mortification. "I don't think Jolene knows anything. She laughed off my insistence that Nash was missing. She's familiar with how Nash acts on a case and thinks I'm overreacting."

"That's a relief." Rhonda patted me on the back. "At least, it doesn't sound like he's hiding in Jolene's house. She would have spilled the beans just to gloat more. Who can resist a dig at an ex-girlfriend?"

I winced. "I never thought he was hiding at Jolene's. He must have taken a burn on Dee Dixon and needed a different vehicle. And I don't think I'm an ex-girlfriend."

"It's okay that you think that." She rubbed my back.

"Nash isn't hiding," I insisted. "He's missing. And he's not anything worse than missing because Nash is resourceful and resilient."

"It's okay you think that, too." Rhonda hugged me. "All these murdered people could get you down. But you're doing real good with all that."

"I need you to look up vehicles registered to Jolene. She has a Lexus GX, but I want to know if she has another vehicle that Nash borrowed."

"We can look Jolene up on our skip tracing app," said Rhonda.

"I'll enjoy that," said Tiffany.

"Only look at her vehicle registrations," I warned. "Even if we don't like her, Jolene hasn't done anything wrong. We can't invade her privacy."

"You're no fun, Maizie Albright," said Rhonda.

"I should have looked up Jolene's registrations as soon as I knew about Nash's truck, but too much has happened too fast. I told Ian where Nash had parked his truck. But the police are focused on the Dee Dixon manhunt. I feel like I keep spinning my wheels while all my leads just fly away."

"You've got a lot going on with getting burned up in fires and dead bodies and whatnot," said Rhonda. "I wouldn't be so hard on yourself."

"Did you find anything about Randy Mercer's second postmortem?"

"Not yet," said Tiffany. "Anything else we can do?"

"I need to learn more about Randy Mercer to understand Dee's motives. I tried talking to Daddy, but didn't have the heart to push him after yesterday's health scare."

"How's he doing?" said Rhonda.

"He's out of the hospital, at least. His hypertension is stress-related. Carol Lynn's forcing him to go to Pigeon Forge to get away from DeerNose. With Dee Dixon on the loose, I encouraged her to leave immediately."

"Pigeon Forge won't help him with his stress," said Tiffany. "Not with that traffic this time of year."

"Oh, man." I slapped my forehead. "The furniture didn't match."

Rhonda blinked at me, then turned to Tiffany. "Do you think she's losing it? I heard some people get a little nutty with grief."

"I'm not grieving. There's nothing to grieve. Nash is just missing. And Cuddles. And Daddy will be fine if I can clear up this DeerNose mess."

"It's okay you think that, Maizie." Rhonda reached to pat my shoulder again, but I pushed her hand away.

"Dee Dixon bought her family's property in Little Gap. The new cabin built on the old grounds is modern, but the furniture didn't match. Who buys a Scandinavian Modern and fills it with rustic antiques?"

"Someone who doesn't care or know what Scandinavian

Modern is?" said Tiffany. "Like most people who buy a new place but have to put their same old furniture in it."

"Exactly, except Dee Dixon is a designer. I think she'd care. She's righting wrongs. Except she said, 'some wrongs can't be righted.' Like returning family furniture to a new house."

"You've lost me," said Tiffany. "What does that have to do with anything?"

"The Mercers had more than the cabin. Someone said they were town people. The factory was in Shake Rag. The Mercers had a house in one of the nearby towns."

"You think Dee Dixon bought their other house, too?"

"There's a good chance. She bought the Little Gap property. Nobody is using the factory, but it's clean inside, not looking abandoned. Someone must have bought it and is maintaining it. I think Dee, but it would be too obvious for Dee to hide there. We need to look at other properties, too."

"We're on it," said Rhonda. "What are you going to do now, Maizie?"

"Keep looking for Nash."

My view of the case had magnified. Dee Dixon was near the center. But she was orbiting around our fathers' relationship.

———

I LEFT the girls to continue with their Mercer research and drove to DeerNose, hoping to poke around while the building was empty. I wasn't the only one. Someone had parked a large black truck in front. I left the Impala at the back entrance and entered with the passkey. I couldn't image Dee Dixon parking a stolen truck in front of the building, but I crept through the building, anyway.

In the executive hall, Marshy's door was open. I spied him at his desk, studying his computer. When I knocked, his head jerked up and his glasses slid down his nose.

"Maizie, what are you doing here?" He adjusted his glasses. "I heard you'd gotten hurt. Something about a fire?"

"I'm okay. The emergency responders were just being cautious. I'm looking for Nash." I sat in a chair before his desk. "What are you doing here on a Saturday?"

He glanced at his monitor and turned it off. "Nash isn't here. When was the last time you spoke to him?"

"It's been a while for me, too. That's why I'm looking for him. I'm worried." I leaned forward. "Give me more details about the sabotage attempts by CrossHair Marketing. Daddy showed me the ruined samples. I also saw the tags they've been putting on your apparel. I'm hoping to trace Nash's investigation to find him."

Marshy pulled off his glasses, rubbed the bridge of his nose, and slid them back on. "I understand corporate espionage. I don't understand these kinds of attacks. They're almost silly. Rivals have seeded bad reviews using click farms, but this is beyond the pale. At first, I thought it might be some anti-hunting organization. Guerrilla strategies. But no activist claimed the attempts."

"Do you understand who CrossHair is, the company behind this? Why it was necessary for the police to get their warrant for Nash's computer?" His eyes had hardened at the mention of the warrant. I adjusted my tone. "I don't think you understand the seriousness of the situation, Marshy. I found something about DeerNose in my investigation. It's sensitive. And it involves Daddy."

"What are you talking about? Some scandal you've dug up?" Marshy scowled. "You've got to be joking if it's about Boomer Spayberry, young lady."

"I think Randy Mercer's daughter is behind these guerrilla tactics. She's trying to destroy DeerNose or at least humiliate Daddy as an act of revenge."

"What?" He shook his head. "Deanna Mercer?

"Please tell me what you know. It could help me discover what happened to Nash. And help my father and DeerNose."

"It's confidential, Maizie. I have to consider our investors." Marshy pulled off his glasses, pinched his nose again, and considered me before sliding his glasses back on. "I haven't told Boomer everything because of his health situation. Once we get this taken care of, then I'm going to give him the full report. Nash was under strict orders only to report to me. I'm asking you to do the same."

As uncomfortable as the secrecy made me, I nodded at him to continue. I wouldn't promise anything verbally, though.

"Let me start at the beginning. DeerNose has been attacked at sites across the country, including this area. It started with vandalism at a warehouse in Spokane. The police called it tagging because the same mark was used."

"A gun site with a bloody deer?"

Marshy nodded. "The police didn't take it seriously. The vandal painted the security camera's lens so we couldn't see them. Not unusual for graffiti artists. Very discouraging. We took it as a one-off. But then the same tag appeared in Montana, Illinois, and Arizona. Not just warehouses. Billboards, freight trucks, and a high-profile banner for a sporting goods convention we were sponsoring. A boutique shop in Colorado had it drawn on their window, another had it chalked on the sidewalk in front of their door."

"Nash only told me he was working on a big project."

"The vandalism started a few years before he came on. In the beginning, it was random and more of a nuisance. These crimes were low penalty, you see. Misdemeanors. We hired Nash when sporting goods box stores across California reported they had fliers inserted between stacks of our clothes. A fake notice about defects in our brand. It didn't feel like activism anymore—more like corporate sabotage. He found similar acts throughout the US, but by the time we heard about it, the perpetrators moved on to another location.

"Then a shipment was hijacked. Although when it happened, it wasn't reported as a hijacking. Someone had stolen a box and replaced it with another from the back of a truck waiting to be unloaded. The driver didn't notice. Neither did the store until it was too late. Our shipping facility had a similar issue. Someone reported the tags on our apparel soon after that."

"CrossHair was ramping up their efforts. Committing felonies."

"But not federal. Always after the shipment was delivered, not before. One box at a time. Pretty sneaky, eh?" Marshy leaned back in his chair. "No one had claimed these acts. Nash tracked down the culprits individually, but couldn't tie them together. Not at first. Many of them were involved in other activist campaigns, you see. Kind of mercenaries for hire."

"Activism is a part-time job for some. They network through group chats. I heard about it when I was taking classes at CSU Long Beach."

"Nash had a list of fifteen people he was investigating. Only one was in Georgia."

I nodded. "Luella Haney."

"But Nash said she differed from the others. He believes she's the one who'd slipped the fliers in our apparel in the California stores months ago. Luella was brasher than the others. That's how he caught her. He found her in Gilmore of all places."

"Gilmore." Even if he didn't know Kristi's real name, Nash would have eventually followed her to the Johnson house in Black Pine. "When did this come to light?"

"Recently. A week or two ago, maybe?" Marshy tipped back in his chair. "You have to understand, it was a lot of work to get this list. The only evidence we had was the resultant acts. These people were careful not to be seen on camera. Except for Luella Haney. For the rest of them, Nash pretended he was hiring for similar jobs. He narrowed these folks down in a massive amount of interviews."

"That would have taken forever."

"Looking for a needle in a haystack." Marshy nodded. "But I have to hand it to Nash. He was determined to catch them. He's like a dog after a bone."

"Maybe too much," I muttered.

"If it wasn't for this local gal, Nash wouldn't have found the guy we're after."

"Simon Craig? He runs CrossHair Marketing. I found him, too, while I was watching an infidelity subject."

"He was cheating on his wife, too?" Marshy shook his head. "Nash said the guy has a rap sheet in the UK. Did time in prison in his youth. I'm surprised they let him into Canada. That's where he crossed into the US after changing his name."

"He's married—" My words came out in a jumble. How had I not found this out? "Wait. What? Simon's an ex-con? He came here from Canada?"

"Nash had to pull some strings to get that information," Marshy preened, like he'd done it himself. "He's got some pretty good connections. Simon Craig—not his real name, by the way— was running this sham company that's basically a gun for hire in corporate sabotage."

"Marshy, CrossHair was only interested in taking down DeerNose. His partner was Deanna Mercer. She's going by the name Dee Dixon."

"Dixon." Marshy slapped his hands on his desk. "That's Simon Craig's real name. Or at least the one on his Canadian passport."

"They were married. He'd leased the apartment to Luella, who was Kristi. And might have been having an affair with Kristi. Kristi had been playing up the spy-life, maybe for Simon. Flaunting it on social media…"

That confirmed Dee's motive for killing Kristi and Simon. I shuddered and wondered if Ian and the Gilmore deputies had caught Dee.

"Deanna Mercer," Marshy continued while my thoughts wandered. "I often wondered what had happened to her. I guess her mom took her to Canada? Or maybe she met Simon Dixon somewhere else. Doesn't matter. If she owns CrossHair, she's a reprobate. I am truly sorry to hear that. But DeerNose hasn't been the only company CrossHair attacked. They're the type of company you hire to dig up dirt on your competitors and use tactics that go far beyond comparative advertising."

"Marshy, I don't think you're getting it. Dee Dixon has her own sporting goods clothing label—Triple D—that specializes in camouflage activewear."

"Triple D?" Marshy scowled, grabbed a pen, and scribbled on a pad of paper. "That's why they're after us. She's an up-and-comer. Triple D is a rising brand. Nash didn't mention that in our meetings."

"There's more to it than that. Dee had a personal reason to attack DeerNose. Maybe it's why she created an opposing brand." I took a deep breath and blinked back a few tears. I didn't want to sully my father, especially to his best friend. Marshy and Petey didn't know this awful truth. How could they? It would hurt them, like it had hurt me.

It sickened me to expose my father. But knowing what Daddy had done sickened me more. I'd have to force this burden out of the shadows and into the light to find justice for Randy Mercer. Just like I was trying to expose Dee Dixon to free Derek Johnson.

I realized this was why Nash loved detective work, and why I wanted to become an investigator. I might use deceit to do my job, but I believed in discovering the truth. Even if it made people uncomfortable. Or angry. Or sick. This was the reason I kept hounding Nash about what was going on in DeerNose. The truth needed to be exposed. Even at the expense of our relationship.

Even at the expense of my father.

FIFTY

"MARSHY," I continued. "This won't be easy to hear. I found evidence about Randy Mercer's death. Dee Dixon—Deanna Mercer—had his body exhumed. The new autopsy showed the supposed self-inflicted gunshot didn't kill him. He was already dead, killed by a TBI in his frontal lobe."

"TBI?"

"Traumatic brain injury. He had a skull fracture. The gunshot wound disguised the actual cause of death. The fire probably didn't help either. It very well could have been an accident that killed him. I think it probably was. But then someone tried to cover it up. To make it look like a suicide."

The text tone on my phone trilled. I ignored it. Marshy shoved his chair back, stood up, and paced to his window.

"I'm sorry," I continued. "I know it's terrible. Awful. Just sickening. I can barely stand it."

"You didn't know Randy Mercer, though," said Marshy.

"Sorry?" I stood up, but he'd turned. His expression kept me rooted in place.

"Randy Mercer inherited Mercer Textiles. He ran it into the ground. We made the deal to work out of his factory to help him out. Felt like a win-win for both parties." Marshy pulled off his glasses, pinched his nose, and took his time wiping the lenses. "We felt bad for his girl. Deanna. Dee Dee, he called her. Her momma was one of those country club-type gals. Beauty queen and thought she was better than everyone. Kind of like Vicki, but nowhere near as smart."

That stung. There was no love lost between my mother and Marshy. The beauty queen part was true, but her parents couldn't afford a country club. They couldn't even afford her pageants. That's what drove her. Like Daddy, she'd always worked. She wanted more than a country club lifestyle. She'd wanted to own the country club. And now she did. A small one in Mexico.

"Jenny Mercer spent money like it was water. Nothing was too good for her or Dee Dee. Randy went right along with it. He liked living high on the hog, too. You know, DeerNose paid the electric bill at his house for a while. Couldn't keep the lights on, but his wife had a brand new BMW the next month. The man couldn't balance books to save his life."

"Okay," I said. "But that still doesn't mean he committed suicide."

"Maybe Randy was going to commit suicide and fell," said Marshy, replacing his glasses. "Odder things have happened. Those brain injuries don't always cause instantaneous death. Don't forget he left a note."

"How could—"

"Maizie, it does no good bringing this up. That's all in the past. The fact of the matter is, Randy Mercer is gone. He lost everything, including his wife and daughter, and he's gone. There's no point in digging into this mess." He shook his head. "Anyway, if Deanna Mercer is the one trying to ruin our business, she needs to be stopped."

"Wait. What?"

"You need to leave this alone. Let the police handle it."

"But…" I squeezed the back of my neck. My phone buzzed again. This time I checked. Ian. I shoved my phone back into my pocket and gazed at Marshy, not knowing how to proceed. Why did I think telling the truth would be easy?

"Let the police handle it, Maizie," Marshy repeated. "You did good. You figured out who's been sabotaging DeerNose. Quicker than Nash did. We can put that to bed. We'll prosecute her."

He turned back to the window.

I wasn't getting anywhere with him. I stared up at the ceiling. Sighed and checked my text messages. "Shiz—"

Clutching my phone, I rushed to the window and grabbed Marshy's arm. "The police didn't find Dee Dixon at Windmere. She abandoned the car there. She's gone."

He looked at me, uncomprehending.

"Deanna Mercer's out there. You need to get out of here. Go somewhere safe. Tell Petey, too."

"Peters is in Atlanta. She was so upset about Boomer, I convinced her to stay at a friend's for the weekend," said Marshy. "I'll meet you at the cabin. That place is a fortress with Boomer's gun collection. Should be safe enough."

"Daddy's already gone. Carol Lynn made him go to Pigeon Forge. He didn't tell you?" I hesitated. "Maybe you should get out of town, too."

"Where are you going?"

"I've got to keep looking for Nash." What else could I do?

———

WITH MY HEART beating in my throat, I hurried toward the factory exit. I felt safe enough in DeerNose, but the woodsy paintings on the walls no longer looked cute. Totally creepy, actually. Like the animals were hiding something, not just themselves.

The secrets in this building were making me a little nutso.

Marshy knew what happened to Randy Mercer. Or he'd guessed. He had to be protecting Daddy. Protecting me, too. Marshy and Petey were loyal to a fault.

A big fault if Daddy had done this horrible crime. I couldn't get it out of my head, yet I still couldn't believe he'd done it. The pain of knowing what had happened to Randy Mercer was almost as unbearable as this pain of not knowing where Nash had gone.

How could I have lost my father, my dog, and my Nash in one fell swoop? In one measly infidelity case?

I called Ian as I climbed into the Impala, then took off for A.S.S.

"We're trying to trace Dixon's movement from Windmere." Ian sounded weary and frustrated. At the hospital, he had less sleep than me. "Nobody saw her arrive or leave. We've talked to Uber and other taxi services and no luck there either. We alerted all area hospitals. Someone must have picked her up. She could be in Atlanta by now."

Atlanta sounded good to me. They had plenty of practice catching criminals.

"What about old friends in the area?"

"From what we've gathered, I don't think she has old friends around here. We'll keep beating the bushes, anyway." Ian's voice deepened, "You still need to be careful, hon'."

"I appreciate that, Ian. I'm focused on figuring out what happened to Nash."

I parked next to Annie's Jeep. But instead of going into the office, I found my feet continuing down the sidewalk and around the corner. They stopped in front of the burned Dixie Kreme Donut shop.

A Bobcat was parked before the building. I supposed that was good news. The insurance would take time to kick in, but Lamar had a lot of fans in Black Pine. The town would support a quick rebuild. The historic committees were always trying to revitalize the old downtown. They wouldn't be sitting on their hands with this kind of destruction to a cornerstone business.

I peered through the front window. A few trays of donuts remained in the glass case. Chairs rested upside down on tables.

Still in place from the evening's cleaning before the arson. But sludge had blackened the floors and counters. Water and smoke had taken a toll.

I grimaced and moved to the old stoop for the second story access. The half-moon window endured, but the door was gone. The stairs were mostly gone, too. Charred wood and unrecognizable rubble filled the little vestibule. I angled myself inside the doorway to glimpse the upper floor, then wished I hadn't.

This had to be personal. Nash worked, slept, and lived up there.

I'd been looking at this all wrong. I might have been good at busting cheaters, but I seemed to be terrible at investigating.

Maybe I'd typecast myself.

———

I COULDN'T pace in the old office—more Nash's thing than mine—so I paced the sidewalk instead. Sucked in air smelling of burnt creosote rather than fried dough, making my eyes water for the wrong reasons.

Think, I urged my brain. Why can't you work through this? Sometime before or during the fire, Nash got out of the building. He drove to Jolene's. Swapped vehicles. And went where?

No idea.

Okay, if Dee Dixon had attacked him and burned down the Dixie Kreme, he would have gone to the police. Unless he didn't know it was Dee Dixon…

Had Nash known about Dee? He'd been tracking the fifteen. Luella led him to Simon. Nash had just started surveillance on Simon. Dee must have been a surprise attack. Nash would swap vehicles and start a new investigation into this mystery woman.

Funny, our paths hadn't crossed, but it had only been a few days. To find Nash, I needed to find Dee Dixon.

But how could I find her if the police couldn't?

Think like Dee Dixon.

Like a homicidal pyromaniac?

Come on, I urged myself. Take a backstory and build a character. You've done it for a million roles. Easy peasy.

Start with young Deanna Mercer. Living lifestyles of the Black Pine old money set. Country Club. Cotillion … hang on. Dee didn't seem like she'd be a fan of cotillion. Her mother made her. Somebody taught her to hunt. Didn't she say she was some kind of rifle champion? Okay, she was in the woodsy old money set. At the Old Mercer Place, they kept dogs and guns. Hunted on the land on weekends. Had a town home for work and school. Dee Dee went to one of the private schools. An idyllic childhood for a wealthy mountain family.

I settled into the role. Raised my chin. Drew back my shoulders. Changed my pacing to a swagger.

A truck drove by. Self-conscious, I crossed the street to make my pacing appear more like walking.

Back to Dee Dee. I closed my eyes, took some deep breaths, and got back into character. There was tension at home. Mom and Randy—Dad—fought over money.

I didn't have an economic grasp on textile factories, but wouldn't a place like Mercer Textile have trouble making ends meet, anyway? Most fabric was imported.

Duh, that's where Dee's interest in design came from. The textile factory. She hung out with her dad at Mercer Textile. But also saw Randy handing out pink slips. Repairing machines himself. Or he hid in the back office, refusing calls from creditors. But when things were at their worst, a savior appears at the factory.

Daddy.

No, you're Dee Dee. Boomer Spayberry appears.

Hang on, first on the scene would be Marshy—Marshall Roth. The DeerNose lawyer would have the offer. Right. Old friends, or at least, old acquaintances. Small world in this industry. Smaller world in this part of Georgia. Boomer, Marshall, and Roxanne Peters would have arrived together. Worked out a deal to use the factory space to get their new company up and running. Great news. DeerNose will keep the lights on and employ the nervous Mercer workers, who could see the unemployment blade hanging above their necks.

I blew out a breath. Straightened my shoulders from their slump. Returned to the swagger. Things were wonderful again. Mom's got a new car. Dad's back to hunting and fishing on his land. Dee Dee can stay in her expensive private school.

But then she overhears her dad talking about DeerNose building on Boomer's land. Mercer Textile was supposed to be temporary for DeerNose, but the brand took off more quickly than Randy thought. Who knew the chemical combination of deer pee could be infused in fabric? Groundbreaking stuff. At least in the hunting world.

They wouldn't find it gross at all. Fellow hunters. Randy would find it exciting.

Or would he? DeerNose was in magazines. Winning awards. The camouflage craze was hitting an all-time high and not just for hunting. Intoxicating times in the outdoor apparel world.

But not in the Mercer household.

DeerNose broke ground on Spayberry land. Dee's mom spent like they still had old Mercer money. Dee's dad returned to hiding from creditors in his office. He knew once DeerNose left, Mercer Textile's situation would get worse. Maybe the popularity of DeerNose would attract other designers who'd want their fabric printed and woven at Mercer Textile. But how long would that last? Still cheaper to get cloth from Asia.

Dee Dee watched her dad spiral. He kept a bottle in his desk and no longer used a glass. DeerNose moved out. Took some of his employees with them.

And her mom said, "Pack your bags, we're moving. Without your father."

My stomach twisted. My throat felt raw. I knew Dee Dee's pain. The pain of separation. Hers differed from mine, of course, but was familiar enough to draw from. Kids were resilient, yes.

But no matter how bad things got at home, they wanted their parents together.

No matter how much I loved Carol Lynn and Remi—which I did with all my heart. I couldn't imagine my life without them—there was still a piece of my soul missing.

The piece that created me.

It was too complicated and deep to say that the missing piece caused me to turn to alcohol and drugs in my teen years. There were other frustrations, like the intensity of my working schedule and the all-consuming need to please everyone while feeling like I pleased no one.

Especially myself.

I didn't know what life was like for Dee Dee after her mother left and divorced her dad. Except that soon after, they got news of his suicide with the double punch that he'd burned her ancestral home to the ground with him.

The home Dee would have inherited. Generational property.

Pain had twisted me in one way. Pain had twisted Deanna Mercer in another.

She wanted revenge.

FIFTY-ONE

#METHODMANIACTING
#GONETOTHEDOGS

I STOPPED PACING and stared at the burned Dixie Kreme Donut building. I had Dee Dixon's character. She was in my head. Time to retrace her steps.

Dee Dixon slips into the Dixie Kreme building. Waited for Nash to leave the office. Coshed him. She could have hid in the hall bathroom. Hard to do, though. Maybe she only wanted information. To see what he knew. How did she get into the office to snoop?

If Nash didn't know her, maybe he let her in. He was always a sucker for a dame.

That's Nora Charles. Back to Dee Dixon.

She talks herself into the office. Nash would have explained he doesn't do private investigations anymore. He turns his back on her and … she pulls a gun? No, she might have fired a gun at me, but a slam to the head was her M.O.

Wait. He's taller than her. Nash's a big guy. A lot bigger than Simon. Simon would be unsuspecting. Nash was wily. How would Dee manage bludgeoning him? She'd have to carry something with her. No fire pokers handy, like at the Old Mercer Place.

Maybe she doesn't attempt murder. Waits for him to leave,

then burns down the building to eighty-six any information about CrossHair.

Except that doesn't make sense.

If Dee knows Nash's investigating CrossHair, she's better off burning down his DeerNose office.

Regardless, where did Nash go after swapping vehicles?

Shizzles. Not making any headway.

My phone vibrated in my pocket. I yanked it out, hoping for Rhonda with more Dee Dixon information. Not Rhonda.

"We got a break," Ian said excitedly. "A Windmere maintenance guy gave a woman a ride. Seems to match your description of Dee Dixon. He assumed she was a victim of domestic violence and didn't ask a lot of questions. She said she needed to get to Black Pine, so he took her to the bus station and bought her a ticket."

"Holy shizzolis. Good work." And great work, Fergy. He'd redeemed himself from the banana incident. "Hey Ian, the Mercers had a house somewhere in the area. Gilmore, Shake Rag, or Black Pine, possibly. Rhonda's looking up Mercer property records for me. It occurred to me, if Dee's on a revenge path, she might go there."

"I'll look into it. But DeerNose makes more sense to me. We checked the old textile factory. Nobody's there."

My thoughts drifted back to the burning of the Dixie Kreme building. "I feel like we're missing something. It's not all connecting. Especially the part with Nash."

"Sometimes a criminal's motives are mysterious, Maizie. Especially in a murder case. What makes sense to them doesn't seem logical to us."

"I guess so."

"I've got to go. I'll keep you updated." Ian hesitated. "Maizie, stay away from DeerNose, the cabin, and your office. Anywhere she'd likely find you. We'll patrol those locations, too."

"Annie's not going to like an officer at A.S.S."

"Tough. She can deal with him or close up shop for the day.

Besides, it's the weekend. Don't y'all ever close? If Rhonda figures out the other Mercer property, stay away from that, too."

"I got it."

"Where are you going? I want to know. I'm speaking as a friend, not a cop."

"Gilmore." The name shot out of my mouth thoughtlessly. "I'm going to look for Cuddles."

"Good idea," said Ian. "Don't worry too much, hon'. He'll turn up. I'll help you look once we have Dee Dixon apprehended."

Once again, I didn't know if Ian meant Nash or Cuddles.

————

I WALKED BACK to A.S.S. to give Annie and the girls the news about their new babysitter.

"Black Pine police will be watching our office. Dee Dixon's headed to Black Pine, if she's not here already," I said. "Fergy got her a bus ticket."

"Fergy," muttered Rhonda.

"He didn't know."

Annie popped her gum.

"Maizie." Rhonda moved out from behind the desk. "I found some stuff you should know. First off, Jolene's other vehicle is a Harley."

"A Harley? Jolene rides a Harley? I can't imagine Jolene on a Harley."

"I can," said Tiffany. "She can pretend she's a badass."

"What kind of Harley?" said Annie.

"A Sportser S," said Rhonda. "Blue."

"Blue's *my* color," I said before I could stop myself.

Annie rolled her eyes.

"Hey Rhon, do me a favor and call Lamar for me," I said, more focused on my to-do list than blustering over my gaffe. "Tell him about Jolene's motorcycle. Because of the fire, I haven't wanted to bother him too much, but he's keeping his ears open for signs of Nash."

"Will do," she said. "I have more information, though. Not about the bike. About the house."

"Lay it on me. I'll give Ian the information about the motorcycle and property, but I might still drive by the place before heading to Gilmore. He'll send a cop to watch that house, too."

"Gilmore?" said Annie.

"I can't sit tight and wait for Dee Dixon to get arrested. I've got to do something."

"Looking for Cuddles?"

I shrugged. "No leads on Nash. What else am I going to do?"

"Maizie, this house," said Rhonda. "It might upset you."

I swiveled my gaze back to Rhonda. "Why?"

"It's in Black Pine."

"We thought that might be the case. Marshy said he and Daddy grew up with Randy Mercer."

Annie motioned for Rhonda to hurry it up.

"It's owned by a Peters," said Rhonda. "Roxanne Peters. Isn't that the woman who works with your dad?"

Stunned, I nodded.

"Why would she buy the Mercer house?" said Annie.

"Maybe to help Randy out? That was the reason DeerNose moved into the Mercer factory for a while. Marshy and Daddy felt bad for Randy's family. Thought it was a win-win for both parties. Randy died in the cabin, so he must have sold the house first."

It made sense, but the thought of Petey living in the Mercer house unnerved me. My stomach churned. I still hadn't brought up the subject to Ian. Was I willing to squeal on my father?

"Sit down," said Tiffany gruffly, but she gently lowered me to a chair. "You're looking whiter than normal under your red."

"I've got to tell Ian right away," I stammered. "I think Petey's visiting someone out of town. I'd hate for her to come back to find her house burned down."

"I'll call Detective Mowry," said Annie. "You call Peters."

"Okay. And Marshy, too." I rubbed my neck and wondered if Annie kept antacids in her lair. I glanced up and caught their concerned expressions.

"Great work, Rhonda," I blurted. "Isn't she doing great, Annie?"

"Yeah," said Annie. "Everybody's doing great. Make your calls and we'll talk after."

———

PETEY DIDN'T ANSWER her phone. I bumbled the first message, called back, and stammered through a second voice mail. "Petey, it's Maizie again. Don't come home. Stay wherever you are. I'm afraid Dee Dixon—Deanna Mercer—will try to … set fire … um … to your house? But maybe not. Don't worry. The police are watching your house, so I'm sure it won't happen. Stay in Atlanta. Enjoy yourself. You know, if you get a chance, be sure to go to Mary Mac's Tea Room. I love that place. Although, you might not be in the mood for fried chicken after this message … shizzles. Your voicemail cut me off. And I should stop talking…"

I tossed my phone on the chair and looked up. Rhonda grimaced. Tiffany's lip had curled.

"Remind me never to have Maizie deliver bad news," said Rhonda.

"I've got to call Marshy."

"Maybe I should do it," said Tiffany.

I shook my head, picked up my phone again, and pressed his number. "Marshy, it's Maizie. The police think Dee Dixon—Deanna Mercer—is in Black Pine. They've got people covering DeerNose, the cabin, and my office. Petey's house, too."

"There's a patrol car in front of my house already," said Marshy. "Impressive response."

"About Petey's house," I tried to remove the squeak from my voice. "Did you know it originally belonged to Randy Mercer?"

"Oh, sure," he said. "I think it actually belonged to his granddaddy."

"Really?" Why was I the only one finding that piece of history disturbing? "There's some concern that Dee Dixon—Dee Dee, you know—might have a desire … maybe desire's not the best way to put it … an uncontrollable urge to, no … um, I guess a possible motive…"

"Spit it out, honey."

"Dee Dixon might want to burn down Petey's house."

"Lord Almighty."

"But the police are on it. I left a message telling Petey to stay in Atlanta." I waited a few seconds. "Marshy, are you still there?"

"Yes, honey. Still here. I'm texting Peters."

"Did she answer?"

"No."

"Do you know where she is?"

This time, the pause was longer. "No. But I'm sure she's fine. I'll call you back later."

FIFTY-TWO

#DOGSOFWAR #SEARCHANDSEIZURE

"PETEY IS NOT ANSWERING HER PHONE." I shoved my phone in my pocket and grabbed my backpack. "I don't care what Ian says. I'm going to her house. If Petey's there, I'll convince her to go somewhere safe."

"Maizie, Mowry's right," said Annie. "This is an area-wide manhunt. Not a good idea for you to go."

"I know the police are going to watch her house, but I'm really worried." I gulped. "No, not just worried. I'm freaking out. Dee Dixon's motive is revenge. What if she's after all the DeerNose founding members? I have to do something. It's like everyone I love is suddenly disappearing…" I bit my lip. "Not everyone."

"Don't get gushy, Maizie," said Tiffany. "We don't do gushy."

"Albright, you don't need to go because I'm going," said Annie. "Focus on looking for Cuddles. I assigned you to him. He belongs to a client."

I gaped. "That's why you don't me to go?"

Annie shrugged and strode to the back room. A few moments later, she reappeared with a backpack and a gun holstered to her belt. "Does Peters live with anyone?

We stared at the gun, not listening.

Annie snapped her fingers. "Albright. Anyone live at that house besides Peters?"

"No." My eyes traveled from the handgun to her face. "Petey lost her husband a really long time ago. Before I was born. They never had kids. She's always lived alone, as far as I know." My voice broke. "Daddy and Marshy are her family."

"You don't have a key to her house, do you?"

"There's a key under the flowerpot on her back stoop. Why?"

"Don't ask me why. But by you telling me where this key is, you're giving me permission to go into her house. Since you're family. Right?"

I looked at Tiffany and Rhonda. Rhonda's eyes had widened and her lips pressed together hard enough to puff out her cheeks. Tiffany was smirking. But it was her worried smirk, not her usual smirk.

"What about the manhunt and letting the police do their thing?" I said.

Annie tossed us a steely look. "They'll need to get permission or a warrant to go into her house if she's in Atlanta. I'm saving them time."

"Why can't I do it?"

"This one's mine." She shoved a new stick of gum into her mouth. "You have someone else to find."

And once again, I wasn't sure if she was talking about Cuddles or Nash.

———

I'D TOLD Ian I'd go to Gilmore. I still didn't have a better idea. After driving by the dog park and Windmere—where I also didn't see any blue Harley sport motorcycles, let alone a giant dog—I stopped at the Embree home. We'd been in contact over the phone, but I thought a face-to-face would make Elaine feel better.

Or make me feel better. I needed an Elaine hug.

"We don't have any news either," said Victoria. "I called all the local vets and rescue folks I know. They're networking for us. Elaine put up flyers."

"I'm not ever giving up," said Elaine. "I know he's not lost. He's on a mission. Cuddles is smart and courageous. The Romans used mastiffs as war dogs. They fought with gladiators in the arenas. They were bred to do everything with their masters—hunting, guarding, even fighting alongside them. In the 1500s, the English bred them with a bulldog for catching poachers. At night, the dogs would hunt the forest, tracking for trespassers. They'd spring on the poacher and hold them until the gamekeeper could come. Isn't that incredible? But the bull-mastiffs are happiest with people. They're an intensely loyal dog."

She might as well have been describing Nash. I wished I could put up flyers for him. "You've done your research."

Elaine nodded. "I read several books and AKC posts, then wrote a paper on bullmastiffs for fun."

Victoria rubbed Elaine's shoulder. "He'll turn up. He's a big dog. Someone will report him. It's only been a day."

"He can track," said Elaine. "That's what he's doing. He'll hunt his way back to us. I noticed how super focused he gets if he's after something. Although it's usually food."

"Maybe we should put up flyers in all the fast-food places," I said, trying to lighten Elaine's spirits.

"That's a good idea." She looked up at her mom. "Can we?"

Victoria nodded, then shot me a look that said if I hadn't been feeding him fast food, that wouldn't be necessary.

"Let me know if you hear anything," I said. "I'll keep looking, too."

In the setting sun, I drove around Gilmore, then motored toward Black Pine. It had grown too dark to see anything. At the exit to Shake Rag, I veered off the highway. The factory was a long shot, but Cuddles had enjoyed the factory.

As I drove through the factory gates, Rhonda called. I parked in the empty factory lot and let my eyes roam the deepening shadows while I talked.

"What's the news?" I said. "Annie? Petey? Nash? Dee Dixon? My dad?"

"Annie's with the police right now. Nobody was in the house. But she found something…" Rhonda blew out a long breath. "Oh, girl."

I hoped it wasn't a body. If it was another body, I would throw up. Or worse. I opened the car door just in case. "Just say it."

"She found gas on the kitchen floor. I don't have any more details."

"Oh, my God. Tell me exactly what she said."

"That's it. She couldn't say more except Black Pine PD was leaving a patrol car at the house. They've already called the fire department."

My heart leaped into my throat. "What about Marshy?"

"There's a patrol car at his house and at DeerNose."

"But where's Marshy?"

"I'm sorry, Maizie, I don't know. Annie said he's not answering his phone either."

"Oh, God." I laid my head on the steering wheel, feeling dizzy. "Anything else?"

"That's it." Rhonda paused. "I'm really sorry, Maizie. Any news about Cuddles?"

"No," I said weakly. "I haven't seen a blue motorcycle either."

"Don't give up hope," she whispered.

"I'm not." I sat up. "Cuddles and Nash are resourceful and courageous. They're war dogs."

"What?"

"Never mind. Are you and Tiff still at A.S.S.? I thought the police didn't want anyone there."

"We took the computer with us," called Tiffany's muffled voice. "We're at my place. Working from home."

"Does Annie know? Never mind. Thank you." My heart swelled at their dedication. When they worked at LA HAIR, they used any excuse to get out of work. Maybe this was a better career for them, too.

I grabbed a Maglite from the console, eased on my backpack, and got out of the car. Striding across the parking lot, I called for Cuddles. At the front steps, I ran the flashlight's beam through the factory's windows. No dog waiting in the hall. I tried the handle and felt surprise to feel the latch give. Maybe the police had forgotten to lock it when they went through the building.

Not something a cop was likely to do, though. They would have secured the premises after their search.

I opened the door quietly. Ran the beam around the entry. Listened. Ducked under the police tape hanging across the frame, and entered. I knew Cuddles wasn't there. If Cuddles was inside, he'd hear me. He had supersonic hearing. He might even smell me at a distance. And if he was napping, I'd hear him snoring, for sure.

The police had already cleared the building. No Cuddles. I could go.

Although, quite possibly, someone else had been here. After the police. My gut said they had. Cuddles or no, I owed it to Nash to look.

And to be careful. Maybe they were still here.

FIFTY-THREE

I GLANCED through the open door of the reception room and ran the flashlight beam around the stillness. At the end of the hall, the door to the back office stood open. The other office doors were closed. I ignored them and slid over to the conference room to peek inside.

Still empty. No. Wait. Three bolts of material—all camouflage, naturally—stood behind the open door.

Did I miss that before? I felt my brows draw together, but my mind drew a blank.

Moving on.

I tiptoed toward the factory. Checked the grimy windows looking out onto the factory floor. Cardboard stacked against the walls. Those had not been there before, either. But they could wait.

On the catwalk, I peered over the edge, then scanned the massive space with my flashlight. The right-side dock door was still ajar. Not as much as when Cuddles and I had originally found it. But a crack. Enough to get a hand underneath. More footprints crisscrossed the dirty floor. And dog prints? I sucked in my breath.

The large prints traveled the perimeter of the space. Probably from earlier. Although …Wishful thinking. I blew out the breath I held and turned toward the offices.

Wary of the closed office doors, I tiptoed through the reception area. My flashlight beam swept the area. The creepy feeling had returned. The right-side offices had the windows looking out onto the factory. I tried the first door on the left.

Locked. Same with the second and third.

At the end office, the dartboard still lay on the floor behind the door. My father's magazine picture was still missing. But a new piece of evidence lay inside the top drawer of the desk. The laptop I had chucked off Dee Dixon's deck. The case was scratched and dented. Screen broken. But a light appeared on the keyboard when I pressed the power button.

I wondered if she'd wiped the files on Randy Mercer. I also wondered if the police could still retrieve them.

In the bottom desk drawer, beneath a curling legal pad, I spotted a piece of rectangular metal. My gut sank. I flipped it over, confirming what I thought. A Georgia license plate. About two-thirds smaller than the size of a regular license plate. Current year. Our county.

My lungs felt like they were seizing and my throat ached. I knew in my heart this was Jolene's plate for her blue Harley.

I cleared my throat and dialed Rhonda. "Any news on the plates for that motorcycle?"

"Not yet. Maizie—"

"Okay. Thanks." I hung up before she could ask me why I wanted to know.

In the bin of mannequin parts, I found a helmet. Blue and black to match the bike. With a big dent on one side. I ran my fingers and the flashlight beam inside. Padding still smooth. No blood. That's why you wear a helmet. The internal cushioning was likely compressed and damaged, but the head was safe from impact.

All good news, right?

I sank on to the desk chair, and with burning eyes, stared at the helmet. Until a flash of light woke me from my stupor.

———

I MOVED TO THE WINDOW. A truck's headlights lit the road. Driving slowly. Could be curious locals who'd heard about the manhunt. They'd see the Impala in the parking lot. I should beat it. Nash would want me to be cautious.

With a final glance around the room, my flashlight beam stopped on the helmet and laptop. Weren't they too obvious? Why would Dee move into the factory so soon? The yellow police tape might make it feel like no one would return. But she didn't lock the door. No key? Had she snuck in through the loading dock, then left the front unlocked?

I didn't care about that. I needed to find Marshy and Petey. Cuddles.

Nash.

The locked rooms. I rushed back to the desk. Dumped out the bin of mannequins. No keys. These were offices with simple doorknob locks. Nash had told me to carry a bump key. Annie didn't find the unlocking of locked doors ethical. I should have listened to Nash. Murder overrode ethics.

I dug in my backpack and found bobby pins. Wiggled two into the first doorknob lock. A bump key would have been easier, but they worked.

Empty room except for a pile of pre-cut cardboard for building boxes.

The second lock was easier than the first. The door swung open, and the fumes hit me. Three red plastic jugs rested near the door. She'd tossed more cardboard for building boxes inside the room.

She meant to burn the factory. Or at least the offices. That's why the rooms in the factory felt staged. Planting flammables. She'd abandoned the BMW at Windmere. She must have transferred the items earlier. Or she was driving something else now…

Who cares? Open the third door. Check the last room. Then get out.

My heart thudded in my chest and blood pounded in my ears while I jimmied the third door's lock. A little trickier, but I got it open.

A cry choked my throat. This room was darker. Someone had drawn the shades. I could make out another desk. The room smelled like kerosene and other things I didn't want to think about.

My flashlight beam found the body on the floor behind the desk. A gun lay nearby.

A woman dressed in camo activewear. Her body, stiff and cool. No way to recognize her by her face. No visible ripped cloth or bite wounds—evidence from Cuddles' attack at the Mercer fire.

Petey?

A wail swelled in my chest, but I shut it down and used my elbow to wipe my tears. I had a job to do.

Leaving the room, I called emergency services. I couldn't handle talking to Ian just yet. It would make me emotional. I didn't have time for emotions. I had more people to find. Another building to check. I wasn't hanging around this one, even knowing the police wanted to question me.

I opened the front door. And the glass exploded behind me.

FIFTY-FOUR
#GRANDTHEFTMADNESS
#GIVEADOGABONE

I ALMOST TURNED to check the broken window, but instinct dropped me to the ground. Crouching low, I reached for the door, yanked it open, and slithered inside. Another bullet cracked the glass. The door slammed shut. I hopped up and ran through the factory. Dashed onto the catwalk. Pounded down the stairs. At the loading bay, I pushed up the rolling door. Wiggled my shoulders through and peered outside. The security lights didn't reveal any moving shadows. I gripped the edge, slid my torso halfway out, and stopped. A faint drumming sounded nearby.

Holy shiz. Not drumming. Feet pounding on the blacktop. She was coming around the side of the building. I scooted back. A shot pinged off the bricks near my head, raining dirt into my hair.

Back inside, I clambered to my feet. Ran for the stairs. Used the railing to whip myself onto the catwalk and hustled out to the front door. Dashed through and pelted across the parking lot toward the Impala.

The burning Impala. The backseat was on fire.

Shiztastic.

I kept running. Wasn't it hard to shoot a moving target?

I hoped so.

At the gate, I barreled through to the street and plunged into the dark weedy lot across the road. A big truck was parked down the street. I pelted in the opposite direction. Toward a group of trees. Heard the retort of the rifle. Flinched. Couldn't tell where the bullets hit.

My lungs were seizing. My heart had tightened. I was a craptastic runner.

I had no idea where I was going and feared tripping in the dark. Tall weeds whipped my legs. My jeans chafed my thighs. My backpack jangled and creaked, banging against the small of my back. If I could make it to the trees, at least I'd have some cover.

More shots went off. Would someone hear them and report the shooting?

Probably not. There weren't any houses near the factory. Just some crumbling brick buildings and derelict garages whose heyday had come and gone.

I plunged into the stand of trees and found the biggest oak to hide behind. Panted and tried to listen over my wheezing. The deep rev of a truck roared from the street.

How long would it take for the police to arrive?

My legs felt like jelly and my lungs still burned. But I pushed deeper into the trees, using my hands to feel my way. Afraid to use my flashlight. Afraid not to use it. The trees thinned. I spied the outline of a building. Drew closer. An old metal shed. I crept around the side and listened for the truck. Darted across the street toward another thicket. Tree-hopped until I reached a clearing and saw another road lit by a faint streetlight. From behind a tree, I studied the empty street, then pulled out my phone to locate my position.

Craptastic, I was back on the Mercer Textile Factory road.

At least the truck had gone. Gone because it was looking for me. No police car yet. I couldn't risk waiting. The truck could return. Or I'd get stuck in a patrol car when I needed to get back to Black Pine.

I needed to get to some kind of haven. A haven where an Uber could find me.

IN ALL OF GEORGIA, there were only about 10 streets that ran in a straight line. They were all in downtown Atlanta. Didn't help me any, especially in the unplanned community of Shake Rag. Using my flashlight, I worked my way behind dilapidated buildings and small forested areas, somewhat parallel to the path I had driven to the factory. Sweat-soaked and grimy, I approached a house with two cars in the drive and more parked in the front yard. I knocked on their back door, unwilling to expose myself to the street. A youngish man wearing rural Georgia's ubiquitous uniform of a ball cap and beard answered the door.

"Yeah?"

"Can I come inside for a minute?"

"Who are you?"

"I'm Maizie Albright." I blinked off tears. "I live in Black Pine. Can I wait for a ride here? My car's on fire."

———

WHILE THE UBER burned the miles between Shake Rag and Black Pine, I silenced my phone and barraged the driver with a steady stream of chatter. While keeping watch out the back window as unobtrusively as I could.

However, in the forefront of my mind, I played out what I'd found in the Mercer Textile factory. I'd interrupted plans to burn the building and the evidence inside. The murders had always been staged with clues pointing toward someone else. Starting with the first murder, a long time ago.

Deanna Mercer Dixon had been bent on revenging her

father's death and to gain back the family inheritance she'd thought stolen from her. Righting wrongs in her mind. She'd created a rival company and used unethical and illegal marketing tactics to upend DeerNose business. I believed Kristi Johnson had been caught sneaking into DeerNose. Caught and squealed on CrossHair.

That must have been the real motive for killing Kristi Johnson. Although I questioned whether her death had been planned like the other coverups. Regardless, Derek had been a convenient and unintentional fall guy for Kristi's murder.

Now that I'd shaken off the fear from Shake Rag, a new emotion caused my stomach to clench, my neck to ache, and my skin to flush.

Anger.

Anger didn't suit my personality, but it stormed through me. I felt furious over Randy Mercer's possible manslaughter coverup. Outraged over Derek Johnson sitting in jail, accused of killing his wife. Even more incensed over Kristi's murder. An adulterous and witless actress's poor decisions didn't qualify death (where would the entertainment industry be if that were true?). Even the murder of Simon the ex-con galled me. The body I found at Mercer Textile sickened me. And the helmet and license plate?

Infuriated me.

Not that I had given up hope on Nash. I refused to give up hope.

But at the top of my list? Jolene's refusal to give me *or the police* any information about Nash. Admittedly, I'd screwed up that chance. My anger wasn't rational. Murder should top the list, not ex-wife pettiness. I was too exhausted for that kind of self-examination.

Not too tired to take action, though.

It was late by the time we reached Black Pine. The driver dropped me off at a random address near Jolene's subdivision. I hiked into the trees, hopped the low brick fence into the golf course, then found the golf cart path leading into her subdivision.

Lot of good the boujie security box did.

Nash's truck was no longer in Jolene's drive. I stood on the street, crossed my arms, and drummed my fingers on my biceps. Her security system records would have been in the old office. Burned in the fire. I could Uber back to A.S.S. and research how to disable her system. Another possibility, try to hack into Nash's database through the Cloud and root around in his files for her security passwords—if he kept any on his computer and if the police weren't monitoring his systems.

Or I could throw a rock through a window and break in.

I'd have to be quick. I didn't have time for an arrest.

In her garden, I found a softball-sized chunk of granite. Positioned away from doorbell camera range, I heaved the rock at a garage window. It didn't sail like a softball. It bounced off the frame into the bushes below.

Of course, it did.

I crept up to retrieve my rock. Peeked into the window. There was his truck. Parked in her garage.

The back of my neck burned, my lips tightened, and my brain fritzed out. Like an out-of-body-experience, I saw my arm swing and my hand release the rock.

The glass shattered. I brushed off the glass, reached inside the window to unlock it, and climbed in. Marched over to the Silverado. Wrenched open the door. His keys were lying in the cupholder. I didn't even need Roger Rabbit. I stalked over to the house entry door and smacked the garage door button. The door rose. I backed his truck out of the garage.

And got the Hades out of there.

ONCE SAFELY OUT of Jolene's neighborhood, I parked at Hot Clucks. Used the key to open the console between his seats.

Then pressed the code in the built-in safe and took out his .38 Special.

Nash hadn't been carrying when he disappeared. He must not have thought he was in danger.

That had been a mistake.

Or not.

My pink .38 Special—a surprise Sweet Sixteen gift from Daddy that wasn't the car I hoped for—had been locked in the safe at the old office. I didn't care what Jolene thought. Nash had left me his truck keys on purpose. He wanted me to have his truck and everything inside.

Like he knew I might need them.

In the safe, he'd also left a box of bullets and a holster. I loaded the gun. Found a bottle of water and a box of protein bars in the glove compartment. I crammed one in my mouth and chewed. Must have fallen asleep. When I woke, it was four in the morning.

I was still angry. And had terrible cottonmouth.

I started the truck. A prickly feeling about DeerNose attacked me, and I crawled past the building on the way to the cabin. Two trucks were parked on opposite sides of the lot. Both big and black. One in a back corner. The other, near the front door. A little unusual for anyone to be there before five. On a Sunday.

I didn't stop. But I'd return. In a different vehicle. I didn't want to risk someone setting fire to Nash's truck. He'd kill me.

No patrol car at the cabin or DeerNose. Presumably, the police called off the manhunt. They would have found the body at Mercer Textile by now. Identification would take longer. Or maybe not.

If the coroner did a careful check, they'd find evidence of a staged suicide. Maybe a dent in the back of her head. Or maybe not. Didn't matter. That was for the medical examiner to figure out and a good attorney to prove.

What mattered to me was finding Nash. I hadn't given up hope. Obviously, he didn't have Jolene's motorcycle anymore.

Maybe she'd stolen the plate from it. Planted clues in the office. The helmet could be a red herring.

Survival was key now. If it wasn't too late.

No, I wasn't thinking that.

AT THE CABIN, I tapped the code for the gate, drove to the house, and parked Nash's truck. My arrival woke the Jack Russells. Barking and bounding over one another to get out the doggy door, the terriers appeared, sniffed me, then ran into the woods. My heart squeezed, thinking of Cuddles. I'd find him, too. But later.

I checked the Jacks' water, fed them, and continued my trajectory toward the big shed that housed extra vehicles. Started up Daddy's Polaris, bringing back the dogs. I headed through the forest to DeerNose, hoping I'd not lose the path in the dark.

The dogs ran alongside me. Before arriving, they cut back toward the cabin. There was no fence between DeerNose and the cabin. They were all one property. DeerNose was Daddy's life as much as his family was. The same for Marshy and Petey. They were also founding members. They'd helped him build something from nothing. Their employees were a second family. The hours spent weren't just an investment. Their lifeblood ran into DeerNose. For good or for bad.

Although now it didn't seem too good.

When I parked behind the factory, I could hear the dogs barking in the distance. I pulled my shirt over the gun holster and left my backpack on the UTV.

My stomach hurt and my chest ached. My anger was losing steam. Marshy and Petey had been at the hospital the day I was born. I'd spent every Christmas Day with them. Every Fourth of July, too. They were family.

And one of them wanted to kill me.

FIFTY-FIVE

#CHAFED #UNLEASHED

THE KILLER WAS AT DEERNOSE. I'd confirmed the truck during my drive by, but in a sense, I'd realized who it was earlier. I wanted to believe it was Dee Dixon. The killer wanted me to believe that, too. They didn't want to kill me. Not unless they absolutely had to. Obviously, we were past that point now.

I had to die because I'd betrayed DeerNose.

My stomach roiled. No, not DeerNose. My father.

A distorted love born from a warped loyalty, I supposed. I hadn't noticed before because I'd grown up accepting it. The secrets were out, but it still didn't matter. Nash and I were the enemies. Our investigations weren't about protecting DeerNose or my father. We'd been trying to discover the truth.

We were being punished for learning the truth.

———

I ENTERED through the factory door, using my key. I was a little surprised it still worked. Safety lights lit the hall. I'd left the Maglite in my backpack, not wanting to carry it. Already, the weight of the revolver drug my waistband down. How did gunslingers stand their muffin top rubbing against the holster?

Gary Cooper, as Marshal Will Kane in *High Noon*, carried a revolver, too. Not a .38, but a .45 Long Colt. Gary Cooper was too lean for muffin top chafing. Harry Callahan in *Dirty Harry* had a shoulder holster. That was smart. He also had a Smith & Wesson revolver like Nash and me, but his was a gigantic .44. Maybe the shoulder holster chafed his armpit. Except rangy Clint Eastwood didn't have side boob to worry about.

Side boob, Maizie?

Easier to think about holster chafing than facing off with a killer who used to babysit me, I guessed.

But like Dirty Harry and Marshal Will Kane, I headed to a standoff. Those lawmen had courage and resolution about the sacrifice they were making. I didn't want to make that sacrifice. I wanted to live. Hoping for the best, but with the grim resolution of Dirty Harry and Marshal Kane, I was ready to face the worst.

I was going to have to be okay with that.

Silver lining, no chafing in heaven.

———

IN THE EXECUTIVE HALL, arguing voices came from Petey's office. I shook out my hands, did a few quick Ujjayi cleansing breaths. Got into character. Stepped into the doorway.

In her chair behind the desk, Petey stared up at Marshy. Her gaze swiveled to me.

"The police said—" Marshy cut off his words. "Maizie. What are you doing here? Everyone's been looking for you. The police called. They found Dee Dixon at Mercer Textile. She's … she killed herself, honey. It's over, though."

"Not over." My voice sounded eerily calm. I couldn't tell who I was pulling from—Gary Cooper or Clint Eastwood. Maybe a mashup of both.

"It's done," said Petey. "It's done and we can all go home. Marshall was right to send me to Atlanta, but now I can go home."

"Not yet." I strode over to Marshy, grabbed his arm, and pressed the gun into his side. "I want Nash. Now."

"What in the hell are you doing, young lady?" said Marshy. "If this is your idea of a joke, it's a poor one. Where did you get that .38?"

"I want Nash. That's all I want." I jerked Marshy's arm and rotated him toward the doorway, keeping my back to the wall. "Let's go, Petey."

"What are you talking about?" shouted Marshy. "You've lost your mind. Stop this right now. Do you know how dangerous it is to point a loaded weapon at someone?"

"I'm not the one whose lost their mind." I flicked a hard look from him to Petey. "Last night, someone I love shot at me. I wasn't armed. I am now. And prepared to do what's necessary."

Petey rose. "Your father is going to be very disturbed by this, Maizie."

"Where is Nash? A storeroom?" I dug the muzzle into Marshy's side, making him grunt. "What are you waiting for? Let's go. Petey, get in front of us."

"Fine, fine," she hurried around us. "Stay calm, Maizie."

"After all that's happened, how can you do this to me?" moaned Marshy. "To us?"

"I've been asking that same question." I edged him into the hall behind Petey. "Nash and I have just been doing our jobs. He had suspicions that something stank at DeerNose for a long time. When Kristi Johnson died, he went into full investigative mode. She was caught here, wasn't she?"

"Didn't you say her husband killed her?" said Petey.

"I don't know what you're talking about," growled Marshy.

"Derek didn't kill her," I stated. "You followed her home, returned later, and killed her. Then started a fire the next day to cover it. Dee Dixon would have burned at Mercer Textile if I hadn't come along when I did. Simon Craig was killed the same way. So was Randy Mercer."

"I told you Randy Mercer wasn't murdered." Marshy stumbled and glared at me when I yanked him back. "It's the truth."

"It may have started as involuntary manslaughter, but the coverup makes it murder. The coroner's report said the blow to his head killed Randy. But the truth would have made DeerNose look bad."

"Not just DeerNose," said Petey grimly.

"I don't care about that right now. Where's Nash?" I jabbed the gun into Marshy, making him grunt.

Petey's brows pulled together. "We don't know where Nash is. I don't know why you're doing this. You've been so high-strung lately. You need to calm down."

Doubts assaulted me. I was no Marshal Kane, let alone Dirty Harry. My ears throbbed from the hammering of my heart. I swallowed, tasting the bile that rose from fear. They could easily overtake me. Two against one. They were being careful because of the gun. I tightened my grip on Marshy's arm. Maybe I should have tied them up. Locked them in an office. Searched DeerNose myself.

Wait. An office.

"We're going back." I yanked on Marshy and wheeled us to the wall. "Petey, get ahead of us. Back to my father's office."

"No. Enough. We know that you and Nash broke up. Obviously, he's left and you're handling it badly."

"Stop saying we've broken up," I yelled. "We haven't broken up."

"For Boomer, we've tolerated this ridiculousness, but enough is enough."

"Move," I said to Marshy. "Daddy's office. Now."

"Don't do this to him, Maizie," said Petey.

I had the gun. *Dirty Harry* time. Time to ask myself one little question: "Do I feel lucky?"

Not really.

FIFTY-SIX

#BUMPSETKILL #DOGEATDOG

USING THE REVOLVER, I pushed Marshy toward the office at the end of the hall. Sweat wet his brow. His arm felt slick. He'd fixed his mouth in a grim line, and his face had paled. I couldn't allow myself to feel any sympathy. I refused to feel anything until I had Nash.

"Open the door." I looked back at Petey. "Get over here."

"You're making a big mistake." She strode toward me. "That's not just your father's office. It's his sanctum. Don't ruin it for him."

"And yet, he prefers to design at home. He wants to stay away from this building as much as possible," I said bitterly. "Do you know why his blood pressure is so high? Why he doesn't like coming to work anymore? Because it's no longer his. He loved building this little empire because he loved working with the people who helped him build it. Creating specialized apparel for people like himself. And you and Marshy. You all loved hunting and fishing together. Hiking the trails. Watching the birds. Checking on the habitats. But he doesn't even have time for all those outdoorsy things he loves. He's caught up in a rat race because you two kept pushing the vision to new heights."

"Boomer does it as much for the community as for himself.

You can't understand because you didn't grow up here," said Petey. "You're just like your mother. The Albrights only care about making themselves look good. You don't have an ounce of Spayberry honor."

"You know, history is great and all, but you need to stop judging people by how their ancestors acted." I nudged Marshy. "Open the door."

"It's locked," he mumbled and wiped his brow.

"Are you okay, Marshall?" said Petey. "You're looking puny."

"I know you have keys, Petey." I moved us to the side. "Unlock the door."

She pulled the keys from her pocket, unlocked the door, and opened it. I glanced inside, hoping to see Nash. It had seemed logical a few moments ago. Daddy had left town. No one would disturb his office.

No Nash. Of course, not. She'd never allow a body to rot in there.

Not that Nash was rotting. I'd never think that.

A sigh squeezed from my chest and caught in my throat just as my peripheral vision caught movement behind me. Marshy jerked, cried out, and teetered forward. My hand skidded on his slick arm. Petey grabbed for the gun. Her hands clamped over the revolver and wrenched it away. Marshy bent to grab the door frame. Petey swung high and sprang forward. The gun butt crashed against his skull, and she landed against him, shoving him into the room. He collapsed, sprawled on the floor.

I whipped around to face her as she pulled the door shut. "Why would you hurt Marshy? I put the gun on him because I thought you wouldn't chance him getting hurt."

"He'll be fine. I didn't hit him that hard. Just enough to knock him out. Give me your phone."

Goosebumps broke on my arms, and the hair on my neck stood up. "You just spiked Marshy's head like it was a volleyball at Huntington Beach."

"Don't be so vulgar," she scoffed.

"Open this door. I need to check on Marshy."

"No. We're leaving. I won't let you sully DeerNose."

"You just coshed Marshy in DeerNose. I think you've sullied more than the building."

"Marshall's got a hard head. He'll be okay. Besides, as far as he knew, you had the gun. You hit him. He knows I'll take care of this situation. I've been doing just that since the beginning."

"You mean *you* covered up the murder of Randy Mercer." My stomach churned. "This company was founded on the blood of an innocent man."

"Randy was not innocent. That greedy guts was going to sue us. He had nothing to do with the DeerNose formula, other than we used his presses to penetrate the scent into the fabric. We paid him for that. He had no right to claim anything more."

"Oh God," I whimpered. I didn't want to know, but I had to know. "What happened? Did Daddy argue with him? And what? It got physical?"

"Boomer?" she looked astonished. "Boomer doesn't argue. Or fight. What's wrong with you? How could you think such a thing? All Boomer did was placate Randy, that good-for-nothing. Feel sorry for him. He was going to employ Randy Mercer, of all people. Make him a vice president. Operations." She hissed, "that's Marshall's title."

"So Marshy argued with Randy, not Daddy?"

"Oh, Maizie," she sighed. "Marshall doesn't have to argue with anyone. He's too smart for that. Stop yammering. Let's go." She grabbed my arm, dug the gun into my side, and yanked my phone from my back pocket. Pushing me, she sent me stumbling ahead of her.

I'd always known Petey as strong and athletic. She golfed, hunted, and fished with the guys. She played in mixed racquetball and basketball leagues at the club. She'd overpower me easily. And she had Nash's gun.

I was in a lot of trouble.

———

WE HURRIED through the lobby toward the back door. "Where's Nash?" I said. "Can I see him first?"

"Go." Petey shoved me. I tripped and my knees hit the floor. "Get up." She motioned with the gun. "We don't have time for last requests. Let's go."

I placed my hands on the floor. Instead of pushing myself up, I spun and shot out my right leg. An old *Kung Fu Kate* move. Intended to knock Petey off balance so I could spring forward and push her down.

She hopped over my outstretched leg and kicked me over. I fell on my back. Sprawled with my legs up, cockroach-style. Unfortunately, Petey had dutifully watched all my *Kung Fu Kate* episodes. She was also light on her feet from racquetball.

I rolled to my side, ready to spring to my feet. She kicked me back and slammed a foot on my chest.

"I don't want to shoot you here, Maizie. Not only will it besmirch the factory, your blood will seep into some crevice or a bullet could lodge somewhere. The police will find it. I've watched enough of those CSI shows."

"Then don't shoot me." I stared up at her. "You have choices. You could come clean. It will make you feel a lot better."

"I feel fine," she snapped. "I'll feel better knowing I'd protected Boomer from your interference. You saw that picture on the dartboard. He needed my protection. Especially with his heart issues."

"Are you insane?" Hello, Maizie. Why ask a question when the answer was obvious? "I'm his daughter. He's going to hate you for killing me."

"He'll never know. Marshall will keep quiet so not to upset Boomer."

"That makes Marshy complicit with murder. Again."

"Watch your mouth," she shouted. "He doesn't know anything. I never told him."

"Wait. You deliberately murdered Randy?" My stomach tightened. "It wasn't an accident you were covering up?"

She lifted her foot and motioned with the gun. "Get up. Time to go."

While I lay on the floor, I'd examined her. Active wear leggings were not forgiving when it came to revealing bumps and creases. A bandage showed beneath her leggings. Had to be the bite mark from Cuddles at the Mercer fire.

I moved as if to get up. Lunged and head-butted her in the thigh. She scrambled backwards. Grabbing her leg, I gouged my fingers into the wound. Her fist swung. I ducked. Dodged between her legs and upending her.

The gun went off. Plaster and other debris sprayed us from the ceiling.

"Dammit," she cried and clambered from the floor, waving the gun.

I skittered backwards. "Where's Nash?"

"You'll see him soon enough." She looked up at the ceiling. "I didn't want to make a mess in here. Now look what you've done."

Look what I'd done.

I'd put the man I loved in danger with my carelessness. I'd put work before my relationship—not even real work, just my mission to learn what secrets Nash hid—and now faced off with that big secret.

Nash had wanted to handle this delicate matter of Petey. He'd needed evidence to prove his theory. His hunt had been for that evidence. I'd come barreling in, guns blazing—almost literally—destroying all his careful work just to prove something to him.

Prove what?

That I was honest? A good teammate? Could keep my mouth shut? I wasn't reckless?

Nope.

I'd just been trying to out-sleuth him. Show him I could

investigate on my own. Annie accused me of getting cocky after a few successes. She was right.

Who does that to someone she wants to partner with?

The awful answer was me.

I'd done this to Nash. I'd put him in danger.

And (hopefully not) had gotten him killed.

FIFTY-SEVEN
#ALLABOARD #NEWTRICKS

"MOVE." Petey motioned with the gun and pushed open the door. Sunrise broke over the trees. A cacophony of barking and growling carried in the cool air. The dogs were after something.

"Oh no, the Jack Russells followed me here." I halted on the sidewalk and glanced over my shoulder at Petey. "Please. I should check on them. Send them home."

"You're being crafty. I know you, Maizie." She gouged the barrel of the gun into my back. "If they followed you here, that means you came from the cabin? On the four-wheeler?"

I nodded.

"I'll take care of that later. Let's go. The dogs won't mind us. It sounds like their attention is on something else."

We moved across the parking lot. Petey had parked her truck at the back of the lot. A black Lariat. The smaller—yet still big—version of Daddy's truck. That thought sickened me, but my attention snapped to the spot she'd chosen. Why so far from the building?

"Where are we going?" All the shows about not getting into vehicles with kidnappers swam through my brain.

"I've had to scramble to set this up, but I've gotten good at it.

Project management, Maizie. Organization is the key to efficiency."

I really needed some organization in my life. Efficiency, too. When I realized the body at Mercer Textile didn't have a bite wound, I knew the killer was Petey. Earlier would have been a lot better. Was there a project management app for investigations? Probably.

Wait. What was I thinking? Too late for that. She was going to kill me.

No app could help me now.

We moved through the empty parking lot toward her truck. "Don't do this, Petey. The police are going to figure this out. They've already found Dee Dixon's body. You know this won't end well for you."

"I've thought about nothing else for the past week. I've barely slept, getting everything in place. As soon as I found that woman in the factory, I knew someone had to stop them. Mr. Nash certainly wasn't doing his job. Someone had to get her to talk. It didn't take much either. She told me everything. No surprise to learn a Mercer was behind all this."

"How would Kristi Johnson know that Dee Dixon was Deanna Mercer?"

"She didn't. Kristi Johnson was an idiot. I followed you to the Mercer property and Mercer Textile, then put two and two together. Of course, a Mercer would be behind all this horrible sabotage business. What I didn't expect was your betrayal. You could have left well enough alone. That awful woman's husband was no longer your client. You and Mr. Nash didn't have to continue looking into the Johnson fire. That's the job for the police. It's so frustrating when people don't mind their own business."

"You'd let an innocent man take the fall for his wife's death?"

"Mr. Johnson wasn't so innocent," she barked. "Before she got hurt, that woman told me her husband was cheating on her. She took the CrossHair job because she was lonely and it was a way to develop her acting. Mr. Johnson was rarely home."

Rhonda wouldn't like that news.

"Although," continued Petey. "I think that woman was unstable. When I visited her home, she told me all kinds of things about being a corporate spy. You know, she had the gall to call DeerNose an 'evil empire?'"

I couldn't blame Kristi for that one.

"And you and that dog," she muttered. "Everything was going so well. It was all arranged. I was almost done. Before I could finish, I caught you trespassing at Deanna's house. Isn't that violating your probation?"

"Yes, but…" Wait, why defend myself?

"I called the fire department, I'll have you know." Petey jabbed the gun in my arm, making her point. "I allowed you and your dog to escape. And what thanks do I get? Now you've given me more work to do. Your father is going to be so upset. He liked Mr. Nash."

"Wait." I stopped and spun around. "What are you saying?"

"It would have been better for Boomer if it looked like Deanna had done all this. Now poor Boomer will suffer."

What the hellsbah did that mean?

I trudged toward the truck. In the woods, the terriers still scrapped. Yipping, growling, and barking. A lower grumble and thrashing accompanied their racket.

"I'm worried about the Jacks," I said. "It sounds like they've found something big."

"Those dogs can handle themselves. I've seen them trap wild hogs. Once they treed a black bear. You're wasting time." She shoved me forward, and I stumbled again. "No funny business getting in the truck."

"Where are we going?"

"I wanted to do this at the Mercer Textile factory, but you showed up too soon. Why are you always where I don't want you to be?"

"I have a knack for investigating?"

"I don't think so. Dumb luck, I would say." She sighed. "I can't do this at the cabin. Pollute your father's home? Unfortunately, the Dixie Kreme building is gone."

"Because you burned it."

"Mr. Nash had DeerNose information in that dirty office. That sneaky man. The building was old. Unfortunate for Lamar, but I started the fundraising and orchestrating the community project for his new place. All's well that ends well."

"OMG." She was a lunatic. How could we not see that?

"Language, Maizie." She stopped me and opened the passenger door. "I had to come up with something on the fly, so to speak. Jolene Sweeney's house seemed appropriate. She's never home. It'd been easier if you had your own place, Maizie."

"You're going to shoot me at Jolene's house? She's not going to like that one bit." I bit my lip. Why was I allowing myself to get pulled into these crazy train arguments?

"I watched you go to her house with Remi. Nash's truck is there. It seems appropriate. I know the history. Everyone does."

"You … How…" Wow. I was much worse at surveillance than I thought.

"They have these little video devices that let you watch and hear everything. I think you told me about them once. I clipped one in that nasty car you've been driving. It's so helpful how much you talk to that dog."

"You've been spying on me?" Oh, craptastic. Irony is a kicker.

She smiled, and I shivered. Her lipstick remained unsmudged, but her grin looked demented.

Hindsight was also a kicker.

FIFTY-EIGHT

TIME for some *High Noon* action. *Dirty Harry* wasn't working for me.

Except Marshal Will Kane had his gun, and I didn't.

I would not get in that truck. I'd rather have her shoot me in the DeerNose parking lot than at Jolene's. Bad for my father, but easier for the police.

Although Jolene had been a pain in the butt about sharing information about Nash, so it would be a told-you-so sort of ending.

Jeez. That was no way to think. Especially when about to die.

The barking and yelping had grown louder. The terriers were moving closer.

A distraction.

"The Jacks are coming." I planted my right foot on the running board and grabbed the truck door to pivot toward her. "You know they'll try to pile in the truck. They love a ride."

"I told you not to worry about the dogs," she snapped and stepped forward. "Get in."

Her right hand gripped the gun, but her elbow had drawn against her side to steady it. Still holding the door handle, I raised my left foot and pushed off with my right. Tackled her to the ground, pinning the gun against her chest. She squirmed and struggled beneath me. My dead weight kept her hand pinned, but I knew it wouldn't last long. I was a lot softer than Petey.

Beneath me, the sinewy muscles tried to slither the gun arm out. She pounded my back. Kicked. Snapped her teeth.

I pressed harder. Then pulled my head back. Slammed my forehead against her face. Felt a wet crunch. She stilled for a moment, then resumed struggling. My forehead ached and felt slimy. If I even shifted my shoulder, her gun arm would slide out.

A distant crashing and a hollow thudding broke through the sounds of our struggle. Like a stampede.

We froze. Something heavier than the little terriers ran toward us. The Jacks herded it forward. Their yips and little toenails clattered against the blacktop, chasing the bigger animal.

I couldn't focus long enough to peer beneath the truck to see what was coming. Petey's free fist pounded my kidneys. Her legs wrapped around mine, trying to flip me. I rose cobra-style to slam into her face again. This time, she rolled to the side. My forehead smacked the blacktop. She wriggled beneath me. Shoving me aside, she scrambled to her feet.

I stared up at Nash's gun in my face. I'd only made her nose bleed. Some blood had seeped through her camo leggings, but that was the old wound. Cuddles could claim that one.

"Why won't you just do what I say, Maizie?" She shook the gun at me. "Why is that so hard for you?"

Something I'd heard from directors in the past. And Vicki. Generally, I was docile. But sometimes I bucked, knowing they were mistaken. Wrong direction ruins a movie. Wrong advice ruins a career.

In this case, it was very wrong to assist in my own murder.

"I'm sorry, Petey." I resorted to *Julia Pinkerton* snark, my fallback character in times of panic. "Screwing up your plans again. Looks like you'll have to kill me here. If I'm going to get shot, I want my blood to soak into DeerNose ground."

Snarling caught my attention. I angled my head to gaze under the truck, squinting in the faint morning light. The Jack Russells chased a monstrous beast. I felt my eyes widen and my jaw slacken.

"Holy Cujo, Batman," I murmured.

The run was more of a gallop. His eyes narrowed on his prey. Cuddles looked like he'd grown three sizes bigger. His bark had grown more ferocious. His coat looked darker. Dirtier.

Petey talked, but I wasn't listening. How had Cuddles gotten here? I'd hear stories of dogs traveling across the country to return home. Little Gap to Black Pine wouldn't be that big of a stretch, but still. Amazeballs! How had he found me at Deer-Nose? Had he checked all our stops along the way?

He drew closer. The whites around his eyes showed. Jowls flapped. Foam spewed. His stiffened tail stood high. His open mouth exposed his teeth. He looked crazed. No wonder after the miles he'd put in and finally found me.

That sweet dog ran all this way to see me. I smiled. Caught myself.

Frigtatstic. Cuddles and the Jacks were about to witness my murder.

I brought my attention back to Petey. She was saying something about blood and office hours.

"Excuse me," I interrupted, pushing myself up. "I changed my mind. You can't kill me here."

The truck blocked Petey from Cuddles' view. And she couldn't see him. I couldn't risk him or the Jacks getting shot. Accidentally or on purpose.

Something thumped the rear of the truck. As I craned my neck in that direction, Petey kicked me in the stomach. I doubled over, rolling back to the ground.

"You don't get to decide," she shouted. "You're not listening to me. I don't want to shoot you here. It's not what I had planned, but I will. I'll just have to set things up differently."

"You know, you're worse than a James Bond villain," I

gasped. "Just let me get up and into the truck. Then you can explain your evil plan on the way to Jolene's house. We need to get out of here."

"I have been saying that all along," she bellowed. "This is why I've never liked children. I warned Boomer against marrying your mother. He should've listened."

I rose and limped to the open door. Inside the truck, I looked for the dogs. The thumping I heard earlier resumed. I couldn't see Cuddles. The terriers had spread out. Three had gotten distracted and veered back to the woods. One Jack stood nearby, eyeing the truck and wagging his tail. A pair bounded toward Marshy's truck.

Where was Cuddles?

I turned back to Petey. She faced the rear of the truck bed. Her arms dropped to her sides. Body still. A heavy growl crescendoed. I leaned out the door. Cuddles had moved around the back of the truck to face her. Tail stiff. Hackles raised. Teeth bared.

Shizzles.

Petey's left hand moved toward the revolver in her right hand. Cuddles' growl deepened. She froze. He barked once—deep and ferocious—and cut it off with a frothy snap. Padded a step closer. Her left hand closed over the gun butt. She was steadying her grip before raising it.

"Cuddles! Go!" I screamed and launched myself at Petey again.

The gun went off. A scalding pain rocketed through my shoulder. Petey toppled back. My body slammed onto the pavement. And I closed my eyes.

FIFTY-NINE
#MUMMYCURSES #THEBLACKDOG

I OPENED MY EYES. Cuddles stood on top of Petey. Foamy drool dripped onto her face. She lay still. And bleeding.

I rolled to grab Nash's .38 that had fallen from her hand. My left shoulder throbbed, hot and sharp. The arm dangled at my side, numb and useless. Ignoring the pain, I used my right elbow for leverage and stumbled to my feet.

"You're such a good boy. Good boy, Cuddles. Poor baby, looking for me for a long time. You could've just gone to Elaine's house. She's been looking for you, too."

His head jerked up, and he smiled at me.

"I promise. Later." I turned my attention to Petey. My head-butt had left blood smeared around her nose. A tiny stream of blood trickled from her neck. I assumed that was from Cuddles. "Where's Nash?"

She closed her eyes and firmed her lips.

I couldn't hold a gun and rummage through her pockets. "I need your help again, Cuddles. Lay down. If she moves, I'll give you the attack command."

He plopped his haunches down. She grunted. He scooted, made himself comfortable, and collapsed on top of her.

Petey moaned but didn't speak.

"You wouldn't stop talking before, but now—" I stopped. The thudding had resumed. "Shizzles. A Jack got in the truck bed. Cuddles, stay. There could be evidence back there. I don't want anything messed up."

I backed toward the rear of the big truck. The bed had a metal tonneau cover. "How did it get in there?"

The noise resumed. "Holy schmolies," I cried and darted to the tailgate. "Nash? Are you in there?"

The thumping stopped and a faint sound came from inside.

"I'm here. I'm here." I jammed the gun in the holster to use my good hand. The cover wouldn't move. "Hang on. I can't open it. It's locked and heavy."

I hustled back to Petey. "How do you open your truck bed cover?"

She tipped her face away from me. Her hands had balled into fists.

From his perch on top, Cuddles watched me.

"I need my phone and her keys. You'll have to move, but stay close." I eyed Petey. "I've got the gun on you and this dog would love to rip out your throat if I say the word. Don't try anything."

I pointed. Cuddles climbed off her torso to sit on her arm. Stuffing the gun into its holster, I knelt and dug through her pockets. Yanked out my phone and her keys. Difficult with one hand. I laid the keys and the phone on the ground and pulled the gun from the holster. Gave a cry of frustration. Shoved the gun back, tapped on the phone, and leaned my face over it. Scrolled to Ian's number. Shoved the phone into my pocket. Scooped up the keys and ran back to the tailgate.

"Ian," I yelled. "I'm at DeerNose. Mrs. Peters has Nash locked in the bed of her truck. Cuddles is standing guard over her. I've got Nash's gun, but I don't trust her. Please send someone immediately. I'm calling you from my pocket ... my phone's in my pocket. I can't hold it, so I can't hear you."

While I spoke, I studied her key fob. Tapped the tailgate icon until I got it to unlock and lower. The thick metal cover created a dim cavern. Various shapes had been wrapped and secured to the bed. One had to be a body. Mummy-bound in tarp and duct-tape. Flattened with a crazy amount of cargo straps. Surrounding the body-shape were various other pieces, also wrapped in tarps and strapped to the bottom of the bed. Odd shapes.

I felt tears welling, but I shook my head to refocus. No time for emotions. And no time to wait for the cavalry. This was a crime scene. But the tight wrapping didn't give me a lot of hope that Nash had room to breathe. I had to work fast.

Tossing the keys onto the tailgate, I peered around the truck to check on Petey and Cuddles. He appeared curled up at her side, sleeping, but his massive body hid her right arm. She wasn't going anywhere. I returned my attention back to the body in the tarp. One end of the mummy rose a few inches and dropped back, creating the thumping sound.

"Oh, Nash. Don't worry, I'm going to get you out," I soothed.

I only had one working arm, though. I yanked my phone from my pocket and took a picture for evidence. Disregarding the voice still on the line, I tossed the phone onto the bed and climbed onto the tailgate. Petey had used heavy-duty ratchet straps looped through tie-downs, creating a taut spider-web over the wrapped figures.

I tried unhooking a strap with my fingers and gave up. Ran back to the truck cab and dug through her seat console. In her backseat, I found a toolbox. Flipped it open and grabbed a utility knife. I scooted out and zipped to the tailgate.

My shoulder felt like it was on fire. I couldn't feel my left arm or fingers. I'd been allowing it to flop around as I ran back and forth, trying to ignore the damage I might be doing. My right shoulder still bore a scar from a similar injury. This one felt different. The pain I remembered hadn't been so intense. The arm hadn't felt so useless.

I bit my lip and used my good arm to haul myself onto the tailgate. Returned to attacking the cargo straps.

The utility knife wouldn't cut through the heavy-duty straps. I stabbed the tarp closest to me and ripped. Beneath was a bent and mangled motorcycle wheel.

"Oh God," I cried. "What did she do? Run you off the road?"

The mummy lifted his feet in response, but the thump had reduced to a tap. He couldn't raise his feet more than a few centimeters. Panicking, I tossed the wheel onto the ground and used the space to climb closer. I couldn't risk stabbing through the tarp. It was too tightly bound around his body. I grasped and tugged the tarp, but the straps and duct tape wouldn't give.

"Please hold on. I'm trying to get you out." I sliced through the tarp at his feet. Freed the soles of his boots. The straps kept his ankles bound. "Nash, are you still with me? Lift your heels."

His feet didn't move.

"Nash, please. The police are coming. Just stay with me." I grasped his heel and shook it. "I'm sorry for everything. I should've trusted you. I was showing off. And annoyed at you, so trying to show you up. So stupid to play games. And dangerous. I haven't proved anything other than I have a lot more to learn. You were trying to do what was right. I should've respected that. Even if I thought you were acting Neanderthally. 'Protecting me was a privilege that I not only took for granted, I abused and rejected.' Just look at what that rejection did."

I rubbed my nose on my shoulder.

"Okay, I'm sorry. Those lines were from the Lifetime Original I did a few years back. And *My Bodyguard* wasn't great mainly because of the writing. But I meant it. The little successes in my career made me cocky. What kind of success is busting cheaters? 'Nothing compares to the success I felt with you…' The hells. That's also a TV movie line. Oh God, what I'm trying to say, I've been lying to myself all along. 'I thought I was all that, but I'm nothing without you.' Sorry. Another line, but I meant it. I need you. I love you. Please, just move your feet a little teeny bit, so I'll know you're going to be okay. That's all I care about."

I placed my hand on top of his thick boot. Closed my eyes to concentrate. Focused on feeling for the slightest tremor.

Nothing.

I had found him. But couldn't save him.

SIXTY

#SILVERLINING #DOGWITH2TAILS

A HAND FELL on my shoulder. "Maizie."

I screamed, opened my eyes, and drew the revolver. Spun to the right.

"It's me. Hold your fire. Didn't you hear me?" Ian wrenched the gun from my hand. I toppled back on Nash. Screamed again. My shoulder felt like it had ripped from my body.

"What happened?" Ian reached for me, then drew his hand back. "What's wrong with your arm?"

"I don't know. It doesn't matter. Help me get Nash out of this. He can't breathe. I think he may have … Help me, please."

I grabbed the hand he held out, but his focus had moved to the lashed tarp I lay on.

"Holy—" He pulled me forward, helped me off the truck, and jumped onto the tail bed. "I've got this. I need you to call off Cuddles. Help my men. And send someone over here."

I tottered around the truck. Cuddles stood over Petey, doing his thing. Growling. Snapping. Drooling. "Cuddles. Come."

He looked from me to the policemen. Glanced down at Petey, who remained lying with her eyes closed—likely project-managing her alibi. He shook off the drool, splattering Petey and the nearby cops. Sighed. Stretched. And padded over to plop onto my feet.

"You're a good boy." I squatted to bury my face in his neck. "We'll get you fixed up and fed in a bit."

I'd been so consumed with Nash that I hadn't heard the cruisers and Ian's truck pull into the parking lot. Now I heard ambulance sirens racing toward DeerNose. I spun back to the truck where Ian and another officer were unlatching the straps.

"How is he?" I called, but they ignored me. "Is he … can he breathe?"

"Get the EMTs," Ian barked at a patrolman. "Now."

I turned toward the arriving ambulances, but a female officer stepped in front of me. "Ma'am. Come with me."

"But," I motioned toward Nash, "I need to be with him. I finally found him. I just couldn't … My arm. I couldn't get him out with one hand."

"You're hurt. And in shock," she soothed. "Come with me."

She led me past two policemen squatting over Petey. "Wait," I halted. "There's someone else. Marshy. He's in my father's office. Marshall Roth. Petey knocked him out, and—"

"He called us. We sent an ambulance to the building and someone's attending to him. You need to come with me now so the medics can look at you."

"I…" I glanced at the truck. Ian and his partner tossed pieces of the mangled motorcycle over the side. The paramedics had hoisted their gurney even with the tailgate and were sliding their bags into the bed. "I want to stay here. I have to stay here."

Cuddles licked my hands and nudged me.

"You can't help him like this, you know." The officer moved to block my view. Her warm brown eyes captured my gaze. "You're bleeding, and you appear to be in pain. You need to take care of yourself before you can help him."

"But that's what I've been doing all along," I wailed. "When I should have been putting everyone else first."

———

MY DISLOCATED shoulder had been relocated. The bullet burn treated and my arm set in a sling. Other parts of me had been liquid-stitched and patched with more than a few bandaids. An ambulance tailgate triage because Cuddles wouldn't allow anyone to take me inside the truck.

Petey had also been patched up, then moved into the back of a squad car. Marshy had refused his ambulance to leave in another cruiser. Ashley Reynolds—the officer charged with my care—said Marshy had summarized the incident, but wanted to make an official statement quickly. He also wanted to break the news to my father himself.

I had apologies to make in that regard. My relief that Daddy had done nothing worth covering up was overcome by the guilt and anguish of believing such a thing. I also needed to speak to him about other truths. We'd both put our careers before our relationship. We'd mend that fence, though. Ironically, I had Petey to thank for shining a light on that breakthrough.

But the talk with Daddy would come later.

Right now, I had other concerns.

The first was Nash, who had been whisked away in the ambulance before I could see him. No one would tell me his condition. Ian had ridden with him. I didn't bother trying to call. Ian needed his focus on helping the paramedics.

The other concern needed a lot of care as well. We left in the back of a police car, too. A second car followed, carrying six Jack Russell terriers I'd helped to round up. At the cabin, I herded Cuddles into the kitchen, set the Jack's breakfast outside, and locked the doggy door to let him eat in peace. He looked up at me, then kicked the empty food bowl.

I placed a donut in it. "I shouldn't give you this. But you deserve a desert."

He grinned up at me. Sprinkles covered his muzzle.

"You were courageous. A hero. You did exactly what you

were bred to do. Protect. Amanda should have socialized and trained you differently. To be honest, I always thought she was unhinged. I'm pretty sure she set you up to take down Brian at the Bark and Brew. She set up the A.S.S. Angels, too. We should've been more careful about Amanda. I'm making sure she doesn't get you back when she's out of jail."

He shook and splattered donut drool over Carol Lynn's immaculate floor.

"I love you, Cuddles. But here's the thing. I am not good for you." I sighed. "At least right now I'm not. I've messed up my life so much, I can't even live on my own because of my probation. I'm trying, though. You deserve better than me. You need plenty of room, attention, and exercise. There's a little girl who will give you everything you need and more. Except donuts and chicken sandwiches. And that habit's also my fault."

He put a paw on my leg.

"No, no. Don't try to comfort me. It's important that I do what's best for you and not what makes me feel good." I scrubbed behind his ears. "I'll visit you plenty, I promise. You have to promise you won't come looking for me on your own. I have a feeling you won't, because you're going to be so happy in your new home."

I sniffed and wiped an eye with the heel of my hand. "Although first we're going to meet E.L.A.I.N.E. at the V.E.T. That's for your own good, too. You walked twenty miles. Who knows what you ate along the way."

Cuddles cocked his head, squinted at me, and looked at the door.

"That's right. Elaine. We're going to see Elaine. You're going to live with Elaine."

He danced in place, toppled the water bowl, and rushed to the door.

I didn't cry.

Okay. Maybe a little.

———

AT THE HOSPITAL, Ian stopped me before I found Nash. "I know you're in a hurry to see him, but I want to catch you up."

"Please, tell me quickly. Is he conscious? He couldn't breathe…" I took in a deep breath and swallowed hard. "What did she do to him? Mrs. Peters planned on making our deaths look … I don't know, like a homicide-suicide? Double homicide? It didn't make sense. I think she originally planned on framing Dee Dixon for killing us, but … Ian, she was … It was like … like I didn't even know her. Like she'd gone all Annie Wilkes or *American Psycho* or something."

"Whatever she planned doesn't matter now. You caught her and survived. How's your arm?"

"In a sling, but not for long." I waved off his concern. "Petey … she's okay?"

"Barely a scratch on her. Minor bruising. Bite on her leg. A broken nose, I think. Puncture wounds in her throat. Nothing compared to her victims."

"Nash?"

He led me to a bench. I caught a flash of sorrow before his steady gaze resumed. "Nash asphyxiated in the back of the truck. When we got him into the ambulance, he was unconscious. It looked pretty bad. His blood pressure had dropped and heart had slowed. They had to administer CPR on the way to the hospital."

I buried my face in my hands.

He placed a hand on my good shoulder and squeezed. "The good news is, he never flatlined. He didn't stroke out. Those are all positive signs for recovery."

I raised my head and wiped my eyes. "Okay."

"Don't be shocked when you see him, though. He's a mess." Ian rubbed my shoulder. "He's got a leg fracture. A lot of road rash from the motorcycle accident. We found tire marks on the business highway near Peters' house. He must have been doing surveillance on her nearby. From what the reporting officer pieced together, Nash wasn't going very fast, so that's lucky. She T-boned him, though. My partner found a spot of blue paint on her front bumper."

"I just can't believe it." I shook my head. "I caught her gaslighting me a few times, but she could be like that. The passive aggressive type. I never imagined anything like this. She's always been there, taking care of Daddy and Marshy. Always a little frustrated with them, but protective. Loyal. A tiger mom. Except Daddy and Marshy weren't her children."

"Carol Lynn never liked her."

I felt my eyes round. "Carol Lynn never told me that."

"She wouldn't."

That was true. Carol Lynn was a big believer in the eighth commandment.

I rose from my chair, and we continued our trek toward Nash's room. "DeerNose will have a lot of rebuilding to do. They'll have to figure out how to run things without Mrs. Peters."

"Maybe they'll sell."

"I doubt that. They care about their employees too much."

"People change." Ian stopped before the door. "Things don't always stay the same. Your dad needs time to heal. Marshall Roth, too. In any case, DeerNose will be closed until my investigation finishes."

"I guess so."

"You might think about doing the same," said Ian. "Make some changes, I mean. You haven't seemed happy. Not like before. I worry this job is making you … I don't know, darker? Seeing the crooked side of people will do that."

"Tiffany and Rhonda used to say I lived in a bubble. Maybe the bubble's popped." I gave him a bitter smile. "But don't worry, I'm always going to look for silver linings. I just need to be honest with myself about who I really am."

SIXTY-ONE
#ANGELS&DEMONS #HOTDOG

I STUDIED Nash from the hospital doorway. His leg was in traction. An IV in one arm. However, the steady blip of his heart monitor reassured me. His face looked drawn but unmarked, and I thought about that helmet Petey had planted at Mercer Textile. A clue to lead the police to believe Dee Dixon had run him off the road. A dumb clue. Why keep the helmet and license plate from someone you've hit? I supposed Petey planned to dump his body and the motorcycle parts in another location.

That was before I stopped her plans.

The thought didn't cheer me. What cheered me was seeing the Paul Newman-blue eyes alert and staring back at me.

He motioned me over. "Miss Albright."

I hurried to bend over him. "I was looking for you. I didn't give up. I didn't lose hope."

"Of course you didn't. You're the sunny-side-up girl," he said and pulled me onto the bed next to him, careful of my arm in the sling. "I knew I could count on you when things got dicey. Mowry gave me the rundown. Why are you sunburned?" He touched my temple. "That bruise looks nasty. How's the shoulder? Same one from that other time?"

"Nope. Opposite. How about your leg? Same or different from when I accidentally shot your foot?"

He scowled. "Same."

I grinned. "I'm getting to be like you, with all the scars and war wounds from this job."

His return smile didn't reach his eyes or make the dimple pop near the scar that ran from cheek to chin.

"I know what you're thinking. Ian said as much. Private investigating is changing me. And not just because of the injuries. I haven't been myself."

His face had tightened, but he nodded for me to continue.

"I could go on about a voyage of self-discovery, but you'd hate that. It's a little true. I was never myself in California because of the work I was doing. When you're a child actor, everyone is shaping and molding you. You spend a lot of time trying to think like someone else, so you can act like them. I jumped from that into the party scene where I didn't have to think at all. Now, I'm free of all that. So I molded myself into a Nash-Annie mashup and thought I was a hotshot investigator out for the truth, no matter what."

"I don't want to think of me mashed with Ms. Cox." He winced. "All investigators get cocky when they have some success, though. I should have been honest with you from the start." Nash smoothed my hair back and cupped my cheek. "I was making you crazy. I'm too stubborn for my own good."

"I'm too nosy. I should have been focused on my work at A.S.S. and left you alone."

He kissed my nose. "A good investigator is always nosy."

"Not that kind of nosy. I didn't trust you or anyone else to do their job. I need to apologize to Annie, Ian, and Daddy, too. I was getting ahead of myself. Thinking I knew more than I did and not listening to anyone." I blew out a long breath. "Boy, did I blow it."

"Let me tell you how I blew it first." His arm snaked around my waist and pulled me against him. "I said I was trying to protect you, when maybe I was trying to protect myself."

"What do you mean?"

"What *do* I mean?" He looked up at the ceiling and grimaced. "I was committed to the DeerNose security job, but it was boring."

"You were looking for a case."

"I already had one. The corporate espionage stuff began before I got there. That's why they brought me in. But it made no sense to me. Of course, I wanted to catch the culprits so we could prosecute, but I wanted to know why they were doing it. I finally narrowed it down to Simon Craig and CrossHair through the 15 saboteurs, namely Luella Haney. I never made the connection between the Mercers and CrossHair."

"You didn't know about Randy Mercer's murder? I thought that must have been the big secret."

"That was all you." He kissed my cheek. "The corporate sabotage was just the job for me. I just let you think that was the big secret. A little subterfuge on my part. But I was having fun with you, which was irresponsible. I broke some of my own rules."

"I forced you to break them. I wore you down."

"I enjoy that kind of wear and tear." He flashed me a tempting smile. "But my evasion backfired. I was trying to protect you from my suspicions about Peters. She caught my attention at DeerNose from the start. She was overly protective of Marshall and Boomer. Weirdly so. You probably didn't see it because you grew up with her. Everyone else had worked with her for years. I was the new guy. I noticed. And she noticed me noticing."

I shivered.

He threaded his fingers between mine and laid them on my thigh. "In meetings, when I questioned Marshall or Boomer, she kept quiet. But later, I'd get a passive aggressive email. Those really ticked me off. If I all out disagreed with Boomer or

Marshall, she'd—very carefully, mind you—make me look bad in front of them."

"Oh no," I said. "But I don't think Daddy would ever think that."

Nash shrugged. "I thought she was checking up on me, so I started leaving traps. She was going through my files. Emails and notes, too. You were, too, so it made the tracking confusing."

"I'm so sorry. And mine were illegal."

He kissed me again. Longer this time. "I thought she was protecting them because one or all were embezzling. Or something similar. I couldn't find anything. The accounts were clean as far as I could tell. But she could barely hold herself together. She seemed desperate to have a go at me. I knew there was something more there. I just didn't know what. And I couldn't tell you. No evidence, just suspicions. Only feelings, not facts. You loved her. I thought if I could figure it out and wrap it up quietly, it'd be for the best."

I squeezed his fingers between mine. "Of course you did."

"It wasn't for the best. She was a lot craftier than I gave her credit for. I should've told you sooner. Should've trusted you to listen to me. I'm too used to doing everything on my own."

"I was trying to do the same thing. It's so stupid. Infantile."

"Trying to prove yourself is not stupid," said Nash gently. "It's only how you go about it that can be stupid."

I opened, then closed my mouth.

"I said that wrong," he grimaced.

"Not really. It's the truth. I've done a lot of stupid things."

"But you corrected and did right."

"I still can't wrap my brain around how Petey hid this part of her personality. Maybe she was triggered into killing Randy Mercer and covered it up in her panic. But she'd covered it too well. That evil must have festered within her for twenty years."

"We don't know that Randy was her first kill. Wasn't she a widow?"

"I don't want to think about that. I've had too many dark

thoughts lately. Those thoughts led me to thinking my father could have done something heinous."

"I told you in the beginning, this business was bad for someone like you. You're too angelic." He touched my face. "You shouldn't let your wings dip into this world."

I shook my head. "You and Ian want to think that. But I grew up in Hollywood. My parents split up early, and it's not been amicable until recently. I've been treading dark waters all my life. But my personality is … buoyant. I'm naturally positive. I'm going to try really hard to let this go. Daddy will need my help. He'll need me to shake off the gloom."

Nash's face had darkened.

"What is it? Are you in pain?"

"Ian? You're lumping me with Ian again?"

"Don't do that." I hardened my gaze. "Not after I had to steal your truck from Jolene's."

"I knew you'd get my Jessica Rabbit hint," he smirked. "I figured no one would look for me there. Except you."

"Forget it. You better hope she doesn't press charges for breaking into her garage." I laid my head on his chest. "I have an offer for you."

He stroked my hair. "Personal or business?"

"Both."

He sighed. "I don't want to think about business right now."

"Annie has contractors expanding the office—"

"I'm not working for Annie."

"What about being partners with Annie?"

"I thought we were going to be partners?"

"When my apprenticeship is done. It may take that long to rebuild your old office. The partnership with Annie could be temporary. You've been saving money since working at DeerNose."

"Annie doesn't own the business. Vicki Albright does. And there's no way in—"

I silenced him with a kiss. "What about renting a room at

A.S.S.? We have more work than we can handle. Annie will cut you a deal. I think she feels bad about the Johnson case. It's a good time to take advantage of that guilt."

"Miss Albright, you're such a schemer." He chuckled. "Mrs. Peters isn't the only one managing other people's lives."

"She project managed deaths." I glared at him. "Besides, I'm transparent with my scheming. I promise, from now on, I'm all about openness and honesty."

"Me, too." He kissed my nose. "Although some of my plans involved that DeerNose savings you seem so eager to have me spend."

"What kind of plans?" I said dreamily, my thoughts filled with Vera Wang and Tiffany.

"Plans that will have to wait another few years, I suppose." He studied me. "But I could pull a few ideas together for the present. I'm thinking of something right now."

"But Mr. Nash, we're in a hospital." I squirmed against him.

"Get your mind out of the gutter, Miss Albright. I was thinking of talking to Ms. Cox." He leaned forward to kiss me. "You're right, you're no angel."

"And you, Mr. Nash, are no devil." I gave him a playful pout. "But sometimes I wish you'd try a little harder."

The End.
Until you read 20 CARATS, A Maizie Albright Star Detective
"Between Cases" Novella.

Did you figure out the 19 CRIMINALS?
Go to a hidden page on my website to see if you got all 19 and
I'll reward for your efforts!
www.larissareinhart.com/the19criminals

ON WRITING 19 CRIMINALS

This book has been a long time in the making. Two years is even longer than the first full book I attempted to write! (This is also the longest book I've written, but the time had nothing to do with the length.) As I hope Maizie learned, we should prioritize people over our own desires. Although I was often frustrated by my lack of progress and concerned that I was letting down my readers, I don't regret the way my time was spent in the last two years.

I think you'd agree that taking care of your people is life's biggest reward.

However, I hope to write a lot faster in the years to come! LOL

But your patience, my dear reader, can be rewarded in another way. Did you figure out the 19 criminals? There is a hidden page on my website that only you can find by typing into a browser:

www.larissareinhart.com/the19criminals

See if you solved the mystery and follow my instructions to get your reward!

If you enjoyed 19 CRIMINALS, would you leave a review? Thank you so much! Your kindness is greatly appreciated by me and other readers!

Thank you!
Larissa

THE PIG'N A POKE
A Finley Goodhart Crime Caper prequel

When a winter storm traps ex-con Finley at the Pig'n a Poke roadhouse, she finds her criminal past useful in solving a murder.

Free for my VIP Readers!

Go to Larissa's website and tap the big pink button at the top of the page or type www.larissareinhart.com / larissasreaders in a browser to join Larissa's email group, where she shares exclusive content, news, and giveaways. You'll receive *The Pig'n A Poke* as a gift.

Note: Larissa will not share your email address and you can unsubscribe at any time.

MOVIES & TV SHOWS MENTIONED IN 19 CRIMINALS

American Psycho

Barefoot in the Park

Beetlejuice

Breaking Bad

Charlie's Angels

Cujo

Dancing With the Stars

Dirty Harry

Ellen

Factory Girls

Golden Girls

Grey Gardens

High Noon

Indiana Jones and the Temple of Doom

Intimate Apparel

James Bond

Julia Pinkerton, Teen Detective

Kill Bill

Kung Fu Kate

Love Island

Misery

Mr. & Mrs. Smith
My Bodyguard
My Brother, the Vampire Hunter
Real Women Have Curves
Red Speedo
Say Anything
The Deliberate Stranger
The Dressmaker
The Equalizer
The Good, The Bad, and The Ugly
The Maltese Falcon
The Seamstress
The Shining
The Thin Man
Turner & Hooch
Who Framed Roger Rabbit

LARISSA'S SERIES

15 MINUTES

16 MILLIMETERS

NC-17

A VIEW TO A CHILL

17.5 CARTRIDGES IN A PEAR TREE

18 CALIBER

18 1/2 DISGUISES

19 CRIMINALS

20 CARATS

21 GUNS

"Child star and hilarious hot mess Maizie Albright trades Hollywood for the backwoods of Georgia and pure delight ensues. Maizie's my new favorite escape from reality."

GRETCHEN ARCHER, *USA TODAY* BESTSELLING AUTHOR

Ex-teen TV and reality star, Maizie Albright, returns home to Black Pine, Georgia, determined to start a new career as a private investigator, modeled after her childhood starring role as "Julie Pinkerton, Teen Detective." Unfortunately, Maizie's chosen mentor, Wyatt Nash of Nash Security Solutions, is not a willing teacher, and her learning curve includes becoming her own person after spending life under the thumb of managers, directors, and producers, particularly her stage-monster mother.

ABOUT THE AUTHOR

Wall Street Journal bestselling and international award-winning author, Larissa Reinhart writes humorous mysteries and romantic comedies including the critically acclaimed Maizie Albright Star Detective, Cherry Tucker Mystery, and Finley Goodhart Crime Caper series. Her works have been chosen as book club picks by *Woman's World Magazine* and *Hot Mystery Reviews*.

Larissa's family and dog, Biscuit, had been living in Japan, but once again call Georgia home. See them on HGTV's *House Hunters International* "Living for the Weekend in Nagoya" episode. Visit her website, LarissaReinhart.com, join her VIP Readers Group, and get a free short Finley Goodhart story.